Discover more at millsandboon.co.uk

SLOW BURN

JANICE MAYNARD

VOWS IN NAME ONLY

NAIMA SIMONE

MILLS & BOON

First Published in Great Britain 2020
by Mills & Boon, an imprint of HarperCollinsPublishers,
1 London Bridge Street, London, SE1 9GF

Slow Burn © 2020 Harlequin Books S.A.
Vows in Name Only © 2020 Naima Simone

Special thanks and acknowledgement are given to Janice Maynard for her contribution to the *Dynasties: Seven Sins* series.

ISBN: 978-0-263-28008-1

1120

MIX
Paper from
responsible sources
FSC™ C007454

SLOW BURN

JANICE MAYNARD

This book is dedicated to my wonderful readers.

2020 hasn't been the year we all envisioned for ourselves. In the midst of uncertainty and change, I am so grateful for your love of books, and I'm thankful that we take this journey together!

One

Jake Lowell had circumnavigated the globe more than once in the last fifteen years. He'd traveled everywhere and seen everything. Well, except for Antarctica. That continent was still on his bucket list. But of all the cities and countries he'd visited and/or put down temporary roots, the one place he *absolutely* thought he'd never return to again was Falling Brook, New Jersey.

The town's name was idyllic. Jake's memories weren't.

He'd left his birthplace at twenty-two, in the midst of scandal and tragedy. And he'd never returned. Until today. Under duress.

When his stomach growled for the third time, he pulled into a gas station and topped off his tank. The credit-card machine on the pump was out of paper, so he wandered inside for his receipt and to grab a very late lunch. In the end, he decided a candy bar would do for now. He'd always had a sweet tooth.

As he paid for his purchases, the stack of newspapers near the checkout stand caught his eye. The usual suspects were there. *New York Times. Wall Street Journal.* But it was the small-town paper that gave him heartburn. The headline screamed, "Vernon Lowell Lives! Black Crescent Fugitive Located in Remote Caribbean Location."

Jake's stomach churned. The story had broken over a week ago, but the local news outlets were milking it daily. He'd had time to get used to the incredibly upsetting news, but he was still in shock. For a decade and a half, he had known his father was gone. Probably living it up in the bowels of hell. Now the dead had come to life.

When the cashier handed Jake his receipt, she gave him a curious look. Too late for him to realize he should have paid cash. Would the woman see the name on his card and put two and two together? Was she part of the always speedy Falling Brook grapevine?

The name *Lowell* wasn't all that unusual, but here in Falling Brook it was radioactive. Fifteen years ago, Jake's father, Vernon Lowell, had absconded with an enormous sum of money—the assets belonging to some of Falling Brook's most high-profile citizens. A dozen or more elite clients had entrusted Black Crescent Hedge Fund with their fortunes and their futures. Vernon, along with his CFO and best friend, Everett Reardon, were financial wizards who founded Black Crescent and made piles of cash for everyone involved.

But, inexplicably, something went very wrong. The money evaporated. Everett Reardon was killed in a car crash while fleeing police. And Jake's father disappeared from the face of the earth, presumably dead.

The living were left to clean up the mess. And what a mess it was.

Jake drove aimlessly, tormented by the memories even now.

Falling Brook was a small enclave, still not much more than two thousand residents. Jake had done his due diligence before returning home. He'd waded through enough online research to know that not much had changed. This town with the rarefied air and high-dollar real estate still protected the famous from the outside world.

For a few moments, Jake parked across the street from Nikki Reardon's old house—a mansion, really—letting the engine idle. Nikki's world, like Jake's, had been destroyed by her father's misdeeds. Fifteen years ago she'd fled town with her mother, their lives also in ruins.

When Jake allowed himself to remember Nikki, he experienced the strangest mix of yearning and uneasiness. Because his father and Nikki's had been business partners and best friends, it was inevitable that the two families spent a considerable amount of time together while Jake was growing up. But what he remembered most about Nikki was his one wild night with her in Atlantic City five years ago.

Though she was four years younger than he was, she had always been mature for her age. Eons ago, she had been his first real girlfriend. Despite all that, the alluring woman he'd hooked up with in a brief, unexpected, passionate reunion in a casino hotel was far different from the redheaded, pale-skinned beauty he had known as a very young man.

That new Nikki had dazzled him. And scared him.

Muttering under his breath, Jake made himself set the car in motion. Nikki's ghost might still wander the halls of that glamorous house, but she was long gone.

His immediate destination was a small boutique hotel known for its discreetness and luxury. Jake needed the first and would enjoy the second. Though he possessed the skills to live off the land, these days he much preferred a comfortable bed at the end of the day.

Once he checked into his spacious, beautifully appointed room, he sat on the edge of the mattress and stared at his phone. He needed to let Joshua know he had arrived. Joshua Lowell. Jake's brother, his twin. The only characteristics they shared were dirty blond hair, their six-foot-two-inch height and eyes that were a mix of hazel and green.

When Josh had called to say their father had been found, Josh asked Jake to come back to Falling Brook, and had invited him to stay in his home. But the invitation was obviously issued out of duty. The brothers hadn't been face-to-face in fifteen years. Other than the occasional stilted text or email on birthdays and Christmases, or the very recent phone call, they might as well have been strangers.

Over the years, Jake had made himself hard to track down. On purpose. He had cut ties with his siblings, and now he knew little of their personal lives. When he was twenty-two, he hadn't fully understood that family was family, no matter what. He also hadn't realized that being a footloose, rolling stone would eventually lose its appeal.

Now that he was a seasoned man of thirty-seven, he was hoping to mend fences, especially since Joshua wanted Jake's input on the CEO search at Black Crescent. It felt good to be consulted.

Joshua had agreed to meet in the hotel restaurant at seven. The entire place was dark and intimate, but even so, Jake offered the hostess a fifty to seat him and his prospective dinner date at an inconspicuous table. If anyone saw two of the three Lowell brothers together again, tongues would wag.

Jake hated the paparazzi. In the aftermath of his father's disappearance, reporters had hounded every member of the Lowell and Reardon families. In fact, *any* family connected to the scandal was targeted. Jake, a newly minted university grad at the time, had already been planning to backpack around Europe, so he simply moved up his timetable and fled.

Josh—good old dependable Josh—had been left to clean up the mess. The guilt from that one decision hounded Jake to this day. His brother had rebuilt Black Crescent bit by agonizing bit. Joshua had stayed the course, faced the accusers and cooperated with the police. Despite having incredible artistic talent, he had put his dreams on hold and tried to make up for their father's despicable deeds.

Jake had done nothing but pursue a selfish agenda.

Sometimes, the truth sucked.

When Joshua arrived, Jake leaped to his feet and hugged his brother awkwardly, feeling a tsunami of emotional baggage threaten to pull him under. "Long time no see." He winced inwardly at what must have sounded like a flippant comment at best.

The two men sat, and a hovering sommelier poured two glasses of a rare burgundy that Jake remembered his brother enjoying. Although, who knew? Fifteen years was a long time. Tastes changed.

Josh downed half the glass, leaned back in his chair and managed a small smile. It seemed genuine enough. "You look good, Jake."

"So do you."

A few seconds of silence ticked by.

"This is weird." Joshua raked a hand through his hair. He wore an expensive sport coat, dress pants and a crimson necktie. Jake, in jeans and a rugby shirt, felt scruffy in comparison. But that had always been the difference between them. Josh dressed the part of a wealthy man. Jake preferred to be unfettered by society's dictates.

He straightened his spine as tension tightened his jaw. "Here's the thing," he said abruptly. "I might as well get this off my chest. I'm sorry, Josh. I'm sorry Dad screwed us over, and I'm sorry I let you do the heavy lifting. I abandoned you. But I'm here now. For what it's worth."

His brother's smile was strained. Born first by three minutes, Josh had often taken the role of "older" brother seriously. He sighed, the sound a mix of resignation and something else. "I quit being mad at you a long time ago, Jake. We all choose our own path in life. Nobody made me stay and sort through Dad's screwups."

"But we both thought he was dead." It was true. Their mother, Eve, had hired private detectives fifteen years ago. The feds had searched for months. No sign of Vernon Lowell anywhere.

Joshua's gaze was bleak. "It would have been easier if he *was* dead, wouldn't it?"

The harsh truth hung between them. Jake's stomach clenched. Authorities had recently located Vernon Lowell on a remote Bahamian island and extradited him to the United States. Currently, the patriarch was languishing in federal custody. And he wanted to see his two oldest sons.

Oliver, their younger brother, had made the pilgrimage recently. It hadn't gone well.

"We have to go, don't we?" Jake said.

Josh shrugged. "He can't make us."

"On the other hand, telling him to go to hell might give us closure."

His brother's lips twitched. "You have a valid point."

"I guess these last six months haven't been easy for you after that damn reporter wrote an anniversary piece about the Black Crescent debacle. I didn't see it until recently."

Joshua's smile broadened. "Actually, I have no complaints. I'm now *engaged* to that damn reporter."

Jake's jaw dropped. "Seriously? Why didn't you tell me that when you called?"

"You and I hadn't spoken in forever. I wanted to give you the news in person. We're planning a wedding very soon. Sophie is great. You'll like her. And you might as well know, she's the one who encouraged me to resurrect my art career. That's why I'm giving up the helm of Black Crescent."

"That explains the CEO search. I was wondering why now." If anybody deserved to follow his dreams, it was Josh. "I'm happy for you. What will happen to the company, though?"

Joshua didn't answer immediately, because a waiter dropped off their appetizers. A few moments later, Josh drummed his fingers on the table, his unease palpable. "You've played the part of a dilettante well over the years. No one realized you were a financial wunderkind." Joshua's smile was wry.

Jake tried not to squirm. "Why would you say that?"

"I've been doing some digging, baby brother. You're an uncannily successful day trader. Probably richer than I am. At the risk of insulting you, I'd say you've inherited some of Dad's business savvy. But not his morals," Josh said hastily.

Jake told himself not to overreact. "I've had some success," he said mildly. "And I'm *not* your baby brother."

Joshua stared at him, gaze clear, jaw firm. "I want you to take over Black Crescent."

What? "Oh, no," Jake said. "Oh, *hell* no." His hand fisted on the table. "Surely, you have other possibilities."

"We do, actually. I've been interviewing candidates for some time now. But I don't know that any of them are exactly right."

"Well, you're dead *wrong* if you think I'm the man."

"Maybe." Joshua's expression was hard to read.

"What about Oliver? I'm guessing he doesn't want to give up his photography?" The youngest Lowell brother had been affected deeply by their father's betrayal, perhaps even more than Josh and Jake. His anger and despair had led him into addiction. Fortunately, he'd been clean for a very long time now.

"Oliver is finally in a good place. Finding out Dad is alive has been hard for him. He's dealing with a lot of the old anger. But he's handling it well."

Eventually, the meal came to an end and Joshua insisted on picking up the tab. A nice gesture, but unnecessary. Awkwardness returned.

Joshua frowned as he slid his credit card back into his billfold. "I need to talk to you about something important," he said. "Something I didn't want to say over the phone. But not here."

"More important than the fact our father has returned from the dead?"

Jake expected at least a smile for his snarky question. But Joshua was serious. "Perhaps. How 'bout we walk while we talk?"

With his mind spinning, Jake followed his brother through the restaurant and outside onto the sidewalk. The air was crisp, though not unpleasant. It was early November. A few businesses had already begun to decorate for the holidays, getting a jump on the busiest season of the year.

For fifteen Decembers, Christmas had been a painful season for Jake, presumably for the rest of his family, too. It was a reminder of all he had lost. The memories of happy times with the Lowell family of five gathered around the tree had faded beyond repair. In the golden years of Jake's childhood, there had been spectacular gifts: ponies, guitars, racing bikes. Everything a kid could want.

And then it was all gone. Even worse, other families, innocent families, had been hurt. Jake and his siblings and his mother had been innocent, too, but no one had wanted to believe that. They were vilified, scorned. Hated.

Jake hunched his shoulders in his jacket and matched his brother's stride as they set off down the street. He didn't want to think about the bad times, but the memories clung to him like cobwebs. There was no peace to be had in Falling Brook.

Even so, it felt good to get some exercise. For three blocks, Joshua didn't say a word. Jake tried to wait him out, but his patience evaporated quickly. "Why are you being so mysterious?"

Joshua halted suddenly, beneath the soft illumination of a streetlight. "I don't know how to tell you this."

"What? Am I dying?"

"This isn't funny."

"How am I supposed to know that? You haven't said anything yet."

Josh leaned against the light pole, his features betraying tension and exhaustion. For a man in love, he didn't look all that carefree.

He shrugged. "When that article came out back in the spring, the story omitted one very big bombshell."

"Oh?" Jake shoved his hands in his pockets, trying not to react to the gravity in his brother's voice.

"Sophie had DNA evidence proving that I had fathered a child."

"Hell, Joshua. Why didn't you tell me?"

"At first, she wouldn't reveal her source, but when she and I got closer, she finally admitted that Zane Patterson had given her the DNA analysis."

Jake was more than shocked—he was suspicious. "Zane Patterson from prep school? He was a year behind Oliver, right? What would he have to do with any of this?"

"Zane received the report from an anonymous source. He was still angry about everything his family lost when Dad disappeared with the money. So Zane saw this as a chance to stick it to me and Black Crescent. Only Sophie decided not to include Zane's info in the article."

"But surely, you've had time to prove it's a hoax. That's been, what? Six months ago? It's bogus, right?"

Joshua shook his head slowly, his jaw tight. "The report wasn't fabricated. It was the real deal. Somewhere out there is a four-year-old girl who shares my DNA. So I discreetly began investigating any woman from my past who might have matched the timing of this pregnancy. The list wasn't that big. I came up with nothing."

"So it *is* a fake report then." Jake was starting to feel as if he had walked into an alternate universe. Joshua wasn't making sense.

His twin straightened, giving Jake a look that made his stomach clench and his skin crawl with an atavistic recognition of danger.

Joshua's expression finally softened, revealing the oddest mix of sympathy and determination. "The report is legit, Jake. But I'm not the kid's father. You are."

Nikki Reardon glanced at her watch. In half an hour she would have to pick up her daughter, Emma, from

Mom's Day Out at a local church in their tiny town of Poplar Ridge, New Jersey. Emma loved her twice-a-week preschool and had made several sweet friends.

The classes had also given Nikki some valuable alone time. Between her job as assistant manager at the diner four days a week, caring for her daughter and dealing with her mother's needs, it was hard not to feel stretched thin. When Nikki worked the overnight shift, her mother came and stayed.

It wasn't the best arrangement in the world, but it sufficed for now. Sometimes Nikki felt guilty about using her mother for a babysitter so much of the time, but she also believed that being with Emma gave her mom a healthy focus in a life that was empty.

Nikki's attention returned to her iPad, where she was reading a story that brought up too many bad memories. A few days ago she'd discovered that Vernon Lowell wasn't dead. Today's front-page article claimed he'd been found hiding out in the Bahamas. After a speedy extradition, Vernon now waited in federal custody for his trial.

She wanted to talk to him. He was the only person who knew the truth. Vernon and her father, Everett, had been best friends and business partners. But her father was dead. She had seen the body, suffered through the funeral. The world thought Vernon was dead, as well. But now he was back.

Thinking about the Black Crescent scandal inevitably made her think of Jake. Beautiful, stubborn, wandering Jake. Her first boyfriend. She understood why he left. Reporters had made his life miserable. She had only seen him once in the intervening years.

It had been both the best and worst night of her life.

A loud knock at the door demanded her attention.

Sometimes the UPS guy did that. But this knock sounded more peremptory than a package delivery.

Cautiously, she peered through a crack in the inexpensive drapes. *Dear God.* It was Jake. In the flesh. Why was he here? His family still lived in Falling Brook, but that was over an hour away. Why had he come? Her secret threatened to choke her with anxiety.

She opened the door slowly, trying to project mild curiosity even though her heart nearly beat out of her chest. "Jake," she said. "What a surprise."

His greenish-hazel eyes bored into her. "Is it true?"

Her brain processed a million reasons why he might be on her doorstep. "Is what true? Why don't you come in and have something to drink?"

As she stepped back and opened the door wider, Jake entered her small living room and paced, his furious gaze cataloging and dismissing the contents of her modest home. "I want to know why you sent Zane Patterson anonymous information claiming Joshua was the father of your baby."

All the blood drained from her head, and she forgot about offering Jake a cup of coffee. She sat down hard on the sofa. "My baby?" She hated the quavering tone in her voice. She had done nothing wrong.

"Don't give me that." Jake shook his head, scowling. "I know it's true. What did you hope to gain by blackmailing my brother?"

Nikki straightened her spine and glared. "If you want to sit down and discuss this civilly, I'll listen. But you're way off base. I've never had any contact with your brother or Zane, not since we were teenagers. I don't know what you're talking about."

At last, Jake plopped down in a chair and drummed his fingers on the arms. His whole body radiated strong emotion. As she tried to catch her breath, she absorbed the look of him. He was a beautiful man. Always had been. Today he wore a scuffed leather bomber jacket and jeans so old and faded they molded to his legs, and other parts, as if they had been made just for him. His soft cotton button-down shirt was pale green, the color of vintage glass bottles. Deck shoes with no socks exposed his tanned ankles.

He was tanned all over, in fact. The man had spent his life outdoors. Or much of it. His streaky blond hair needed a cut. In the summers when they were kids, the sun would bleach Jake's hair gold. Now it was more subdued.

She glanced at her watch, trying not to panic. Did he know the truth about Emma, or was he fishing? She wouldn't lie about her daughter, but she wasn't going to volunteer any unnecessary information at this point. "I have an errand to run," she said calmly. "This will have to wait."

His jaw tightened. "Then I'm coming with you."

Her stomach clenched. Having him close made her senses go haywire. Why was it so hard to be sensible when Jake Lowell was around? "It won't take me long. I could meet you for dinner later."

"I'm not letting you out of my sight, Nikki Reardon." His gaze was grim. Implacable. As if he was the hunter, and she was the prey.

"Fine," she said. She stood and retrieved her purse and keys. She had no idea what he would think when he saw Emma, but she would put one foot in front of the other until she figured it out. Her mother had pressed her to contact Jake and ask for child support, but Nikki had been too proud to beg. When Jake walked away from her five years ago without a word, she had known he was still running from his past. And that he was never going to be the man she needed him to be.

Outside, she grimaced when she saw his fancy black sports car, a rental no doubt, parked at the curb. The sleek vehicle looked wildly out of place on this middle-class street. Her own mode of transportation was a fifteen-year-old compact model with a car seat in the back.

She unlocked her car and watched as Jake folded his body into the passenger seat. He was a couple of inches over six feet, so he was not going to be entirely comfortable.

Good.

"Where are we going?" he asked.

"I have to pick up Emma from preschool."

"Emma?" The word sounded strangled.

She shot him a sideways glance, noting his sudden pallor.

"Yes. Emma. My daughter."

Two

Jake watched through the windshield as the gorgeous red-head and the bouncy little girl walked toward the car. He felt queasy. A host of other emotions swirled in his chest.

The brief ride from Nikki's house to this pleasantly ordinary brick building had been silent. Nikki's knuckles were white as she gripped the steering wheel.

Now he tried to study her dispassionately. In the midst of his clinical visual survey, the memories hit him hard and fast. Nikki naked. Sprawled across his hotel bed. Smiling. Warm and sated from their lovemaking. Her pale, pale skin like porcelain.

It had been one night. One extraordinary night almost five years ago. And now he was a father? Why hadn't Nikki told him? Or was this all just a misunderstanding? Even as he tried to rationalize her behavior, he couldn't get past the anonymous emails that were eventually passed on to his brother.

Despite Joshua's insistence that a baby existed with Lowell blood, Jake was by nature a suspicious man. Being betrayed by his father had taught him not to trust easily.

The rear car door opened, and Nikki helped the child into her car seat. Though Emma had been chattering excitedly, she fell silent when she spotted the stranger up front. Her eyes were green. That meant nothing. The color could have been from her mother as easily as from Jake's DNA. But the girl's blond hair was nothing like her mother's.

Jake wanted to say hello. The word stuck in his throat. Instead, he gave the kid a quick nod and turned back toward the front. He wanted to stare at Emma. To examine her from head to toe. To see if there was anything of him in her. But he didn't want to make the child uncomfortable. No point in both of them feeling weird.

Back at Nikki's house, Nikki lowered her voice as she parked the car. "I usually give her a snack, and then she'll go play in her room for half an hour or so. You and I can talk then."

Jake nodded brusquely, not entirely sure what he wanted to say. Crazy revelations were popping up in his life like rodents in an upsetting game of whack-a-mole. His father was alive. Nikki had a kid. The child was Jake's? It was too much to process.

He shoved his hands in his pockets as the unlikely threesome walked across the lawn into the house. Once inside, Jake escaped into the small living room with a muttered excuse. Even at this distance, he could hear mother and daughter in the kitchen debriefing Emma's day at school. When Nikki finally returned, she looked tired, but resigned.

She took a chair across from him and gracefully curled

her legs beneath her. Her steady green-eyed gaze and long, wavy red hair made him clench his fists as an unwelcome wave of desire swept through him. He remembered burying his face in that hair. Inhaling the scent of her shampoo. Feeling for a brief moment in time as if everything in his world had finally popped into sharp focus.

In his early twenties, he had loved her with a ferocity that was equal parts lust and devotion. He'd been waiting for her to grow up. His nightly fantasies had featured Nikki, and no one else. But just when his desire had almost come to fruition, both of their worlds had been torn apart.

Running into each other in Atlantic City a decade later had been a shock to his system. The very best kind of shock. Even now, his hands tingled with the need to touch her. But, in the end, he had been wary of the new Nikki, unable to handle how *together* she was, how grown up. She hadn't been a frightened teenager anymore. She had moved on. And she knew exactly who she was.

The new Nikki had been even more appealing than the girl he remembered. But the changes spooked him, as did the depth of his feelings, so he ran. The same way he had so many times before.

He cleared his throat. "I'll ask you again. Is it true? Is Emma my daughter?"

Nikki paled, making her skin almost translucent. "You weren't making sense earlier. I don't know why you're here. What does your brother have to do with this?"

"Don't be coy, Nikki. You sent Zane DNA results and notes that threatened Joshua. But Josh eventually concluded that he couldn't possibly have fathered a four-year-old child. So that left me. His twin. Why did you try to blackmail my brother and not me?"

As he watched, Nikki's lower lip trembled, and her

eyes glistened with tears. "I have no clue what you're talking about, and I don't appreciate your accusations. If that's all you have to say, Jake Lowell, you can get the hell out of my house."

A tiny voice intruded. "You told me not to say that word, Mommy."

Both adults jumped. Emma stood in the doorway, visibly distressed.

Nikki swiped a hand across her face, drying her eyes. "You're right, baby. Mommy goofed. I'm sorry."

Jake left his seat and crouched beside Nikki's daughter. "Hi, Emma. I'm Jake…a friend of your mother's."

Emma stared at him solemnly, her gaze filled with suspicion. "Then why did she tell you to leave?"

The irony didn't escape Jake. Were all four-year-old kids this aware of social cues? He cleared his throat. "We were having an argu—"

Nikki stood abruptly, halting his explanation with a chopping motion of her hand. She ruffled her daughter's hair. "Em, would you like to watch a *Peppa Pig* episode on my phone?" Nikki gave him an exasperated look. "I don't allow her much screen time, but it would give us a chance to finish this conversation."

Emma's face lit up. She smiled at Jake, distracted by the promised treat. "They're called 'Peppasodes.' Get it?"

Jake grinned for the first time, his mood lifting despite the situation. The child's charm and obvious intelligence delighted him. "I get it, munchkin."

He stood and gave Nikki a measured glance, trying not to notice the way her soft, fuzzy sweater delineated her breasts. He wanted to hold her, to relearn the contours of her body. The sexual awareness threatened his focus. "I have another idea. If you can get a babysitter on such short notice, I'll take you to dinner."

Now Nikki's face showed no emotion at all. Her gaze was level, and her arms wrapped around her waist in a defensive posture. After a couple of heartbeats, she took her phone from her pocket, tapped a few icons and handed it to Emma. "You may take it to your room, sweetheart. Fifteen minutes. No more. I set the timer."

When Emma was gone, Nikki sighed. "The truth is, Jake, I can't afford a babysitter right now. The holidays are coming, and I'm saving every penny for Emma's gifts from me and from Santa. Can't we just wrap this up? I honestly have no clue what you're talking about. I've never been in contact with your brother about *anything*."

Jake pulled a sheet of paper from his pocket. Earlier, Joshua had printed out one of the incriminating emails. "So you deny sending this?"

Their fingers brushed when Nikki took the note. She glanced down, read the contents and moaned. If she had been pale before, she was ashen now. "Oh, my God."

Her obvious distress convinced Jake she was telling the truth. But that only deepened the mystery. "Let me pay for a sitter," he said urgently. "We need to clear the air." He pulled a business card from his wallet and gave it to her. "This is my cell number. I'll grab coffee somewhere and return a few phone calls. Let me know when you work it out. I can pick you up at seven."

She shook her head vehemently. "No. If we do this, I want to be back home to do the bed-and-bath routine with Emma. We would have to eat early. Five thirty."

He blinked. "Ah. Okay. Call me."

That beautiful bottom lip trembled again. "I'll see what I can do," she whispered.

He was incredulous to realize that he was aroused, hard and ready. It had been five years since he had made love to her, but it might as well have been yesterday. It was difficult to cast Nikki as the villain when he wanted her even now. Was he so besotted that he could ignore her lies?

Her anguish touched him despite the turmoil she had caused his family. He brushed her soft cheek with a single fingertip. "It's not the end of the world, Nik. But I do want answers. Don't try an end run. I'm not leaving town until you and I get a few things straight."

Once Jake said goodbye, Nikki made the necessary phone call and fretted. She knew a threat when she heard one. Even if it *was* couched in seeming cordiality. Jake was not a man who bluffed.

She remembered watching him play poker with other guys in high school—*after* class mostly, but whenever they could elude faculty detection. All the parties involved had been highly privileged teenagers with virtually unlimited resources.

Jake had taken bragging rights as top dog, and he loved it. People *thought* he bluffed…and would bet against him time and again. But his lazy, chilled attitude concealed an amazing skill with numbers.

Was that why he had been in Atlantic City? To gamble? If so, he would have won. She knew that much.

But gambling had been the last thing on his mind the night the two of them had gone up to his hotel room. When a hot shiver worked its way down her spine, she knew she was in trouble.

Reluctantly, she dragged her attention back to the present. Emma was bouncing with glee that her favorite babysitter was coming over. Nella was a college-aged woman who lived just down the street. She had five brothers and sisters and was no stranger to caring for little ones. Nella adored Emma and the feeling was mutual, so Nikki was free to have dinner with Jake.

Despite the gravity of the situation, she couldn't squelch a little flutter of anticipation. As she showered and changed, she vacillated between fear and excitement.

She had known this day would come eventually. But not like this.

Since giving birth four years ago, her social life had been mostly nonexistent. The only remotely suitable outfit she owned for having dinner with Jake Lowell was a sophisticated black pantsuit that she paired with an emerald silk chemise and spiky black heels. She left her hair down and added a spritz of her favorite perfume. She probably shouldn't be dressing up at all, but maybe deep down inside she wanted Jake to see what he was missing.

The scent was for *her* benefit, not his. She needed a confidence boost.

He arrived at five thirty on the dot. Nikki didn't give him a chance to come inside. She hurried out to the car, almost tripping on the sidewalk in her haste to keep him from seeing Emma again. She would protect her baby girl at all costs.

Jake hopped out and opened the passenger door of the sinfully luxurious roadster he was driving while in New Jersey. When he helped Nikki in with a hand under her elbow, she was wrapped in the smells of soft leather and warm male.

She was glad when Jake closed the door and went around to the driver's side, though it wasn't much of a reprieve. The car's interior was intimate. With every breath, she inhaled him. Not that his aftershave was overpowering. In fact, she wasn't sure he wore any. She might only be smelling soap on his skin.

Either way, she was susceptible to his considerable appeal.

"Why did you change clothes?" she asked. He now wore a conservative dark suit, though most restaurants seldom enforced any kind of dress code these days.

He shot her a cautious grin. "Because I knew you would look nice. You always did enjoy sprucing up for an evening out."

What could she say? He was right about the old Nicole Reardon. That teenager had owned two closets full of designer clothes. Nikki had lived in a pampered world that seemed a lifetime away.

Intentionally, she drew his attention to the night that had gone so well and ended so badly. "Things are different now. In Atlantic City I was wearing a cocktail waitress uniform when I ran in to you. Not exactly haute couture."

He shrugged, his sideways glance filled with dark male interest. "I can't say that I noticed. I was more interested in getting you out of *whatever* you were wearing."

That shut her up. He was right. They had both been intent on one thing. The results had been spectacular.

Tonight, Jake had made reservations at an upscale seafood restaurant with white linen tablecloths and plenty of candlelight. The ambiance made Nikki the slightest bit uncomfortable. She and Jake weren't a typical couple. And they certainly weren't celebrating anything.

Once they were seated at a table overlooking a small manmade lake, Jake gave her his undivided attention. But his face was hard to read. "Thank you for coming. I know this was last-minute."

"My sitter was available. It worked out."

"Good."

The conversation was painfully stilted. Memories of

the last time they had been together swirled beneath the words. "Do you think about Atlantic City?" she asked quietly.

His jaw tightened. "Don't be coy, Nik. Of course I do. We hadn't seen each other in a decade, and there you were. Wearing one of those provocative outfits. Your legs were about a million miles long."

The flash of heat in his eyes told her he remembered *everything*. She hadn't been sure until right now. For her, the night had been a watershed moment, the culmination of all her girlish fantasies. But Jake was a man of the world. She had assumed their tryst was another notch on his bedpost.

"It seemed to embarrass you," she said hesitantly. "That I was working as a waitress in a casino. You acted very odd at first."

He nodded slowly. "I was startled. I'll admit it. I went to Atlantic City for some fun. Just a quick flight in and out. Seeing you was a punch to the gut. The girl I used to date was wealthy and pampered. I was aware that you and your mom lost everything. But witnessing the personal cost of your father's deceit stunned me. I didn't know what to do with that information or how to relate to you."

Nikki shrugged and snagged a fat boiled shrimp from the appetizer plate. "You don't have to feel sorry for me, Jake. No one *wants* to be poor, but the rapid fall in my social position taught me a lot."

"Like what?"

He seemed genuinely interested.

"Well…" She paused, thinking back. "I learned there are many very nice people in the world. And a few jerks, of course. I learned how hard a person has to work to earn five hundred dollars a week after taxes. I learned how scary it is not to have a safety net."

His gaze darkened. "Those are some damn serious lessons."

"Maybe. But I also learned my own resilience. I discovered that although I had been a pampered princess, it felt good to be responsible for myself… To know I was stronger than I knew."

Their meals arrived, momentarily interrupting her self-analysis. Despite the gravity of this encounter with Jake, she spared a moment to appreciate the quality of the food. Her scallops were plump and perfectly grilled. She enjoyed every bite. Jake would probably be astounded if he knew how many nights she shared boxed macaroni and cheese with her daughter.

Over coffee and dessert, Jake pressed for more. "When I showed you that email, you were clearly shocked. No one is that good an actress. So, if you didn't send it, who did?"

Nikki's cheeks heated with embarrassment. "Possibly my mother."

"Why?"

"About a year ago I lost my job. I was unemployed for almost ten weeks. Money was tight. Mom kept pressing me to ask for child support from Emma's father. I put her off and put her off, but she wouldn't let it go. Finally, after she had badgered me incessantly, I told her that Joshua was the father. Your brother. That he and I weren't ever a couple, but we had been intimate for a brief period. I said he didn't know about the baby. I thought that would be the end of it."

"But it wasn't."

"Obviously not."

"Why would you lie to her?"

"Because I didn't want her to know the truth."

"And that was?"

Nikki inhaled sharply. "That *you* are Emma's father."

* * *

Jake had heard the truth from his own brother. He'd had a little time to get used to the idea. But in this moment, he realized it had all seemed like a remarkable fiction until Nikki told him straight out. He felt sick and angry and everything in between.

"Damn you, Nikki. How could you not tell me I had a child?"

If he'd been expecting her to look guilty, he was way off base.

His dinner companion stared at him with cool hauteur reminiscent of the old society princess she'd been. "A little while ago you told me you still remember our night in Atlantic City. If you'll recall, you disappeared afterward. I woke up in your hotel room *alone*. The only thing missing from that scenario was a stack of hundreds on the nightstand to make me feel like a hooker you hired for the evening."

"I had a very early flight," he muttered, guilt making him ashamed. He'd acknowledged to himself at the time that he was behaving badly, but he hadn't known how to deal with the all-grown-up Nikki, so he had left her sleeping, her vibrant red hair spread across his pillow. The provocative image had almost been enough to make him stay and miss his flight.

But he had left her, anyway.

Nikki shrugged. "It doesn't matter. That night was a long time ago. I've moved on, believe me."

Something struck him. "We used protection," he said, feeling suspicion creep back in. How could he trust her? Did he know her at all after fifteen years? If he was really the father, why the secrecy?

"Not every time." She stared him down. "It doesn't matter if you believe me or not. Emma is the result of our reckless reunion. You and I were both curious, weren't we? And blindsided by sexual attraction. A decade before that night in the casino, we had been on the verge of a physical relationship. But then your father and mine destroyed everything. I suppose Atlantic City was closure, in a way. We came full circle."

They finished their meal in silence, the mountain of regrets and what-ifs too tall to climb. Jake was achingly aware of Nikki's beauty, her poise, her intense femininity.

When Nikki was almost eighteen, Jake had fled Falling Brook never to return. Even then, he had understood what he was giving up, but his father's actions had made staying impossible. The closest Jake had come to Falling Brook in the intervening years was a visit to Atlantic City five years ago. Running into Nikki had knocked him off balance. The long-ago feelings, the yearning and the need for her, had come roaring back to life.

He and Nikki had reminisced. When Nikki finished her shift, she went to his room at his invitation. They had showered together, tumbled into bed and screwed each other until dawn. Even now, the memories made him hard.

He cleared his throat. "I'm sorry I left without saying goodbye."

She grimaced. "You're forgiven." Her gaze was filled with something he couldn't decipher. "It would have been a very awkward morning after if you had stayed," she said.

"And then you found out you were pregnant. That must have been a shock."

Her face flushed. She nodded slowly. "You have no idea. Telling my mother was hard. After Daddy died in the car crash, she imploded emotionally. Our roles reversed. She has helped me enormously with Emma, of course, but Mom leans on me."

"It makes sense. She lost her whole world and way of life. Except for her daughter." He paused, swallowing hard. "You and I didn't do much talking that night in Atlantic City. What happened to you after you left Falling Brook? Before I met up with you again?"

"Nothing earth-shattering. I made it through four years at a state school. Got my degree. Mom and I worked multiple jobs to cover tuition and to handle our living expenses."

He had a gut feeling there was more to the story. So he pushed.

"And after you finished school? I count at least five or six missing years until I ran into you in Atlantic City."

"I got married."

"Married?" He parroted the word, feeling like somebody had punched him in the belly. "Married?" So Emma did have a dad after all. Anger returned, mixed with an emotion he didn't want to examine too closely. "I'm surprised your husband is so open-minded. Letting you go out to dinner with another man..."

His sarcasm didn't even make her blink. Nikki Reardon was a cool customer. "The marriage didn't last long," she said. "Two years. He resented my privileged past. Had a chip on his shoulder about my upbringing. I realized I had said 'I do' because I was lonely. Our relationship was doomed from the start."

"I'm sorry," Jake said stiffly. He was still coping with the fact that he was *jealous*. Jealous of a faceless man who had slept with Nikki. Since when did Jake get jealous about *any* woman? He was a love-'em-and-leave-'em kind of guy.

She cocked her head. "And what about you, Jake? All I

know is that you travel the world. I'm not sure how that's a full-time occupation, but it sounds like fun."

The note of criticism stung. "I'm lucky," he said lightly. "I learned about day-trading early in my life. And I have a knack for it. In among my many adventures, I made a few bucks here and there. Enough to eat and hit the road whenever the mood strikes me."

Nikki's smile mocked his statement. "You're wearing a limited-edition Rolex. I may not have money anymore, but I haven't lost the ability to recognize luxury when I see it."

"Being comfortable isn't a crime. I like to think I'm generous with my money. I don't maintain a huge house. So I wander. I value experiences. Learning my way around the planet has changed me and made me a better person. At least I hope so."

The way Nikki stared at him made him itchy and uncomfortable. It was as if she could see through to his soul. When was the last time he had ever articulated so honestly what he wanted from life? Never?

"You're fortunate," she said slowly. "And I don't blame you a bit. You're still a young man. Healthy. Wealthy. Unattached. Why not enjoy what the world has to offer?"

Something about her response bothered him, but he couldn't pinpoint his unease.

"We need to make some plans," he said.

Nikki lowered her fork, her expression wary. "Plans?"

"Plans for integrating my life with Emma's. I've missed four years. I won't miss any more. She's a part of me."

Every bit of color leached from Nikki's porcelain complexion. Now he could almost count the smattering of freckles on the bridge of her nose. "Absolutely not," she said, her tone fierce. "I won't have you playing at fatherhood and then walking away. Emma is happy and well-adjusted. She doesn't need you, Jake."

Perhaps Nikki realized her rejection was harsh. She circled back to the beginning. "You're a good man, but you're not father material. Emma is better off having *no* father than one who flits in and out whenever the wind blows."

He ground his jaw, trying to control his temper. "You're making a lot of assumptions about me, Nik."

"It's been fifteen years since you walked away from Falling Brook. From your family. From me. You've never been back. Not once. You juggle demons, Jake."

He felt raw. Only someone who had known him so well would dare to diagnose his behavior. "At least I don't keep secrets," he muttered.

She stood abruptly and gathered her coat and clutch purse. "Take me home, please. I want to go now."

Three

Nikki was angry. And scared. Once upon a time Jake had held her entire heart in his hands. She had adored him. They had been friends forever, and then, just as she began to grow into her feelings for him in a very adult way, their fathers had ruined everything. Jake fled, and Nikki and her mom had fled, too.

But not in the same direction.

As they walked outside, Nikki barely felt the cold. At least not on her face, hands or feet. Her chest felt frozen from the inside out. How dare he blame her? Didn't he know how many times she had cried herself to sleep, wondering again and again if she had made the right choice for her daughter? For the absent Jake…

Jake started the car but left it in Park. He reached for her wrist, not letting go even when she jerked backward. "I don't want to fight with you, Nikki." He rubbed his thumb over the back of her hand with a mesmerizing stroke. "The past is the past. We can't change any of it."

In the dimly lit interior, his face was hard to read. "But your father is back," she said quietly. "That's why you're here. In New Jersey, I mean. To see him?"

Jake shrugged, his posture and expression moody. "Joshua and I are being summoned to the prison tomorrow. But to be clear, I came back because Josh asked, not for my rat bastard of a father."

His palpable misery twisted her heart and dissolved some of her animosity. She flipped her hand over and twined her fingers with his. "I'm sorry you have to see him. But maybe it will help. For closure, I mean."

"He won't answer our questions. We'll never know why he did it or what happened to the money. I can tell you that right now. My father never let us boys talk back to him…ever. He was always king. Arrogant. Proud. The worst part is, he turned his back on our mother, and for that alone, I'll never forgive him."

Nikki cupped his cheek with her free hand, feeling the late-day stubble. "Forever is a long time. Bitterness and anger poison your soul. I want you to be happy, Jake."

It was true. Despite everything that had happened, Nikki didn't want Jake Lowell to suffer. She could have found him when she turned up pregnant after their night in Atlantic City. Possibly. And told him he was a father. But he had hurt her so badly once in her life, she had been reluctant to trust him with the truth. Instinctively, she had known he could hurt her again. And she knew it now.

Jake sucked in a sharp breath. Audible. Ragged. "You're right. It's time to take you home." He released her, so she was no longer touching him.

Something shimmered in the air between them. Was

it sexual chemistry that refused to die? Nostalgia, grief and hormones were a dangerous combination.

Nikki cleared her throat. "Sure," she said.

Jake put the car in motion. Traffic was only now beginning to taper off as commuters found their way home. Nikki stared out the window, searching for answers. Was she wrong to keep Jake away from his daughter?

When he parked in front of her house, she bit her lip and stayed put. "I'll have to think about it," she said. "You and Emma. I need time. Please."

"Okay." His voice was quiet. "I don't blame you for not telling me earlier. But I know *now*, and we'll start from here."

The following morning, after a sleepless night, Nikki drove to Falling Brook. The small community where she and her mother lived was about an hour's drive away. Her mother was with Emma at the moment. Nikki's shift at the diner didn't start until eight tonight, and it was a short one. She felt the tiniest bit guilty about leaving her daughter. But this errand was important.

At ten to nine, she pulled up in front of Black Crescent headquarters. The building had been a source of conflict over the years for the way its modern architecture stuck out jarringly in the midst of Falling Brook's mostly traditional landscape.

Nevertheless, it was an impressive structure.

Nikki had dressed in the same black pantsuit from last night. But she had exchanged the sexy stiletto heels for espadrilles, and her sleeveless blouse underneath the jacket was simple white cotton.

There would be two obstacles between her and her destination. The first was a young receptionist at the front desk.

Nikki gave the barely twentysomething kid a confident smile. "I have an appointment with Mr. Lowell at nine. Is it okay if I go on up?"

The smile faltered. "His assistant will have to okay you."

"No worries. They're expecting me."

It was only partly a lie. She *had* called Joshua to tell him she needed fifteen minutes of his time. If he wasn't in, his assistant would surely have listened to his messages. So either way, Nikki wouldn't be a total surprise.

She climbed the stairs to the second floor. The executive assistant at the desk outside Joshua's office was familiar. Nikki smiled. "Haley Shaw? You're still here?"

Haley was only a couple of years older than Nikki. She had been working at Black Crescent as a college intern when Vernon and Nikki's dad, Everett Reardon, had disappeared. Well, Nikki's dad had *tried* to disappear. He'd fatally crashed his car into a tree while fleeing the police.

Nikki hadn't been inside Black Crescent headquarters since she was a senior in high school. Nothing much had changed. Her father's old office was at the opposite end of the hallway. She didn't look in that direction. Her heart was already beating too rapidly. Being inside this building brought up painful memories.

Haley had a puzzled frown between her eyebrows. "I'm sorry, I—"

"It's me. Nikki Reardon. I'm here to see Joshua. Very briefly."

The other woman's face lightened. "Nikki, of course. How nice to see you again." Her gaze went to the computer screen at her elbow. "I don't have you on his calendar…"

The door behind the desk opened, and Joshua Lowell poked out his head. "Thanks, Haley. Please hold my calls. Nikki, it's good to see you after all these years."

Nikki entered Joshua's office and waited as he closed the door. "I won't take much of your time, Josh," she said quietly, conscious of the gatekeeper just outside the door.

Joshua waved her to a comfortable seat in front of his massive desk. "No worries. Let me have your coat. What can I do for you?"

She shrugged out of her thigh-length parka, handed it to him and sat down. Joshua was Jake's twin. By all accounts, she should be feeling the tug of sexual attraction. But despite the fact that both men shared an unmistakable physical similarity, they projected a different vibe.

Josh was very handsome, confident and appealing. But he projected authority and a no-nonsense air of being all business. Where Jake was funny, and at times outrageous, Joshua was more reserved.

Nikki folded her shaky hands in her lap. "I'm sure Jake has already talked to you since last night. I owe you an apology," she said bluntly. "He showed me one of the emails my mother sent. I knew nothing about them, and I am so very sorry. I'm going to speak to her firmly and warn her never to do anything like this again. She was trying to help me, but it was wrong. I hope you can forgive me."

Joshua leaned back in his chair and smiled wearily. "I think you and I both know that parents don't always make good choices."

"Touché."

"How did my brother react when you told him he's the father? He wasn't forthcoming about that part of the evening."

Nikki tried not to fidget. Joshua Lowell was a powerful man. "Well, you had already given him a heads-up.

I suppose me telling him wasn't news. He says he wants to be part of Emma's life."

"And?"

"And I'm not sure. You know your brother, Josh. What your father did—what my father did—sent Jake running fifteen years ago. As far as I can tell, the only reason he's back at the moment is because you asked him to go with you to see Vernon. I don't think he's father material."

"You could give the guy a chance."

The suggestion was couched in mild tones, but Nikki felt the unspoken edge of criticism. Her defenses went up. "I have to protect Emma. She's my first priority."

"I understand."

"May I ask you a personal question?" she said, taking a deep breath.

His eyes widened fractionally, but he nodded. "Yes."

"Is it true that you're giving up your position here at Black Crescent? That you've been interviewing potential replacement candidates?"

Joshua nodded slowly. His gaze narrowed. "Yes. I have."

Nikki leaned forward, feeling an urgency that was perhaps not hers to feel. "Have you thought about asking Jake to replace you? I know he likes to pretend he has no depth, but he's whip-smart. Especially with finances. He could do this job and do it well. Maybe the challenge would be enough to make him stay. To put down roots."

Jake's twin sighed, and his expression filled with sympathy. "I get where you're coming from, Nikki. And, yes. That would be a great plan. But I already offered him the helm of Black Crescent, and he turned me down flat."

"Oh." The bottom fell out of her stomach. Suddenly, she realized she had been naive. She knew it was stupid to think she and Jake could have a relationship after all this time, but her need for him continued to sabotage good sense. Clearly, Jake only wanted to leave. Again.

She stood abruptly, near tears. Her sleepless night was catching up with her. "I should go. Thank you for your time."

Before Nikki could move, the door burst open and Jake strode into the room. He pulled up short when he saw her, his gaze narrowing. "What are you doing here?" The question was just short of rude.

Nikki hitched her purse on her shoulder. "I wanted to talk to Joshua. Don't worry—we're done. I'm leaving—"

Josh interrupted before Jake could speak. "It's my turn to ask *you* something, Nikki. Jake is here now, because he and I are headed into the city to see our father. It occurs to me that you might want to ask a few questions, too. Since your own father can't answer them. My dad owes you that much."

Jake's face had frozen in stone. "I don't think that's appropriate. Vernon asked to see us. No one else."

Nikki flushed, mortified. "Thank you, Josh, but Jake is right. This will be a family moment. I don't want to intrude." She scooted toward the door.

Josh snorted. "We're going to see the worthless son of a bitch who for a decade and a half let his own wife and kids think he was dead. I doubt we'll share any Hallmark moments today. You're welcome to come."

Nikki was torn. She did have questions. A million of them. Why did the two partners steal from their clients? Why did they run? Why did Vernon never come home? Why did he and Everett think it was okay to destroy dozens of lives? And for what?

Jake sighed. "Come if you want. I doubt he'll talk, anyway. He won't want to incriminate himself."

The cynicism in Jake's voice didn't entirely conceal

a son's pain. Vernon Lowell had betrayed his own flesh and blood. How could he have been so selfishly cruel?

"My mother is with Emma. Let me see if she can stay." Nikki stepped out into the hallway and called her mom's cell. It wasn't hard to fabricate an excuse. Besides, Roberta loved spending time with her granddaughter. Not to mention the fact that Nikki partially supported her mother. Other than a small government retirement check, Roberta had no income. The woman who had once been a society maven and influencer now shopped for groceries at a discount store and drove a ten-year-old car.

Nikki liked to think her mother had adapted to their new reality, but the truth was, Roberta never gave up hope that one day she might reclaim what she considered to be her rightful place in the social scene.

When Nikki returned to Josh's office, the two brothers had their heads together and were talking in low tones. They both jerked upright with identical guilty expressions on their faces.

"Am I interrupting?" she asked wryly.

"Of course not." Jake gave nothing away. "We're ready to head out. You okay with the plan?"

He didn't mention Emma's name. The oblique question was odd. "I'm good," she said.

Downstairs in the employee parking garage, Joshua motioned to a large black SUV. "We're taking mine. Jake is leaving his car here. He spoke to our security guard and asked him to feed your parking meter. I hope that's okay."

"I appreciate it." She wasn't going to jockey for shotgun position. Before either man could say a word, she climbed into the back seat. The interior was nice. It reminded her of a Secret Service vehicle. Nothing wrong with that.

Falling Brook was an hour from New York City, depending on traffic and the destination. Once Joshua put the SUV in motion, Nikki fell dead asleep…

She roused as the car slowed and turned a corner. Up ahead, she saw a sign for the correctional facility.

Jake shot her a glance over his shoulder. "You okay back there?"

She nodded, rubbing her eyes and smoothing her hair. "Yes. I can't help thinking about all the times my mother and I came to the city for a play. Or shopping. Those days seem like another lifetime, another person. I was spoiled and naive."

He frowned. "Don't beat yourself up. You were the only child of wealthy parents. Of course they gave you the best of everything."

Until they didn't.

This prison, among others, made the news now and again for overcrowding and poor treatment of inmates. Nikki shivered. Her own father could have landed here before his certain conviction. Maybe death had been a kinder sentence.

When the three of them exited the parking garage a short time later, Nikki huddled into her coat. The wind whistled through the streets between tall buildings. The sun was out, but it shone hazily behind a thin veil of clouds.

Once inside they had to go through a security checkpoint with a metal detector. She began to wish she hadn't come, but it was too late to back out now.

Joshua signed a visitor log for the three of them, and then they sat in a waiting room. About fifteen minutes later, a uniformed security officer appeared in the doorway and called Joshua's name. Jake and Nikki stood, too. Her stomach fell to her feet.

Without overthinking it, she slid her hand into Jake's. He was about to see his father for the first time in a decade and a half. What was he thinking? His fingers gripped hers tightly.

The officer's face was stoic. "Mr. Lowell has changed his mind. He doesn't want visitors today."

After a moment of silence, Josh cursed beneath his breath. He and Jake had both gone pale. Joshua straightened his shoulders. "Perhaps you misunderstood. My father *asked* us to come today. We're here as a courtesy to him."

The man shrugged. "I don't know what to tell you. Mr. Lowell was perfectly clear. He's in his cell, and he doesn't want to be disturbed."

Nikki could feel the tension in Jake's body. "Well," he said, his tone gruff. "I guess that's it." He turned on his heel, dragging Nikki in his wake.

Joshua followed them out onto the street. They all stood on the sidewalk, stunned. Nikki let go of Jake's hand, self-conscious now that Joshua might notice.

Jake exhaled and stared at the ground. "I'm not sure why we're surprised. The old man is a class-A bastard. We've done our duty. Now we're off the hook."

Joshua shook his head slowly. "I can't believe it. Why would he ask us to come and then refuse to see us?"

"Maybe he's ashamed," Nikki said. She tried to put herself in Vernon's shoes, but couldn't imagine it. What kind of parent abandoned his family?

Jake made a face that could have meant anything. "It's freezing out here, and I'm starving." He gave Nikki a quick glance. "You up for walking a couple of blocks?"

"Of course."

They ended up at a little hole-in-the-wall place the Lowell brothers remembered from their teen years. Jake actually smiled when they entered. "We used to come here on the weekends and eat pizza and play pool. We felt like such rebels."

"Why was that?" she asked.

"Because it was a million miles from Falling Brook," Josh answered. He looked around the crowded, dimly lit room with a grin. The booths were covered in faux green leather. The wooden floor was scarred. The dartboards on the far back wall might have been relics from the Second World War.

There was an awkward moment as they were being seated. A booth for three meant that two people were cozy. In this case, Jake and Nikki. She squeezed toward the wall and tried to pretend she wasn't freaked out by the fact that his leg touched hers.

He helped her take off her coat.

Though Joshua seemed oblivious to any undercurrents, Jake's gaze, intense and warm, held Nikki's for long moments. Thankfully, the waitress came, and Nikki was able to catch her breath.

It occurred to her that the three of them had been frozen in time. Jake and Nikki had left Falling Brook fifteen years ago, headed in opposite directions. Joshua had stayed behind, the dutiful son, though Nikki had to wonder if his sacrifice had been worth it.

And now, here was Nikki, pressed up against the man who made her quiver with awareness and need. She'd had a taste of intimacy with Jake…in Atlantic City. Though she didn't want to admit weakness—even to herself— the truth was, she wanted more, even if her brain was shouting *danger, danger, danger*.

"This is a weird reunion, isn't it?" she said, clearing her throat. They had finished ordering, and now her stomach growled as they waited for their meal.

Joshua nodded. He gazed at his brother. "Weird, but satisfying. I'm sorry it's taken us this long to reconnect."

Nikki hesitated and then decided to indulge her curiosity. "Tell me, Josh. How have the finances at Black Crescent recovered? I felt so guilty for years that those families lost everything."

Jake slid an arm around her shoulders, resting it on the back of the booth. "My saint of a brother has been able to repay a lot of the money."

Her eyes widened. "Really?"

Joshua grimaced. "Well, not at first. Although I wasn't implicated in the crime, the feds were all over me for several years."

Jake nodded. "Everything was liquidated, including your home, as you know, Nikki. Our cars, yachts, vacation properties. Oliver's remaining tuition for Harvard was canceled. Luckily for our mother, our home was in her name, since it had been in her family for generations. There were some Black Crescent assets liquidated, too, but not enough to cripple the company. It was in everyone's best interest to keep things afloat so Josh could start rebuilding."

"I'm glad to know that you were able to make at least *some* reparations," she said.

The food arrived, and serious talk was sidelined in favor of hot pizza.

Eventually, Joshua picked up the earlier thread. "Because of the nature of the crime, Black Crescent has been bound by some pretty stringent rules. Thankfully, I've been able to pay all the people our father cheated at least eighty or eighty-five cents on the dollar. It's not everything, but our clients signed off on the agreement. They were thrilled, actually, to know that they would recoup most of their investments over the long haul."

Jake's expression darkened. "I still want to know what happened to the money."

"Living off the grid for fifteen years isn't cheap," Nikki said.

"But he took millions." Jake shook his head slowly. "I doubt we'll ever know."

A silence fell, rife with unspoken emotions. Nikki wondered what Jake was thinking. Perhaps he was deciding how soon he could get back to his travels. Suddenly, her throat was tight. "I hate to break up the party, but I need to get back to Emma."

"Of course." Joshua raised his hand for the check, and then pinned Nikki with a determined gaze. "I was glad you turned up in my office today. I'd been planning to talk to you, anyway. Now that I have finally fulfilled all the company's legal obligations, Black Crescent will begin paying you and your mother a monthly stipend. You were victims, too."

She opened her mouth, stunned. "Oh, no. My father was one of the perpetrators. Mom and I are fine. Don't be ridiculous. We don't need the money."

Jake's eyes snapped with displeasure. "You're working in a diner, and you can't afford a babysitter. You are definitely *not* fine. My brother is doing the right thing."

Nikki straightened her spine, her cheeks burning with humiliation. "My life may not look like much to you, Jake Lowell, but I'm proud of what I've accomplished. The good things in life aren't always measured by dollars and cents."

Both Lowell twins were formidable when they put their minds to it. Joshua wouldn't be moved. "What you do with the money is up to you, Nikki. Put it away for Emma's college, if you want. But you deserve to regain what you lost."

Four

Nikki didn't sleep on the way back home, but this time, she sat quietly, listening to the two brothers' conversation. It had been a strange and unsettling day. She wanted to spend time with Jake, but she was confused and worried. If she let him come around to see his daughter, Nikki might be tempted to sleep with him again.

Joshua had offered his brother a permanent, full-time, challenging opportunity, but Jake had turned him down. Wanderlust. That's what it was. Jake didn't know how to stay in one place, and he was far too old to learn new tricks now.

In the parking garage at Black Crescent, Joshua said a quick goodbye and ran upstairs. He was late for a meeting. That left Jake and Nikki standing awkwardly.

"Let me take you to dinner tonight," Jake said. "We still have plenty to talk about. And I've missed you, Nikki."

The raw honesty in his words seduced her more than anything. "I'm sorry," she said. "I have to work."

He scowled. "Are you blowing me off?"

She lifted her chin. "I'll spend a couple of hours with Emma, and then I have to go straight to the diner."

"I see."

"How soon will you be leaving?"

His face reflected shock. "What do you mean?"

"You came home to see your father. That didn't work out. I assumed you'll be heading out again soon."

"No." He leaned back against a concrete pillar. "Are you trying to get rid of me, Nik? Is that what this is about? Are you afraid of what I make you feel?"

"I'm not afraid of you," she said, the lie sticking in her throat.

He stared at her so long she began to get fidgety. "I'm staying for my brother's wedding and my father's trial. Both of those are soon. In the meantime, maybe you and I could reconnect."

"Reconnect?" She parsed the word for meaning.

He straightened and took the few steps that separated them. "I want to touch you. Kiss you. Get to know you again. Atlantic City was only a start."

When his lips settled on hers, warm and firm, her legs threatened to buckle. Just like five years ago, this sexy, desirable man knew how to cut the ground from under her feet.

She pulled away, wiping her mouth with the back of her hand. Words came tumbling out. Words she should have censored but didn't. "I missed you so much, Jake. I fantasized about you. Wanted you. But you left me twice. Once fifteen years ago, and again in Atlantic City. Only a foolish woman would place a bet on a man who flits around the globe."

He shoved his hands in his pockets, his expression stormy. "I couldn't save you, Nikki. I couldn't save *us* back then, so I ran. I couldn't bear to stay in Falling Brook one more day. Everywhere I turned, there was another damn reporter. Digging. Poking. Prodding. Wanting every detail of our bleeding lives."

"And yet you abandoned me to the wolves."

He blinked. "Ouch. The old Nikki I knew wasn't so harsh."

"The old Nikki was a child, Jake. I had to grow up fast. It wasn't fun, and it wasn't easy. I survived, though."

"Yes, you did. You're an extraordinary woman."

Something pulsed between them. Awareness. Need. He looked so sexy she wanted to climb him like a tree and never let go. If it had been only her, perhaps she would have rolled the dice. Taken a walk on the wild side.

The kind of selfish pleasure she had embraced in Atlantic City was not a choice now. She had her mother to look out for, and she had Emma to raise. Nikki's wants and needs had to come in dead last.

"I should go," she muttered, looking at her watch. "I'm sorry your father wouldn't see you today."

"Like I said, I'm not surprised." He reached for her hand and squeezed her fingers.

"Think about it, Nikki. Not just me and Emma, but you and me. I want to spend time with both of you."

"Because you're bored and at loose ends?"

His eyes flashed. "Because she's my daughter, and you're my past."

Nikki played Barbies with Emma, started dinner and then dashed to work, leaving her mother in charge. Roberta Reardon wasn't incompetent. She was merely fragile. As Nikki poured coffee and took orders—because one of her best waitresses was out—she chatted with regulars. Half of her brain was occupied, trying to cope with the ramifications of the email she had seen on her phone just before she left the house.

It was from Black Crescent Hedge Fund—from Joshua Lowell, in particular. As he had promised, the attachment to the email was a very official-looking document. Beginning January first, Nikki and her mother would both be receiving checks for ten thousand dollars a month for a period of ten years.

The math was staggering. In the first twelve months alone, the two women together would have just shy of a quarter of a million dollars. There would be money for her mom to have almost anything she wanted, within reason. Nikki would be able to quit her job and spend these last precious months before kindergarten with Emma.

They would have financial freedom.

Why did the prospect seem so threatening? Perhaps because Nikki knew what it felt like to lose everything. She was superstitious about this extraordinary windfall. It was great that Black Crescent had recovered enough to restore much of what was lost. But Nikki's father had participated in the con, the scam.

She felt guilty.

It was late when Nikki got home, so her mom was sleeping over. That was often their pattern. Even though Roberta spent a lot of time with Emma, it was healthier for the two grown women to maintain separate residences. That hadn't always been possible in the beginning. Back when their lives had fallen apart, and Nikki had barely been an adult, they had needed to save every penny.

Eventually, things had changed.

And now, they were about to change again.

Nikki wanted desperately to go to bed, but she knew she would toss and turn if she didn't tell her mother what was about to happen. "Mom," she said. "Can I talk to you for a minute?"

Her mother raised an eyebrow. "So serious, sweetheart. What's up?"

"I had lunch with Joshua and Jake Lowell today."

Her mother paled. "Oh?"

"I found out about the emails. Your emails. And I apologized to Joshua."

Roberta Reardon went on the attack. "Well, I *won't* apologize for wanting to protect my daughter and granddaughter. Joshua Lowell is a scoundrel. He should be supporting his baby girl."

"Mom…" Nikki rubbed her temple, where a sledgehammer pounded. "Joshua is not Emma's father."

"Of course he is. Don't try to cover for him. You told me the truth."

"I lied."

Roberta Reardon stared at her daughter. "I don't understand."

"You kept badgering me when I lost my job. Trying to get me to ask Emma's father for child support. I didn't want you to know the truth, so I finally told you what you wanted to hear. I never dreamed you would try to blackmail him."

Her mother was visibly offended. "It wasn't blackmail. I never *asked* for money. I just wanted him to know he had a child."

"But he didn't."

"So, who *is* the father?"

Nikki felt her face heat. She was a grown woman, but this wasn't an easy topic to talk about with her mother. "Jake," she said quietly. "*Jake* Lowell. Not Joshua."

Roberta put her hands to her cheeks. "Well, that makes a lot more sense. You always did love that boy. He left Falling Brook, though. He's never been back. Right?"

"That's true. But about five years ago I ran into him when I was working at the casino in Atlantic City."

Her mother looked shocked. "A one-night stand? Oh, Nikki."

"I couldn't resist him, Mom. I made a mistake. But trust me, Jake hasn't changed. He's still the proverbial rolling stone. I can't risk being with a man like that."

She was strong. She could let Jake come over, let him spend time with Emma, but Nikki wouldn't risk her heart. She wouldn't give in to sexual attraction. Not this time. The stakes were too high.

Her mother's gaze judged her. "Emma deserves a father. Even one who's not around much. He's her blood kin. What did he say when you told him?"

"Not much. I only confirmed what Jake had already heard from his brother. But Jake is only here for the trial. Then he'll be gone again."

"Life is never easy, is it?" Her mother's eyes were filled with resignation.

"It felt easy when I was a kid. You and Daddy gave me a perfect childhood."

"Nothing is perfect, Nikki. I thought I had a perfect marriage, but look how that turned out. It's hard to know what's inside a person's heart."

"I'm sorry, Mom. You deserved better."

"And so do you, my dearest girl. So do you."

Jake was answering emails in his hotel room when his phone dinged. It had been twenty-four hours since he had seen Nikki. Now she was texting him.

If you don't have plans, you're welcome to come over for dinner. Maybe even read Emma a bedtime story. As a friend.

Jake shook his head wryly. He did have plans, but he would cancel them. Nikki had made an overture. He wouldn't miss this chance.

When he showed up at her house at five o'clock, he saw neighborhood kids playing outside. The weather had shifted, and the late-afternoon temps were in the upper fifties. He reached into the back seat and grabbed a shopping bag. He had bought Emma a treat for just such an occasion.

Nikki opened the door before he could ring the bell. Her face was flushed, her fiery red hair pulled up in a ponytail. Wispy curls escaped around her forehead and cheeks. Those emerald eyes searched his soul.

"Hi," she said, giving him a wary look.

Emotion gut-punched him. This woman. What was it about this woman? She was dangerous to him, to his emotions, his good sense, his need for self-preservation.

As Nikki stepped back to let him in, he saw Emma, half hiding behind her mother's leg. He squatted, greeting her at eye level. "Hey, there," he said. "I'm Jake."

Her eyes were big, her gaze solemn. "I remember. Is my mommy gonna be mad at you again?"

Jake glanced up at Nikki. "I hope not."

Nikki shook her head ruefully. "I have to finish dinner. Why don't you two get acquainted?"

Jake rattled the shopping bag. "Would it be okay if we played outside? I hate to miss this weather. And I brought Emma a ring-toss game."

Emma's face lit up. "It *is* okay." She took his hand. "We have to go to the backyard, 'cause there's a fence."

"Presents, Jake?" Nikki's expression said she disapproved.

"Relax. It was less than fifteen bucks. I have a few friends with kids. They always tell me simple toys are the best."

Nikki spied unashamedly out the window over the sink. Emma didn't always warm up to strangers, but perhaps Jake's thoughtful gift had lowered her defenses. Nikki wouldn't be so easily convinced. Jake was a loner, a man who deliberately stayed away from any kind of home base, any kind of tie. She wouldn't let him hurt her or her daughter.

Even so, Nikki had to admit he was good with the little girl. Patient. Kind. Time and again, he showed her how to position the ring horizontally and how to hold her hand sideways to fling it. Emma got closer and closer. When she finally landed the first one, father and daughter did a spontaneous victory dance.

Moments later the duo came inside, their body language relaxed. Nikki was bemused by the way her daughter had taken to Jake. Did Emma feel some mystical bond? Did she recognize her father on some visceral level?

Nikki tried to swallow her misgivings. "Wash up, please. This will be ready soon."

Jake gave her an odd glance. "Emma wants to show me the butterflies in her room. We won't take long."

Nikki followed them, unable to squash her anxiety about seeing Jake inside her house. Emma loved butterflies. Always had, even as a toddler. On her fourth birthday, Nikki had let Emma redo her room. Bedspread, posters, mobiles hanging from the ceiling.

Jake whistled long and low. "This is amazing, Em."

Nikki waited for Emma to correct him. No one short-ened her daughter's name. But Emma simply beamed. "I can name fifteen different species on flash cards," she said, "and I'm working on the others. Some of the words are hard."

Jake seemed surprised. "You're reading already?"

Emma gave him the kind of eye-rolling look that pre-cocious kids have been giving parents since the begin-ning of time. "I started reading when I was three. It's easy, Jake. Don't you love books?"

He nodded. "I do, at that. And I'm glad you do, too." He stared around the room, taking in every bit of it. "Emma," he said, "I have something to show you." He sat in the rocking chair, the one Nikki had bought at a thrift store when Emma was an infant. He lifted Emma onto his lap.

She squirmed and got comfortable. "What is it?"

He pulled his phone out of his pocket. "You know the monarchs, right?"

"Of course. They're the easiest ones."

"Last year, just about this time, I was in Mexico." He pointed to the large map on her wall. "It's that pink coun-try under the United States."

"I know," she said. "There's a kid at my preschool named Matias. He and his mom moved here from Mex-ico when he was a baby."

"Ah. So you know geography, too." The expression on his face when he glanced over at Nikki made her shrug and grin. Emma was very bright. And endlessly curious.

"What's jog-raphy?" Emma asked, perplexed.

"Never mind, kiddo. Here. Look at this." He cued up a video and Emma zeroed in.

"Wow," she said.

"It's part of the monarch-butterfly migration. People come from all over the world to see it."

Emma's intense absorption tugged at Nikki's conscience. Travel was something she hadn't been able to afford. At least not anywhere out of state.

Her daughter looked up at Jake, wonder in her eyes. "Do they really fill up the whole sky?"

"It seems that way. It's so beautiful, your heart wants to dance."

"And maybe you wished you could be a butterfly, too?"

His voice got all low and gravelly. "Maybe I did."

Nikki tried to swallow the lump in her throat. "Will you help her wash her hands? I've put pasta in the pot. We'll eat in five."

In the kitchen, she concentrated on her task, but her brain raced like a hamster in a wheel. Jake had so much world experience to share with his daughter. Nikki had traveled as a teenager, but taking trips had ground to a halt when she and her mother had been sent away from the only home Nikki had ever known.

Her father had cleaned almost everything out of the checking and savings accounts. Her mother had been forced, by necessity, to sell most of her jewelry that first year so she and Nikki wouldn't starve.

When Nikki's two dinner companions returned to the kitchen, they were discussing the merits of brownies versus cupcakes.

Emma took her usual seat at one end of the table. "Mommy makes both of them good. You'll see."

"No pressure," Nikki muttered. Her daughter wouldn't understand that a man like Jake had dined on the world's finest cuisine in dozens of the most cosmopolitan cities.

But Jake was unfazed. "Comfort food is the best,"

he said, digging into his spaghetti as soon as Nikki was seated. "This is amazing, Nikki."

"I'm glad you like it." She had set the table so that Emma was between her two parents. Maybe Emma didn't feel the weight of the moment, but Nikki definitely did. Judging by the look on Jake's face, he did, too.

During the entire meal, he watched Emma with a combination of pride and wonder that would have been adorably macho if Nikki hadn't been so torn about the future.

When the meal was over, Nikki put on her stern-mommy look. "Into the shower with you, ladybug. And don't forget to brush your teeth."

When Emma disappeared, Jake raised an eyebrow. "Isn't she a little young for that?"

Nikki picked up the plates while Jake gathered the silverware. "Three months ago, she informed me that baths were for babies. She's trying her best to grow up as fast as she can, and I'm trying my best to slow her down."

Jake watched Nikki put the dishes in the sink, then he dropped the silverware and pulled her close, tucking a stray strand of hair behind her ear. "You've done a great job with her, Nikki. She's smart and funny."

"I'm glad you think so." Nikki backed away. She was supposed to be focusing on her daughter, but with Jake this close, all she could feel were her wobbly knees and sweaty palms. After fifteen years, she should have developed some kind of immunity, but whatever pheromones he'd been blessed with made her crazy.

They weren't touching. Not really. Not anymore. But the eight inches of air between them vibrated with deep emotion. She wanted him.

Did he feel the same urgency?

"I need to check on Emma," she croaked. "Don't

worry about the kitchen. Make yourself comfortable in the living room. I have basic cable."

His lips twitched. "Go, little mama. Look after your chick."

The whole time Nikki supervised Emma's drying off and choosing clean pajamas and picking a bedtime book, her skin quivered. Jake was in the next room. Waiting. He was staying to talk about Emma. She knew that.

Maybe Nikki was the only one in this house acting immature.

When Emma was completely ready for bed, Nikki kissed the top of her head. "Would you like Mr. Jake to read your bedtime story tonight?"

The little girl's face brightened. "Sure. But I need to get a different book."

Nikki glanced at the picture book in her daughter's hands. It was a Caldecott Medal winner about Irish fairies and sliding down rainbows—one of Emma's favorites.

"I don't understand, sweetie. You love this book."

"Yeah, Mommy. But it's kind of *girly.* Mr. Jake is a boy, and he's real smart. I've got other books he'll like better." Before Nikki could stop her, Emma was tearing through her bookcase, moving and tossing and stacking until she found what she wanted. "Here it is."

Nikki frowned. "I thought we agreed that book was a little too hard for you to read right now. Maybe next year, Emma." It was a thick, several-hundred-page volume about the solar system.

"But I'm *not* reading it, Mommy. Mr. Jake is."

"It's far too long, baby."

"He can do just a few pages."

Nikki knew when she was beaten. She followed her daughter to the front part of the house where Jake was sprawled on the sofa resembling the dangerous male animal he was. He hadn't bothered turning on the TV. Instead, he was staring at his cell screen.

When they walked into the room, he immediately dropped the phone. "Hey, there."

Emma walked right up to him and handed over the book. "Will you read me a story? I picked this one for you," she said, beaming. "Because you told me you liked zubzertories."

Nikki shot Jake a puzzled glance.

He smiled. "Observatories. And I'd love to read this to Emma."

"Ah. Well, twenty minutes, no more, please." Nikki needed to get Jake out of her house before her resolve cracked.

Even when she left the room, Jake's low, masculine voice carried in the small house. It was impossible to ignore him, impossible to pretend she didn't react to him strongly.

Fifteen minutes later, Nikki returned to her daughter's room. "Time for bed, Emma."

"Just one more chapter, please, Mommy."

Nikki had played this game far too many times. "Now means now. Tell Mr. Jake thank you."

Emma slid off Jake's lap. "Thank you, Mr. Jake," she said, her expression doleful. The sad-little-girl act sometimes won her five extra minutes, but Nikki held firm this time.

Nikki managed a smile for Jake, though she was nervous and jittery. "There's beer and wine in the fridge. Help yourself."

He gave her a slow, sleepy smile. "I'm good. Take your time."

Emma yawned. "Can Mr. Jake tuck me in?"

Nikki froze. She was pretty sure Jake did, too. It was one thing for a visitor to read a book. Tucking in was for family members. "Um, no, sweetheart. That's for mommies and little girls." She picked up her *baby*, who was getting almost too heavy to carry like this. "I'll be back, Jake."

Five

Jake stood and paced. Suddenly, this small house felt stifling. The home-cooked meal. The cute kid. The beautiful mother. All the things he had managed to avoid in his life.

In Atlantic City five years ago, Nikki had appeared as a sexy woman from his past. A chance to indulge in some hot and heavy no-strings sex. But now, Nikki had changed. She had moved on. She had grown up and matured. Or maybe she had already changed five years ago, and he hadn't seen it.

Though Jake admired her for the life she had created despite her father's deeds, he was wary. He'd been on the run for far too long to be seriously tempted by the idea of *settling down*. It would be unfair to let Nikki think that he might. Better to keep his distance and fight the sexual hunger that consumed him.

Maybe Nikki was right. He had no business playing "Daddy" unless he was ready to go all in. And he wasn't.

Returning to Falling Brook had been hard enough.

This little blue-collar town where Nikki lived, Poplar Ridge, was less than an hour away from where she had grown up, but by every other measure, it might as well have been on a different planet. Jake had hung his hat in all kinds of communities over the years. He'd enjoyed luxury, and he had found meaning in testing himself with deprivation. But all the while, he had known he had a safety net. He always had money.

Even when he fled Falling Brook and the reporters that were hounding him, he'd had secret money saved from playing poker. Jake had used his skills in day-trading and gradually built his fortune.

But Nikki and her mother had been left with virtually nothing.

Roberta Reardon had come from a social background and a generation where trophy spouses entertained and visited the spa but weren't employed. Nikki had been seventeen, almost eighteen, when her father disappeared. Not a child, but certainly not a full-grown adult. In the midst of grief, her whole world had imploded. At the time, Jake had insisted she was partly to blame. Even now, he regretted that.

He had lashed out at his teenage girlfriend, because the truth was too much to bear. Vernon and Everett had embezzled money and left their families behind. In search of what? If Everett Reardon hadn't been killed, if he had joined his partner in the Bahamas, what were the two men hoping to accomplish?

That unanswered question had shaped Jake's life. Bitterness and angry regret kept him on the run. Or maybe it was the memory of the woman he had lost that locked him in a lonely cage of his own making.

Thinking about the past was never fruitful. Jake

shoved aside the baggage and sprawled in a chair, his focus returning to the present. What would Nikki and Roberta do with their windfall from Black Crescent? Jake had thought about asking if Joshua could add Nikki and her mom to the list of people Black Crescent was repaying, but Josh had beaten him to the punch.

Would Nikki and Roberta want to return to Falling Brook?

His turbulent thoughts were eventually interrupted when Nikki appeared in the doorway. Her ponytail was mussed from being in bed with her daughter.

"Is she asleep?" he asked.

"Close," Nikki said. "She played hard today."

Jake patted the sofa beside him. "Come sit with me."

Nikki hesitated, but did as he asked. It didn't escape his notice that she left a good four feet between them.

Didn't matter. He felt connected to her and drunk with wanting her. He didn't know what to do about that.

"Emma is delightful," he said gruffly.

"Thank you." Nikki's response was subdued. In fact, she seemed to be having trouble looking at him.

He sighed. "You're right about me. I don't know that I'm father material. I'd still like to hang out with her now and then while I'm here. But I won't cross any boundaries, I swear. I would never tell her she's mine. That would be cruel."

Finally, Nikki lifted her head. "I don't know if you saw it, but what happened between you two tonight was extraordinary. She's usually shy with strangers, especially men. But with you, she was happy. Excited. How can I *not* tell her the truth?"

Now the roles were reversed. Nikki wanted full disclosure, and Jake was uncertain about the future. "Let's give ourselves time," he said, feeling some unseen noose tighten around his neck.

"So, what? You'll just stay away until we figure it out?"

"Do you have a better idea? If our goal is not to hurt our daughter, we both have some thinking to do."

She nodded thoughtfully. "I suppose you're right."

"But let me be clear about one thing."

Her eyes widened. "Oh?"

He reached for her hand, stroking the back of it with his thumb. "I don't think I can stay away from *you*. I'm feeling the same things I felt five years ago. Seeing you face-to-face destroys me. Everything inside me says, 'Hell yeah!' I want to make love to you, Nikki. Rather desperately, in fact."

Her eyes flashed with anger. "Those feelings in Atlantic City didn't last 'til morning, Jake. You're a flight risk."

"What does that have to do with me wanting you? Besides, I don't think this attraction is one-sided…is it?"

Tears sheened her eyes. Her chin wobbled. Her fingers curled around his. "No. But at what cost?"

"It will be our little secret. Just the two of us."

"We both know that secrets can tear a family apart." Her gaze clung to his, begging for assurance.

"Not this one. I give you my word. Come here, Nik. Let me show you."

They met in the middle of the sofa, a ragged curse from him, a low moan from her. He wrapped his arms around her and pulled her close, kissing her recklessly, telling himself there was no danger. Sex was good. Sex was healthy.

Her body was soft, pliant. Her scent tantalizing.

She was perfection in his arms. That one night in Atlantic City had haunted his dreams. He told himself he had embellished the memories…the way their bodies seemed to recognize each other. But something had been different that night, and it was different still.

He wanted Nikki to be his teenage sweetheart, but she was not the same woman now. She had made a life for herself. What had Jake ever done but run?

Despite his unease, he couldn't walk away. Touching her, kissing her, needing her. It was as simple and perfect as falling asleep in a feather bed. But the dark edge of lust was something more. Dangerous. Powerful. He was a man who respected women, yet in this fraught moment, he felt capable of behavior that frightened him.

Why, after so many years, did Nikki still have the power to push him beyond all reasonable boundaries?

When she put a hand to his chest and shoved, he was almost relieved.

"Wait, Jake. Please."

He released her instantly, still recognizing the beast inside him. "You changed your mind." His tone was low and flat, his mood mercurial.

She met his stormy eyes bravely. "I want you every bit as much as you want me. But I don't have the same freedom you do. Every choice I make, every road I take, affects at least two other people. My life is inextricably tied to my mother's and to Emma's. I don't have the luxury of spontaneity or reckless pleasure. As much as I wish things were different, I have to face the truth."

"So you *won't* make love to me?" He was frustrated now and trying to pretend this conflict wasn't proof of all his misgivings.

"I don't know," she said, the words taut with misery.

"That's no answer, Nik."

"Then how about this? Not now. It's too risky."

"Does Emma wake up during the night? Is that it?"

"Not usually. But it feels wrong with her in the next room."

"How can it be wrong if our being together created that perfect little girl?" Nikki was pale, obviously distressed. It was all he could do to keep his distance.

"Jake," she said quietly. "This thing between us is like sitting in front of a fireplace on a cold night. Even though we scattered the logs years ago, and the blaze went out, somehow, a couple of small embers stayed close enough to create danger. I can't explain it. We're a weird paradox. Virtual strangers who somehow know each other very well."

"You don't feel like a stranger to me." It was the God's honest truth. One encounter in fifteen years? They should be awkward together. Instead, touching her was the easiest thing he had ever done. He wanted to drown in her.

"Maybe we need to back up. Spend some time talking. Getting reacquainted."

"Talking?" He clenched his fists. "What will that accomplish?"

She lifted her chin. "You think you know me, but you don't, Jake. We can't pick up where we left off fifteen years ago. And not even where we were in Atlantic City. Time changes people. I've changed."

His body vibrated with sexual tension. He was hard and desperate—a toxic combination. There was the tiniest possibility she was right. Only in Jake's case, he had dealt with the tragedy in his past by moving slowly through the years. He'd made plenty of money. But he lived from day to day. Alone. Sometimes in the midst of a sea of people, but alone.

Now he was back in New Jersey. What was his next step?

Emma complicated the outcome. Enormously.

Maybe Jake could be a lover, but not a dad. It was painful to admit.

He exhaled and told himself no man ever died from unfulfilled lust. "What do you want to talk about?"

"Would popcorn make you feel better?"

His nose twitched, already imagining the scent. "With real butter?"

"Sure."

He followed her into the kitchen. Nikki's body language was wary, as if she knew he was on a short fuse. As he watched, she pulled out an old-fashioned aluminum popper. She added oil, seasoning and kernels, then put a chunk of butter in a tiny pan and set it to low.

Her small dinette chair was barely big enough to support his weight. He sat, anyway, his knee bouncing under the table with nervous energy.

When there was nothing to do but wait, she joined him, her body language guarded.

Jake plowed ahead. "What shall we talk about?"

Nikki shrugged. "You first."

"Will your mom want to go back to Falling Brook now that money won't be an issue?"

"Honestly? I don't know."

"I guess she's made friends here."

"Not really. We've moved around a lot, at least we did before Emma was born. For years, we used my mother's maiden name. A dozen different apartments. A dozen not-so-legal leases. She was terrified that someone would recognize her from the news."

"That's understandable." Wasn't that why Jake, himself, had fled?

The sound of the first pops ricocheted in the small room.

Nikki jumped to her feet. "You want wine?"

"Coke goes with popcorn. If you have any…"

She cocked her head. "Jake Lowell is asking for a sugary soft drink?"

He crossed his arms over his chest. "It's been a stressful week. I think I'm entitled."

"That's an understatement, for sure. Here you go." She got a can and handed it to him, then reached up into the cabinet for bowls. "I'll let you salt yours how you like it."

"Thanks." The fact that Nikki's brief, light touch affected him so deeply meant he was in real trouble.

Moments later they were enjoying their snack in silence.

His throat tightened. "Your turn," he said gruffly.

"I'm surprised you're willing to answer questions."

He frowned. "What does that mean?"

"Fifteen years ago, it was like you disappeared off the face of the earth."

The tops of his ears got hot. "It wasn't that extreme," he said, feeling guilty all over again. "I sent the occasional text or email to my brothers. First question, please."

"I know you're good at playing the stock market. But day-trading isn't a full-time occupation, at least not in your situation. What else have you done for the past fifteen years? I wanted to write to you, but I never worked up the nerve to contact Joshua and ask for your addresses, snail mail or otherwise."

"Why would you have to 'work up the nerve'?"

She gnawed her bottom lip. "You blamed me for what happened. I thought Josh might, too. Believe me, I've wished a million times that I could turn back the clock and beg my father not to get involved with yours."

Jake's chest was tight. Mostly because he knew Nikki was right. Even as a twenty-two-year-old, Jake had known that his dad must have orchestrated whatever convoluted plan led to the painful implosion of Black Crescent. With Vernon Lowell missing and presumed dead, and Everett killed in a car chase, the details weren't all that important.

"I can't believe I'm saying this," he muttered, "but I'd rather talk about me than what happened fifteen years ago."

Nikki nodded. "Fair enough." She poked at the unpopped kernels at the bottom of her bowl. "You can hit the high spots. What does a twentysomething do when he sets out to seek his fortune?"

Jake leaned his chair back on two legs, completely willing to narrate a travelogue. That was a hell of a lot easier than dealing with messy emotions. "Everyone expected me to head to Europe, so I started out in Wyoming instead," he said simply. "Working for a mountain-climbing school. Teaching inexperienced tourists the basics, so they could climb Grand Teton. It was a dangerous job at times. And I pushed the edge more than I should have. I wasn't suicidal. But I didn't really care what happened to me at that point."

"How long were you there?"

"About eighteen months. One day I heard some guys whispering and snickering. They shut up when I walked by. I found out later that one of our climbing school pupils was from Jersey and recognized my face and my name from the news."

"That must have been awful."

"It was shocking. Humiliating. So I decided that North America was too close. I set out for Australia. I always wanted to travel more, so that's what I did. A couple of weeks here. A month there. Gradually, I worked my way around the globe."

"Sounds like fun."

"It was. Mostly. Still, there were days I was so home-sick I could hardly stand it. It was as if I was living life in slow motion. But that slow pace was the only way I knew how to handle the upheaval. Every time I thought about flying back to New Jersey, I remembered there was nothing left to return to."

"How can you say that? Joshua and Oliver were here... and your mom."

"I sent Oliver a few texts over the years, but he never answered. I thought he was still angry with me for leaving, but now I know he was busy partying, doing drugs. And I couldn't face Joshua. I had run out on my twin... Left him to clean up my father's mess."

"My father's mess, too..."

"Yes."

"What about your mom?"

"She was in deep denial when I left. The few times I called home it was the same. 'Vernon will be back. This is just one of his stunts.' After six months, I still called her occasionally, but I quit talking about anything that happened at Black Crescent. I didn't mention my dad's name. It was too damn sad."

"I'm sorry, Jake."

"She and Oliver went to see him recently. Before I got back. Joshua couldn't get any details out of them."

"In a way, your mom was right. Vernon *did* come back. Don't you wonder what happened to the money?"

"Every damn day."

After a heartbeat of silence, Nikki smiled. "Still my turn," she said. "What about you, Jake? Did *you* ever get married?"

The question stopped him dead in his tracks. "No," he said bluntly.

"Any close calls?"

The expression on her face reflected mild curiosity, but he suspected she was hiding her true feelings. "None. I like my freedom too much."

Nikki surprised him when she reached across the table and squeezed his arm briefly. "We have to get past this and move on. We've both played the hands we were dealt. I don't hold any grudges, Jake. You are who you are. Maybe we could tell Emma the truth when she turns eighteen."

"And have her resent me for missing her childhood?"

"You can't have it both ways."

He had to get out of this house. His head threatened to explode with a million unanswered questions, and his libido wanted to get laid.

Not with just any woman. With Nikki. Nikki of the pale white skin and the fiery hair and the eyes that went moss green or forest green depending on her mood. She was a fascinating, desirable female.

Even though he had gone an entire decade without seeing her, he could have used the encounter in Atlantic City to build something new, something more than his vagabond existence offered him. But he hadn't had the guts to try again.

His own lazy, selfish choices had brought him to this point.

Jake had run away fifteen years ago. He had wanted to be left alone, and he had succeeded in his quest. As he wandered the globe, he'd kept his friendships and his sexual relationships on a shallow plane. Expedient. Disposable. Forgettable.

The one woman he had never been able to forget was Nikki Reardon.

Now it was too late.

He stood up abruptly, nearly tumbling the chair. "I need to go," he said. "I'll call you later."

Nikki stood, too, seeming hurt or relieved or maybe both. "Okay."

"Joshua is getting married soon. I'll need a plus-one."

She gave him a loaded look. "Is that an invitation?"

"You know it is," he said, feeling more irritated by the minute.

Nikki shook her head slowly. "Charming. You sure know how to make a girl feel wanted. I'll think about it."

"What's to think about? Who else would I take?"

Nikki poked her finger in the center of his chest. "You need to learn some manners, Jake Lowell. I don't know what kind of women you've been hanging around with, but I'm not some floozy you can pick up and put down when the mood strikes you."

"Floozy?" He laughed out loud despite his uncertain temper. "This is the twenty-first century, Ms. Reardon. Women aren't judged for their romantic entanglements anymore. Haven't you heard?"

She poked him a second time, eyes flashing. "You know what I mean. You're the absolute definition of a man who keeps a woman in every port. Just because you and I share a history doesn't mean I'm going to let you push me around. Are we clear?"

They were toe-to-toe now. He could feel her breath on his skin, hear the uneven hitch in her angry words. "Poke me one more time, Nik. I dare you."

Her chest heaved as she sucked in a breath and exhaled. "I'm not scared of you." One feminine finger prodded his sternum.

"Well, you should be, you frustrating woman." He groaned the words and snatched her up in his arms, backing her into the refrigerator. "Because you make me insane."

Six

Nikki was a rule follower, a straight arrow.

Even as she recognized that Jake was neither of those things, she was drawn to him inescapably.

He hitched her legs around his waist and buried his face in the curve of her neck. "You smell good, Nik."

As he nibbled the sensitive skin below her ear, she shuddered. "You like the scent of tomato sauce?"

"On you I do." He caught her earlobe between his teeth. "Tell me to go home." He begged her with as much sincerity as she had ever heard from him.

She smoothed his hair. "You told me you don't have a home."

"You know what I mean."

He let her slide to her feet, but where their bodies were pressed together, she could feel the hard length of him. Her memories of Atlantic City undermined her good sense. "I've dreamed of you holding me like this, Jake."

"I did more than hold you five years ago," he said huskily.

She unbuttoned two buttons of his shirt and slipped her hand inside to test the warm contours of his chest. "Yes, you did. I was there, remember?"

Sexual tension pulsed between them.

Jake shifted his feet. "At the risk of jumping the gun, are there any condoms in this house?"

"What do *you* think?" She kissed his chin and tasted his lips, loving the way he shuddered at her touch. "Don't you have one or two?"

"Not on me."

His disgruntled response might have been funny if Nikki wasn't so wound up. Being a single mom for the past four years had been a monastic existence. Life was hard. Busy and good, but hard. Not much time for a woman to indulge her sexual needs. And now here was Jake—sexy, gorgeous, every inch the man of her dreams.

She wanted badly to undress him and explore his taut, hard body. But if she wasn't going to have sex with him, there were rules to follow. Fair play. Self-denial.

Though it took remarkable willpower on her part, she moved away. "Would you like some coffee?" she asked, trying to pretend as if everything was normal.

Her kitchen looked the same as always, despite Jake's presence. Pine cabinets. Faded Formica countertops. Beige walls. This little house was dated and homely, but the community was friendly, and crime was low. Nikki's neighbors were Black and white and Hispanic. Young and old.

The man with the laser gaze stared at her, his jaw rigid. "Coffee? That's your answer?"

"I don't want to fight with you, Jake."

"And you don't want to have sex with me."

She shook her head slowly. "Not like this." She dealt with the coffeepot and turned it on. When she faced him again, he was leaning in the doorway, arms crossed over his broad chest, a dark scowl doing nothing to diminish his sexual pull. "Have you bought a return airline ticket?" she asked. No point in pretending.

"I have an open-ended one. Because the judge has fast-tracked the trial, I want to catch the opening arguments. Apparently, my father is planning to make a statement. Given the nature of the case, the judge is also allowing wronged parties to face the man who stole from them. Perhaps even let them speak."

"Poor Vernon."

Jake raised an eyebrow. "You have more charity than I do. My father *deserves* public condemnation. In fact, that's the tip of the iceberg. He should be—"

Nikki held up her hand, halting the flow of angry words. "Stop." She poured a cup of coffee and handed it to him. "Bitterness will destroy you. Mom and I spent the first several years of our exile constantly in the midst of grief and emotional upheaval. It was only when we decided to forgive my father that we were finally able to move on."

"I've moved on," he said, his tone defensive.

"You moved *away*," Nikki said. "Ran away. By your own admission. It's not the same thing. I know you're in Falling Brook for a brief time, but why don't you use these weeks to find closure with your dad? Actually, closure with the whole dismal experience?"

He stared down at his coffee, his expression moody. "Can we take this outside? I need some air. It's not all that cold."

"Sure." She grabbed a coat and the baby monitor. Jake retrieved his jacket from the living room.

"A baby monitor?" he said. "Still?"

"It gives me peace of mind."

"I can understand that."

They settled on the porch, skipping the swing in favor of sitting on the top step. Nikki didn't bother with the light. Because the stoop was narrow, she and Jake were hip-to-hip. She wanted badly to lean her head on his shoulder and dream of a future that included everything she wanted.

But that was futile. She sipped her coffee in silence. They weren't the only people taking advantage of the unexpectedly mild evening. Older kids still played up and down the street.

Without warning, Jake put a hand on her knee, making her jump.

"Why don't you and Emma come to Switzerland with me when this is all over?" he said. "For a visit," he clarified, as if wanting to make sure she understood. "The mountains are magnificent, and I think Emma would like it."

"What's in Switzerland?" Nikki kept the question light and casual, though her guts were in a knot.

"I own a small house there. I have a great housekeeper who handles things when I travel."

When I travel. There it was. The truth of Jake Lowell.

Nikki clenched the handle of her cup. "I have a job," she said evenly. "And other responsibilities."

"Emma's not in regular school yet. Besides, with the money from Black Crescent, you could quit the diner, right? I'll cover all the Europe expenses."

She sucked in a breath. "Being poor is not as bad as you think it is, Jake. But even if I decide to take the money from Black Crescent, it's a long time until January. Besides, I think Emma is a little young for a trip like that. I appreciate the offer."

They were both being so damn polite. As if roiling currents of emotion and discord didn't threaten the foundation beneath their feet.

Jake stood abruptly and set his empty coffee cup on the porch railing. "When can I swing by tomorrow?"

Nikki stood, too. The night was cloudy. She couldn't read his expression. "Tomorrow is not good. I work a double shift. Maybe you could come to a movie with Emma and me late Friday afternoon."

"Joshua's bachelor party is Friday night."

"The wedding's so soon?" The prospect of seeing people from her old life sent anxiety coursing through her veins.

"The actual ceremony is a week from Saturday. You never answered me. Will you be my date?"

She saw a challenge in his eyes, a dare. She weighed the prospect of attending a romantic wedding with Jake against her very real concerns. "I will," she said. "But I'll be nervous about seeing Falling Brook folks."

"You didn't do anything wrong. We'll face them together."

"Okay." It might be the only carefree time she had with Jake. An evening that would have to sustain her for the long, lonely years to come. "Good night," she muttered. Jake was too tempting. Too everything.

He cupped her neck in his big, warm hands and pulled her head to his. "I'll dream about you, Nik."

This kiss was lazy and slow. As if he had all the time in the world.

She put her hands on his shoulders to steady herself when her knees went weak. He tasted like coffee and dreams. Her dreams. All the ones that shattered when Black Crescent imploded, and Jake left her.

For long seconds, she let herself kiss him back. It was exhilarating. Toe curling. She felt like a princess at the end of a fairy tale. A very hot, flustered, needy princess. Only this particular prince was never going to stick around for the happily-ever-after.

When she realized she was running her fingers through his hair, she made herself step back. Take a breath. Reach for reason. "I should go in," she said. "I have a few mommy jobs to accomplish before I head to bed."

"I'll pay child support," he said gruffly. "Even if we decide not to tell her."

Nikki's temper flared, but she held her tongue. He was trying to do the right thing. "I don't need your money, Jake. Emma and I are fine. A child is a huge responsibility, but money is the least of it."

"You're saying you want emotional support?"

Is that what she was saying? She honestly didn't know. Having Jake around as a part-time dad would be awkward and painful. Maybe it *would* be better if he simply went away. She was convinced he still saw her as a version of her teenage self. He didn't understand or want to admit how much she had changed. "I only meant that it's eighteen years of hard work."

"Longer for some families whose kids never move out."

"I suppose so. Either way, I need you to know that you're off the hook. Your life doesn't accommodate fatherhood. Let's think about it. Maybe we can come up with a solution that suits us both."

"And Emma."

"Of course."

He moved toward the sidewalk. When a streetlight illuminated his features, she saw that Jake looked tired, sad. Maybe even uncertain. She had never seen him so vulnerable. Her heart squeezed. "You're good with her," Nikki said. "Truly, you are. She's lucky to have your brains and your fearlessness."

"You're wrong about one thing, Nik."

"Oh?"

He shoved his hands in his pockets and kicked at one of the small rocks Emma loved to collect. "I'm not fearless at all right now. Falling Brook. My father. My brothers. You. I feel like I'm stumbling around in a fog. I'm not even sure if I should have come back."

This time, her heart hurt when it pinched. "I'm glad you came, Jake. Really glad."

Jake always slept with the drapes open in a hotel room. In big cities, he liked seeing the array of colored lights on decked-out skyscrapers. Here in Falling Brook, the lights were fewer and less impressive, but they still lit the night with a comforting glow.

He was lying on his back with his hands behind his head. It was three in the morning. He'd barely slept. A few days ago, when he was flying across the ocean, he'd worried about reuniting with his twin. But the thing with Joshua had gone well.

The two brothers had fallen into their old relationship without drama.

Jake still had to face his mother and Oliver. Those reunions weren't something to dread, not really. The harder encounter had been finding out that he and Nikki had created a child, a daughter.

Suddenly, unable to be still a moment longer, he rolled out of bed, threw on some clothes and went down to the twenty-four-hour fitness center. On the treadmill, he set a punishing pace. If he ran hard enough and long enough, maybe he could outrun the demons at his heels.

At last, exhaustion claimed him. Back in his room, he showered and tumbled into bed, comatose almost instantly. When the alarm went off at eight, he opened his eyes and groaned. Insomnia had rarely been a problem in his adult life, except for the occasional bout of jet lag. Clearly, being back in Falling Brook was bad for his health.

He sat up on the side of the bed and reached for his phone. If peace and closure were his aims, he needed to work his list. Oliver was Jake's next priority. After thinking for a moment, he sent a text asking if his younger sibling could meet him at the Drayhill Quarry at ten thirty. It was a spot where the three Lowell brothers had often hiked and played around.

On one memorable hot summer day, they had even taken a dip despite the warning signs posted everywhere. Their mother had found out and grounded them for a month. After that, they still returned now and again to the abandoned quarry, but not to swim.

What appealed most was the isolation. At the quarry, they were free to be on their own. No parents breathing down their necks. No teachers demanding excellence.

But that was a long time ago.

Jake dragged his attention back to the present. While he was brushing his teeth, the text *ding* came through. Oliver would be there.

Jake was nervous. Once upon a time, the three brothers had been tight. But Jake had let his father's actions drive him away. He'd lost Nikki, his brothers, everything. Now a chance for reconciliation beckoned. Jake knew he didn't deserve anyone's forgiveness—least of all, his baby brother's.

After a few sprinkles of rain overnight, the mild weather had continued today. A weak sun shone down, making the morning slightly more cheerful. The drive out to the quarry was familiar but different. The old rutted road was worse now. Jake's fancy rental car took a beating. He parked by the gated fence and waited.

Soon, Oliver showed up in a late-model sedan. When the other man climbed out, Jake felt a wave of emotion he rarely allowed himself to acknowledge. This was his sibling, the man who was part of him. His blood and kin.

The two men embraced without speaking. Jake's eyes were damp when he pulled back. "Good to see you, Ol."

Oliver's brilliant blue eyes twinkled with happiness. "Took you long enough to contact me. I started to think you hadn't really come home at all."

"Sorry about that. I had to deal with some urgent business first."

"Yeah. Joshua told me. You have a baby. Right?"

"Well, Emma is four. But yes."

"Must have been quite a shock." Oliver's eyes held empathy.

Again, Jake's throat was tight. "On a scale of one to ten, I'd say a fifty. I don't know what I'm going to do about it."

"Joshua told me Nikki Reardon is the mother?"

Jake nodded. "I assume you remember her?"

Oliver snorted. "Are you kidding me? Of course I remember Nikki. You panted after her for years. It was painfully obvious that you were a one-woman kind of guy."

"Well, I screwed that up, too. I abandoned her just like I abandoned my brothers. I'm sorry, Oliver. Sorry for what happened to you."

"I doubt you could have done anything. Josh tried to

reach me. Mom did, too. But I was so damn angry. The anger ate me alive."

"Will you tell me what happened? If you want to," Jake said quickly. "I only had snippets from Josh."

"Sure," Oliver said. "But do you mind if we walk out to the falcon? I need to stretch my legs."

They climbed the fence and set off, striding along the makeshift trail that wound around the quarry. The underbrush was heavy. At times they had to scale fallen trees. After three quarters of a mile, they reached their destination. The falcon was an enormous boulder, shaped vaguely like Han Solo's famous spaceship. The broad, flat surface was perfect for hanging out, drinking beer or simply enjoying the summer sun.

Today, the November water below wasn't blue. It was murky and threatening. No temptation at all to chance a swim.

They sat down and got comfortable.

Oliver pitched a pebble into the quarry, his expression pensive. "I headed out for Harvard just a few weeks after you left. I was glad to leave Falling Brook, even though my tuition was only paid up for a year. I was furious with Dad. That anger moved with me, fueling the usual freshman-year screwing around. But I couldn't let it go, even though those feelings were poisoning me. Drugs and alcohol dulled the pain."

Jake's stomach twisted with guilt. He was silent for a moment. Stunned. "I'm sorry I wasn't there for you."

Oliver shrugged. "I needed to sort myself out. Things are good for me now, and I've been sober for years. I'm finally happy. But our father still has a lot to answer for."

"Josh said you went to visit him?"

"I did. He looked old, Jake. Old and pitiful. But when I saw him, all that anger came back, and it scared the hell out of me. He immediately criticized me for being a photographer. Same old crap. I asked about the stolen money. He said it was his. At that point, I knew he'd never change. I walked out. I won't let him destroy me a second time."

"I'm really proud of you, you know. You're very good at what you do. Our father is an asshole. Josh and I went, too," Jake said slowly, remembering and sorting through his own emotions. "Actually, we were summoned. But when we got there, the old man apparently changed his mind. Sent us away."

"What a bastard. But then again, perhaps you were lucky. Did you really want to talk to him?"

"Maybe. I don't know. I became a man without a country because of him. Falling Brook was unbearable. I went on my graduation trip and just never came back. Because of him, I've lived my life in slow motion. Slow to forgive, slow to process my feelings. Slow to mend the rift with you and Joshua."

"And Nikki?"

"Her most of all. I ran into her five years ago in Atlantic City. We had a…thing. But I let her slip through my fingers again. When Josh called and said Dad had been found, I took it as a sign that maybe it was time to deal with my own failures."

They sat there in silence. Although Jake couldn't speak for Oliver, he suspected the two of them were juggling the same mishmash of regrets.

Finally, Jake exhaled. "So, are there any women in *your* life?"

Oliver's broad grin caught Jake off guard. "As a matter of fact, there *is* a woman. Samantha. We just got engaged. And we're expecting a baby."

"Well, hell, man. You buried the lead. Congratulations."

Jake envied the fact that his brother was clearly thrilled about fatherhood. Oliver wasn't conflicted, like Jake.

"Sammi is a firecracker. You'll love her. She's had a tough life, but she's one of the strongest women I know."

"How did you meet?"

Oliver ducked his head, his expression sheepish. "A one-night stand. But it turned into something more, really fast."

Jake winced inwardly. His one-night stand with Nikki was at the root of his troubles. Did he regret it? How could he? It was arguably the best night of his life. But he'd been terrified by what he felt for her after a decade of nothing. She had changed, grown up. Though he wouldn't have thought it possible, she'd been even more intensely appealing than the teenage girl he had known all those years ago.

The tsunami of feelings had swept him under, drowned him. And so he had run.

Was he any better equipped to deal with her now?

Since there were no clear answers to his current dilemma, he changed the subject. "I assume you're going to the bachelor party tomorrow night?" One of Joshua's friends had put together a fun evening in Atlantic City.

"I'll be there," Oliver said. "It's not every day a Lowell man gets married. How about you?"

"Yep. I'm coming. Have you bought him any kind of gift?"

"No. Damn. I'll get something tomorrow."

"Well, here's the thing. When I was in Paris earlier this fall, I stumbled on a small Matisse at auction. It's a window scene from Morocco. I immediately thought of Joshua. You know how much he always loved Matisse. Of course, I had no idea Josh was going to get married soon, but when he told me, I had my assistant package the painting and send it to me. I should have it at the hotel tomorrow morning. I'd like to put your name and mine on the gift. You know, to acknowledge the fact that Josh is starting a new career, a new life. We left him to clean up the mess fifteen years ago. I know he didn't have to do it, but he did. What do you think?"

The words had tumbled out in a rush.

Oliver nodded. "That's perfect."

"Good. I want this gift to come from both of us. Together. I want to mend fences. To heal our family. We used to be the three Lowell brothers, unbreakable, unshakable. I'm sorry for my part in breaking us up. This is a gesture. A peace offering. Are you in?"

"I'm in."

Oliver ran a hand through his hair, his profile stark as he stared out across the quarry. Jake felt the coals of guilt burn hotter. Oliver had been a teenager when Jake left. Jake had failed him. Had failed Joshua. And Nikki. And his mother.

Could he ever do penance for his neglect? Sometimes he thought he'd simply been too lazy to look for a reason to return home. The truth was…he'd been scared. Scared that the people he loved would judge him. Or turn their backs on him.

Now it seemed that both of his brothers were willing to forgive and forget. That realization filled him with quiet satisfaction.

But what about Nikki? He had wronged her, most of all.

Would the mother of his child be willing to accept his regrets and his determination to do better?

And, if she did, was Jake willing to deal with the consequences?

Seven

It had been a very long time since Nikki shopped the designers on Fifth Avenue or Madison Avenue. But some memories never faded.

If she was going to Joshua's wedding—as Jake's date—nothing in her closet was remotely suitable. She had a credit card for emergencies. This didn't qualify. But even if the promised payments from Black Crescent didn't come through, Nikki could pay off a purchase over the coming months.

She had trained herself, out of necessity, not to live on credit. Today, she was going to break her own rule. A woman deserved the occasional fantasy, and this was hers.

After working the very early morning shift at the diner and then spending time with her daughter, Nikki changed clothes and said goodbye to her mom and Emma. Because the wedding was close, she decided to postpone the movie date with her daughter. Catching a train into the city at one o'clock didn't leave Nikki much time for shopping.

She dozed en route, exhausted. Yesterday's double shift, followed by a 4:00 a.m. alarm this morning, had drained her. Even so, adrenaline pumped in her veins when she arrived at Grand Central.

In better days, Roberta Reardon had employed a full-time chauffeur. Now, Nikki was happy to use the subway. It was cheap and easy and took her where she wanted to go.

The first two stores she tried were a bust. Her mother had shopped with her at both when Nikki was a teenage girl. But Nikki's tastes had changed.

She was getting discouraged when she spotted a small boutique wedged in between two well-known fashion houses that took up most of the block. The modest shop had a name on the glass door that Nikki didn't recognize. The items in the window told her to go in and take a look.

Inside, a pleasant saleswoman honored Nikki's intent to browse undisturbed. There were casual outfits aplenty. Deeper into the salon, Nikki found what she was looking for. Jake had told her the wedding would be in the early afternoon. Which meant tea-length was perfectly appropriate. The dress she spotted was a beautiful shade of ivory. Strapless. With a ballerina skirt that frothed out in layers of soft tulle.

"I'd like to try this one," she said impulsively, although the price tag made her gulp.

"I'll put it in a changing room for you," the woman said. "And if you're interested, that small rack over there is marked down. Last year's items. You know the drill."

Nikki wondered if the clerk had scoped out her customer and noted the inexpensive jeans and generic top. It didn't matter. False pride was a commodity Nikki couldn't afford. Though she had planned only to flip through the discounted items, her hand landed on a scoop-neck red cashmere sweater that might or might not clash with her hair. The black wool pencil skirt was a no-brainer. It would go with everything.

In the curtained cubicle, she tried the sweater and skirt first. They fit perfectly. A small pulled thread on the sleeve of the sweater and a missing button on the skirt explained another reason the items were on sale. The small imperfections didn't daunt Nikki. She had learned to be handy with a needle. Jake wanted to see her again. If that involved a night out, this outfit would bolster her confidence.

Her choice for the wedding was even better. She smoothed her hands over the skirt and tugged at the bodice. The only thing holding her back was the color. Some people insisted that only a bride should wear white to a wedding.

The saleslady knocked on the door frame. "Any luck?"

Nikki held back the curtain. "I love this, but I don't know if I can wear it to a wedding. You know, because of the color."

The woman tilted her head and studied Nikki. "It fits you like a dream. And I don't think most people care anymore. Besides, it's a deep, rich ivory, not white. What if you add a pop of color? Hold on."

When the woman returned moments later, Nikki nodded. "That might work." She took the proffered scarf and draped it around her shoulders. It was soft, watered silk in pale, pale pink. When Nikki looked in the mirror, she smiled. "Thank you. I'll take it."

As the clerk rang up the purchases, Nikki battled her conscience. Any extra money she made over and above her household expenses went to doing things with her daughter and her mother. Movies. Meals out. This self-indulgence was hard to justify.

The saleswoman excused herself for a moment to deal with a call on the store's landline. While Nikki waited perched on the edge of a chair, her cell phone dinged. Her heart gave a funny little jump. It was a text from Jake...

Dinner tomorrow night? Just us? Let me know...

There was no reason to get flustered. Jake wasn't making a romantic overture. He clearly wanted to speak with Nikki about the future and how he would be a part of Emma's life. Or how he might not. Nikki knew it was an important conversation. One she needed to have with Jake alone. She would have to act like a mature thirty-something single mother and not the giddy cocktail waitress who had still adored Jake Lowell and let him coax her into bed.

Even more importantly, she absolutely *had* to decide what it was she wanted from him. She needed his body, his intense lovemaking. His rakish charm. But common sense said she couldn't sleep with him and still make smart decisions about Emma.

What happened if Nikki didn't make the right choice?

If she agreed to this dinner, she had little more than twenty-four hours to figure it out.

Other customers entered the store, and Nikki got up, rattled by the unexpected text. When the employee handed over two lilac-and-navy shopping bags, Nikki winced inwardly. On the other hand, a little part of her was already thinking about how perfect her new sweater and skirt would be for a night out with her daughter's father.

Elegant. Not too fussy. Nothing that would suggest

Nikki misunderstood Jake's motives. But definitely flattering.

Outside, the wind had picked up, and the sky was gray. The pleasant temperatures were gone, replaced by a bone-chilling cold. Nikki leaned against the building only long enough to answer the text.

She dithered over what to say, even as her fingers began to freeze. Finally, she pecked out a response…

Dinner is fine. Can we do seven?

Her phone dinged again…

Works for me. I'll pick you up then.

She gnawed her lip. But decided to add one more note…

Have fun at Joshua's bachelor party!

After a long silence, all she got was the thumbs-up emoji. Jake could be busy. Or he wasn't interested in a long text exchange.

No need to feel rejected.

When she glanced at her watch, she saw that she had a little time to kill before she caught the train. Too bad the Rockefeller Center tree wasn't up yet. Maybe she could bring Emma in a few weeks. At four, her precocious daughter was more than old enough to enjoy the treat.

Since Nikki's shopping errand had been accomplished with time to spare, she decided to walk despite the gloomy weather. She could definitely use more exercise. Everywhere she looked, retail establishments were beginning to deck the halls for the holiday season.

Thanksgiving was the weekend after Joshua's wedding. Barely two weeks away. Nikki and Roberta never made a big deal about the holiday. Nikki often baked a pumpkin pie. And sometimes they cooked a small turkey breast. But the celebration was low-key.

When Nikki was in high school, she remembered huge Thanksgiving spreads, mostly put together by the Lowell cook and housekeeper. As a kid, Nikki had never really thought about the work it took to pull off something like that. Or the expense.

Vernon Lowell had loved hosting lavish celebrations and inviting fifteen or twenty of his friends and business associates. The enormous cherry dining-room table could seat two dozen. The chandelier was actual Venetian glass. The priceless Persian silk rug and the enormous sets of china, crystal and heavy silver had all been sold off after the patriarch's disappearance.

Nikki had nothing of that era to pass down to her own daughter.

It didn't matter, she told herself firmly. Emma knew she was loved, and that's what mattered.

Eventually, Nikki made her way back to Grand Central and caught the train home. This time she didn't sleep. She worried. Did she and Jake have anything in common anymore? Could she step back into his world even temporarily? Could she sleep with him and let it be no more than that? And what about the fact that he didn't understand how much she had changed?

She knew he wasn't staying. But she badly wanted him to acknowledge all the ways she had survived and thrived. Something deep inside her craved his approval and his love.

And if that wasn't the most dismal admission a woman had ever made, she didn't know what was.

Arriving on the doorstep of her familiar small house calmed some of Nikki's nerves. She and Emma had made it this far and had a good life. Whatever came next, they would handle.

When Nikki opened the front door, the aroma of homemade chicken-noodle soup wafted out. Though her mom and Emma had finished eating, the soup was still warming on the stove.

Nikki shrugged out of her coat and hung it up on a hook near the door. Her shopping bags went in a nearby closet. Then she hugged Emma and smiled at her mom. "Thanks for keeping her this afternoon." She tried never to take her mother's help for granted, even though Roberta enjoyed time with Emma.

Emma demanded to be picked up. Nikki nuzzled her daughter's hair. "You smell like dessert," she teased.

The routine of the next hour and a half was comfortable and familiar. At Nikki's request, Roberta stayed. When Nikki told her mother they needed *to talk*, Roberta raised an eyebrow, but nodded.

At last, Emma was asleep. The two women made their way to the tiny living room, turned on the gas logs and put up their feet.

Roberta sighed. "This is nice. Did you find a dress for the wedding?"

"I did," Nikki said. "I'll try it on for you sometime soon. Thanks again for keeping Emma. I tried to get back as quickly as I could."

Roberta cocked her head. "You said we needed to talk. Is this about Jake?"

"Not directly. He and I are having dinner tomorrow night to discuss Emma and the future."

"What's to talk about? He's her father."

"Jake being Emma's daddy isn't what I wanted to talk to you about, Mom."

"Oh?"

Carefully, and as calmly as possible, Nikki shared what Joshua had told her about his plan to compensate Roberta and Nikki for all they had lost. She went on to explain that all of the Black Crescent clients who lost money fifteen years ago had received payments at an agreed-upon rate. It had taken Joshua a very long time, but the ethical and legal obligations had been met.

Roberta listened in silence, though her eyes widened, and her cheeks flushed.

When Nikki finished, Roberta sat up on the edge of her seat, clearly agitated. "Vernon stole that money. Why should you and I get anything?"

"That's what I told Joshua, Mom. But he says Dad stole from us, too. Joshua wants to do this."

"Dear Lord." Roberta seemed dazed.

"The payments will begin January first. It's a lot of money. Not like what you had before, but plenty if we're careful. We'll need to invest some and save some. You don't want to get to the end of the ten years and find yourself right back where you are now."

Roberta nodded. "I didn't know a single thing about finances when I married your father. I've regretted that more than once since he left us."

"I'll help you. And I suspect Joshua will be willing to advise us."

"And Jake, too. If he's such a financial genius."

"Yes," Nikki said hesitantly. She'd told her mom how Jake had supported himself for years by day-trading. "Jake, too. Think about it, Mom. You can go back to your old friends. Pick up the good pieces of your old life."

Roberta's face hardened. "They turned their backs on me."

"No. To be fair, you and I disappeared. We didn't give anyone a chance to help us. We were embarrassed and too humiliated to show our faces. I'm sure there were a few of your friends who might have shunned you for what Daddy did, but I have to believe that at least some of them would be glad to reconnect. I think that's true even now. But we haven't wanted any contact. Maybe we were wrong, Mom."

"I suppose."

It was a lot to digest. Nikki was glad her mother didn't turn the tables and ask what Nikki wanted to do. Life was comfortable now. Hard and demanding, but comfortable in its predictability.

Did Nikki want to uproot all she had worked for and return to the town of her childhood? Emma could attend the same Falling Brook prep school where her mother got a good education. Nikki could be a stay-at-home mom for a few years. Volunteer at school. Pay attention to her physical and mental health. Not be so exhausted all the time.

Maybe see Jake when he came home to visit his mother and brothers.

Nikki yawned. "We've got a lot to think about. Thankfully, nothing has to be decided tonight."

The more important questions surrounded Jake. Despite the changes happening all around her, Nikki was most conflicted about Jake. Fascinating, sexy, unpredictable Jake Lowell. What would tomorrow night bring?

Jake sipped his scotch and loosened his tie. Joshua's bachelor party was proving to be a good distraction from thinking about Nikki. A friend of Joshua's had reserved a large room on the top floor of one of Atlantic City's glitziest casinos. Jake didn't know the man. It was someone Josh had become friends with after college—a relationship that began after Jake had left Falling Brook.

The dress code tonight was upscale, but Jake noticed that several guys had already shed their jackets. Enormous flat-screen TVs covered the walls, tuned to various sports channels. The open bar was stocked with top-shelf booze. Three beautiful pool tables were busy. Half a dozen female servers wandered among the partygoers handing out delicious hors d'oeuvres and smiles.

At the far end of the room, elegant tables were set for the steak dinner to come. Jake sat in a bubble of quiet at the moment, observing. He knew most of the men in the room, or he had at one time. Many of them had greeted him cordially tonight. They were understandably curious about Joshua's absent twin. When Jake left Falling Brook, he had cut all ties with surgical precision, preferring to look forward rather than dwell on the past.

That recollection brought him right back to Nikki. She, like Jake, had abdicated her place in Falling Brook society and had gone into hiding. Maybe that was a dramatic way of phrasing it, but the result was the same.

A waitress stopped at his elbow. "Would you like anything, sir?"

He looked up, noticing the woman's surgically enhanced breasts and the flirtatious look in her eyes. At one time, he wouldn't have thought twice about getting her number and hooking up after the party was over.

"Thanks, I'm good," he said, giving the woman his best noncommittal smile. Despite the fact that he was in the midst of a dry spell, sexually speaking, he wasn't interested. Nobody but Nikki pushed his buttons. Knowing that she was so close and yet so far away made him grumpy. Their brief text exchange had revved his motor to an embarrassing degree.

He found himself obsessing about tomorrow night's date. Clearly, he and Nikki had to come to a decision about Emma. Maybe Jake was a total jerk to think so, but dealing with his small daughter wasn't nearly as worrisome as understanding his feelings for Nikki.

Seeing her in Atlantic City five years ago had been both exhilarating and unsettling. He hadn't stuck around long enough to find out what was going on in her world. Despite the incredible sex, he'd been afraid to hear that she had a life that didn't include him, which was stupid, because of course she did.

His stomach tightened unpleasantly as he finally admitted the truth to himself. One reason he had stayed away from Falling Brook for so long—among many— was that he'd been afraid to come back and see that Nikki had moved on with another man.

And she had. By her own admission. She had married and divorced.

That was more of a relationship than Jake could claim. His hopscotching travels had, by design, left him little opportunity to get attached to any one place or person. He had anesthetized his pain over his father's betrayal with new experiences, fresh vistas.

For a very long time, he had been satisfied with the status quo. Or, at least, he had convinced himself he was. When Joshua's phone call came out of the blue saying that Vernon was alive, it had been an electric shock to the system.

The Jake who lived day by day and never worried about anything was suddenly jerked back into the truth that he was indeed tied to other people. Despite time and distance, he was still a son, a brother. And now, a father, too.

What he was to Nikki remained to be seen…

Oliver approached him and bumped his knee. "Play me some pool?"

Jake finished his drink and set it aside. "I'd be happy to kick your ass. Lead the way."

It wasn't as easy as he had imagined. Though Jake was a shark when it came to the pool table, his baby brother was a different kind of wizard. Jake lined up his shots with cool precision, sinking ball after ball.

Oliver, on the other hand, played wildly, taking dumb chances that paid off. After four games, they had each won twice. Both men had shed their sport coats and rolled up their shirtsleeves. Jake raised an eyebrow. "Best three out of five?"

"Nope."

"Nope?"

Oliver wiped his forehead with the back of his hand. "I learned in recovery to be satisfied with 'enough.' That who I am is sufficient. Now, when those competitive rushes try to drag me into deep water, I step away."

Jake frowned. "You know we weren't playing for money, right?"

"Doesn't matter. I still have that killer instinct. And it can get me in trouble. So I stop and take a breath and ask myself what's really important. You should try it, Jake. It's good for the soul."

Oliver excused himself, leaving Jake a lot unsettled and a little bit pissed. He was damn glad his sibling had beaten addiction, but Jake didn't have similar problems. He didn't drink to excess. He'd never done drugs. Why did Oliver's implication sound so judgmental?

Maybe Jake was making a big deal out of nothing. So Oliver didn't want to play the tiebreaker. So what?

Jake was leaning against the momentarily empty pool table, brooding and watching the nearest TV screen, when the man of the hour crossed the room in his direction. Joshua looked relaxed and happy. For a split second, Jake was jealous. Jealous that his twin had found love and challenges and purpose in his life.

The truth was, if anybody deserved that trifecta, it was Josh.

Jake grinned at him. "I still can't believe you're getting married. And leaving Black Crescent."

Joshua lifted an eyebrow. "The job is still yours if you want it."

The urge to say yes came out of nowhere. Jake quaked inside. Here was an opportunity to fit back into the fabric of Falling Brook, to grow close to his family again, to build a bond with his daughter. To make Nikki proud. The temptation dangled. But it would require stepping up to the plate. Changing. Growing.

His gut clenched. *Back away.*

"Lord, no," he said, managing a chuckle. "I'd be terrible at it. It's one thing to take risks with my own cash. I wouldn't want the responsibility of handling other people's money, but I don't mind helping you with the CEO search."

"Then what *do* you want to do, Jake?"

The serious question caught Jake off guard. He hadn't expected to be grilled in the middle of a party. "Same thing I always do, I guess. Be me."

Joshua's gaze showed concern. "We all have to move forward. Whether we want to or not. Don't let Dad control your life."

The expression in his twin's eyes baffled and bothered Jake as much as Oliver's pseudo lecture about being *enough*. "That's bullshit," Jake said angrily, keeping his voice low. "Dad doesn't control me. I haven't seen the man in fifteen years. Are you nuts?"

"He casts a long shadow. And now even more. He's going to spend the rest of his life in prison, by all accounts. It would be foolish of us to let him affect our choices. I'll admit that I'm being selfish. I lost you for a decade and a half. I don't want to lose you again."

Joshua bumped Jake's shoulder with an affectionate fist and walked off, leaving Jake with the strongest urge to run out the door and keep on running. That's what he did when things got tough. But this was his brother's bachelor party. His twin. His other half. He couldn't bail on Joshua. Not tonight. He'd done it too often already. He owed Josh.

He certainly didn't *deserve* Josh's goodwill and forgiveness. Jake had left his brother holding the proverbial bag. When Vernon disappeared, Joshua had dealt with the feds and the insurance companies and their mother and everything else in the midst of panic and grief and confusion.

What had Jake done to help? Nothing. Nothing at all… He had disappeared, severing the ties that might have sustained him in his grief. He might be slow, but he was finally beginning to understand how much he had lost.

Eight

The bachelor party was a huge success. Even the guys who imbibed heavily were classy enough not to get falling-down drunk. Or maybe Joshua picked his friends carefully. Maybe he surrounded himself with men of depth.

Whatever the reason, the evening was going well.

When it was time for dinner, the men moved as one to the tables, where shrimp cocktails and Caesar salads sat waiting. As everyone dug in, Jake noted that Joshua had perhaps intentionally *not* set up a head table. In most families, the groom-to-be might be flanked by his two brothers. But the Lowell relationships, though cordial, were strained by the events of the past.

Jake sat with Oliver to his right and a Black Crescent employee he had just met on his left. The meal was fabulous. And it must have cost a fortune. Again, Jake felt guilty. *He* should have been the one paying for this spread. He could certainly afford it. But, heck. He hadn't even known his brother was getting married.

Jake had kept himself out of the loop.

When the steaks and potatoes were only a memory, and there was a brief lull before dessert was served, Jake seized the moment to say a few words. He stood and cleared his throat. "As the twin brother of the groom, I believe it's my duty to make a toast."

Joshua grinned, his expression a mixture of surprise and pleasure. "By all means," he said. "But if you start telling childhood stories, I'll plead the Fifth."

Ignoring laughter and a few catcalls, Jake began his spiel. "Joshua…you were known as the good kid, and I was the bad apple. I guess some things never change."

A titter of laughter went around the room.

Jake continued. "For a decade and a half, you've managed to find the best in a really crappy situation. Now, although I've only met Sophie briefly, I can already tell that the two of you are a perfect match."

"Thanks," Joshua said, his posture slightly guarded as if he didn't know what was coming next.

Jake reached beneath the dinner table and picked up the small package that was loosely wrapped in brown butcher paper. "Oliver and I want to give you something to mark this occasion. It's not exactly a wedding gift. It's more of a thank-you for being a damn good human being, and our steady-as-a-rock brother. We love you, man."

Jake walked past several people and handed over the small package, then returned to his seat.

Joshua stood and carefully peeled back the paper. He examined the painting intently, his fingers clenched on the frame. His face went pale. He looked up, startled, staring at his two brothers. "My God. Is this really a…" He trailed off, his expression gobsmacked.

"It's a Matisse," Jake said quietly. Joshua's reaction made him damn glad he'd come up with this idea.

Oliver, shoulder-to-shoulder with Jake, spoke up. "We're pumped as hell that you're jump-starting your art career, and I hope you know we'll both be first in line to hang a few Josh Lowell masterpieces on our walls."

Jake lifted his glass of champagne. "To Josh. May your marriage be as long lasting as this old master."

"To Josh." The chorus rose around the tables.

Amid the laughter and applause, Joshua stood and hugged each of his brothers tightly, then pulled them both in for a triple embrace. "Thanks, guys. This means the world to me."

Oliver held up his hands. "We're heading for the mushy zone. Time for more red meat and male bonding." He returned to his seat with a chuckle.

Joshua kept his hand firm on Jake's shoulder. "I'm not letting you hold me at arm's length ever again. You got that?"

The words were low, only loud enough for Jake to hear. But they packed a punch. Jake nodded, his throat tight. "Understood."

The remainder of the evening passed in a haze for Jake. He was more of a watcher than an active participant. The men in this room admired Joshua. It was evident in the way they joked with him and laughed with him and thanked him for inviting them to be part of his bachelor celebration.

Oliver was equally popular and social, though he drank nothing stronger than sparkling water. Jake wondered how his brother felt being present at an event where the alcohol flowed freely, but Oliver never seemed tempted.

The room was booked until midnight. Gradually, the

guests began making their goodbyes. Oliver had come with a trio of guys and was the designated driver. Eventually, quiet fell. Only Joshua and Jake remained.

Joshua yawned. "That was fun. But I sure as hell am glad the wedding is not tomorrow. I'm going to go home and crash hard."

"Sounds like a plan," Jake said. "You want me to drive you? I switched to coffee a couple of hours ago."

"Sure. I'd like that. My driver is waiting, but I'll send him on."

In the car, Jake adjusted the heat and made his way out of the crowded parking garage. "This may take a while," he said, grimacing at the line of cars.

Joshua took off his tie, reclined his seat a few inches and sighed deeply as he stretched out his legs. "If you had told me six months ago that I'd be getting married soon, I'd have said you were crazy." He shook his head, but he seemed more smug than reflective.

Jake swiped his credit card and waited for the arm to raise. "What does it feel like?" he asked, easing out into the traffic. "Knowing that you've found someone for a life partner? Isn't it scary? What if you've made a mistake?"

"I know the statistics. But I also know Sophie. I didn't even realize I had been waiting for someone like her. She argues with me and pushes me and makes me a better person. Plus, she's hot as hell. Not that I'm bragging."

Jake horse laughed, wiping his eyes with one hand. "Of *course* you're bragging. That's what a groom is expected to do."

"And what about you and Nikki and Emma?"

Josh shrugged, keeping his eyes on the road. "Nikki and I are having dinner tomorrow night to talk about the situation."

"A date?"

"Not a date." The clarification was irritating, mostly because he had asked himself the same question a dozen times.

"What are you going to say? About the daddy thing, I mean."

Jake rotated his shoulders. He felt as tight as if he had been driving for hours. "I'm not sure. I don't think I can walk away from my own flesh and blood."

Several seconds passed. Long, suddenly awkward seconds.

Joshua ran a hand across the back of his neck. "Not to belabor the point, bro, but you did before. I can understand where Nikki is coming from. She wants to protect her daughter from getting hurt."

Suddenly, all the warm fuzzies Jake had been feeling as he reconnected with his twin evaporated. Was he always going to be the bad guy? Was there nothing he could do to make up for his fifteen-year hiatus? Nikki insisted she had changed, but did no one entertain the possibility that Jake might be changing, too?

He reached for the radio and tuned it to a station that played current music. It wasn't long before Joshua was snoring.

It was just as well. Jake knew where he stood now. He was always going to be on the outside looking in, wishing for something he couldn't even name...

Nikki worked the eight-to-four shift on Saturday, then rushed home to shower and change. Emma was pouty because her mom was leaving again, but it couldn't be helped. And, honestly, except for work, Nikki seldom left her daughter to go out. Mommies had needs, too.

She gave herself a mental slap. Tonight wasn't about a

single mother's *needs*. She and Jake were getting together to discuss his role in Emma's life, her future.

The red sweater and black skirt, both newly mended, gave Nikki's confidence a boost. She paired the outfit with spiky black heels and silver snowflake earrings. Her black wool coat was at least seven years old, but it had classic lines. The forecast called for spitting snow, so she had no choice but to dress for the cold.

Roberta had been with Emma during the day, but Nella came over at five thirty to help with Emma's dinner and stay until Nikki returned.

"Enjoy yourself, Ms. Reardon," she said. "I brought stuff to do when Emma is in bed. If you're late, it won't matter. I'll doze on the sofa."

"Thanks," Nikki said, hoping her cheeks weren't as red as her sweater. "Text me if you need anything. And I'll check in with you a time or two." When the doorbell rang, Nikki kissed her daughter. "Be good, sweetheart. You and I will spend the day together tomorrow, I promise. Bye, Emma."

When she went through the house to the front door, she slipped her arms into her coat, then picked up her cell phone and purse. Jake wasn't coming in. Not with a babysitter who might or might not gossip.

As she pulled open the door, she smoothed a flyaway strand of hair. "Hi, there. I'm ready." Though she thought she was prepared, the sight of him made her weak. Those beautiful greenish-hazel eyes. The tousled hair. Broad shoulders. Flat belly. She felt the zing between them and forced herself not to react.

He blinked when he saw her, as if he, too, felt something. She saw the muscles in his throat work. "You look nice, Nik. I hope I didn't rush you too much."

"Not at all. Actually, I'm starving." They were back

to being polite again. She hated it. At least when they fought, they were honest with each other. Now she felt the need to guard her words to preserve the peace.

Jake had suggested eating at the restaurant in his hotel. Nikki looked it up online while she was getting ready. It was one of the top-rated eateries in Falling Brook. Upscale. Jackets and ties required.

The fact that Jake had a king-size bed a few floors above was incidental.

"How was the bachelor party?" she asked when they were in the car.

Watching Jake's capable hands on the wheel made her tummy feel funny. *Sexual attraction. Animal attraction.* She recognized it for what it was, just like she had recognized it that night in Atlantic City. No point in denying the truth. But her physical response to Jake complicated the conversation about Emma.

When he helped her out of the car at the hotel, he put his hand under her arm momentarily. She came close to leaning into him the way she used to when they were together as teenagers, but she stopped herself.

He smelled warm and spicy and masculine. As they walked quickly toward the building, icy snow pellets dotted her coat. She turned up her collar and shivered. Neither of them was wearing gloves. When they entered the lobby and were enfolded in warm air, she inhaled the scents of fresh gardenias and furniture polish.

They bypassed the registration desk and walked down a long, carpeted hallway. The decor was understated and elegant, with no expense spared. It had been a very, very long time since Nikki had found herself in such sophisticated surroundings.

Their table was waiting for them. A single white orchid bloomed alongside a lit hurricane lamp. The restaurant was already swathed in holly and gold ribbons. The smells wafting from the kitchen promised culinary delights.

When Jake helped Nikki out of her coat, the warmth of his breath on the back of her neck made her shiver. He draped the coat over one of the extra seats and held her chair as she sat down. Then he took his place on the opposite side of the table and stared, his gaze hot and hungry.

"Don't," she said.

"Don't what?" His eyes danced, though he didn't smile.

"Don't look like you're going to gobble me up. It's disconcerting."

"I'd forgotten how beautiful you really are."

"I'm older and five pounds heavier, and I have stretch marks."

Now his beautiful lips curled upward in a sexy grin. He shrugged. "I know what I see, Nik."

"Can we eat right away?" she asked, unable to look straight at him. It was as dangerous as peering at the sun. Everything inside her heated and churned. "I don't want to be out too late." Was she reminding herself or him?

"Of course." Jake lifted a hand and summoned the waiter. "My friend is famished. We'd like to order, please."

"Yes, sir. As you wish."

Nikki glanced blindly at the specials. "I'll have the prix fixe menu," she said. "Bruschetta. Shrimp bisque. The chicken piccata."

The dignified older man nodded. "And for dessert?"

"I'll decide later if that's okay."

The server turned to Jake. "And you, sir?"

"I'll order the other choices, so we can try them all. A house salad, the sweet-potato puree and the pork tenderloin."

Soon, Nikki and Jake were alone. Again. She worried her bottom lip with her teeth. "This feels awkward."

Jake nodded solemnly. "Very. Shall we discuss Emma now or later?"

"Let's get it over with." She clasped her hands on the table and took a deep breath. "Have you thought about who you want to be in her life?"

His response was instantaneous. "I'm her father," he said firmly. The possessive words sent a thrill through Nikki. They had made a baby together. "That's who I am and who I want to be," he said. "But I understand that I'm new to this game. I don't want to step on your toes or cause a problem for you."

Too late. Nikki kept her dark humor to herself. She cleared her throat, acknowledging the butterflies in her stomach. Though she spoke prosaically, she wanted to crawl across the table and drag his lips to hers. "I'm glad. A girl needs her father. How often do you think you might be available? I know you live a long way from here, and you have a busy travel schedule."

"It's the twenty-first century. We have jets and Wi-Fi conversations. I'll make time for Emma, I promise. I want to know her. I want to know her well."

Nikki found herself on the brink of tears. She realized in that moment that she hadn't known for sure Jake would claim his fatherhood. The fact that he had made her wildly emotional. "I'm so glad," she said, her throat tight. "I suppose we can work out the details later."

"I suppose we can." He reached across the table and took one of her hands, stroking his thumb across the back of it, giving her goose bumps. "Now that we've settled the big topic, let's talk about us."

"Us?" Her heart raced.

His tight smile held a hint of determination. "I ran away from you twice, Nikki. Once in Atlantic City, but even worse when you were almost eighteen."

They both winced. By the time Nikki's birthday rolled around that June, she had lost her innocence, but not because of Jake. Her world had been in ashes. Law-enforcement vehicles in her driveway. Uniformed men and women inside her house, boxing up her father's office. Opening the safe. Confiscating computers.

"I wish I could have spared you all the awfulness," he said, the words gruff and raw. "You were in so much pain. It broke my heart."

"You stayed for the funeral before you took off. I always appreciated that."

"It was a circus, as I recall. Paparazzi everywhere we turned. My mother and your mother weeping in a corner. I still get nauseous when I smell carnations."

"It was all a long time ago," she said softly. "We're different people now."

Suddenly, their food arrived, and the intimate conversation was shelved. Though Nikki was the furthest thing from calm, she ate, anyway. Soon, the flavors and textures of the various dishes coaxed her into enjoying the meal.

Beneath their conversation, a current of heated lust ran strong. She saw it in Jake's laser gaze, recognized it in her trembling body. They laughed and flirted and shared something rare and wonderful.

But Nikki knew in her heart it was temporary. Ephemeral.

Jake seemed relaxed, more relaxed than she had seen

him since he had returned to Falling Brook. She asked the question she had been avoiding. "What did you do Thursday when I was working? I felt bad about turning you down."

"You have a job, Nik. I understand that. Oliver drove in from Manhattan, and we reconnected. Then we went to my mom's."

"How did that go?"

"Mom hugged me. Cried a little. I'm worried about her, Nik. A few years back, my father was declared legally dead. Mom took off her wedding ring. Thank God she didn't date anyone seriously. It would have killed her, I think, to know she had committed adultery."

"Is she glad your father is alive?"

"I'm not sure. It's a devil of a mess. The hell of it is, there's not much my brothers and I can do for her."

"Except be there."

"I suppose."

"Sorry," Nikki said. "I didn't mean to ruin the mood."

Jake's face lightened. "Well, that's promising. I didn't even know we had a mood," he said, teasing. "Have I told you that your very lovely red sweater gives me all sorts of naughty ideas?"

"It's new," she admitted. "I bought it even though I shouldn't have, because I wanted to look good for you."

"Mission accomplished." The words were intense. Now he had both of her hands in his.

"Seeing you again after all this time has surprised me, Jake."

"How so?"

"You know the phrase *slow burn*?"

"Of course."

Her bottom lip trembled. "You severed our relationship. But the burn didn't end. I used to fantasize about you sometimes when I was having sex with my husband. How awful is that?"

He went pale. His pupils dilated. "Why are you telling me this? The truth, please."

She pulled her hands away and wrapped her arms around her waist, trying not to fall apart. "I know there's nothing between us, Jake. You've been gone almost half my life. Fifteen years. We've lived apart. Separate. No connection at all except for that one insane night in Atlantic City five years ago. But that slow burn rekindled when I saw you again. And I have to know. Do you feel it, too?"

Now his face was grim, almost angry. "You know I do."

She swallowed hard, wondering if she was making a huge mistake, but feeling the urgency of the moment. "I'd like to sleep with you again. I'm living like a nun. I miss physical intimacy. I miss you."

The server brought dessert. For a moment, Nikki thought Jake might come unglued. The glare he gave the poor man sent him scuttling away.

"This looks good," Nikki said inanely.

Jake's jaw was hard as iron. "Please tell me you don't really expect me to eat anything right now."

"Shall I ask for to-go boxes?"

The sexual frustration and hunger rolled off him in waves. She had unleashed a sleeping dragon. A beautiful creature capable of creating great destruction.

He stared at her, his gaze hot. "Fine."

This time, Nikki was the one to summon the waiter. Soon, the check was taken care of, and Nikki had a paper bag in front of her. It was imprinted with the restaurant's name and held two clear plastic boxes, one with tiramisu, the other pecan pie.

She stood up on shaky legs. "Are we done?"

Jake stood, as well. His feral smile made the hair rise on the back of her neck. "We're *not* done, Nikki. Not even close."

Nine

Jake wondered if he was dreaming. He'd had a number of vivid dreams about Nikki Reardon over the years. With color and sound and all the visuals he could handle. But tonight was different. She stood at his elbow in the elevator, her gaze downcast, her fair skin tinted with a noticeable flush.

When the elevator stopped on his floor, they both got out, but still he didn't touch her. His hand shook as he tapped his key card on the electronic panel and waited for the tiny light to turn green.

Inside, he turned on lamps and kicked up the heat a couple of notches.

"This suite is amazing," Nikki said.

"I'm glad you like it."

Suddenly, he found himself looking at the room through her eyes. He wasn't the neatest traveler. His laptop was plugged in on the desk by the window with papers scattered nearby. His suitcase was open on a luggage stand revealing his tumbled clothing.

For a man who traveled constantly, he'd never had any interest in being anal about organization. He was more likely to toss things in and hope for the best. His system hadn't failed him yet.

Now that he finally had Nikki within ten feet of his bed, his brain seized up and threatened to shut down. He was hard all over. And breathless. A thirty-seven-year-old man who could barely speak.

"Um," he said, as he undid his tie and tossed it aside with his jacket. "Would you like something to drink?"

Nikki set the desserts on a table and removed her coat. "I'd rather not. That's what got us into trouble in Atlantic City. If we're doing this, I want to be all in, not woozy."

"Fair enough." So much for smoothing anyone's nerves with alcohol. "There's an extra robe in the bathroom. If you'd like to get comfortable."

She kicked off her sexy high heels and padded across the room to where he stood. "I kind of thought you'd be the one getting me out of my clothes."

Holy hell. "Nikki…" He nearly swallowed his tongue when she placed her small hand, palm flat on his chest, right over his heart. Her fingers burned his skin through the expensive fabric of his dress shirt.

She went up on her tiptoes and kissed him. "I have a babysitter on the clock. And I'm *interested*." She hesitated. "Have I shocked you?"

"Lord no." He lifted her off her feet and walked toward the bed, her legs dangling. When he set her down, the smile she gave him fried a few more synapses. "I didn't think this would happen tonight," he said. "Or ever. Forgive me if I'm off my game."

She ran her hands through his hair while he reached

behind her to unbutton her skirt and lower the zipper. What he saw then paralyzed him even more. Nikki stepped out of the skirt casually, as if undressing for an audience was no big deal.

The lacy white garter belt, thong panties and silky stockings she wore were pure fantasy. He touched her warm thigh. "Damn, Nik. If I'd known you were hiding this, we'd have skipped dinner altogether."

Her small smile was smug. The little tease was enjoying his discomfiture. "I ordered all of it online after you left my house Wednesday. I'm glad you approve."

He removed her sweater next, lifting it over her head, trying not to mess up her hair. The bra he found matched the rest of her undies. Except that it had a panel of fine mesh on the top edge that revealed her raspberry nipples.

With his heart slugging in his chest, he scooped her up in his arms, folded back the covers one-handed and laid her gently on the bed. "Don't move," he croaked.

He began to strip with a marked lack of coordination, tossing pieces of clothing wildly until he was down to his black knit boxers.

Nikki no longer smiled. Her gaze fixed raptly on his erection, outlined in stretchy cloth. "You are a beautiful man, Jake Lowell," she said softly. "I thought I might have embroidered the memory of you naked, but it seems not."

He dispensed with his underwear and joined her on the bed.

When he touched her, he understood that time really could stand still. The room was hushed. Traffic noise from the street below barely penetrated his consciousness.

He ran his fingers through Nikki's golden-red tresses,

spreading her hair on the pillows. She was a sensual woman. A siren. A goddess.

He refused to dwell on his grief for the years he had missed.

Timing. It all came down to timing.

"Jake?" She said his name softly, with concern. As if she could sense his turmoil. "Are you okay?"

He nodded slowly, running one hand from her shoulder to her belly to her silken-clad legs. "Oh, yeah," he said. "I'm good." He removed the panties but left everything else in place. When he played with her nipples through the bra, she moaned and arched off the bed. Her cheeks flushed. Her eyelids fluttered shut.

For one breathless moment, she was there in front of him. Ripe for the taking.

That one night in Atlantic City was a blur to him now. This felt like another first. A second chance. Was karma offering him closure, or an opportunity for redemption?

Slow burn. Yes. That's what it was. The need to take her rose through him like a forceful, uncontrollable wave.

"Nikki…" He whispered her name, not even sure what he wanted to tell her. If he hadn't run away all those years ago, *this woman* might have been his.

Emotion burned his throat, scored him with pain, but not as much as the regret crushing his chest.

He wouldn't let the negative emotions ruin this. Not now. Not tonight.

Carefully, he touched her center and found her wet and slick with heat.

Belatedly, he remembered the condoms in his shaving kit. He rested his forehead on her belly, breathing hard, shaking like he had a fever. "I'll be right back."

When he returned seconds later, Nikki turned her head

and smiled at him. The look in her eyes nearly brought him to his knees.

He joined her again, but when she tried to curl her fingers around his shaft, he grabbed her wrist and held her at bay. "Later," he said gruffly. "I don't think I can wait."

He took care of protection and moved over her, spreading her thighs and fitting the head of his sex at her entrance. They both gasped when he went deep. So much for wooing her with his technique.

Nothing about this was smooth or practiced. Just two people yearning, straining against each other. Her skin was soft and warm. When he lifted one stocking-clad ankle onto his shoulder, the sight of her shot another bolt of heat through his gut.

"I adore these stockings, Nikki. You look like a pinup girl from a wartime calendar."

Her smile was sleepy and happy. "Glad you approve." She raised her hips, urging him on.

Fear like he had never known intruded—a fear he didn't want to admit. This was a mistake. Like that night in Atlantic City, he was rocked with wild emotions. He didn't know how to control the feelings. This was more than sexual desperation. So much more…

What did it mean?

Now he and Nikki were forever connected because of Emma. He couldn't pretend he was a ship passing Nikki's in the night.

He had left her twice before.

In the midst of unprecedented passion, the knee-jerk instinct to run was strong. But even scarier was the yearning, the need to stay.

She cupped his face in her hands, testing the late-day stubble on his chin. Her eyes searched his. "It's okay, Jake. Don't worry about it. This is just you and me scratching an itch. No declarations. No promises. Give me what I want."

"Gladly." He closed his eyes and pumped his hips, breathing raggedly, blind with need and confusion. Nikki's body welcomed him, drew him in, squeezed him. If he had been the kind of man to believe in love, this might have changed him.

But he wasn't and he didn't, so he concentrated on taking Nikki with him to the top and then holding her as they tumbled over the edge.

When it was over, they were both breathing heavily, the sounds audible in the silent room. He felt dizzy and warm and limp with satisfaction.

As he rolled onto his back, Nikki curled her body into his, her head resting on his shoulder. "Wow. You're good at this."

"I'm glad you think so." He mumbled the words, his eyes closed. He was so tired suddenly that he teetered on the brink of unconsciousness.

After a few moments, Nikki stirred. "I have to go, Jake. It's a long way back. Please don't get up. You're in a warm bed. I'll grab a cab or a ride share."

He tried to process her words. And then it hit him. Nikki wasn't free to spend the night. He knew that, of course, but the knowledge had been pushed to the back of his brain. "I'll take you," he said.

"No, really." She climbed out of bed and scooped up her underwear and clothes, then went toward the bathroom, still wearing the garter belt and stockings. God help him. "Stay where you are," she said. "I'll text you when I get home."

He stumbled after her, pulling up short in the doorway to the small en suite. The long mirror over the sink reflected a woman who looked like a weary angel...if angels had red hair and white skin and a stubborn tilt to their chins.

"Don't be ridiculous," he said. "I'm getting dressed."

His clothing was scattered all over the floor and the furniture. He grabbed everything except his sport coat. When he was ready, he avoided looking at the bed. Would he be able to sleep there tonight?

Nikki wasn't like the other women he had bedded. She never had been.

What was he supposed to do with that knowledge?

They made their way down to the car in silence. The snow had picked up, but it wasn't sticking to the roads.

Nikki tried once again to convince him to let her leave without him. He shut her up by leaning her against the car and kissing her hard. Then he tucked her into the passenger seat and closed the door. Once the engine fired, he turned up the heat.

"You okay, Nik?"

She nodded. "I'm good."

When she reached out and put a hand on this thigh, he felt like he had won the lottery. "What's your schedule like this week?" he asked.

"On Wednesday, I only work half a day. I could fix dinner and you could have some time with Emma."

"Any chance I might spend the night?" His hands gripped the steering wheel.

The long silence made his stomach curl. He heard his passenger sigh. She sounded conflicted. "I'll have to think about it, Jake."

"Is there a downside?" He asked the question lightly, as if he was merely curious instead of stung by her palpable reluctance.

"I want you, but I don't want to get involved. My life and yours are both complicated. You've left me twice now. And both times nearly killed me. So I like to think I'm smarter than I used to be."

"You don't think much of my character, do you?"

"It's not your character. It's *my* self-control."

The rest of the trip passed in silence. Jake chewed on her words, unable to put a positive spin on them. She cared about him, but she didn't want to get hurt when he inevitably left again.

She wasn't wrong. He wasn't cut out for Falling Brook. Hell, he wasn't cut out for anywhere permanent. That was why he wandered. But could he change? Did he want to?

"Will you still come to Joshua's wedding with me?" he asked.

"Of course. I said I would. Besides, it will be fun. Your brother is a super guy. I'm so glad he and Sophie found each other."

The snow was coming in heavier bands. Jake focused his attention on the road, glad of the excuse to drop the conversation. Talking about his brother's happy nuptials made his own life seem empty and meaningless.

When they finally pulled up in front of Nikki's modest house, she leaned over and kissed his check—a brief peck, nothing to get hot and bothered about.

"I enjoyed tonight, Jake. Thanks for dinner…and everything."

"I'll walk you to the door," he said.

"No. Keep the car warm. I'll talk to you soon."

And then she was gone, though her scent lingered.

Jake waited for the front door to open and close. Then he put the car in gear and headed back to Falling Brook. The long drive gave him plenty of time to think. Too much time. Why were people so complicated?

As soon as Josh's wedding was over, there would be

no reason to stay. Except for the trial, of course. But even those legal proceedings didn't demand Jake's presence. He didn't care what happened to his father.

Not at all...

But he couldn't lie to himself. He was falling for Nikki all over again. Which scared the hell out of him...

Nikki spoke briefly with Nella, and then urged her to go home before the roads got any worse. She handed the girl an envelope with cash in it. "Thank you so much for staying late. I really appreciate it."

"No problem, Ms. Reardon. She was a lot of fun, and she went to sleep as soon as I put her to bed. Call me again anytime."

When the babysitter left, Nikki closed the front door and leaned her back against it. She had shed her coat when she walked in, but now her cashmere sweater and wool skirt felt too hot. Nella must have run up the thermostat.

It was fine, really. Emma sometimes tossed off her covers during the night. Nikki wanted her baby girl to be warm.

In the bathroom, she tried to avoid looking at herself in the mirror. She felt as if she was wearing a neon sign—*I had sex tonight...with Jake Lowell.*

Who really cared? If Nikki kept her head in the game and didn't lose sight of the fact that Jake would leave New Jersey sooner than later, she couldn't get hurt. Right?

After a long hot shower, she put on her oldest, comfiest pair of flannel pajamas and climbed into bed. When she closed her eyes, Jake was there in the bed with her. He had touched her hungrily but with such tender care. As if she was breakable.

She wasn't. Not anymore. Life had knocked her down more than once, but she had picked herself up and kept going.

Though it was late, and her daughter would be up early, Nikki couldn't sleep. She replayed the night with Jake over and over, stirring restlessly in her lonely bed.

No other guy she knew was as smart or as funny…or as dangerously masculine and attractive.

The sex tonight had been revelatory. Nikki responded to Jake like no other partner she had ever known. Not that there was even a handful to compare.

He drew something from her. Some deep expression of her femininity. With Jake, she felt sexual, sensual, elementally human in the best possible way.

For the first time, she let herself wonder if there was a way forward that included the two of them as a couple. They shared a child. It wasn't so far-fetched an idea. They certainly had sexual chemistry. And a deep history. Similar backgrounds. Shared values.

What if she allowed herself to open up to him? To drop her resentment and anger and disappointment? What if she took Jake into her bed and into her life with a blank slate? Was there any possibility she might really be able to love him again? Did there exist a part of her that never *stopped* loving him?

If she lowered her defenses and let her emotions run wild, would Jake be able to reciprocate? It was scary to think of saying "I love you" and then being rejected.

When he had suggested that she and Emma visit Switzerland, the invitation had been couched in very temporary terms. To say Jake was skittish about commitment was like saying a zebra had stripes.

Nikki wanted more from a man. She deserved more.

A life partner. Someone who would encourage her to grow and flourish, and who would love and support her.

Being honest with herself about the current situation was getting harder and harder. She wanted to dream.

By the time Wednesday rolled around, she had second-guessed herself a million times. She picked up Emma after Mom's Day Out, stopped by the store and then rushed home to throw together a homemade lasagna. Soon, the kitchen was all warm and cozy and filled with the wonderful smells of tomato sauce and cheese and garlic.

Jake had sent a text, offering to pay for a babysitter so they could go out to dinner again, but Nikki had declined politely. Perhaps it was unfair, but she felt the need to test Jake's reactions in a boring family setting. He couldn't always splash his money around and expect to make problems go away.

Nikki liked being pampered as much as the next woman, but this relationship with Jake had three sides, not two. Tonight's focus would be Emma. After Emma went to bed, all bets were off. Nikki hadn't planned that far ahead. Some things were best left to chance.

Jake hadn't asked again about staying over, and she hadn't brought it up.

Unfortunately, the weather had taken a raw turn. The flurries they'd had for a few days were predicted to become accumulating snow sometime during the night. She wondered if Jake would cancel, and then felt sheepish when she realized how very much she dreaded that phone call.

She could tell herself all she wanted that she was keeping an emotional distance, but the truth was far different. Jake was deeply involved in her life already. She had allowed it, encouraged it and enjoyed it.

The real question was…did she want him to *stay* involved?

When the doorbell rang at five thirty on the dot, she dried her damp palms on her pants and took a deep breath. Emma was playing in her room, but she would soon be asking for dinner.

Nikki had decided to dress casually. Her stretchy black leggings and gold ballet flats were comfortable and cute. The off-the-shoulder sweater was turquoise. She looked like what she was—a middle-class suburban mom home for the evening.

The bell rang a second time. Evidently, she had dithered too long.

Scuttling through the house, she swept her fingers through her clean hair and checked her reflection in the hall mirror. Not bad. Her eyes were perhaps too bright, her smile too big. She inhaled sharply and let the air escape slowly. *Calm, Nikki. Calm.*

It took her two tries to grab the doorknob. At last, she flung open the door, letting in a rush of cold air and revealing the identity of her visitor, not that she'd had any doubt.

"Jake. Hi. Come on in."

In a quick glance, she saw everything about him. Leather jacket unzipped over a tailored blue cotton shirt. Jeans that were just the right amount of worn. Jeans that hugged his legs and man parts in a very distracting fashion. And my gosh, were those…?

She blurted it out. "Are you wearing *cowboy boots*? Mr. Sophisticated World Traveler, Jake Lowell?"

"Let me in, Nik. It's freezing."

"Sorry." She stepped back quickly.

He brushed past her, bringing in the scents of the outdoors. "These are for you."

The large bouquet of deep yellow roses definitely didn't come from a run-of-the-mill supermarket. The blossoms were huge and fragrant. She took them automatically. "You didn't have to bring me flowers."

He shot her a glance that included irritation and banked lust. "I know that. Put them in water, Nik." He glanced down the hall. "I brought Emma something, too."

"Honestly, Jake. Gifts aren't necessary. She'd just a little kid."

Without warning, he kissed her, his lips lingering, pressing, summoning memories of the night in his hotel room. "She's more than just a little kid. She's my daughter."

Ten

Jake noted the stricken look on Nikki's face, but he couldn't quite pinpoint the cause. Was he being too abrupt about claiming his parental rights? Did his words sound like a threat? He hadn't meant them that way.

Giving Nikki a chance to regain her composure, he shrugged out of his jacket and rolled up his sleeves. The little house was cheery and warm. "Dinner smells amazing."

At last, Nikki's posture thawed. "I hope you like lasagna."

He followed her into the kitchen and watched as she rummaged under the sink for a vase. Her position gave him a tantalizing view of her perfect, heart-shaped ass.

Just as his libido began to carry him down a dangerous path, little Emma appeared in the doorway. "Is it time, Mommy? I'm hungry." She turned to Jake. "Hi! Are you eating with us?"

Jake nodded. "Sure am. And *I'm* hungry, too. Maybe we should get out of the way for a bit and let Mommy get everything on the table." He shot Nikki an inquiring look. "Unless you need help."

Her cheeks were pink. "I'm good. Give me five minutes."

In the living room, he handed Emma the gift that was wrapped in shiny red paper.

She cocked her head in a movement eerily reminiscent of her mother. "It's too early for Christmas."

"This isn't a Christmas present. It's just something your mom told me you liked." He had wrestled with his conscience and finally decided he wasn't above buying a child's affection if it landed him a few extra points in a sticky situation.

Emma's excited screech brought her mother running. Nikki stopped in the doorway, her expression frazzled. "What's wrong?"

Emma beamed and held up the toy, not realizing she had scared her mother. "Look what Mr. Man got me!"

Nikki mouthed at Jake, *Mr. Man?*

He shrugged. "I thought you told her to call me that."

"No."

Emma demanded her mother's attention. "Look, Mommy. It's the special one."

What Jake had procured at an appalling price was the princess from the latest animated movie. She was the deluxe edition with eyes that opened and closed and a fancy dress with two additional outfits. The doll had been advertised heavily on television and was out of stock in stores across the area despite the fact that Black Friday hadn't even happened yet.

Nikki squatted to give the princess her required admiration. "She's beautiful, Emma. Did you thank Mr. Jake?"

Without warning, Emma whirled and wrapped her arms around Jake's knees. "Thank you, thank you, thank you."

He touched her head, felt the long, soft golden hair. "You're very welcome." Emotions buzzed inside his chest. Alien emotions that weren't particularly welcome. He had decided he wanted to know his daughter. But that had been a cerebral decision. He hadn't anticipated actually *feeling* things.

Nikki rescued him. "Dinner's ready," she said calmly, rising to her feet. It almost seemed as if she could detect his internal agitation.

The meal could have been awkward. Emma's nonstop chatter made it less so. The roses were displayed in an inexpensive glass container. They matched the yellow stripe in Nikki's woven place mats.

Emma turned up her nose when her mom put a small serving of salad on her plate. It must have been a battle the two females had fought before, because the younger one sighed and gave in to the older.

The three of them ate in harmony, though Jake was unable to keep from imagining Nikki naked and at his mercy. Such inappropriate mental pictures probably reflected poorly on his qualifications to be a dad, but he couldn't help it. Three entire days and most of a fourth had passed since he had seen his lover.

Though Jake had kept busy, the mental movie reel made him itchy and restless and disrupted his sleep. He'd brought an overnight case this trip and left it in the trunk of the car. He couldn't read Nikki on this particular subject, but he wanted to be prepared.

Emma liked her mother's lasagna and cleaned her plate.

Jake ate three helpings himself and groaned when he

finally pushed back from the table. "I had no idea you could cook like that."

"Thank you." Nikki served her daughter a very small dollop of warm apple pie with ice cream.

When she offered some to Jake, he shook his head ruefully. "I overdid it with dinner. I'll have to wait for some of this to shake down."

"Of course."

Emma asked to be excused and was given permission. Just like that, the atmosphere in the kitchen went from homey to horny. At least on his part.

Nikki's face wasn't giving away anything.

Jake finished his glass of wine and poured himself another. "I'm glad she liked the doll."

Nikki stiffened visibly. "Presents aren't a substitute for quality time."

He stared at her. "I only found out I was a father a short time ago. You could cut me some slack, Nik. Are you trying to pick a fight with me?"

All that wild red hair was caught back in a ponytail at her nape, but it didn't take much effort to remember it fanned out across his sheets.

Her jaw jutted. "I want to make Christmas special for her. You just undercut me."

He frowned. "Were you planning to give her that doll?"

"No. You know I can't afford it. But now, whatever Santa brings will look paltry in comparison."

"I doubt she knows the word *paltry*, and you're her mom. She's going to love whatever you and the jolly old man put under the tree."

Nikki's ire deflated visibly. "Whatever." She chewed her lip. "You could make it up to me."

He grinned. "I like the sound of that."

"Get your mind out of the gutter, Lowell. I'm talking about actual useful *work*."

He glanced around him at the dishes. "You want me to clean up the kitchen? Sure. I'd be happy to—"

"No. Not that. I need help with the Christmas tree."

"What Christmas tree?"

She looked at him and rolled her eyes. "The one in the closet. I like to put up the tree the day after Thanksgiving. But since I've asked off for the wedding this coming Saturday, the diner has me down to work Friday *and* Saturday of Thanksgiving weekend. With you here tonight, we could put up the tree together in no time, and Emma could hang a few ornaments before she goes to bed."

"If you want, I could buy you a tree, fully decorated, and have it delivered tomorrow." Which would free up time for the two grown-ups to fool around later.

Nikki touched his arm briefly, making his skin hum. "Trimming the tree is part of the magic of Christmas," she said. "I appreciate the thought, but I love decorating. It makes me feel good."

"I get it. But why artificial?"

"For one, Emma has allergies. Besides, a live tree can't go up this early. They dry out. Surely, you've done this before."

"As a kid," he said, feeling defensive and trying not to show it.

Nikki stared at him, her beautiful eyes wide. "Are you telling me you haven't put up a Christmas tree in fifteen years?"

"Why does that shock you, Nikki? I live alone. I'm always on the road. It's a lot of hassle for one person."

"But what about the holidays? What about Christmas Day? How did you celebrate?"

Her inquisition brought back memories that weren't always exactly pleasant. "Well, for starters, sometimes I'm in a country that doesn't observe the Christmas holiday."

"Okay. I get that. But other years?"

"Occasionally a friend will invite me over. Or if I'm traveling, I'll find a church and go to a service. It's not a bad thing to skip the commercialism and the sappy sentiment. I haven't missed much."

Her eyes darkened with some emotion he couldn't name. "Oh, but you have, Jake. You just don't realize it."

"Where's this damn tree?" he growled. "Let's get it over with."

Nikki pointed him toward the closet, though she seemed troubled. Jake carried the long, rectangular box into the living room and opened it. Fortunately, the tree was one of those prelit deals. All he had to do was lock together the three sections and make sure the stand was attached tightly.

At Nikki's direction, he positioned it in front of the window. Though he wouldn't dare say so out loud, the poor fake evergreen was not the snappiest tree in the forest. Honestly, it looked a bit dilapidated. Even sad…

"I know it's not great," Nikki said, studying the tree with her nose wrinkled. "I got it on clearance the year I was pregnant with Emma. But the decorations cover up its imperfections. Emma," she called. "We're ready to put ornaments on the tree."

Emma came running, holding her doll from Jake. "Can I do the first one?"

"Sure, baby."

Jake had planned to sit back and watch while the womenfolk did their thing. He was sadly mistaken about his role. First Emma, and then Nikki, chided him.

Soon, he was selecting ornaments from a jumbled plastic container and placing them on the tree. When the ornament box was finally empty—hallelujah—the adults added shiny silver tinsel, starting at the top and winding it around the tree. Nikki got down on her stomach and spread out a red velvet tree skirt, twitching and pulling until it was straight enough to meet her exacting standards.

Jake would have offered to help, but he was afraid he would be tempted to do more than twitch if he was down on the floor with Nikki. She looked like a holiday treat in her fluffy turquoise sweater. It was the color of the Aegean Sea. Maybe he could convince her to take a trip with him to Greece. Sunshine. Warmth. Blue skies.

He cleared his throat and tried to think about icebergs and cold showers. "Are we done?" he asked.

Nikki stood, stretched her back and nodded. A piece of her hair had tangled with one of the lower branches. Jake smoothed the strand and rubbed his thumb over her cheek. "The tree looks great, Nik."

It was true. Somehow, the collage of ornaments had transformed a shabby artificial tree into something beautiful.

Emma stared at it, her doll in her arms. "Turn the lights off, Mommy."

In the dark, the tree was even better. Jake pressed a surreptitious kiss beneath Nikki's ear and nipped her earlobe with his teeth. "I keep picturing you naked," he confessed, his words too quiet for the child to hear. He slid a hand under the back of Nikki's sweater and caressed the length of her spine.

Nikki shivered, but didn't move away. Instead, she leaned into him, letting him support her weight. Her hair tickled his nose.

Finally, she turned in his loose embrace, touched his lips with her fingers and spoke as he had, in a low voice.

"It's snowing really hard now. You shouldn't drive back to Falling Brook. Why don't you spend the night?"

A rush of heat settled in his groin. His mouth dried. "On the sofa?"

He saw the multicolored lights from the Christmas tree reflected in her laughing eyes. "In my bed."

"What about Emma?" His voice sounded funny, perhaps because he was struggling to breathe.

Nikki gave his chin a quick kiss, then eyed her daughter. "We'll set an alarm," she muttered. "You can move to the sofa at five. It will be fine."

Nikki bathed her daughter, washed her hair and dressed her in warm pajamas. The temperature was dropping and would soon leave a crust of ice on the new-fallen snow. As Nikki tucked Emma into bed, her daughter cuddled the new doll sleepily. "Why isn't Mr. Man reading me a story tonight?"

"It's late, baby. Decorating the tree took all our time."

Emma yawned and snuggled deeper in her covers. "I like the tree. It's bootiful."

Nikki grinned. "Yes, it is. But remember, it's still a long time until Christmas. We put up the tree a little early this year. You and I will enjoy it every day and every night, and I'll let you know when it's time to look for Santa."

"I can wait, Mommy. I'm good at waiting."

"Can I ask you a question, love?" She smoothed her daughter's still-damp hair. "Why do you call Jake 'Mr. Man'?"

Emma yawned again, her eyelids drooping. "He's a boy and we're girls. I like Mr. Man."

Nikki managed not to laugh. "Fair enough."

When she turned off the light and tiptoed out, she was

pretty sure her daughter was already asleep. Nikki found Jake in the kitchen wiping the last of the countertops. The dishwasher was humming, and the kitchen was spotless.

"Jake," she said, feeling guilty. "You're our guest. I would have done all this."

His grin curled her toes. "First of all," he said, "I needed to earn my keep. And second of all…" He crossed the room and scooped her up on her toes for a fast, breath-stealing kiss. "I wanted you to be free for whatever comes next."

"And what would that be?"

"Lady's choice."

She nuzzled her cheek against his broad, hard chest, listening to the steady *ka-thump* of his heart. "What if we start by drinking cheap wine in the dark and enjoying the Christmas tree?"

"Cheap wine?"

"You tell me." She threw open the cabinet where she kept a single bottle of red and then opened the fridge and pulled out two bottles of chardonnay. "Your pick."

He winced. "I could have brought some."

"I suppose a man who visits fancy vineyards in France and Italy is above five-dollar vino?"

Jake's expression was droll. "If you paid five dollars for these, you were robbed."

His disgust made her giggle, though she was breath-less with wanting him. "How about coffee? I have some beans in the freezer. And a grinder. Though it's probably dusty," she admitted.

He cupped her face in his big hands and kissed her eyelids one at a time, his expression searing and intense. "How about a glass of water, and then we go make out on your couch?"

"I'm fine without the water," she gasped. They were

pressed together so closely she could feel the hard length of him against her abdomen. "And we *could* go straight to the bedroom."

Jake was suddenly the one with patience. "Tree first, woman. We worked hard on that masterpiece."

He took her by the hand and drew her down the hall to the living room. Nikki had opened the drapes before she put Emma to bed. Now, streetlights illuminated the heavily falling snow. The tree cast a warm glow over the room.

"You couldn't have driven home, anyway," Nikki muttered. "Look at it out there. Did you bring an overnight bag? You should grab your stuff from the car before it gets any worse."

Jake sat down and pulled her onto his lap. "You agreed to make out with me. Don't change the subject. And yes. I packed a few things. Just in case."

Nikki shivered. How many times over the years had the two of them fooled around like this? When she was in high school and Jake was in college, she had lived for the weekends when he came home to Falling Brook. He'd told his mother he needed to wash clothes. He'd told Nikki he needed *her*.

Now, Jake's hands were everywhere…caressing, arousing. When he stroked the center seam of her leggings, the one that lined up with her aching sex, she arched into him and whimpered. "Yes, Jake. Yes."

They kissed ravenously, straining to get closer and closer still. His lips bruised hers. His hands tangled in her hair. "I want you, Nik. I haven't been able to think about anything else but making love to you since I brought you home Saturday night. Please tell me I'm not the only one with this obsession."

"You're not," she panted, her tongue soothing the

small hickey she had left on his neck. "Where are the condoms? Don't say they're in the car."

He shoved her aside and jumped to his feet, reaching for his billfold. "Two," he croaked. "Right here."

"Good." She stood also, then stripped her sweater over her head. The house was warm, but her nipples furled tightly when Jake reached for her, his gaze hot.

"Let me help you with that bra," he said. Seconds later, the bra was in the air and Jake was sitting on the sofa again with her on his lap so he could play with her breasts. He plumped them between his hands and buried his face between them, inhaling her scent. "You still wear the same perfume," he said softly.

"Yes."

"I caught a whiff in a department store one time and got a hard-on. I love the way it smells on your warm skin. I could eat you up, Nik." Then he caught one nipple between his teeth and tugged. That simple contact sparked fireworks all over her body.

When she cried out, he glanced up at her, his cheeks flushed. "Too much?"

She smoothed his hair with a shaky hand. "No, Jake. Never too much."

He rewarded that confession by giving the neglected nipple equal time. In moments, Nikki's knees were weak and the thrum of arousal low in her belly was impossible to ignore. "Take off my pants," she begged, standing up clumsily.

The stretchy fabric cooperated easily when Jake slid his hands inside and dragged her pants down her legs. He took her ballet flats, too, leaving her in nothing but a pair of lacy black undies.

"God, you're beautiful," he breathed, his expression reverent.

"You have too many clothes on."

She started unbuttoning his shirt, but his patience ran out. "I'll do it."

Suddenly, she realized the drapes were still open. "Oh, my gosh." The living room was dark, but still. Scuttling backward into the shadows, she hissed at Jake. "My bedroom. Now."

They tiptoed down the hallway, past Emma's closed door, and made it unscathed into the master bedroom. *Master* was a misnomer. The bedroom was scarcely larger than Emma's, but it did have a bathroom, so the lady of the house didn't have to use the one in the hall.

Jake exhaled. "Does this door lock?"

The room was dark. "Yes. Hang on." She found the bedside table and turned on the lamp. When she saw Jake's face, her heart stopped. He looked like a pirate intent on capturing a prize.

Rapidly, he removed the rest of his clothes. He made her feel young again, and reckless.

She turned back the quilt and the sheet and climbed onto the bed.

Jake joined her quickly. "This feels good," he said as they rolled together, their limbs tangling.

"The mattress isn't great," she mumbled, wrapping her hand around the most interesting part of him.

He shuddered. "I don't give a damn about the mattress. I'd take you outside in the snow if that was the only way to have you. You excite me, Nik. I guess that's obvious. I'd like to see you sunbathing nude on a private terrace in Greece. Just the two of us. Drinking ouzo and eating cheese. How does that sound?"

Since he was touching every erogenous zone on her body and a few that were surprisingly mundane most of the time, she was in a cooperative mood. "Sounds won-

derful. Would you buy me a gold anklet and let me ride
a donkey down to the sea?"

He choked out a laugh. "I'd buy you a whole damn
town. And every man who walked by our dinner table
at night would see you in candlelight and be jealous that
they weren't me." He moved away long enough to don
protection, then came back to her.

Reclining on his hip, he entered her with two fingers,
feeling the slick warmth of her body. Gently, he stroked
the spot that centered her pleasure. "I want to take you
hard and fast, but I also want it slow and easy."

Nikki skated her palm over his sculpted, warm shoulder, loving the feel of him, the intimacy. "Why choose?"
she asked quietly. "We can have it all."

He rose over her and thrust hard, making both of
them gasp. She wrapped her legs around his waist. The
movement forced him deeper. He thrust again, and she
climaxed, the world going hazy as she concentrated on
wringing every bit of pleasure from her release. It had
come too fast. She wanted more. But already Jake was
finding his own nirvana, taking her body and making
it his own.

At last, breathing hard, he rolled away, linking her
hand with his. "That was amazing, Nik." The words were
slurred. His breathing deepened as he fell asleep.

She reached for the lamp and turned it off. Then with
one hand, she set an alarm on her phone. In the dark,
tears stung her eyes. Christmas was the season of mira-
cles, but something told her Jake Lowell wouldn't stick
around long enough for Santa to show up.

Nikki squeezed his hand, holding on as if she could
keep him forever. "I love you, Jake," she whispered.

Eleven

When Jake opened his eyes, he was disoriented by the dark. This wasn't his hotel room. And then he was fully awake.

Shifting carefully to the side of the bed, he stood and stumbled to the bathroom. When he returned, his eyes had adjusted fractionally to the black of night. Nikki must have installed room-darkening shades on her windows.

A glance at his watch told him it was only two. In the silence, he could hear the almost imperceptible sound of Nikki's breathing. He climbed back under the covers and turned into her warmth. The curves and valleys of her body had him hard again.

But he was cold inside, and there was a block of ice where his heart should have been. Nikki had thought he was asleep when she said those four incredible words. *I love you, Jake.*

Had she really meant it? How could she? After everything that had happened…

As he tried to steady his panicked breathing, a memory popped into his head. He'd been twelve, maybe thirteen, camping with a friend and his family at Yellowstone. A park ranger gave a talk about the west's low humidity and had warned that if the remnants of a campfire were not separated and scattered well enough, an ember, a slow burn, might remain for hours, days. And then spring back to life when the wind conditions were right.

Now here Jake was. Did he still love Nikki? Or did he even care enough to try? And with a kid in the mix, what was the fallout if he wanted to be the man Nikki deserved, but failed?

His erection mocked his indecision. *Take her*, the devil on his shoulder urged. *Protect her*, said his better self.

In the end, he knew the answer. Moving her gently in the bed, he shook her awake. "I need you, Nik. Again? Please?"

She nodded sleepily, murmuring her pleasure when he kissed her long and deep, teased her lips, thrust his tongue inside to stroke her tongue. The fire burned hot again.

Reaching for the nightstand on his side of the bed, he found the remaining condom and managed to rip it open. When he was ready, he faced her on his side. Carefully, he lifted her leg over his hip, pulled her close and joined their bodies.

It was perhaps the most intimate thing they had done. Their breath mingled. They met as equals. Neither in charge. Both of them taking pleasure and giving it in return.

Nikki curled her arm around his neck and kissed him. "I'm glad you stayed tonight," she whispered.

Her kiss took him higher. He felt invincible. "Me, too, Nik," he groaned. Fire swept down his spine, flashed in his pelvis. His fingers dug into the soft curve of her ass. He wanted to say something, to tell her how he felt, but the storm swept him under. He came so hard he might have lost his wits for a moment.

He rolled to his back at the end. Her cheek was smashed against his chest. Stroking her glorious hair, he tried to steady his breathing. His brain spun out of control, and he tasted fear. How could he hurt the woman who had been his whole world?

"Jake?" she said, petting his chest like he was a big jungle cat.

"Hmm?"

"I'm wide-awake now. Tell me about the wedding. I know you said it's at two o'clock, but is it going to be a huge affair? Where are they getting married?"

He tried to focus. "You remember the Bismarck Hotel downtown?"

"Yes."

"They've remodeled the top floor into a large entertainment space. Josh and Sophie had the choice of including only family and close friends or planning for a crowd of a thousand or more. You know how it is in Falling Brook. Once you start inviting people, it's hard to draw the line. Plus, with all the Black Crescent mess in the news again this year, my brother and his fiancée thought it would be in poor taste to spread a bunch of money around. Last I heard, the guest list hits around fifty. Small and intimate."

"What about a rehearsal dinner?"

"Nope. Not even that."

"Good for them."

The conversation was a pleasant diversion, but Jake

had arrived at the moment of truth. Things were getting far too cozy. He released her and scooted up against the headboard, forcing himself not to touch her.

Nikki reached for the lamp and flipped the switch. He hated that. He didn't want her to see what was coming.

If he had any guts at all, he wouldn't let her have hope. He raked his hand through his hair, feeling the cold sweat on his forehead. "I don't think I'm going to stay for my father's trial, Nikki."

She sat up, too, pulling the sheet to her chest, covering her breasts. Her hair was a tumbled, fiery cloud around her face. Her eyes were huge. "I don't understand. Why not? You need closure, Jake. If you don't face Vernon, you'll never get over what he did. He'll always be the bogeyman."

Perhaps there was truth in what she said, but he didn't want to hear it. He didn't want to admit it. "He's nothing to me. I don't care what happens to him. He destroyed us, Nikki. I can't forgive him for that."

Every bit of color leached from her face. He thought for a moment she might be sick. "That's not true," she said. The words were sharp.

He stared at her. "Of course it is."

The heartbreak dawning in her eyes was familiar. He'd seen it fifteen years ago. He might have seen it five years ago in Atlantic City if he'd left when she was awake. She lifted her chin, visibly angry. "*You* destroyed us, Jake. Not your dad. He disappeared, but you could have come back anytime, and you didn't."

The attack came out of nowhere.

He gaped at her. Nikki was always on his side. Always. "I *had* to leave. He'd made my life impossible. Every-where I went, reporters followed me. One of them shimmied up a ladder and tried to climb into my bedroom. It was hell, Nikki. And all of it, his fault."

"I know it was hell. I was there, remember?"

"Well, at least your dad died. He paid for his sins. You didn't have people thinking that you and your mother were hiding a fortune somewhere."

"That's a terrible thing to say." Her pallor increased. "I loved my dad, even though I hated what he did. I also hate how your dad and mine tore lives and families apart. But time moved on, Jake. I'm not stuck in the past. I've had to build a new life from the ground up. I have a child who loves me and a mother who depends on me for emotional support. I'm not that frightened high-school girl anymore."

"The implication being that I'm a coward?" His temper simmered.

She hesitated. "Not a coward. No. Not that. But you're emotionally stunted. You've had every resource in the world at your fingertips, and yet you couldn't bring yourself to grow up and come back and do your part. We all needed you, Jake. Oliver. Your mother. Joshua. Me."

Her words chipped away at him, exposing his weaknesses. It wasn't that he'd been too lazy or immature to share the burden—he'd been afraid. Afraid that he would come home and make things worse. "I offered Josh my help more than once. But he assumed I was a screwup, so he wasn't interested."

"That was in the past. My God, Jake. He offered you the helm of the company recently. How much more does he have to do to prove he believes in you?"

"I've lived on the road too long to change my ways. People aren't always who you want them to be, Nikki. You expect too much."

Her eyes were wet. Her jaw wobbled. "Do I? Maybe

so." One tear broke loose and ran down her cheek. "I think you should go sleep on the sofa now."

There it was. The death blow.

He had brought it on himself. Provoked this confrontation. The ice in his chest melted, leaving a gaping hole. It hurt. Dear God, it hurt. But he didn't know how to fix it.

Nikki stared at him, anguish on her face. "What about Emma?"

"I'll still see Emma. She has nothing to do with my father."

Now Nikki's smile was bitter. "I think you're wrong, Jake. How you relate to your daughter has everything to do with this chip on your shoulder. You've carried it far too long. It's crippled you."

He took the hit stoically, but he fought back, lashing out. "What did you say your college degree was in? Surely, not psychology." He heard the sarcasm and condescension in his words, but he couldn't seem to stop this train wreck of a conversation. "I'm a grown-ass man, Nikki. I think I can handle my own life."

She huddled against the headboard, her knuckles white where she gripped the sheet. "Maybe you can. But I have to ask, what about the wedding? I don't want to be rude to Joshua and Sophie."

"You'll come to the wedding with me. My family is expecting it. I've told them about Emma, so they'll want to see you."

"Won't that be fun," she said bitterly. "I'll find my own way there, Jake. I wouldn't want to inconvenience you."

"Don't be absurd. I'll pick you up at noon."

"And what happens to you and me after the wedding?"

He saw it then. Despite everything he had said and done, in Nikki's despairing gaze he saw one last remnant of hope amid her pain. "I don't think there is a 'you and me,'" he said, the words brusque and flat. "Lots of people share custody of children. I know who I am. And who I'm not." He slid out of bed and found his knit boxers. Grabbing up his shirt and pants, he started getting dressed.

Nikki wrapped the sheet around her body, toga-style, and went to her closet. "I'll get you some sheets for the sofa," she said.

Suddenly, he couldn't stand to be near her for another second. It was tearing him apart. "No," he said curtly. "I'm leaving."

She whirled around, frowning. "Don't be stupid, Jake. The snow is deep. And it's still coming down. You'll wreck your car."

He shrugged, staring at the woman who had shown him a glimpse of what his life *could* be like. "Don't worry, Nik. I always land on my feet."

As he grabbed his cowboy boots and the rest of his things and walked to the living room, he waited for her to follow him. Instead, the house was still and quiet. It would be a few more hours until dawn arrived. No need to worry about Emma getting the wrong idea. By the time she woke up, Jake would be back in Falling Brook at his impersonal hotel.

The Christmas tree mocked him with a cheerful glow. It was still lit, because Jake and Nikki had been too desperate for each other to pay attention. When he was completely dressed, he listened one more time to see if Nikki was going to waylay him. To lecture him about road safety. To tell him what a stubborn, closed-off bastard he was.

But nothing happened.

The front door had one of those twist locks that didn't require a key to be secured from the inside. When he was bundled up, he opened the door, stepped out into the hushed silence and waded through the snow.

He was alone in a deserted landscape.

Nikki cried for an hour, cried until her nose was stuffed up and her chest hurt. For long minutes, she had expected a knock on the front door. She had strained to hear it. Because it would be Jake admitting that the weather was too bad to leave.

Apparently, risking life and limb was preferable to staying with her.

How could he make love to her so beautifully and feel nothing?

If Jake had shown any glimmer of interest in a permanent relationship, Nikki would have fought for their future. She would have traveled anywhere with him. Emma hadn't started school yet. And Roberta might soon be going back to the friends she had known for decades.

But Jake had run from Nikki yet again, because of shadows from his past. She was long beyond what had happened fifteen years ago. She wasn't reliving old hurts, not anymore. She deserved a man who would love her, body and soul. Maybe he was out there somewhere.

In the meantime, she had to let Jake go. The hurt was like severing a limb, but it would only hurt worse if she refused to face the truth. Jake Lowell didn't love her. He couldn't. He was too empty inside.

The trouble with heartbreak and emotional meltdowns was that the world kept on turning. Emma bounced into Nikki's bedroom at seven, her impish personality bolstered by a good night's sleep.

Nikki managed not to groan. "Hi, baby."

"Where's Mr. Man?"

"Why would you ask that, hon?"

"It was snowing last night. You told me we couldn't drive in snow. Remember?"

"Ah. Well, that was us. Mr. Jake is a very good driver. So he went home after you were in bed."

"When is he coming back?"

"I don't know." Nikki, in desperation, changed the subject. "Let's get you some breakfast, so you'll be ready to play when Grandma gets here."

In typical Jersey fashion, the weather pattern had shifted again. It was too early in the season for sustained cold temps. The snow was already melting, and the sun was out. The streets were a slushy mess. But not particularly dangerous.

Nikki's shift at the diner started at ten today. Though she was glad it wasn't any earlier, she still didn't know how she was going to make it through eight hours of on-your-feet work. Lots of caffeine maybe. And a stone-cold commitment not to think about stupid, emotionally stunted rich men.

Roberta Reardon didn't spare Nikki's feelings when she arrived. "You look terrible. Are you getting the flu?"

"No, Mom. I'm fine. I just didn't sleep well."

"I see you have your tree up. How did you manage that since I last saw you?"

Emma answered, innocently. "Mr. Man helped."

Roberta's eyebrows went up. "Mr. Man?"

"Jake. He had dinner with us." Nikki glanced at her daughter. "Go take off your pajamas and get dressed, please."

When Emma headed for her bedroom, Roberta pressed for more. "And?"

"And nothing. He's getting to know Emma. He wants to be part of her life."

Her mother's smile was gentle. "You don't seem happy about that."

"It will be difficult," Nikki admitted, her throat tight.

"Because you're in love with him?"

"Mom!" Aghast, Nikki turned to look down the hall, making sure Emma hadn't picked up on the adult conversation. "She'll hear you."

"So it's true?"

"No, Mother," Nikki lied. "Jake and I are friends who share a child. That's all we'll ever be, and I'm okay with that."

She waited for the lightning to strike or for a huge sinkhole to open up and swallow her for telling such a whopper.

Roberta seemed disappointed. "Okay then. I believe you."

"I have to finish getting ready."

Nikki fled the room, telling herself she absolutely would *not* break down and cry. She was a grown woman. Not some fragile schoolgirl fixated on romantic fantasies that had no base in reality.

She made it to work with ten minutes to spare, so she grabbed a cup of coffee and took it to the storeroom. This place, this small restaurant, had become a familiar home. She liked her coworkers, and she liked her customers. The days had a comfortable routine.

Everybody needed to eat. And, surprisingly, a lot of people needed someone to talk to when their lives were empty. Nikki could do worse than stay here at the cozy retro diner indefinitely.

But the truth was, the salary for assistant manager wasn't all that great. When Emma was older and her needs were more expensive, Nikki would need a different job. Perhaps one that made use of her degree in communications.

She had thought about working for an ad agency. Maybe doing PR for a local business. She was a decent writer, and she didn't mind speaking in public.

Her moment of quiet time ended abruptly when one of the line cooks swung open the door and grabbed a can of baked beans. He glanced at the clock with a grin. "You hiding out in here, Nikki? Rough morning?"

Her face must have looked worse than she thought. She managed a smile. "Not enough sleep. You know. Kids…"

"Don't I ever."

The door closed, and she took a deep breath. Nothing had to be decided today. She would stay the course until after Christmas. January was a good month for resolutions and starting over. Maybe Falling Brook was the answer. Maybe Joshua really would offer Nikki and her mother a lifeline. Who knew what the future held?

The only certainty was that *Nikki's* future didn't include Jake Lowell.

Twelve

After Jake left Nikki's house in the predawn hours, he made a concerted effort to spend time with his family. If he was leaving after the wedding, he needed to fulfill his responsibilities as a son and a brother.

Oddly, the movie with Oliver, the rushed lunch with Joshua at Black Crescent and the afternoon tea at his mother's Friday afternoon were cathartic. He'd had in mind offering his support to *them*, but he ended up being the one who felt comforted.

His mother, especially, surprised him. They bypassed the pleasantries quickly and waded into deep water. "How are you doing, Mom? Really, I mean. I know you went to see Dad."

Eve Lowell looked much as she always had. Younger than her years. Dignified. Stylish. She was older now, of course. But she still had the posture of a beauty queen.

She wrinkled her nose at his question. "It was all small

talk. But enough to show me that it's time to move on. I'm not the same person I was. It took me a long time to find my strength, but I did. I still have my rough days, but I'm in a good place now, just like Oliver. When Oliver told me about his visit and how he came to the same conclusions, I was glad he went. It was healthy and positive for both of us."

"Do you still love Dad?" Jake hadn't known he was going to ask that question. When his mother was silent, he wished he hadn't. Finally, she shook her head slowly. "It depends on what you mean by love. Your father was declared legally dead. I'm no longer bound to him by law. But I said vows a million years ago. Vows I meant at the time. I certainly didn't know my husband was going to become a felon."

"So, is that a yes or a no?"

She looked at him wistfully. "We can't always choose whom we love, and we can't always stop loving them simply because they don't deserve our love. I know your father sent you away, Jake."

"He didn't send me away." Anger snapped in each word. "He left. He left you. He left me. He left all of us. And I couldn't handle the gutter press. They hounded our family and made us miserable. Because of *him*." Jake shook with sudden fury—fury he hadn't realized he'd pushed down, and had pushed down forever, it seemed.

"My poor boy. He left you homeless, didn't he?"

Jake felt raw suddenly. And he hated that vulnerability. "I owe you an apology, Mother," he said formally. "I never should have left you to face everything on your own. I'm sorry I didn't stay. I'm sorry I didn't come back."

"I had Joshua," she said, waving a hand. "We got by." Though her words weren't meant to wound, Jake felt them cut deep. He loved his brother dearly, but always being cast as the screwup was not a role Jake relished.

"Is there anything you need?" he asked. "I've done well financially."

"Jake, dear boy." She patted his hand. "Over the years you've sent me jewelry and artwork for my birthdays and Christmas. I never felt forgotten. I knew why you couldn't come home. But I hoped that one day the hurt would fade." She paused, her expression turning crafty, mischievous even. "Now tell me about Nikki and this baby of yours. Joshua has filled me in on the basics."

Jake hunched his shoulders. "Emma is four. She's mine. I'm making arrangements with Nikki, so I can fly in for the occasional visit. And, of course, we can video chat."

His mother's face fell. "I don't get to see my granddaughter?"

"I suppose that's up to you and Nikki."

"It strikes me that I haven't heard you talk about Nikki and *you*."

"There's nothing there, Mom."

"You made a baby together."

"That was five years ago. We bumped into each other one evening in Atlantic City and…well, you know."

Eve's smile was sweet. "I may be getting older, son, but I do understand sexual chemistry."

"We've been apart fifteen years. Whatever we had is gone."

"I find that hard to believe."

"Why?" He frowned at her.

"Because you've never found another woman to settle down with and make a home. That strikes me as odd. You have a huge heart, Jake. A generous spirit. And though you'd chew glass before you'd admit it, you're a sensitive and loving and wonderful man."

"I thought you were disappointed in me," he said gruffly, caught off guard by her praise. "I failed you."

"Nonsense," she said stoutly. "You followed your own path. Don't hide in the shadows forever, dear boy. You may not get too many chances for happiness. Seize this one before it's too late."

In that moment, he knew he was tired of running, tired of being so slow to change and grow. Despite all evidence to the contrary, he felt a fillip of hope that something new might be close at hand. He was ready to reach for happiness. But he still wasn't sure he could handle it or how to get there.

Maybe it was too late…

Though Jake appreciated his mother's support, his intentions were all over the map. Maybe Falling Brook wasn't as bad as he remembered. After all, the town had been nothing more than an excuse, a convenient bogeyman.

He'd had no contact at all with Nikki. He couldn't bring himself to text her. What would he say? Her words still rang in his ears. *You destroyed us, Jake. Not your dad.*

Apparently, Nikki Reardon was not as forgiving as Eve Lowell. Mothers always made excuses for their misbehaving sons. Lovers simply walked away.

Though, in all fairness, Jake had been the one to leave. He'd given up the wild, glorious uncertainty of Nikki's bed for the cold comfort of his iron-clad, selfish rules.

Never stop moving. Never put down roots. Never look back.

On the morning of the wedding, he ran out of options. He sent a brief text: I'm picking you up at noon.

It took ten minutes for Nikki's reply: I'll be ready.

He sighed. Thanksgiving was five days away. Maybe he should get out of New Jersey. The sooner, the better. Nothing was the way he thought it would be. Too many messy emotions. Too many people. Too many regrets.

He pulled up in front of Nikki's now-familiar house at twelve sharp. Before he could exit the car, she started down the walk, her long legs shown to advantage in silver heels. He met her halfway. "Hello."

She eyed him coolly. "Hello."

Though she carried a winter coat over her arm, the silvery-pink scarf around her shoulders protected her from the light breeze.

She looked stunning. Her golden-red hair was caught up on top of her head in a fancy knot of loose curls. The lustrous strand of pearls around her neck complemented the fabric of her dress. He wondered if Roberta had managed to hang on to one piece of valuable jewelry for her daughter, or if the pearls were costume.

The dress's strapless bodice and fitted waist fluffed out in what Emma would probably call a princess skirt. It ended midcalf. Jake opened the passenger door for Nikki and helped her in, carefully tucking in her skirt so the door wouldn't catch it.

When he ran around and slid behind the wheel, Nikki's familiar scent enveloped him. Her perfume wasn't heavy. Perhaps she had barely spritzed her throat. But he was intensely aware of it. And of her.

He started the engine. "You look beautiful, Nik. That dress was made for you."

She stared out the windshield. "Thank you."

"Are we going to act normal today?"

"I don't know. You tell me."

"C'mon, Nikki. Can't we call a truce?"

Now her head snapped around in his direction. Her eyes shot fire. He'd always thought that was just an expression, but Nikki nailed it. "You mean a truce during the wedding or until you leave town?" she asked.

He counted to ten. "For my brother's wedding. It's an important day."

"I know what weddings are, Jake. I had one, remember?"

The reminder hit him hard. He'd tried to forget that. "I know," he said, reeling from the pain of imagining it. Suddenly, he wanted details. "Was it a big wedding?"

"Mom and I were broke. Timothy and I went to the courthouse."

"I'm sorry it didn't work out." He said the words quietly, but he meant them. "You deserve to be happy."

"Thank you." She crossed her arms. The curves of her breasts peeked over the silky fabric that covered her chest. She looked lush, untouched, intensely feminine.

She belonged to him. The certainty came out of nowhere. Implacable. Undeniable. What was he going to do about it?

They arrived in Falling Brook and parked in a garage near the hotel. The half-a-block walk wasn't bad. Nikki put on her coat. Jake helped. The bare nape of her neck gave him ideas, but he reined in his impulses. It would be hours until he could get her alone.

Weddings happened every day, all the time. Half of them ended. He hoped his brother and Sophie would not be one of the failures, but who knew? Jake wasn't a sentimental man, or at least he hadn't been. But today, the woman beside him and his brother's big day were making Jake *feel* things.

At the Bismarck, they left Nikki's outerwear at the coat check in the main lobby. In the elevator, riding up to the twentieth floor, he studied her. She wasn't looking at him, so it was easy to sneak a peek.

She was so beautiful, it made his chest hurt. As a seventeen-year-old teenager, she had been cute and pretty and full of life. Now, she carried the maturity of a woman—a woman who had faced many of life's challenges and persevered.

Her magnolia skin, so often associated with redheads, was still the same. Soft, unblemished. Begging to be touched. Lust stirred uneasily in his gut. Today was about his brother, his twin. But despite the occasion, or perhaps because of it, Jake was drawn to his wedding date, his Nikki. He had missed her fiercely the last two days. The strength of that feeling convinced him he needed to move forward carefully.

He cleared his throat, feeling claustrophobic in the small space. "Joshua and Sophie asked their guests, in lieu of gifts, to make a donation to Haley Shaw's charity. I wrote a check. But I also sent Sophie a large potted orchid this morning from you and me with best wishes for a wonderful wedding day."

Nikki's head came up, and she actually smiled. "That was a lovely gesture. Thanks for including me."

The elevator dinged, and they exited. The entire top floor of the Bismarck had been completely transformed. Plate-glass windows in every direction showcased the view. One section of the giant room was set up with rows of white chairs and a center aisle marked with a satin runner. At the front, seasonal live flowers covered a trellised arch. Along the center aisle, candles burned inside crystal globes atop brass stands.

"This is beautiful," Nikki said, scanning the room with interest.

"C'mon. Let's get a seat." The front row on the right-hand side was reserved for Jake's mother, for Oliver and his fiancée, Samantha, and for Jake and Nikki. Jake watched as Nikki greeted each member of his family. Then they sat down.

Eve shot her son a knowing glance, but he ignored it.

The area set aside for the ceremony filled up quickly. The guest list might have ended up closer to sixty than fifty, but the crowd was still small enough to be described as intimate. A buzz filled the space as anticipation mounted.

Suddenly, Jake needed air. He had been blind for far too long. He was beginning to know what he wanted, but he had to make plans. Now he was trapped by the time. Three minutes before the hour.

From a side alcove, Joshua appeared, beaming. The minister accompanied him. The two men took their positions. A stringed quartet had been playing for the last twenty minutes. Now they paused and began the first notes of "Pachelbel's Canon."

Nikki touched his forearm. He jumped at the unexpected contact. His skin felt too tight for his body, and his chest was constricted.

She looked at him with concern. "Are you okay?" she whispered.

Nikki knew without any doubt that Jake was definitely *not* okay. He ignored her question. They stood with the other guests as the bride began to walk down the modest aisle. The expression on Sophie's face when she looked at Josh made Nikki's eyes damp with emotion.

Weddings always got to her, but this one more than most. Joshua had borne the weight of his father's sins and had worked for years to restore the community's trust in Black Crescent. He deserved to be the man of the hour.

His bride was stunning in an off-the-shoulder white satin gown with dozens of cloth-covered buttons down the back. Her hair was twined with tiny white flowers. She had opted for no veil.

Sophie and Joshua held hands and faced the minister. Their voices as they spoke their vows were clear and strong. They had chosen a traditional wedding liturgy with phrases like "love, honor and cherish" and "'til death do us part."

At last, the minister placed his palm over the couple's hands for a blessing. Then he said words that rang out over the small assembly: "I now pronounce you husband and wife. You may kiss the bride."

Everyone cheered and clapped. Josh bent Sophie over his arm and kissed her enthusiastically, not seeming to mind that they had an audience.

Nikki, without thinking, twined her fingers with Jake's, fighting a flood of feelings that threatened to overwhelm her. When he shot her a surprised sideways glance, she realized what she had done and dropped his hand immediately. But it was too late. She had inadvertently let him know how much she cared about him. Her face heated with humiliation.

The bride and groom exited. Everyone stood up and moved toward the reception area, talking and laughing.

Nikki spoke in Jake's direction without actually looking him in the eye. "Excuse me," she said stiffly. "I'd like to speak to Haley Shaw." She fled, managing not to run.

Fortunately, Haley was nearby. She had been sitting with Chase Hargrove. But Chase had moved away to chat with someone else.

"Hi, Haley," Nikki said. "You look beautiful."

Haley beamed. "Thanks. So do you."

"I didn't get a chance to say everything I wanted to the day I showed up at Black Crescent to talk to your boss."

Haley seemed surprised. "Oh?"

"I never thanked you for all those years you've stood by Black Crescent. Your loyalty to Vernon and my dad. And the way you stayed to help Joshua after everything fell apart."

Haley grimaced. "Well, I felt guilty, to be honest."

Nikki gaped at her. "Why?"

"Because I saw both of them that morning—Vernon and your dad. And I knew something was going down. But I never said anything to anybody. And then it was too late."

"Oh, gosh no, Haley. What could you have done? None of us had a clue what they were planning."

"Maybe. But you should know—I stayed with Black Crescent because I loved working there, and Joshua is a great boss."

Nikki shook her head slowly. "Life is strange. I've felt guilty all these years, too. I was still living at home back then. I overheard pieces of several odd phone calls. Conversations that made me uncomfortable. But I never said anything, either. I blamed myself afterward. Jake blamed me, too."

"Well, he must have gotten over it. The way he looks at you gives me the shivers. The man is in love with you in a bad way."

"Oh, no," Nikki said quickly. "You're mistaken. We're old friends, that's all. He asked me to be his plus-one because he's been gone forever and doesn't really know any women in Falling Brook."

Haley wrinkled her nose, unconvinced. "I think you're kidding yourself. Chase and I had our ups and downs and misunderstandings before we got engaged. Relationships are difficult. We had to learn to trust each other."

"I didn't know you were engaged."

Haley held out her hand, showing off her ring. "Yep. No wedding date yet. I'm waiting to see if Josh is going to be able to find a new CEO before making plans."

"I thought he had been interviewing candidates."

"He has. For months. But it has to be the right fit. Look at the Lowell men over there. It's probably what they're talking about right now."

The groom had separated from his bride for the moment. Sophie was surrounded by a crowd of family and friends. Joshua stood in a tight circle with Oliver and Jake. The three men were gorgeous. With both twins in dress clothes, Jake looked far more like his identical brother than usual.

"You're probably right," Nikki said. "I think I'll go get some food. I skimped on lunch. And I see that your handsome fiancé is headed this way."

Joshua, Jake and Oliver were deep in conversation when Nikki slipped past them. She picked up enough words here and there to know Haley was right. They were talking about the CEO search. Maybe the Lowells should sell Black Crescent. She wondered if any of the three had floated that idea.

Feeling somewhat out of place, Nikki picked up a plate and began filling it with appetizers. The cake would be cut later. She found a corner and sipped her champagne. The day, unlike the expensive alcohol, had gone flat. She shouldn't have come. Things with Jake were rocky at best.

She was looking down at her glass when a deep voice startled her. "There you are."

"Jake," she said.

"So you do remember my name. That's a start."

His attempt at humor failed.

"Don't feel like you have to entertain me," she said. "I know you have lots of catching up to do with old friends." Even after fifteen years, she and Jake knew many of the guests personally.

"How about a dance?" he said, taking her empty plate and glass and setting them on a nearby tray.

"I don't think so."

"We agreed to a truce, remember?"

His gentle smile and half-hearted grin made her stomach curl with anxiety and heartbreak. "Sure."

He tucked her tiny beaded clutch in his jacket pocket, then took her by the hand and led her out onto the dance floor. Other couples had the same idea. Jake put an arm around her waist and pulled her close. The string quartet had yielded to a bluesy band that began playing romantic standards.

When the musicians launched into "I Only Have Eyes for You," Nikki stumbled and gasped. "I don't want to dance," she said, trying to pull away.

Jake held her tightly, looking almost as miserable as she felt. "Dance, Nik. For old times' sake."

He might as well have stabbed her through the heart. She wanted to run away. This was agonizing. She loved him, but he didn't feel the same.

No matter the pain, she wouldn't cause a scene at Josh and Sophie's wedding.

She kept her gaze focused on the third button of Jake's pristine white dress shirt, trying not to cry. His body was big and hard and warm, and he smelled amazing. His hand clasping hers was strong and tanned. He had mentioned Greece. Probably because he had a favorite villa there that he rented whenever the mood took him.

What kind of women did Jake *entertain* when he went

to the Mediterranean? The odd thing was that Nikki didn't really care about all those faceless females. She loved him as he was—imperfect, fierce, generous, sweet with Emma…and the perfect lover in Nikki's bed.

Once, he had been her whole world. Having him back in Jersey now, even fleetingly, had shown her why her marriage hadn't worked out. It had also underlined the truth that some feelings never die. She loved Jake Lowell, and she probably always would.

The dance finally ended. Jake and Nikki stood at the edge of the floor, not speaking, and watched as the bride and groom enjoyed their first dance. After that, the tempo picked up. Alcohol flowed freely, and the crowd became more raucous.

"I have to go to the restroom," Nikki said. She pulled her clutch from Jake's pocket and slipped away before he could say anything. In the ladies' lounge she found a seat and repaired her lipstick. One glance in the mirror told her she was hiding her feelings fairly well. Only her eyes gave her away. She pinched her cheeks and put a wet paper towel on the back of her neck.

She wanted badly to go home. But it was a very long way. If she hired a car, it would cost a fortune.

When she returned to the reception, Jake was nowhere in sight. Some kind of buzz circled the room. Clumps of guests stood here and there, looking either startled or worried or both.

Nikki found Haley, who looked shell-shocked. "What happened?" Nikki asked. "I can't find Jake. What's going on?"

Haley lowered her voice. "Somebody just brought word that Vernon has escaped from custody."

"Oh, no. Poor Joshua. Poor Sophie. What a dreadful thing to happen today of all days."

Suddenly, Joshua strode across the room in their direction. His face was stormy. When he stood right in front of the two women, he sighed. "Jake is gone, Nikki."

She gaped at him. "What do you mean *gone*? I don't understand."

"He and Oliver left to go find our dad."

Nikki shook her head slowly. "No. That doesn't even make sense."

Josh rubbed his forehead and pinched the bridge of his nose. "I know that. Neither of them was particularly rational when we got the news."

"Vernon could be anywhere," Haley said.

Nikki felt sick. "I'm so sorry, Josh. Is Sophie upset?"

At last, he smiled. "My new bride is a saint. We're going to contact the travel agency and delay our honeymoon for a few days. Once again, Vernon has screwed me over. I don't know how this keeps happening."

Nikki touched his arm. "Is there anything I can do?"

"Maybe keep my twin from losing his mind."

She winced. "I don't have any control over your brother. Sorry. He told me he was leaving Falling Brook as soon as the wedding was over. He was pretty insistent about it. I tried to talk to him, but we had a big fight."

Haley frowned. "But you came to the wedding together."

"We had a temporary truce," Nikki said. "I guess it's over."

Joshua glanced over his shoulder, clearly looking for his bride. "I've got to get back to the lovely Mrs. Lowell. Jake sent you a text, Nikki. Check your phone. I'll see you ladies later. God help us if they don't find Vernon. I don't know if this town can handle that kind of news."

Thirteen

Nikki kicked off her high heels and stared at the message on her phone for the hundredth time:

I called a limo to take you back to your place. The driver will be in the lobby to greet you at five. Sorry I had to leave…

She didn't know whether to laugh or cry. Here she was, sitting in a fancy, over-the-top hired car heading home from the ball without the handsome prince. It was a miracle her dress hadn't turned into rags and the car into a pumpkin. In the whole history of bad wedding dates, today had to rank right up there in the top five.

This was the end. Jake was who he was. She was never going to change him. Perhaps she should be glad Jake even remembered he *had* a date. *Damn* Vernon Lowell to hell and back. How could he do this to his sons, his ex-wife, the citizens of Falling Brook? Nikki's heart ached for the man she loved. But at the same time, she was angry and hurt. How could Jake treat her this way? Whatever she thought she had with him was over.

In fifteen years, Jake hadn't managed to deal with his father's betrayal. This stunt would rip open the wound for sure. She wanted to talk to Jake, but she was afraid that if she called, he wouldn't answer. And that would hurt even more.

It was better not to know. It was better to call time of death on this relationship.

She huddled into her coat and listened to her stomach growl. The original plan with Jake had been to go out to dinner after the wedding. As it was, Nikki was destined to eat peanut butter and jelly with Emma.

Finally, the ride ended.

Roberta lifted an eyebrow when her daughter walked into the house. "Was that a *limo*, Nicole Marie Reardon?"

"Yes, Mom." Nikki squatted and hugged her daughter. "Hi, baby. I missed you. But I brought you some bubbles from the wedding reception. And some M&M's." The candy was imprinted with the bride's name and the groom's. Yellow for Sophie. Navy for Josh.

"How was it?" Roberta asked.

"The ceremony was lovely," Nikki said.

"I hear the reception took an exciting turn."

Nikki shot her mom a startled glance. "You know?"

Roberta nodded. "It's all over the internet."

"Oh, lordy. Did you find out any details?"

"No. The story I read said they think he must have paid off one of the guards. The feds are investigating."

"Great. Just great."

"How did Jake react?"

"Not well, Mom. He and Oliver went haring off to try to find Vernon."

"Oh. I'm sorry."

"Yeah, me, too. That was the final straw for me. I can't wait forever for Jake to get his life together. I can handle the future on my own. I don't need a man who spooks like a skittish horse. I wanted him to share my world, but that's not going to happen."

Emma looked up, clearly not interested in the conversation. "I'm hungry. Can we eat now? And is Mr. Man coming over?"

Sunday evening, Nikki sat on the end of her bed and checked her texts…again. Nothing but yawning silence from Jake. Why was she surprised? Though she had hoped against hope that he might lean on her in the midst of his crisis, Jake was on his own…again.

If they'd had any chance at being a couple, it was gone. His silence said louder than words that he didn't need her.

It hurt, far worse than she could have imagined.

In the hours since law-enforcement officials had apprehended Vernon at the Canadian border—midday today—the judge had issued a statement. On Tuesday morning at 10:00 a.m., anyone who had been wronged by Vernon Lowell and his partner, Nikki's father, would be given the opportunity to address the defendant directly. To state their grievances. To bear witness to the misery and pain Vernon and Everett had caused.

The only caveat was that in order for anyone to speak, he or she must first notify the judge via email and receive a confirmation.

Nikki was torn. She called her mother and posed the question. Roberta refused flat out. "I have no interest in going," she said firmly. "Anyone in that room will probably still assume I knew what my husband was doing. They'll hate me for what happened. My being there will solve nothing."

"Are you sure, Mom? Don't you even want to ask Vernon the questions you can't ask Dad? Aren't you curious?"

There was a brief silence, and then Nikki heard her mother sigh. "I can't change the past, Nikki. Go if you want to. I know you're worried about Jake."

"I'm not positive he'll be there. He was pretty insistent about leaving right after the wedding."

"Things have changed in the last two days. It's hard for me to believe he would simply walk away. I'll keep Emma. If it will make you feel better, go. Go see Vernon. Go speak to him. Ask what you want to ask."

"Maybe I will."

"When you sign up with the judge, you can always drop out if you change your mind."

"True."

"Do you *want* to speak to Vernon?"

"Maybe. Mostly, I just want to be in the room and see what happens."

"Then do it. There's not a downside. Judges are leaning more and more toward giving victims the right to face their abusers. Vernon hurt a lot of people and abused their trust. That pain runs deep. You've seen it in dear Jake. Go, Nikki. Be there to support the Lowell boys if nothing else. It will make you feel better, and maybe you'll get a few of the answers you've wanted for fifteen years."

Nikki slipped into the courtroom at twenty minutes before the hour. It had taken longer than she anticipated to get through security. The chamber was crowded, but she found a seat in the back corner. Many of the faces she recognized. Some she didn't.

The Lowell men were sitting in the front row with their mother, Eve. Sophie was there, too. And Samantha. Just looking at the back of Jake's head made Nikki tense and weepy. What was he thinking? How was he holding up?

The bailiff instructed everyone to stand. The judge entered. Then came Vernon Lowell in handcuffs, his gaze downcast. He was wearing a standard-issue orange jumpsuit. His scruffy beard and longish hair were a mix of gray and white. With his stooped shoulders and weary air, it was almost impossible to reconcile this version of the man with his past self.

At one time, Vernon had been one of the richest men in the tristate area. The boutique hedge fund he created from scratch had been wildly successful. It was rumored years ago that there was a waiting list of would-be clients hoping for a chance to "get in."

Nikki didn't know if that was true or not, but it made sense. The very elite reputation of Black Crescent had made it all the more attractive to the high-profile citizens of Falling Brook. Those lucky enough to have their millions in Vernon's care had seen those millions multiply.

But then everything went south. The fiscal dreams rotted on the vine.

Vernon and Everett absconded with money that wasn't theirs.

The judge banged a gavel and made opening remarks, explaining why he had allowed this somewhat unprecedented hearing. Still, Vernon stared at the floor.

Nikki's stomach tightened as the first name on the list was read aloud. The judge instructed Vernon to lift his head and face his accusers. Nikki wondered if there was any particular order. The first person to stand and walk toward the front of the room was Zane Patterson. There was a small podium for the Falling Brook visitors. Zane's words were calm but held an underlying bitterness as he laid out for Vernon a litany of what had happened when the Pattersons lost everything.

Each person on the judge's list was allotted ten minutes. Some took the entire time. Some ended abruptly. Though the wounds were fifteen years old, the stories sounded fresh. Raw.

It was painful to hear. Jessie Acosta was on the list. Like Zane, her father had been a client of Black Crescent.

Nikki was shocked when Chase Hargrove stood. As far as she knew, his family hadn't entrusted their money to Black Crescent. But, apparently, Vernon had involved Chase's father with some scheme that ended with Chase's dad going to prison for fraud.

One after another, the people spoke. Many of them had been in their teens and twenties when the tragedy happened. Their lives had been shaped, broken, damaged by Vernon's actions.

Nikki held her breath, feeling waves of guilt for something that hadn't been her fault at all. But her father had been deeply involved.

Evidently, the judge was saving Vernon's immediate family for last.

Suddenly, the name read aloud was *Nicole Reardon.* She flinched. Why had she signed up? Why hadn't she had them strike her name when she first arrived?

"Ms. Reardon?" The judge repeated her name.

Nikki stood slowly, her heart thumping wildly in her chest. Dozens of people stared at her. Not Jake. He still faced straight ahead. Nikki swallowed, her mouth dry. "You can skip me, sir."

The judge frowned. "This is your moment, Ms. Reardon. I assume it's been a long fifteen years. I'm giving you a chance to speak your piece."

There was no backing out now. Nikki walked on shaky legs to the front of the courtroom. Not once did she cast her gaze sideways to see Jake. She stood at the podium and faced Vernon.

Until this very instant, she hadn't known what she was going to say to him. But the words came tumbling out as if she had rehearsed them for five thousand empty days. Not a single other person had asked Vernon a question. They had vented, accused, mourned. Now it was Nikki's turn.

"Mr. Lowell…" She paused, feeling overwhelmed. Hopefully, she wasn't going to keel over. "Mr. Lowell. You and my father were best friends, colleagues, business partners. Clearly, you both were involved with the destruction of Black Crescent. But tell me this. You got away scot-free. My father crashed his car fleeing the police. Why wasn't he with you?"

For a moment, emotion broke the stoic expression on Vernon's face.

The judge addressed him. "Please answer Ms. Reardon's question. She deserves to know the truth."

When Vernon spoke, his voice was almost defiant. "Everett wanted to say goodbye to you and your mother. I told him he was a fool. Partway back to the house, the chase started. He had to turn around. He never made it."

"Oh. Thank you." Why was she thanking Vernon Lowell? How stupid. She turned to go back to her seat. As she moved, Jake looked at her across the small distance that separated them. He didn't smile. He was visibly ashen.

Nikki kept on walking, comforted in the smallest possible way that her father had wanted to say goodbye.

Next up was Eve Lowell, Vernon's wife. When the judge read her name, she shook her head. Like Nikki, she must have changed her mind. The judge didn't press her. He went on. *Oliver Lowell*.

Oliver stood and shrugged. "I learned in recovery not to blame other people for my addiction," he said. "You're a wretched bastard of a father, and I'll spend the rest of my life trying not to be like you. End of story."

Joshua Lowell. Joshua went to the podium and spoke quietly about his regrets. Mostly, he mentioned his mother and his two brothers. He sat down.

Then came the name Nikki had dreaded hearing. *Jacob Lowell*. Surely, Jake was the last one. It was almost noon.

Jake walked to the podium, his shoulders stiff, his eyes blazing with strong emotion. When he reached the designated spot, he stood there for a moment. The courtroom was completely silent. Hushed. Waiting.

Outside, the noise of New York City was audible, but muted by the thick walls and closed windows.

Even Vernon seemed affected by the somber atmosphere.

Jake shoved his hands in his pockets as if he didn't know what to do with them. "I'm not going to address you as *Father* or *Dad*," he said. "You gave up that right long ago. But I will say that I have hated you for far too long. I've let your shadow hang over my life, blighting it. Constraining it. I told myself I traveled the world because I loved the freedom and the adventure. The truth is that I've been afraid to come home. What you did nearly destroyed me. Not because I was destitute or on the run from the law. But because you convinced me that my

DNA carried some sort of poison. If you could do what you did, maybe I was doomed to be as black-hearted a person as you."

Jake paused, maybe to catch his breath, and then continued. "I'm not a perfect human being. I have my faults, plenty of them. But from this day forward, I will no longer let your treachery determine the course of my life. I don't hate you. I don't love you. You are nothing to me at all…"

The gathered crowd exhaled almost in unison as Jake returned to his seat.

Moments later, the judge tapped the piece of paper in front of him, shook his head slowly and gave the bailiff a nod.

"All rise," the uniformed officer instructed the gathering.

Another set of officers stepped forward, helped Vernon to his feet and led him away.

When the judge and the prisoner were out of sight, the bailiff said, "You're dismissed."

Nikki was sitting in the back corner. No one needed to climb over her. She wasn't in anyone's way. She remained as the room emptied. At last, Oliver and Samantha walked out. Then Joshua and Sophie and Eve.

Jake never stood up. She watched from the back corner of the room as he leaned forward, elbows on his knees, and stared at the ground. His posture suggested that he was unapproachable.

Suddenly, Nikki couldn't bear the thought that he might speak to her or think she had been waiting for him.

She jumped to her feet and slid around the back of the last bench, escaping into the crowded hallway. When she saw the nearest stairwell, she made a beeline for it, not willing to wait for an elevator.

Six flights of steps. The courtroom had been higher up in the building than she had realized. At last, she popped out onto the street. The crisp, cool air felt good on her hot cheeks. She felt weird. Sad. Depleted. It had been an emotional morning.

But maybe there was closure now. Maybe everyone could move on.

She set off down the street, feeling tiny icy pellets of snow land on her face. Nothing that would amount to much. At least the weather felt Christmassy. Every shop she passed was fully decorated. Though Thanksgiving was still two days away, hardly anyone waited for that marker to get ready for the December season.

Behind her, someone called her name. "Nikki. Nikki. Stop. Wait up."

When she turned, she saw that it was Jake. She shivered, a combination of the cold and the way she always reacted in his presence. He'd had plenty of opportunity to speak to her in the courthouse. Why had he followed her now?

She stepped into the sheltered doorway of a large building and waited. This was not a confrontation she relished. Prior to this morning, the last she had seen of Jake was when she went to the ladies' room at the wedding reception three days ago.

He caught up to her, panting. "Where's your car?" His hair was tousled, and his cheeks were ruddy with the cold. He looked like a male model in a winter catalog. Sophisticated. Gorgeous. Out of reach.

"In the garage on the next block."

"We'll take mine," he said, sounding as arrogant as a man who thought he had all the answers. "I'll get one of Joshua's guys to drive yours home."

"No, thank you," she said politely.

She left the alcove and continued her journey.

Jake took her arm. "Don't be ridiculous, Nik. We need to talk. We'll ride together. My car is more comfortable."

Anger swept over her, dissolving any squeamishness she had felt at facing him. "Don't you *dare* call me ridiculous," she said curtly, conscious of the many passersby. "I'm not the one who took a woman to his brother's wedding and then slipped out like a thief in the night."

His jaw tightened. "Maybe a poor choice of words."

"Sorry," she muttered.

"You knew where I was."

"I knew that you and Oliver lost your minds. You hadn't seen your father in fifteen years, and yet somehow you thought the two of you could track down Vernon better than the FBI? Sorry, Jake. That doesn't cut it."

"I made a mistake," he said. "I was running on shock and adrenaline."

"The mistake was mine," Nikki replied, her throat clogged with tears.

"Let me explain," he said urgently.

Nikki refused to be a pushover. "I know you're Emma's father. I won't play the villain. But when you decide on a visitation schedule that fits your life, I'll make plans for you to spend time with her in the company of either my mother or yours. I don't want to see you again."

His face was frozen in tight planes. His eyes burned. "Give me a chance, Nik. I have things I need to say."

She shored up her resistance. "I'm cold, and I'm hungry. Goodbye, Jake." She started walking again, blind to her surroundings. All she could think about was getting away. It hurt too much to be with him.

He followed her, took her arm in a gentle hold and spun her around, his eyes filled with anguish. "Don't go." He kissed her then, a kiss that held more desperation than passion. At first, his lips were cold against hers, but then the slow burn kindled again, and they were clinging to each other like survivors of a shipwreck.

In a way, the comparison was apt. Fifteen years ago, their love had crashed on the rocks of tragedy, and they had been one step from drowning ever since.

Jake's kiss was achingly sweet one second and roughly possessive the next. Nikki went on her tiptoes, striving to get closer. She was courting more heartbreak. She knew that. But how could she be strong when everything inside her was melting with yearning for him?

At last, he stepped back, but he kept her hands in his. "One hour," he said hoarsely. "That's all I'm asking. One hour."

"And you'll feed me?"

Not even a glimmer of humor lightened his face. "Yes."

They ended up at the same scruffy neighborhood grill where the two of them and Joshua had eaten after their abortive attempt to visit Vernon in jail. Jake asked for a booth in the back. As they took off their heavy coats, he tried to sit with Nikki like last time, but she waved him to the other side of the table. She needed a buffer zone.

Jake didn't ask her opinion about the meal. He motioned for a waitress. When the woman arrived, he ordered two burgers, medium, with no onions and extra pickles, plus a couple of Cokes. How many times as teenagers had they ordered that exact meal and then laughed that they were so perfectly matched?

While they waited for the food, awkwardness loomed between them, filling the space, making conversation almost impossible. Finally, Nikki broke the silence. "Have you learned anything at all about the stolen money?"

Jake scowled at his drink, poking his straw through

it. "Mom spoke briefly to the lawyer this morning. According to him, Vernon claims there never was a theft. He told counsel that he and Everett were *hoodwinked* by an unscrupulous deal. They saw a chance to quadruple Black Crescent's coffers and took it. But the investment went belly up, and they were too ashamed to admit the truth, so they fled."

"Do you believe that?"

"I don't know. Maybe. I've read reports from the officers who apprehended my father. He wasn't living in luxury."

"I suppose that makes more sense than the two men suddenly deciding to embark on a life of crime. Doesn't that make you feel better?"

"No. Because they should have stayed and faced the music."

The server arrived with the burgers. Nikki dug into hers, ravenous despite the circumstances. Some women didn't eat when they were stressed. Nikki wasn't one of those. She had gained twenty pounds after her father's death and Jake's departure. Gradually, she had come out of her funk and started taking care of herself again, but it had been a struggle.

She and Jake barely spoke while they ate. The waitress brought drink refills and the check. Eventually, plates were clean, and the awkward silence returned.

Nikki looked at her watch. "It's been an hour," she said bluntly. "I have to go."

Jake frowned. "We haven't even talked."

She glanced around at the bustling eatery. "This place isn't exactly private, and it's too cold outside for a long walk. Let's call it quits, Jake. Please. You. Me. It's a no-go. There's nothing left." Her chest ached.

He was everything she wanted, but there might as well

have been an ocean between them. Soon, there would be…when Jake returned to Europe.

The line of his jaw was grim. He flagged down their server one last time. Jake handed the woman the check and three one-hundred-dollar bills. "We'd like to keep the table for a bit. No interruptions, please."

The woman stared, dazed, at the cash in her hand. "You mean no change?"

"No change. No drink refills. No nothing. Is that okay with you?"

She nodded vigorously, wonder dawning in her eyes. "Yes, sir. Cone of silence. I've got it." Tentatively, she touched the sleeve of his jacket. "Thank you, mister. This will make Christmas pretty special at my house."

When the woman disappeared, Jake shrugged out of his suit jacket and rolled up his sleeves. It was warm in the small restaurant. They were tucked in a far back corner. No one had any reason to pass by their table. Because the lunch rush had now waned, the booth next to them was empty.

The situation wasn't ideal, but under the circumstances, it would have to do. Nikki fanned herself with a napkin, wishing she had chosen something other than wool when she got dressed that morning. She had worn the red sweater and black skirt again with more sensible shoes.

Jake must have read her unease. "I could grab us a hotel room for an hour. If privacy would make you more comfortable."

She gaped at him. "You'd spend two hundred and fifty dollars for one hour in a hotel?"

He shrugged. "More like five hundred probably. It's the holidays. But, yes. If you were there, I would."

Nikki knew what would happen if she found herself

in a hotel room with Jake. The chemistry she had tried so hard to deny would spark and flame. That fantasy wasn't conducive to holding her ground. "No hotel," she whispered. "Just say what you want to say."

Jake stared at her. His eyes were more gold than green at the moment, and his gaze was hot and beautiful and determined. "I'm in love with you, Nikki."

Fourteen

Jake saw his companion flinch and knew he had his work cut out for him. Nikki's body language was guarded in the extreme. Her chin was up, and her eyes were dark with anxiety. He saw her throat work.

"No, you're not," she said quietly. "You've been under a tremendous amount of pressure, and you're trying to make a grand gesture. It's not necessary to placate me in order to see your daughter."

His temper flared. "That's not a very complimentary assessment of my character. I know my past behavior hasn't been exemplary, Nik, but I've changed. Or I'm trying to," he added, in the spirit of honesty. "I love you."

Tears spilled from her beautiful Irish-hued eyes, rolling down her cheeks unchecked. She swiped at the dampness with the back of her hand and reached for her purse and coat. "I can't do this."

"Don't leave me, Nik," he begged, his heart like shards

of glass in his chest. "Don't be afraid of this, of us. We lost it all once before, but our time has come. You have to believe me. Things are different now."

She didn't slide out of the booth, but she was close to bolting.

"What makes you think so, Jake? I don't see it."

He swallowed hard. "I spoke to Josh this morning. Before we went to court. I told him I had changed my mind about Black Crescent. That I was prepared to take over as CEO." Even now, his stomach churned about his decision, but he wouldn't let Nikki misinterpret his nerves. "Josh was thrilled and supportive," he said.

Nikki seemed less so. She gnawed her bottom lip. Her restless fingers shredded a paper napkin. "You'll be bored with it in a month. And you'll disappear again."

It was his turn to flinch. "Wow," he said, stunned at how much she could hurt him. "You're not making this easy."

Now she was angry. "There's *nothing* easy about us, Jake."

"I heard you say 'I love you,'" he muttered. "That night I made love to you at your house. You thought I was asleep."

She closed her eyes and shook her head slowly. When she looked at him again, he finally saw how much his abandonment had cost her. "It was the sex talking."

"Don't be flip. Not now. I heard you say it, and I was too chickenshit scared to say it back. But I'm saying it now. *I love you*. I'm not leaving. I'm not running away. If it takes me ten months or ten years to convince you, I'll do it. I. Love. You."

"Stop," she begged, her gaze agonized.

He clenched his hand on the table as he resisted the urge to pound something. "When we ran into each other in Atlantic City five years ago, it was like being struck by lightning. You were everything I had left behind, everything I had lost. That night we spent together was incredible. But you weren't a teenager anymore. You'd lived your life far more bravely than I had. I was knocked on my ass and swamped with so many feelings I couldn't handle it. I'm sorry I left you, Nikki. I've regretted it every day since."

Nikki put her face in her hands, her shoulders bowed. He couldn't tell for sure, but he thought she was crying again. When she finally looked up at him, her mascara was smudged, and her eyes were still wet. "How can I believe you, Jake? I want to, but I'm afraid. Afraid you'll smash my heart again. I don't know how many more times it can recover."

Slowly, he reached for his wallet. "Maybe this will convince you," he said quietly. He opened the leather billfold and extracted a piece of paper that was ragged at the creases. It was yellow stationery with a row of pink daisies at the top. He handed it to Nikki. "Do you remember?"

She stared at the note, her eyes wide. Though the letter was upside down from Jake's perspective, he didn't need to read it. He had memorized the contents years ago. Nikki had slipped the plea to him at her father's funeral.

In the days before smartphones and texting, she had written, "Take me with you to Europe…"

Her hands shook as she traced the girlish handwriting with a fingertip. "I can't believe you kept this."

He sat back and sighed. "I tried to throw it away a hundred times. The guilt crushed me when I looked at it. Over and over."

"You shouldn't have felt guilty. It was outrageous of me to ask."

"Was it, Nikki?" He cocked his head and soaked in her grace and her courage, painfully aware of how his life might have turned out differently. "I kept this, too." He handed her a graduation picture, wallet-size. It was Nikki, smiling at the camera, her hair vibrant, her eyes filled with joy.

"Oh, Jake." She teared up again.

He inhaled sharply and dropped the last of his protective cloak of secrets. "I love you, Nikki Reardon. I suspected it in Atlantic City. I think I knew it deep down the moment I came back to Falling Brook and saw you face-to-face. And heard I had a daughter. But I couldn't accept the truth."

"But you—"

He waved a hand, cutting her off. "I'm not finished. I've loved you in one way or another my whole life, Nik. Everywhere I traveled, I wanted to share new adventures with you. Sunsets and storms. People and places. You were always in the back of my mind, those big emerald eyes telling me how much you cared. I was wrong, Nicole Marie Reardon. I was a coward. I let inertia keep me on a path that led nowhere." He reached across the table, across the miles and years of loneliness. "I love you. I adore you, in fact. I want to spend the rest of my life with you and Emma."

And finally, at long last, the sun came out.

She smiled at him through her tears. Her fingers gripped his. "Yes," she said, the word barely audible. "I love you, too, Jake. So much it hurts."

They sat there for seconds. Minutes. Their gazes locked. Their hearts healing.

Finally, Nikki glanced around the restaurant, seeming dazed, noting the people going about their business.

She took a sip of her watered-down drink. "If you're still serious about that hotel thing, I'll take you up on it."

And just like that, his body went hard all over. Except for his heart. That organ was embarrassingly soft and filled with love for this incredible woman.

"Let's go," he said gruffly.

Outside the restaurant, he hailed a cab, not wanting to waste the time it would take to retrieve his car. Pulling Nikki against him in the back seat, he trembled when she laid her head on his shoulder.

He directed the driver to one of the city's premier luxury hotels.

Nikki balked briefly when she saw the iconic facade. "We don't have any luggage," she whispered.

"They won't bat an eye."

It was true. The front desk ran Jake's credit card and confirmed his request for a suite. The man handed over two keys.

Jake dragged Nikki with him to the small gift shop. Her face turned bright red while he bought protection.

Then they were on the elevator, streaking toward the top floor. When they were in the room, Nikki exclaimed over the view of Central Park. The light snow had dusted the tops of the trees.

Jake took her hand and went down on one knee. "Nikki, will you marry me? We'll shop for a ring together."

She tugged on his arm. "Yes, yes, yes," she cried. Her eyes glowed with happiness.

He stood and scooped her up. "Is it too soon to try out the bed?"

"Honestly," she said, with a mischievous grin, "I thought you were moving kind of slow for a well-traveled bachelor bad boy."

He carried her into the bedroom. Though the ache in his body urged him to do everything in hyper speed, Jake knew this occasion was too important to rush. He set Nikki on her feet and started undressing her, pausing to caress her smooth skin, soft curves, lush hills and valleys.

Her body was a wonder to him. Feminine. Unbelievably arousing.

While Nikki settled herself in the sumptuous covers, he stripped in record time and joined her. "I'm sorry," he groaned, burying his head between her breasts, feeling the ragged thump of her heart. "I'm sorry we've wasted so much time."

She stroked his hair, shivering when he tasted her nipples. "We've learned a lot, Jake. We've grown up. We've faced battles and won. Life won't ever tear us apart again, because we won't allow it. Make love to me, my dearest heart. Now. Like it's our first time. Like we have forever ahead of us."

"We do, Nikki. We do." He gave her his pledge and entered her slowly, stunned by the pleasure as her body welcomed his. The fit was snug, the stimulation almost unbearable. She deserved romance, but the lust he had bottled up for days and hours roared to life.

They moved together wildly, straining for dominance. It was heat and blessing, madness and perfect bliss. He took them to the peak and then slowed, tormenting them both. Trying to make it last.

Nikki arched and cried out beneath him, her fingernails scoring his shoulders. "Don't stop," she begged. "Don't stop."

He was beyond reason then, blinded by the need to find release, wrapped in the realization that their love had risen from the ashes against all odds.

The end was hot and hard and fast, draining, as close to perfection as mere mortals could get.

He held her after that, his breathing rough and jerky. Though it had been far too long since he had done so, he thanked the deity for not giving up on him.

Nikki's body was a warm, sweet gift in his embrace. "You're everything to me, Nik," he muttered hoarsely. "Now and always. I love you."

She smiled softly and reached for his hand, curling her fingers with his. "Emma and I will go wherever you go, Jake. You don't have to run Black Crescent if you don't want to…"

Shaking his head slowly, he exhaled. "I'm back where I belong. Here with you. And with my family and Falling Brook. I'm not leaving again."

A tiny hesitation betrayed her last reservation. "You're sure?"

He nuzzled her hair, letting sleep take him. "You can count on it, my love. You can count on it…"

* * * * *

VOWS IN NAME ONLY

NAIMA SIMONE

To Gary. 143.

One

"What the hell are you talking about?" Cain Farrell snarled, surging from his chair in his father's library.

His dead father's library.

Barron Farrell had to be dead for Cain to step foot in the mausoleum where he'd suffered a hellish childhood. As soon as he'd graduated from college at twenty-one, he'd left and never returned for a birthday, a Christmas, an Easter or even a potluck dinner. It was bad enough he'd spent twelve-hour workdays with his father at the offices of Farrell International, the conglomerate that had been in his family for four generations. But he'd vowed eleven years ago to never again grace the hallowed halls and marble floors of his father's historic Beacon Hill mansion.

It figured the old man would do something as contrary as having a heart attack and dying just to get Cain to break his promise.

He'd always been a manipulative bastard.

Speaking of bastards…

Cain stalked across the gleaming hardwood floor, ignoring the dark leather furniture gathered around a cavernous fireplace, the winding staircase leading to the next level, the floor-to-cathedral ceiling shelves packed with first editions of the classics his father had never bothered to read. If Cain looked too long, the memories always lurking at the edges of his mind would seize the opportunity to slither in and torment him. To inflict punishments like the ones he'd received in front of the very desk behind which Daryl Holleran, his father's personal attorney, perched.

God, Cain hated this room. This whole goddamn house.

Fury bristled inside him. He drew to a halt in front of a large bay window, but the view of the private walled garden didn't consume his attention. No, the other two men sitting silently in the room claimed that distinction.

Two strangers he'd never laid eyes on before this afternoon. Two strangers whose presence had been requested at the reading of Barron's will.

Two strangers who, according to Daryl, were Cain's brothers.

Half brothers.

"Cain," Daryl said, his smooth baritone placating, as if he hadn't just announced that the multibillion-dollar company Cain had been groomed to run was no longer his. "I know this is surprising—"

Cain snorted, pivoting and jabbing his tightly balled fists into the pockets of his black suit pants. "Surprising? No, surprising is Big Papi coming out of retirement and returning to the Sox. Surprising is finally discovering the location of Jimmy Hoffa's body. Surprising is the Four Horsemen of the Apocalypse riding down Commonwealth. This, Daryl, is bullshit," he snapped.

To his credit, the older man didn't flinch at Cain's caustic tone. But then again, Daryl had been Barron Farrell's lawyer for the past thirty years. The man probably had skin as thick as an elephant's ass.

"Be that as it may," Daryl said, picking up the small stack of papers from the desk, "it was your father's decision, and Barron was adamant and very clear about the terms. Controlling shares in Farrell International are to go to his living heirs. But only if you and your brothers agree to remain in Boston and run the company together for the period of a year, starting from the date this will is read. At the end of the year, you can decide to helm it together, or Cain, you can buy out your brothers' shares and Farrell International is yours. If any of you refuse to adhere to these conditions, then the company and all its subsidiaries will be liquidated and sold to the highest bidders."

It didn't make any more sense the second time around.

"There's one more stipulation," Daryl added.

"Of course there is," Cain growled.

"It concerns you, Cain." Daryl paused, and for the first time, Cain glimpsed uneasiness flash in the older man's brown eyes. Which set off an almost painful tightening of his stomach. If this unflappable man was discomfited, that spelled trouble for Cain. "You must spend the next year here. In this house."

Cain didn't move—couldn't. Because if he even dragged in a breath, he would explode, and the fury that howled inside him would consume this room and the people in it. Barron hadn't been satisfied with hijacking Cain's future. No, he had to manipulate his son into his own personal nightmare.

That son of a *bitch*.

"So just because the asshole who knocked up my mother demands it, I'm supposed to give up my life in Washington and move here?" The bearded giant in the black thermal shirt, faded jeans and battered brown boots who Daryl had called Achilles shook his head. "She might have given me his last name, but that's all I got from him. I don't owe him a damn thing."

Or you.

Achilles didn't say the words aloud, but they quivered in the air, and Cain ground his teeth together. Of course, the possible dismantlement of the business Cain had worked on for most of his life wouldn't affect this man. Losing the business for which he had endured the intolerant, merciless Barron, the business Cain had dreamed of one day heading…that wouldn't concern this man either.

He hadn't suffered for it.

Hadn't sacrificed for it.

But Cain had.

It was his legacy. His due for surviving and outliving Barron Farrell.

And yet, Barron had found a way to rip it all out from under him.

"I have to admit, when I received the phone call to attend this mysterious gathering, I wasn't expecting a family reunion," the second man, Kenan Rhodes, drawled, eyebrows arched over the distinctive blue-gray eyes they all shared. Farrell eyes. "But I have to agree with Achilles, is it?" At the giant's nod, Kenan shrugged a suit jacket–covered shoulder. "I have a position with my family's business. A good one. And leaving it would be like turning my back on them. What would be my incentive to do that? I didn't know Barron Farrell personally, but I am aware of his reputation. And no offense, but I have no reason to give him my loyalty."

Cain stared at the two strangers, and though the will had announced them as brothers, he felt no pull toward them. No familial connection. Hell, except for the eyes, none of them would be mistaken for family.

Kenan, with his light brown skin, close-cropped dark hair and neat goatee, was biracial. Though they all shared tall, muscular frames, Cain and Kenan were wide-shouldered and lean, while Achilles boasted a broad, powerful build that wouldn't be out of place on a football defensive line. Add in the shoulder-length, nearly black, curly hair, beard and tawny skin and he rounded out the most diverse family tree since Brad and Angelina's children.

Still… That Cain's father had cheated on his mother didn't shock him. His infidelity hadn't been a secret in their house. What astonished him was that Barron had fathered not one, but two illegitimate children. Barron might not have cared where he stuck his dick but the thought that he would leave the fate of his company to the whims of men he hadn't known? Cain couldn't line that up with the controlling bastard his father had been.

But then, apparently Barron had been aware of his sons all the time. And he hadn't bothered to acknowledge their existence until it benefited him. Until he could shift and maneuver all three of them like pawns on a chessboard.

Now *that* coincided with the Barron Farrell Cain knew.

"I don't expect your loyalty, and I'm not asking for it," Cain stated. His flat tone belied the anger and yes, fear, roiling in his veins. "Both of you are right—you have your lives. But today, mine just changed forever. Not only did I find out I have two brothers I never knew existed, but everything I've—" *suffered for* "—worked for is suddenly not in my control but in the hands of strangers who, as you put it, don't owe me a damn thing. Yes, you can walk away, and nothing changes for you. For me, though? *Everything changes.* I don't have the option of walking away."

Panic welled up in him. "I don't have—"

A legacy. Control. Power. A voice.

His teeth snapped shut, grinding together, trapping those betraying words inside him. Trapping the plea that would inevitably follow.

Had his father resented him this much—hated him this

much—that even from the grave he relished the thought of Cain humiliating himself to beg these strangers to help him? To save him?

Yes. Yes, he had.

The swift and concise answer rebounded against Cain's skull and everything he'd ever felt for his father—rage, grief, confusion, bitterness and God help him, love— swirled in his chest like a tornado.

"Fuck this," he growled, stalking across the room and wrenching the heavy library door open to storm out. Air. He needed air that wasn't tainted by his desperation and helplessness. By his weakness.

Almost immediately the incongruous sounds of gaiety slapped him as he stepped into the hallway. Right. The reception. How screwed up was it that the circus in the library had temporarily made him forget that over a hundred people congregated in the great room and formal dining room to mourn his father? He snorted. Mourn, hell. From the loud chatter, bright laughter and clink of glassware, he couldn't tell if they were all there to celebrate his life—or his death.

Exhaling, Cain pivoted sharply and strode toward the rear of the house, in the opposite direction of his "guests." In his current mood, he wasn't good company and he damn sure didn't feel like fielding condolences.

At least Barron was in a better place.

If one could call hell a better place.

Two

Devon Cole frowned at the wall of shrubbery in front of her, two thoughts prevalent in her mind.

One, how in the world did the gardener manage to keep the leaves so green and lush in the middle of October? A special fertilizer? A new pesticide? The blood of virgins?

And two, if she waited a few seconds longer, would David Bowie dressed as the Goblin King appear wearing his eyebrow-raising buff breeches and Tina Turner hair?

They were both fair questions considering she stood outside in a garden with high, labyrinthine hedges that formed cozy nooks and convenient, romantic hiding places. Who would've thought such a beautiful, magical place could exist behind a cold mausoleum of a mansion? Unless this was where the owner banished those who displeased him to be devoured by a voracious minotaur?

Oh, and a third thought… She peered down into the flute of red wine she clasped in her hand. Should this third glass of cabernet sauvignon be her last? When a person started wondering about garden tips, David Bowie's codpiece and Greek mythology in the space of ten seconds, laying off the booze might be wise.

Sighing, she stared down into her glass. She'd only briefly met Barron Farrell a few times at the social events her father had browbeaten her into attending, but still… The dead deserved respect. If not for Barron, then at least for the son he'd left behind.

Her belly clenched as an image of Cain Farrell coalesced in her mind. She'd never encountered Barron Farrell's son and heir before today; not surprising since she tried to avoid the galas, charity events and dinner parties her father so loved.

Closing her eyes, she sank to one of the marble benches dotting the cool, shadowed corners of the garden. She'd attended the crowded, solemn funeral at the ornate Catholic church, but only at the graveside ceremony had she captured her first view of Cain Farrell. Even from several rows back, it hadn't been hard to spot him. Not when he towered above most of the people there.

Even unsmiling and stoic, he'd been…beautiful. A lean, angular face with slashing cheekbones, almost brutally perfect lines, a carnal yet hard mouth and a stark, uncompromising jaw. His black, slim-fitting, ruthlessly tailored suit had molded to wide shoulders, broad chest, slim waist and long, muscular legs. A king. He reminded her of a king who bore authority as his birthright, but who'd have no issue with throwing on armor and hefting a sword and shield to fight beside his men. Commanding, formidable, and merciless when warranted. Matter of fact, the only thing soft about him had been the thick, dark waves combed back from his face and curling around his ears and the collar of his jacket. Yet, instead of gentling his imposing, arrogant beauty, those incongruously soft strands only emphasized the blunt, raw strength of his facial features, especially the hint of cruelty in the sensual curves of his mouth…

Shame threaded through her.

He'd been mourning his father, and she'd been ogling him as if he'd been Mr. December in a Billionaires of the Year calendar. Maybe her father was right, and he really *couldn't* take her anywhere.

A piercing longing stabbed her in the chest, and she pressed a palm over her heart, rubbing the phantom soreness. Ten years she'd been in this world of wealth, and she still didn't fit in. No amount of etiquette classes or designer wardrobes could remedy that.

What she wouldn't give to be gone from this Beacon Hill home, hell, from *Boston*, and be back in their old house in Plainfield, New Jersey, that had been full of family, with her and her parents on one side of the duplex, and her uncle, aunt and three cousins on the other. Their home had been crowded, relatives flowing from one apartment to the other with slamming doors, loud voices and laughter. Their home had been happy.

That had been before her mother had died from a lingering cough that she'd refused to see the doctor about. A cough that had evolved into a severe case of pneumonia. That had been before her father had channeled his grief, anger and ambition into growing his chain of electronics stores, eventually selling to a larger company. That had been before he'd invested profit from the sale in a tech company that would lead the industry in defense-level security and go from respectably wealthy to filthy rich.

That had been before he decided Plainfield was too "boorish" for him and his daughter—his words, not hers. She loved her hometown, loved her family. But he'd cut off all ties and moved them to Boston where his job had become infiltrating the rarified ranks of the blue bloods of high society. Ranks into which all his nouveau riche money couldn't buy entrance.

Didn't stop him from trying though.

Hence, their presence at Barron Farrell's funeral. Her father hadn't been able to pass up an opportunity to rub elbows in this affluent circle of businessmen, socialites and celebrities. But to be fair, he wasn't the only one treating the billionaire's death like a tea party.

Heaving another sigh, she picked up her glass and rose from the bench. She'd better head back inside before her father came looking for her with his constantly disappointed and disapproving scowl. Her fingers tightened around the stem, and she briefly closed her eyes, weathering the momentary vise on her heart. God, she remembered a time when only affection, love and pride had brightened his dark eyes. That had been when he'd been a husband and father, content with a couple of stores. That'd been before death had cleaved their lives in two.

Staring at the pointed toes of her black Louis Vuittons, she stepped back on the paved garden path, dragging.

"Damn you."

The low, rumbling growl reached her seconds before a tall, powerful figure stalked around the row of hedges, pausing inches away from her. The corner of the shrubbery offered her flimsy cover, and she clung to it, gaping at the man pacing back and forth. From the bench she'd just vacated to the wall across the slim path and back again.

Not just a man.

Cain Farrell.

Anger seemed to vibrate off his large frame in humid waves. No, not anger. *Fury.* With his black hair, black suit and dangerous stride, he resembled a predator. Sleek, dark and lethal. Waiting for the right prey to cross his path so he could pounce...devour.

Did it make her foolish that she couldn't ascertain if she

wanted to avoid becoming said prey, or…or surrender to the insane need to soothe him? To pet his hair, stroke those broad shoulders? Yes, it did make her a fool. Because one did *not* try and comfort a beast on the hunt.

Even if he was an incredibly sexy beast…

Cain jerked to a halt, pinning her with a narrowed but brilliant stare and jamming her breath in her lungs.

Damn.

"Who are you?" he demanded. His voice was constructed of midnight, the most expensive Scotch…and dark chocolate. Yummy.

"Me?" she rasped. Oh God. She mentally shook her head, but then made the mistake of looking into the absolute beauty of his eyes. Wow. Given the distance between them, she hadn't determined the color at the cemetery. But now… "I'd wondered," she breathed.

Dark, arrogant brows slanted down over his startling, blue-gray eyes. A wolf's eyes. The sense of being in the presence of a predator grew, but instead of fear, excitement tinged with nerves hummed under her skin.

Don't be silly.

"You wondered what?" Cain asked, impatience a tight snap in his voice.

"Your eyes," she blurted out, inwardly wincing and cursing her decision to pick up that third glass of wine. Shrugging a shoulder, she added, "I couldn't tell the color at the graveside service. But now, I, uh, know," she finished. Lamely. Scrounging for a smile, she moved forward, erasing the scant distance separating them. "Devon."

She stretched her hand toward him—the hand not clutching the wineglass for dear life. For several taut seconds, he glared down at it, then slowly lifted his arm.

His long, elegant fingers engulfed hers. Branding her. Fire licked at her palm, blazed up her arm and swirled in her chest like a star seconds from imploding. His gaze rose from their clasped hands and traveled the path the flames had taken. Only his gaze dipped lower, taking in the rest of her petite frame before finally landing on her face again.

Extricating her hand from his, she fought the need to rub her tingling palm against her thigh. She hiked up her chin to meet his wolf's gaze. She knew what he saw. What everyone saw. Short. Nondescript features. She'd overheard one "gentleman" call her forgettable. Breasts and hips too heavy and rounded to be fashionable. Her best feature was the thick, caramel curls that were wrapped in a knot at the back of her head now, but when loose, reached the middle of her back. Her mother's hair.

No, she wasn't a great beauty, and no doubt he dated women whose faces belonged on big screens and whose bodies graced swimwear magazines, but screw it. One of her first lessons after moving to Boston had been never, *ever* let anyone know they could intimidate her. The first whiff of weakness and they circled like vultures over a carcass. Being on the receiving end of that attack one too many times, her motto was now, *Fake it until you get home and barricade yourself in your bedroom with chips, ranch dip and Netflix.*

It worked for her.

Cain stared at her, silent and brooding. And even though she shook inside, she didn't waver. But, damn, those eyes. Eerie in their beauty. Like he could see past flesh and bone, down to her soul…

"Yes, now you know," he drawled, and the flames that had died down to a simmer burst to life…in her face. *Oh God.* He probably thought that was her pathetic attempt at flirting. "What are you doing out here, Devon?" he asked. "The *party*," his lips curled into a faint sneer, "is in the house. Specifically, the great and dining rooms. This part of the property is off-limits to guests."

"Oh, I'm sorry. I must've missed the signs," she apologized. As soon as the words echoed between them, it hit her how flippant they sounded. "I mean, of course there weren't *signs*. But in a house this size, maybe there should be. Or at least little discreet nameplates like on bathroom doors—*oh dammit*."

"Excuse me?" Cain growled, his frown deepening.

She shook her head, holding up a finger in the universal sign of "Wait a minute." And she took that minute to take a deep gulp of wine. And another. "Honest to God, I'm more of a sipper and two glasses is my limit. I don't know what made me think I could handle three. Here." She thrust the goblet at him, and he accepted it. Either that or wear it. "Besides, given you were just damning someone minutes ago, you probably could use it more than me."

Again, more staring on his part. And could she really blame him? She was acting like a lunatic. A tipsy, blathering, garden-invading lunatic.

Slowly, without breaking his visual connection to her, he lifted the glass to his beautiful, cruel mouth. And sipped.

Her knees might not have weakened, but by God, they wobbled. Why that sip was so hot, she couldn't begin to explain. But the heat gathering low in her belly and flowing to all points north and south assured her, it most definitely was.

"You're right," he said. "I need it. Thank you."

The wine. He needed the wine. Not *her*, as her body wanted to interpret his words.

"You're welcome." Unable to maintain peering into his unusual gaze, she brushed invisible lint from the skirt of her dark gray sheath dress. And as she recovered the space she'd placed between them, all embarrassment and disconcerting desire fled. "God, I was so focused on heading back to hell, I forgot." She reached out to him, placing a hand on his forearm. Taut muscle flexed beneath her fingers and his jacket. But she didn't allow it to distract her. "I'm so sorry for the loss of your father. Unfortunately, I know the pain you're feeling, and I wouldn't wish it on anyone."

His scrutiny dropped to his arm, where her fingers still lingered. He didn't move out from under her touch, and though it would've been the smarter option, she didn't remove her hand.

"Heading back to hell?" he repeated, not acknowledging her condolences. She got it; after her mother died, she'd wanted to talk about anything other than her death. "Other than the obvious, where is that?"

She winced, her shoulders lifting to her ears. "Promise not to be offended?" He arched a dark eyebrow but nodded. "That reception. Large social events are my definition of cruel and unusual punishment, but that in there…" She shook her head. "I'm from a big, loud Italian family, so I'm not a stranger to repasts that turn into noisy gatherings with food and laughter. But not like that. There's no one talking about your father, remembering him. There's no sense of sadness that comes with losing someone you love. There aren't any tears with the laughter. There's no comfort from family and friends. What I escaped in there is…ghoulish."

She lowered her hand from his arm and braced herself for his rebuke. Prepared herself for the same chiding smirk she'd received from her father when she'd voiced the same thoughts before seeking a place where she could get a break from the avarice and phoniness of it all.

But the ridicule didn't come.

Instead, Cain studied her with an impenetrable stare that revealed nothing. That must be a handy skill.

She fought not to fidget under his regard, but just as she parted her lips to apologize for her insensitive words, he murmured, "Thank you, Devon."

"For?" Being inappropriately blunt? Trespassing? Handing him secondhand wine? He had to be more specific.

"For having the courage to be honest when the truth isn't pretty." A small, half smile that struck her as a shade grim briefly curved a corner of his sensual mouth. "And for giving me a few minutes' reprieve from my own hell." He stretched the glass of wine back toward her, and as she accepted it, he lifted his other hand and shocked her by stroking the back of his fingers down her cheek. "I appreciate that more than you know."

He stepped away, leaving her skin burning from his caress. She didn't move—couldn't move—as he sharply pivoted on his heel and strode away, disappearing as quickly and quietly as he'd appeared.

Only then did she graze her trembling fingers over the spot he'd touched so tenderly. With gratitude. Because surely, she'd imagined the flash of heat in his eyes. It'd been only a wishful reflection of the unwise and wistful desire that had coursed through her.

Yes, that's all.

Still, what was the harm in believing in that fantasy?

It wasn't like she would see Cain Farrell again.

Nope. No harm at all.

Three

A year.

That was the length of time required of him, and he could endure it. Hell, he'd endured his father for thirty-two years. Twelve more months was child's play.

He could damn well do this.

The mantra marched through Cain's head like a regiment of soldiers on a deadly campaign, and he clenched his jaw so tightly it throbbed. Either that or let loose the string of curses flaying his throat. And he would never give his father that satisfaction. Dead or alive.

"Mr. Farrell, you had several messages while you were in your meeting. I placed them on your desk and emailed them to you as well," Charlene Gregg, his executive assistant, informed him as he stalked past her desk. The polished brunette had been with him for the last five years, and she was a godsend. Her protective, six-foot-four, three-hundred-pound bruiser of a husband and adorable two children thought so as well.

"Thanks, Charlene," he ground out. Another perk of having an assistant who'd been with him so long. She ignored his bad moods. "Hold all calls for the next twenty minutes."

"Of course."

He entered his office, barely managing not to slam the door behind him. Control. He'd spent the formative years of his childhood developing it. Growing up in a chaotic household where the slightest offense—real or imagined—could earn him a verbal, soul-stripping assault or a punch to the chest, he'd been a quick study on reining in his emotions and reactions.

But coming out of a meeting with his… Hell, he still couldn't call them his brothers. Achilles Farrell, the brooding giant who shared his last name, and Kenan Rhodes, the charmer with the wide smile and steely eyes, were strangers. Strangers who, only a week after their initial meeting during the funeral reception, were carving a piece out of his company for their own.

He hated the intrusion.

Guilt thrummed inside his chest, but the simmering anger that had become his constant companion prevented it from sinking a foothold. Logically, he got that his rage was directed toward a dead man who'd screwed him over, but Barron wasn't here. His illegitimate offspring were.

Thrusting a hand through his hair, Cain circled his desk and dropped into his chair. His gaze lit on the thick file he'd been studying for the past week. Immediately after the will reading, Cain had contacted Farrell International's private detective and had him open investigations on Achilles and Kenan.

Achilles Farrell. Born in Boston, but raised by a single mother near Seattle, Washington. Software developer and something of a genius. And an ex-con who'd spent two years in jail for assault. Seemed like a chip off the old block.

Kenan Rhodes. Born and raised in Boston by the wealthy

family who'd adopted him. VP of Marketing in his family's business and brilliant at it. And a consummate ladies' man, according to the number of times he appeared in society gossip pages. Again, chip off the old block.

And once both men had agreed to Barron's terms, they'd informed Cain they didn't plan on sitting back as figureheads while the year crawled by. Each intended to make their mark on the company. Achilles with the IT department and Kenan in Marketing. Everything in Cain howled at handing over the reins of any part of his business to strangers. But, because of Barron's will, Cain couldn't object. Couldn't do anything but sit there, fuming. And powerless. That grated the most. As soon as he left his father's house, he'd vowed never to be weak, vulnerable again. And yet…

He raised his arm, his fingers curled into a fist, and aimed it toward his desktop. But at the last moment, he halted the swift downward motion before his hand could slam onto the wood.

Control. He couldn't lose it.

Heaving a sigh, he leaned back, squeezing his eyes closed and pinching the bridge of his nose. Unbidden and inexplicable, an image of Devon—he never did ask her last name—wavered then solidified across the screen of his mind.

It wasn't the first time the woman who'd appeared in his mother's garden like a pinup version of a fairy featured in his thoughts. Petite, with breasts he suspected would spill into his palms. A cinched-in waist that those same hands could easily span. A delicious flare of hips that completed a wicked hourglass figure. The stilettos she'd worn should've added height to her small frame, but they hadn't. Yet, damn had they done amazing things for her toned, thick thighs.

Yes, Devon possessed a body that made a man jerk awake in the middle of the night, sweating, his dick strangled in his fist. But her body couldn't compare to the beautiful emerald eyes that seemed so innocent yet contained age-old secrets in their depths. Or to the gentle slope of her elegant cheekbones that he hadn't been able to resist touching. Or the lush, damn near indecent curve of her mouth that even now had a dull ache throbbing in his hardening flesh. That top lip–heavy mouth had combatted the impression of purity that stubbornly clung to her.

What man could look at her and not lust to be the one who thoroughly corrupted her?

He wasn't that man.

Objectively, he acknowledged that some men might call her features plain or unremarkable.

And those men would be fucking blind.

Yet… Out of all that, it was the humor, the self-deprecation, the sympathy and selfless comfort she offered in her guileless words and wine that calmed him. A week ago, she'd unknowingly given him the strength to return to that library and face his father's mess.

Cain, who lauded himself on needing no one, clung to the memory of a woman he'd met once and would most likely not see again. The irony was not lost on him.

"Mr. Farrell." Charlene's voice through his phone's intercom ripped him from his thoughts and he jerked forward with a grimace. "I know you instructed me not to interrupt you, but there is a Gregory Cole here requesting to see you. He doesn't have an appointment, but he claims it has something personal to do with your father."

Tension streaked through him, and for a moment a terse "no" burned his tongue. Who just showed up uninvited at the executive offices of a billion-dollar company asking for an unscheduled meeting with the CEO? It could be one of the many journalists he'd turned away with a barely polite "No comment." Hell, it could be another brother.

He jabbed the reply button, irritation swirling in his gut. No, whoever it was could turn around and walk out the way they came in. And if it was that important, he could set an appointment before he left.

"Send him in, Charlene." Releasing the button, he rose behind his desk, growling, "Dammit."

His father. And personal. He wanted to resist the lure of that bait, but couldn't.

Moments later, Charlene entered his office, an older man following close behind her. Tall and distinguished with neatly cut salt-and-pepper hair and clothed in a perfectly tailored suit Cain knew cost at least three thousand dollars, he strode forward, hand outstretched.

"Mr. Farrell, Gregory Cole," he greeted. "I'm glad to meet you, although I wish it were under different circumstances. I was very sorry to hear about your father's passing."

The words were appropriate but his gaze, green and somehow familiar, didn't hold the solemnity that matched. Disquiet crawled beneath Cain's skin as he quickly shook the man's hand and dropped it.

"Thank you, Mr. Cole." He nodded at Charlene who quietly closed the office door behind her. "My assistant said this had to do with my father," he said, sliding his hands into the front pockets of his pants.

No, he didn't invite Gregory Cole to sit down in one of the visitors chairs or on the dark brown leather couch in his sitting area. Call it intuition or plain old superstition, something about the man unnerved him.

"Please, call me Gregory. May I?" He didn't wait for Cain's agreement, but settled into the wingback chair in front of the desk. Crossing one leg over the other, the older man smiled. And superstitious or not, Cain couldn't suppress the shudder that rippled down his spine. "I have a matter regarding my...relationship with your father but decided to wait in deference to your mourning before approaching you."

A whole week. Yes, he was a saint. But given most journalists had been camped out on Cain's doorstep the night of Barron's death, maybe Gregory had been magnanimous.

"Did you have a business relationship with him, Mr. Cole?" Cain questioned, deliberately using the man's surname.

If the slight irritated Gregory, he didn't reveal it. If anything, his smile deepened slightly, and a gleam brightened his gaze.

"I would call it more of an understanding," he drawled, brushing an imaginary speck of lint off his immaculate suit. The gesture was contrived. Deliberate. And annoying. Impatience hummed inside Cain even as Gregory continued, "Mr. Farrell, or Cain. Can I call you Cain?"

"No."

This time the other man couldn't control the brief tightening around his mouth or the flash of anger in his eyes. The telltale signs were there and gone in seconds, but Cain caught them. From the way this man had strolled into his offices with a sense of entitlement, he obviously didn't like hearing the word *no*. Too fucking bad.

"As I was saying… I am a self-made man. I grew a chain of successful electronics stores on my own before selling them and investing the profit in even more lucrative projects. Now I own an exclusive financial and investment firm that has earned my clients and myself millions for the last few years," he bragged.

"Your hard work and determination are very admirable. But I fail to see what that has to do with me or my father. Mr. Cole, I don't want to appear rude and rush you, but I have meetings, so if we could conclude this one…?"

Actually, he didn't give a damn about appearing rude or rushing him.

Again, he caught a glimmer of irritation before something else replaced it. Satisfaction.

Cain's stomach tightened, and though it defied explanation, he braced himself. Because something was coming. And whatever put that gloating shine in Gregory Cole's eyes couldn't mean anything good for Cain.

"By all means," Gregory purred, linking his fingers across his torso. "Before your father died, he entered into a contractual agreement with me. Now that he's gone, it's your responsibility to honor it."

Cain frowned. "That's what we have a legal department for," he said. "If you want to leave the contract with my assistant, she'll make sure it's forwarded to the correct channels—"

"I can do that, *Cain*," he continued, emphasizing the usage of Cain's first name with no small amount of delight. "I thought you might want to keep this particular piece of business private. But if you don't mind your company's attorneys reviewing a wedding contract, I don't either."

Cain blinked. Stared at the man wearing the mocking grin. Shock buffeted him, momentarily rendering him deaf except for two blaring words—*wedding contract*.

What the *fuck*?

That sense of unease exploded into panic and a strangling sensation of claustrophobia. His fingers curled inside his pocket. But ingrained, brutally taught lessons kept him still. Maintained his stoic composure. Betrayed nothing of the fear ricocheting against his rib cage.

Revealed nothing of the weakness.

"What are you talking about?" he asked, voice calm.

"I'm talking about you, Cain Farrell, marrying my daughter. Your father promised you to me. Signed you over to me, actually."

Gregory chuckled as if the thought of a father selling his son like medieval chattel amused him. Hell, since the bastard was doing the same to his own daughter, he probably did find it funny. He opened his jacket and reached inside, withdrawing folded up sheets of paper. Rising, he extended them toward Cain. "I took the precaution of bringing a copy of the contract with me. Please take your time and review it. I assure you it's all binding."

Numb, Cain retrieved the papers and circled his desk. Unfolding the contract, he laid it out and studied it. Silence ticked by in thunderous pulses, echoing the pounding in his veins. And the longer he read, the more consuming his fury became. As he flipped to the last page of the three-page agreement and spied his father's bold scrawl next to Gregory's more elegant signature, Cain's body ached with the force he wielded to restrain himself. To not roar his outrage to the ceiling. To not flip his fucking desk. To not lunge across the space separating him from the smirking bastard across from him and wrap his hands around his scheming neck.

"You call yourself a businessman," Cain ground out, his voice the consistency of gravel. "You forgot to add a couple more names. Extortionist. Blackmailer."

Gregory didn't even possess the decency to appear ashamed of his actions. Lifting a shoulder in a Gallic shrug, he arched an eyebrow. "No need to get insulting, Cain. One thing I learned during my climb up in this world, no one is going to offer handouts to a poor man with a high school education. I made my own success. Forged my own paths when people of *your world* closed them. And I did that by any means necessary. So if you expect me to apologize or feel ashamed for how I got here, then you're in for a long wait that will only end in disappointment."

"Save me that self-serving drivel," Cain snapped, uncaring if Gregory glared at him in return. "There are plenty of people who start from the bottom, who put in the work, the sacrifice to claw their way to the top without resorting to criminal behavior. So you weren't born with a trust fund. Over ninety percent of people aren't. But you deni-

grate their efforts and shame them by justifying this—"
he jabbed a finger at the offensive contract "—with where
you started from."

"Spoken like a man who's never gone a day without in
his life," Gregory sneered, a ruddy color flooding his sharp
cheekbones. A cold rage glinted in his green eyes, and Cain
correctly deciphered the disgust there. For him.

"You don't know a goddamn thing about me, Cole,"
Cain growled, planting his fists on the desktop and leaning
forward. "Because if you did, you would've never walked
into my office this morning. Take this." He flicked the
three sheets of paper, and they slid across the furniture,
teetering on the edge before fluttering to the floor. "And
get the hell out."

Gregory didn't bend to pick up the contract or remove
his stare from Cain's.

"Oh see, that's where you're wrong. I know all I need to
when it comes to you, Cain," he murmured, a corner of his
mouth kicking up in a smirk Cain hungered to knock off
his face. "While your father entered into this arrangement
because of his conceit and ego, he assured me you would
comply because of one thing. Your loyalty to your mother.
A love for one's mother—it's a powerful thing," he continued in a silky tone. "And I don't doubt that you would
do anything rather than see Emelia Farrell's name splashed
across tabloid rags and dragged through the gutter by unscrupulous reporters. They would be relentless if they discovered that she had an affair while still married to your
father. And they would be absolutely rabid if they received
evidence of that affair—pictures, emails, texts…video."

Bile rushed from his stomach in an acidic torrent. It
burned, searing him. For an instant, he caved to the pain
and briefly closed his eyes. But immediately, images of his
mother's face if this news became public swam across the
backs of his lids. Devastated. Humiliated. Broken.

His mother, beautiful, proud, kind and so damn strong. In order to be married to Barron Farrell she'd had to be. She'd been the one stable, loving constant in Cain's life— gentle where his father had been harsh. Affectionate where he'd been cold. Protective when he'd been the aggressor. She'd suffered during her marriage. Once upon a time she'd probably loved his father, but his belittling, verbal assaults and constant infidelities had whittled that devotion to scraps. And his insistence on "making a man" of Cain with his fists had eradicated even those remnants.

His mother had endured for Cain, and the knowledge, the guilt, ate at him. She could've left Barron at any time, but he would've fought her for custody, and with his power, money and influence, Barron would've won. And she'd refused to leave Cain to Barron's "tender mercies." So she'd stayed until Cain had been old enough to fend for himself both financially and physically.

Emelia Farrell had paid her dues.

So no, he didn't blame her for stepping outside her travesty of a marriage and finding comfort where she could. Just… *Christ.* She'd made a mistake choosing this man.

"Another crime you're confessing to, Cole," Cain snarled, loathing scalding him from the inside out. "It's against the law to release that kind of material without the other party's consent."

"Sue me."

Cain straightened. Better to insert as much distance between them as possible. "And your daughter? She doesn't care that the man she's willing to chain herself to is only marrying her because of blackmail? That he doesn't want her, doesn't love her? Or is she like you, and all she cares about is digging her hooks into a wealthy man so she can bleed him dry?"

"My daughter does what needs to be done for her family," he replied, smoothly. "And I don't need your money,

Cain. I have more than enough of that. But if my daughter is married to a Farrell, doors that money can't buy will be opened to her."

"To you, you mean," Cain spat.

Another shrug. "Boston society is clannish, disdainful to those who weren't born in your rarefied circles. You know as well as I do that wealth will only propel a person so far. Will only grant them entrance to the building, but not a seat at the table. If you're born with a setting and a name card at that table, then you can't talk to me about how to gain a place there."

Bitterness tinged the other man's words, and though Cain hated Gregory for his methods, for threatening his mother, Cain had to agree with him on that point.

He understood the cliquish, snobby and classist world he moved in. Understood that more often than not it was the name Farrell and everything it meant—history, heritage, power, affluence—that paved his way, granted him access, afforded him allowances others didn't have.

But nothing, *nothing*, excused Gregory Cole.

He'd threatened the only person Cain cared about. That was unforgivable. Of him and his daughter.

"So when it comes down to it, you and your bitch of a daughter are willing to sell other people's souls for business," Cain said, voice as cold as the sheet of ice spreading through his veins.

"Business. Connections. Power. Influence. Your father understood that better than most," he corrected. The smile curving his mouth disappeared and the humor fled Gregory's eyes. "Enough chitchat. As you mentioned, you have meetings and I have appointments as well. So what is your answer, Cain? Are you going to marry my daughter or am I going to release my information about your mother's dalliance to the media?"

For an instant, Cain transformed into that ten-year-old

boy cowering in front of his father in that damn library. Cowering and crying because he wanted to fight back, to break free and be strong enough to face his father down. But he couldn't then. And he couldn't now. Once more he was as powerless and helpless as that boy.

Gregory Cole had made him go back on his vow never to be that weak, that vulnerable again.

And Cole would pay for that.

He and his daughter.

"I agree to marry her," Cain said, meeting the triumph in those green eyes. "But that's all I'm agreeing to. You've consigned your daughter to a union from hell. I'll make sure of it. She'll get my name and nothing more. You might have forged this farce of a marriage, but she's going to be the one to suffer for it. I promise you that."

Four

"Devon, is that you?"

Devon closed the front door behind her, momentarily holding on to the doorknob. *Lord, give me strength*, she silently prayed. And then grimaced, guilt for the disloyal thought scurrying though her. No matter how…*demanding* her father could be, he was still her father. And even if he'd changed so drastically from the protective, affectionate and laughing man he used to be when her mother was alive, he'd still never abandoned her. He'd provided for her, given her everything any daughter could wish for…everything money could buy.

"Yes, Dad, it's me," she called out, setting her purse on a chair then striding through the spacious foyer of the stately brick town house located in the heart of Back Bay.

Her father had shelled out seven million for the home—and he had zero problems bragging about it to anyone. It was gorgeous; she couldn't deny it. With large, airy rooms and cathedral ceilings, oversized bay windows that offered views of the quiet tree-lined street and the private patio, cavernous fireplaces, beautiful bedrooms and luxurious bathrooms, it was a place Devon couldn't have ever imagined calling home as a little girl. The one-bedroom apartment on the garden level even provided an elegantly appointed home office for her father. Add in the expensive art pieces, opulent furniture and state-of-the-art amenities, it was a showpiece.

And yet, for Gregory Cole, it still didn't seem to be enough. Her father had this yawning, insatiable hole inside him that he tried to fill with money and things. A hole that family used to fill.

Smothering a sigh, she entered the casual living room. Her father stood in front of the dormant fireplace big enough to fit two grown men. Well, maybe one and a half if the men were the size of Cain Farrell—okay, she had to stop thinking about him.

It'd been a little over a week since that impromptu meeting in his garden, and she couldn't eradicate him from her mind. More than was probably healthy, she turned those stolen moments over and over, analyzing them. Trying to convince herself that his gentle stroke to her cheek hadn't meant anything beyond gratitude. That she hadn't spied heat in his eyes. Because to believe the alternative…

"Hey, Dad," she greeted. "Is everything okay? Your message sounded urgent."

"Yes, everything is okay. Better than okay," he said, flicking a hand. A frown creased his forehead as he scanned her from top to bottom. "Good Lord, Devon. What are you wearing? I can't believe you went out looking like that. What if one of my business associates or someone important had seen you?" He shook his head, uttering a low sound of disappointment.

Someone important had seen her. Several *someones* actually. The hundred-plus children she worked with as a youth coordinator at a community center located in East Boston.

"Since most schools are out for Columbus Day, we hosted a play day. Jeans and a shirt are far more appropriate for balloon tosses, three-legged races and kickball than a suit." Very aware of her father's low opinion of her job—a job he viewed as beneath her—she shoved aside the pang of hurt his condescending words elicited and switched the subject. "So what's going on? Why did I need to rush home?"

Before replying, he crossed the room to the full bar built into the wall. Only after he fixed himself a drink and sipped from it did he turn back to her. "I have wonderful news, Devon," he said, lightly swirling the alcohol in his glass. "We're having a very special guest over for dinner. Which means you need to go upstairs, get out of those rags and dress in your best."

"That's the emergency?" She left off the *seriously*. But it echoed in the room. "You have people over for dinner at least three times a week. Why is this so important?"

"Because," he paused, sipping from the glass and studying her over the rim, "the guest is your future husband."

Devon rocked back on the heels of her sneakers in shock. The words boomed in her head, but they didn't make sense. Husband? What the hell was he talking about? She wasn't even *seeing* someone much less thinking about marriage.

Swallowing hard past a suddenly constricted throat, she forced out, "What?"

"I've arranged for you to be married to one of the most sought-after bachelors in this city. Maybe the country. He comes from one of Boston's best families, is rich, successful—you can't do better."

"I—" She shook her head, dread mixing with astonishment. Because he wasn't kidding.

Oh my God, *he wasn't kidding*.

"Dad, you can't just arrange marriages like this is feudal England. I'm a grown woman fully capable of choosing men to date and one to eventually marry. And when I do, his credentials will include more than the number of zeros in his bank account or how far back he can trace his roots," she argued. Wondering why in the world she was actually having this discussion.

"As your father, I have a vested interest in who you marry and who enters our family. This isn't just about you," he persisted. The steely note in his voice had horror coiling around her rib cage.

"Since it will be me pledging my future to someone, living with them, sleeping with them and having kids by them, I would say it's most definitely about me," she snapped, unable to contain her irritation…and growing panic.

His gaze narrowed on her, and he stalked across the room back to the fireplace, where he deliberately set his drink down on the stone mantel. "I have cared for you, provided for you, worked hard and sacrificed for you. There is no better judge of who you should call a husband than me. And that includes you."

You did it all for you. *For your pride, your ego, your never satisfied need for more.*

The scream filled her head. Only sheer will and a deeply rooted respect for his role as her father prevented the words from tumbling past her lips.

"Now," he continued, "after all the trouble I went through to secure this arrangement, you *will* be at your best. You *will* impress him tonight. He has connections that far surpass business. Thanks to me, you will be welcomed into Boston society and have all kinds of doors opened to you. To both of us. I won't allow you to mess that up."

"And what about kindness? Affection? Love? I don't deserve that kind of marriage? Like you had with Mom?" she whispered.

"And you see how well that turned out," he snapped.

"I'm doing you a favor, Devon. Enter a relationship based on mutual benefits and common ground and if, God forbid, you end up a widow, you won't be left devastated and broken. Remember that, Devon. Keep your heart out of this. And you will have the best life I could ever gift you with."

"Dad, are you listening to yourself?" she demanded, disbelief and bone-deep sorrow pulsing in her. "You can't possibly mean any of that." She shook her head. Yes, her mother's death had changed him. But this much? When had he become so...cold? So hard-hearted? "Sorry, Dad. I can't do it. You might think an arranged marriage is some kind of blessing, but to me it would be hell. I won't marry a stranger."

And what kind of man would agree to this archaic and self-serving nonsense? What did he expect from her? More to the point, what did her father promise him to get him to agree to this farce? If he really was one of the country's most eligible bachelors, then he should have his pick of women. Devon was a realist; she was kind, smart and a hard worker. But she wasn't the most connected, the wealthiest or the most beautiful. Why her?

"You'll do it, Devon," he snarled. "Because I've raised you, sacrificed for you."

"You did those things because you're my father," she replied, anger at his attempt at emotional blackmail coursing through her. "It's what fathers do."

"And daughters put their families first," he snapped. Pausing, he drew his shoulders back, visibly calming himself. Turning, he picked up his glass again and drank from it. When he faced her again, he slid his free hand into his pants pocket and quietly studied her. "Devon, you're going along with this—"

"No, sorry. But I'm not," she interjected.

He continued speaking as if she hadn't interrupted. "Because if you don't, I'll make sure the funding for that precious community center you love will be rescinded. And I'll make the rounds with other donors and convince them the center is a bad investment. You know as well as I do that there isn't a lack of charities where that money can be applied."

Anger, so hot, so rich she could taste it, broke over her. A tremble quaked through her, and in that moment, she hated him. For rendering her powerless. For reducing her worth to no more than an asset he could trade or cash in. For who he'd become.

Guilt and shame crashed into her, a churning deluge that damn near drowned her. What kind of daughter harbored those thoughts about the man who'd brought her into this world? Before her mother died, she'd hugged Devon close and made her promise to look after her father. Logically, Devon understood that her mother hadn't meant to place such a burden on a ten-year-old. But that vow had chained Devon to her father all these years. At twenty-six, she still remained with him, worried about how hard he pushed himself, driven by invisible demons.

"Would you really take away my job, the place I care most about?" she asked quietly.

He scoffed, flicking off her question as if batting away an annoying gnat. "I've told you repeatedly you don't need that job. You have your choice of volunteer committees where you could actually bring about change by fundraising and forging relationships with people who matter. But instead, you insist on taking a menial position that anyone with a rudimentary degree could work at. So yes, I would take that away, if you force my hand. Gladly. Because it would be for your own good, which you're too stubborn to see."

Her father was right—this wasn't just about her. Not since he put the future of the community center on the line. For four years, it hadn't only been a place to utilize

her bachelor's degree in urban studies and her master's in
social work—it was also a haven. The staff, the children,
the senior citizens and their loved ones had become sur-
rogates for the family she'd left behind in New Jersey. So
how selfish would it be of her to rip funding out from under
them just to save herself? Employees would have to be let
go. The center would lose programs that served all the de-
mographics of the community, not just youths, but before-
and after-school care, and elderly care.

No, she wouldn't allow her father to harm the center and
all the people it assisted and employed.

She also wouldn't let him determine her future. As he'd
taught her, she'd play the game. For now. But somehow,
she'd find a way out of this sham. How? No clue.

Yet.

"Fine, Dad," she said, curling her fingers around the
back of the couch, steadying herself against the foreboding
that swept through her. As if with those two words she'd
sealed her fate. "You win. If you leave the community center alone, I'll go along with this."

"Marriage, Devon," he stated, a vein of steel threading through his voice. "Not only will you marry the man
I've handpicked for you, but you'll make him believe this
is what you want. You'll convince him your dream is to be
his wife. This discussion stays here between us, Devon.
And I mean that. Do you understand?"

"Of course, Dad," she murmured, the placid tone bely-
ing her death grip on the furniture. "You want me to begin
my future on a lie. Got it."

"Devon," he barked, but the peal of the doorbell broke
off what would have undoubtedly been a scathing dress-
ing-down. He scowled. "Who is that? Are you expecting
someone?"

She didn't have a chance to reply before their housekeeper appeared in the room's entrance. "Sir, I'm sorry to

interrupt you and Ms. Devon, but there's a gentleman at the door. He claims you are expecting him. I placed him in the formal living room—"

"Since I'm practically family, I decided not to stand on formalities," drawled a dark, silken voice of velvet and grit.

She knew that voice.

Heard that voice in her dreams.

No. Oh God, *no. It couldn't be.*

Slowly, she pivoted, as if delaying what her clamoring heart and the heat pooling low in her belly already concluded.

But neither her ears, her heart nor the desire lighting her up like the Boston skyline were lying to her. Only one man had caused her body to tighten with a peculiar combination of anticipation, lust, excitement and trepidation. And he stood in her home.

Cain Farrell.

Delight exploded within her, and the beginnings of a tremulous smile tilted the corners of her mouth. She took a small step forward, but then his words penetrated her shock.

Since I'm practically family...

Wait. She jerked to a halt.

He couldn't possibly mean...

She shot a glance over her shoulder at her father, and the smug smirk confirmed the dread yawning wider in her chest. In her soul.

She returned her attention to the silent, brooding man standing feet from her. Instinct warned her that between him and her father, he was the one who presented the most danger. Not physically. Even though his tall, wide-shouldered frame seemed to shrink the spacious room to a cubbyhole, she didn't fear him using his size against her.

No, the danger he posed was much more nebulous, intangible.

Swallowing, she again moved toward him, his name

hovering on her tongue. But he shifted his gaze from her
father to her. And once more, she jerked to a halt.

Those wolf eyes didn't gleam with humor or admiration
or even bemusement.

Loathing.

He stared at her with pure, unadulterated loathing.

Cain Farrell hated her.

And she couldn't blame him.

Not one bit.

Five

Her.

Betrayal, razor sharp, bit into him. Ridiculous and inexplicable how deep the hurt and bitterness pierced. He'd spoken with her for all of ten minutes, didn't even know her last name. And yet…

Yet, he'd dreamed about her. Built her up in his mind to be this paragon of kindness, innocence and…decency. A paragon of all the things he'd believed were gone from this world.

God, he was such a fool.

He'd thought it would be impossible to be as enraged as he'd been in his office with Gregory. Wrong.

He'd been so wrong.

Before, he'd been enraged.

Now, he was *furious*.

She'd played him. Had probably arranged that little meeting in his mother's garden. Well, she deserved a goddamn award for the performance. He'd fallen for it. Had she and her father laughed about him afterward? Congratulated themselves on a job well done?

Anger, fueled by disillusionment and humiliation, poured through him like gasoline. And the phony shock and hint of sadness in her emerald eyes was the match that had his control on the verge of detonating. No wonder Gregory Cole's gaze had seemed familiar to him. He'd stared into those same green, deceptive depths before.

Never again. Never again would he believe what shone from those beautiful, treacherous eyes or those sensual, lying lips.

"Cain, this is a surprise. We were expecting you for dinner," Gregory greeted, smiling as he crossed the room, his arm outstretched to shake Cain's hand.

Was he fucking kidding?

Cain stared down at Gregory's palm until the other man lowered his arm back to his side. Crimson stained Gregory's cheekbones and twin lines bracketed his mouth.

"You may be blackmailing me into marrying your daughter, but don't for one second believe that makes us friends. Or even friendly. I warned you what you would get from me. My name. That's it. Not small talk. Not pleasantries. And not dinners. I came by to meet the person so desperate for a man and a foothold in society that she would allow her father to take criminal measures on her behalf." He swung his regard back to Devon, gratified to see she'd wiped that attempt at genuine emotion from her face. It didn't fit her. "And now that I have met her, I want a moment alone with my fiancée. Since you've gone to so much trouble, you don't mind, do you, Devon?"

Gregory glanced sharply at his daughter, who did an applause-worthy job of appearing guilty. Her thick eyelashes lowered, and she didn't meet her father's gaze. Nice try, but keeping up pretenses of innocence was unnecessary. That ship had sailed. Just being here in the same room with her father solidified that she was a willing accomplice.

"Devon?" Gregory barked, and though Cain harbored no sympathy for her, he clenched his jaw against the impulsive need to order Cole to watch his tone.

"I have no problem speaking with you," she murmured, ignoring her father and addressing Cain.

The dense fringe of lashes lifted, and he glimpsed determination in her stare. She would need that determination dealing with him. Because he intended to grant her and her father the same amount of mercy they'd offered him.

None.

"Well, I have a problem," Gregory snapped.

"And I don't care," Cain said, not bothering to hide his impatience and disgust for the man. "Either we talk now, or I leave."

Gregory's expression tightened, his facial bones stark under his skin. Cain read the fury in his glare, the taut pull of his mouth and the tense set of his shoulders.

And he relished it.

"Fine," Gregory eventually growled. "Twenty minutes."

He stalked from the room, and Cain snorted. If that was supposed to be a show of parental concern, Gregory had failed. A man like him didn't care about something as tender as his daughter's feelings or well-being. Hell, he was trading both for more business, more wealth and an entrance into an inner social circle whose doors had been closed to him. No, more likely he worried about not controlling the situation.

Welcome to the fucking club.

As soon as he disappeared, Cain turned back to Devon… and slow clapped, the gesture condescending.

"Well done," he drawled. "I congratulate you on a stellar performance. Your father must be proud of his star pupil."

"Cain, I'm sorry," she murmured.

He snorted. "You'll have to be more specific. For what? Lying in wait for me during my father's funeral? For tag-teaming with your father to extort me?"

For making a fool out of me? For making me believe I saw sweetness in you? For every sweaty, hot night I woke up hard and aching for a woman who didn't exist?

As the too-vulnerable questions whispered through his mind, he locked his jaw and strode past her to the bar he'd spied when he'd entered the well-appointed room. Part of him detested partaking of anything that belonged to Gregory Cole—and that included his daughter.

But the other half acknowledged that this conversation required a drink. And that he needed to keep his hands busy—before they acted of their own accord and mapped the dangerous curves showcased by the simple long-sleeved T-shirt and dark, hip-hugging jeans.

She was like the lily of the valley—elegant, sweet, virginal. But if ingested, poisonous.

Tearing his gaze from her, he poured a finger of Scotch into a glass and brought it to his lips. He downed the alcohol in one swallow. Closing his eyes, he welcomed the smooth burn. It warmed him, spreading as it hit his stomach. Anything to distract him from wondering if those beautiful breasts would spill over his hands if he cupped her. If her nipples would be a slightly lighter hue than her caramel-colored hair, or would they be a deep rose.

He poured another drink to try and convince himself he didn't care.

Yeah. Not enough Scotch in the world for that.

"Cain, I know you won't believe me, but I'm sorry you've been dragged into this…" She faltered, not finishing the sentence, and he threw back the second drink, slamming the glass down as the Scotch hit the back of his throat.

"Into this shit show, you mean?" he supplied, arching a brow. "You offer up that pretty apology as if you have nothing to do with this. As if your selfish demands aren't screwing with my life," he growled. "I don't have much of a choice here, but you? All you have to do is tell your father no, that you won't go along with it. But you're not going to do that, are you, Devon? Not when both of you have dollar signs in your eyes."

She swept her hands over her hair, dragging away the few loose strands that had escaped her ponytail. She turned away from him, giving him her profile to study. The high forehead. The impudent tilt of her nose. The top-heavy bow of her mouth. In another era, artists would've competed to paint the elegance of her features and lushness of her body. Now, in this more materialistic and shallow society, beauty like hers earned criticism instead of praise. Which just proved society was dumb as well as blind.

Her curves, dips and hollows would lure men to their downfall like currents sweeping ships to crash against jagged rocks.

Well, screw that. He might find himself shackled to her, but damn if he would be a casualty to his dick.

"No," she said, facing him again, her chest lifting and falling on the audible breath she inhaled. "I can't back out of it."

He'd expected the answer—had known the answer. And yet it still slammed into him, the knowledge reverberating through him like an earthquake. As if there had been a small part of him hanging on to the hope that he'd misjudged her. That he hadn't been so damn *wrong.*

How many times would he be a fool for this woman?

Never. Again.

"Even though the thought of chaining myself to a gold-digging bitch and her bottom-feeder father makes my skin crawl, part of me is glad you said that," he murmured.

Ignoring the jerk of her chin and the slight recoil of her body, he stalked closer, eating up the distance he'd placed between them. She shifted backward, but the couch prevented her from going any farther. And he took advantage of it. Trapping her body between his and the fussy piece of furniture. He stopped just short of pressing his chest to hers, but near enough that her scent—a sultry combination of honey and sharper citrus notes—teased him. Taunted him. Steeling himself against it, he cocked his head to the side and studied her.

Not caring that both his open inspection and the infiltration of her personal space sped past rude and parked next to inappropriate. There was nothing *appropriate* about any of this.

"Because now, when I do everything in my power to make your very existence a living hell, you'll know exactly why you'll receive no mercy from me. I hope you enjoyed that moment of satisfaction when your father told you he got me on the hook. Because that's the last time you'll feel anything close to it again."

"Does it make you feel better to threaten me?" she asked, and he resented her calm, the evenness of her voice. Like he was the only one drowning in emotion.

God, he wanted—*needed*—her to go under with him.

"Yes," he replied, and she blinked at his blunt candor. "But you don't need to bother with this act on my behalf, sweetheart. Pretending to be the sweet, concerned, *honest* woman who introduced herself in the garden—it must've been tiring, maintaining that charade. No need to keep it up when I can see right through you." He lifted a hand and gently dragged the backs of his fingers down her cheek, imitating and mocking the touch he'd surrendered to before. Before he'd discovered that soft heart was actually made of stone and yearning for large denominations. "That might be the one thing you'll enjoy about our marriage. The freedom of no pretense. I'm going into this already knowing you're a coldhearted, greedy social climber who would do anything to get what she wants."

Fire flashed in those eyes and, God help him, excitement twisted with anger in his blood, creating an unholy union. Desire—he recognized it, acknowledged it. He might despise everything Devon stood for, but that didn't prevent lust from locking him in its jaws, from hardening his body to the point of pain.

"Good girl," he purred, rubbing his thumb over that slightly fuller top lip. He pressed gently, testing the texture, the give. Her gasp bathed his skin, and before he could check it, he bowed his head over hers, their foreheads almost touching. "There it is. I want to see that fire you hide behind a purity we both know doesn't suit you."

She slid her arms between them, flattening her hands on his chest and shoving him away. He shifted backward, and the bitter twist of her lips telegraphed what they both knew—she'd slipped away only because he'd allowed it.

"You don't know me," she snapped, crossing her arms over her chest.

On another person, the gesture would've struck him as self-protective. But this wasn't another person; it was Devon Cole, and as he'd learned, she was a master at portraying herself to be something she wasn't.

"Ten minutes in my company doesn't make you an expert on who I am. And don't flatter yourself. You might think you're this wonderful catch that I have to plot and scheme to trap, but you're not the only one sacrificing. Contrary to what you believe, this isn't all about you."

"Prove it," he said. "Call your father in here and put an end to this." When she didn't answer, didn't move toward the door, his lips curved into a mocking, cynical twist. "So much for your pretty speech. Righteous indignation doesn't become you, sweetheart."

Sighing, she pinched the bridge of her nose. "Cain, listen. I—"

"No," he interrupted. Unbidden and without his conscious permission, his gaze raked down her body again. His blood pounded in his veins, his cock. She was untrustworthy, a liar, and he detested that his body could betray him. Could make him weak for her. The fear of that weakness coated his voice in ice as he met her wide eyes. "You listen. Because I want it crystal clear what you're in for if you and your father go ahead with blackmailing me. Like I told your father, you'll get my name, but here's what you won't have from me. Peace. Happiness. Fidelity. I refuse to curb my lifestyle for you. Your father might receive the perceived benefits of me as a son-in-law, but you'll be the one to pay the price. Day in and day out. Consider that, Devon. And decide if it's worth it. I promise you. It isn't."

He pivoted and strode from the room, unable to spend another moment staring into those bottomless eyes. Eyes that had darkened with an emotion he refused to attribute to her. Remorse.

No, she wasn't capable of that.

And he wouldn't fall for her act again. She'd duped him once, had made him believe. Had played him.

She wouldn't receive a second chance.

Six

Devon stepped from the elevator onto the executive floor of Farrell International. Except for soft murmurings and the muted click-clack of fingers flying over keyboards, a silence not unlike a church permeated the expansive area. Her heels sank into the plush dark blue carpet, and on either side of her, artwork that wouldn't have been out of place in a museum graced the dark wood walls. Wide, circular desks manned by professionally dressed men and women dotted the floor, guarding closed double doors that bore gold nameplates.

Power. Wealth. Before arriving here today, she hadn't known they possessed a smell. Lemon verbena and fresh cedar. And something more elusive, indefinable.

It was that something that clung to Cain.

She'd inhaled it when he'd pressed against her in her father's living room. When he'd surrounded her. Touched her. Let her feel the imprint of his thumb on her mouth. After he'd left, she'd swept her tongue over her lip, his caress a phantom weight on her flesh. And even though his hand had long left her, she tasted him. That same scent. Dark. Sensual.

Exciting.

Lord. She barely stopped herself from spreading her fingers over her stomach. What did it say about her that when he'd crowded her, glared at her with those wolf eyes—hell, *threatened her*—she hadn't felt fear? No, it hadn't been that emotion pumping through her blood, tingling her nipples into taut tips, swirling low in her belly...wetting the flesh between her legs.

It'd been lust.

Pure and simple.

Well, if anything that greedy and clawing could be pure.

She'd experienced desire before; she was a twenty-six-year-old woman, and she'd been with a few men. Even enjoyed sex. The connection, the intimacy, the physical bonding—she wasn't ashamed to admit she took pleasure in the act. Especially when love was involved. But it was love that had her steeped in the middle of a year-long sexual drought.

Donald Harrison had been an associate quickly moving up the ranks of her father's firm. When he'd approached her at a business event, she'd been flattered and attracted to him. Why not? With his dark blond hair, deep brown eyes and athletic build, he'd drawn many appreciative glances from women and men alike. But his interest had been solely focused on her. He'd showered her in compliments, gifts and affection. Her father hadn't been thrilled about her relationship with a "mere associate," but Devon hadn't cared. She'd loved Donald. Could see them sharing a future together.

Which had made her discovery so shattering. He'd been using her only to climb the corporate ladder in her father's company.

It'd been a year since her father had slid that file across the dining room table. He'd chosen breakfast to break the news to her. One task to get out of the way over coffee before his day started. He'd nonchalantly eaten a perfectly cooked omelet while she'd read about Donald's fiancée, the house they'd just bought in Charlestown, even a picture of the engagement ring. And while her heart had been crushed, her father had lectured her about not being astute enough to recognize a "chaser" when she encountered one. About being too naive to recognize a man who desired her wealth and connections rather than her.

The irony didn't elude her.

Then, she'd been the one used for upward mobility.

Now, she was doing the using. Not willingly. But in the end, it didn't matter.

Not to her father. And certainly not to Cain Farrell.

At least she entered into this arrangement with her eyes wide open, not blinded by sentiments such as love and loyalty. Cain harbored none for her; the only emotion he possessed when it came to her was hate. And though that stung—God, glimpsing the loathing in his eyes, hearing it drip from his voice had been scalding—maybe, it was for the best.

As of now, she hadn't devised a way to escape her father's plans. Which meant for the foreseeable future, she was trapped, unable to back out and unable to confess to Cain why she had to go through with this.

But given her completely inconvenient desire for Cain, his disdain for her might save her from herself, from her untrustworthy heart. She'd confused physical attraction with love before. But just one mocking caress down her cheek from Cain had stoked her lust hotter than sex with Donald. So if she didn't guard herself against Cain…

She couldn't do anything as foolish as allow herself to

be vulnerable with him. Lowering her guard would be like opening the cage door to a prowling lion.

In other words, stupid as hell.

"Can I help you?" the statuesque brunette behind a large gleaming desk asked Devon as she approached.

Devon glanced at the closed double doors behind the desk. For a moment, panic seized her. Cain had requested her presence with a terse text message, but he hadn't included why. What awaited her? The first step in his plan to begin making her existence a "living hell"?

Anxiety should be the only emotion quivering through her at the thought of his threat. Not anticipation. Damn sure not excitement.

Maybe she was as twisted as Cain believed her to be.

"Hello," she said, smiling at the executive assistant whose nameplate proclaimed her to be Charlene Gregg. "Cain Farrell is expecting me. Devon Cole."

Charlene nodded. "Yes, he told me to send you in as soon as you arrived. Just through those doors."

"Thank you." Devon offered her another smile, hoping it didn't betray the nerves rattling inside her.

Inhaling a deep breath, she walked forward, chin tilted upward, shoulders squared. One of her mother's favorite sayings had been "Faith it until you make it," her twist on the old axiom. Well, Devon would have faith that she wouldn't appear like a lamb heading into the slaughter until she actually didn't feel like one.

No telling how long that would take.

Pulling open the door, she stepped into Cain's inner sanctum. Stalling, she surveyed the spacious office. Glass comprised two of the four walls, and tasteful masculine furniture of wood and leather dotted a sitting area. Instead of the beautiful artwork that decorated the outer office, huge framed black-and-white photographs of historic Boston adorned the walls. Faneuil Hall. The *Appeal to the*

Great Spirit statue in front of the Museum of Fine Arts. The Bunker Hill Monument. The Old North Church. The lighting, the imagery, the tone of the photos—they were all stunning. And seemed out of place in the office of a merciless billionaire.

Her gaze jerked toward Cain.

And immediately she regretted the impulse.

The stirring of curiosity flickered then died in her chest. His cold, narrowed stare extinguished it. Not even two minutes later, and she'd already broken a rule she'd set for herself. Guard against any emotion with Cain. And that included curiosity. Because it was the gateway drug that led to other emotions—interest, wonder, compassion, need...

Do better, she snapped at herself.

Then she deliberately conjured the memory of the heartache that had nearly ripped her in half after discovering Donald's lies. She embraced that ache, let it soak into her skin, her bones. She'd hold on to it so she wouldn't slip again.

"You summoned me here," she said, injecting the calm nonchalance that had abandoned her the second she entered the downtown Boston skyscraper of Farrell International's offices.

That was one lesson she'd come away with from their meeting at her home a week earlier.

Never show weakness in front of this man.

"Can I always expect this kind of pliancy during our marriage?" he mocked. "Submissiveness in a woman isn't something I'm usually attracted to, but for you I could make an exception."

"Making allowances for me already?" She shook her head, tsking, even as a voice inside her head yelled, *What the hell are you doing? Don't poke the beast!* "You're setting a bad precedent. And you know how women like me will take full advantage of that."

He didn't reply, but his intense scrutiny stroked over her, from the center part of her drawn-back hair, down the straight lines of her dress to her dark green stiletto heels. When she'd donned the green-and-white-striped shirt with the big bow tie at the neck and the emerald pencil skirt, the outfit had seemed both professional and flattering. Now, with that blue-gray gaze on her, she fought not to check if she'd left a button or two loose or if her skirt skimmed too tightly over her hips.

His eyes lifted to hers, and her words—*"take full advantage of that"*—seemed to resonate in the office. Suddenly, instead of referring to his permissiveness, it sounded as if she were offering him something else to exploit. Herself.

A dull throb of heat beat low in her belly, edging farther south. Settling deep between her legs. Her mind railed against the implication of her words, demanding she clear up her meaning. But her body, mainly the flesh between her legs, approved of this new plan of action.

She was in trouble.

"While I appreciate the sudden display of honesty, that's not why I asked you here." He picked up a tablet, tapped the screen a few times then rounded his desk, extending the device toward her.

Primal survival instincts cried out that she retreat, hide from the ultimate predator in the room. But pride—foolish, self-destructive pride—kept her feet rooted. She might not have any intention of going through with this disaster of a marriage if she could find a way out of it, but she also didn't intend to start any relationship, no matter how short-lived, cowering from him.

She'd lost her mother as a child, and in every way that mattered, her father, too. And she'd survived it, become a woman who could weather a storm and come out stronger on the other side. Battered maybe, but not beaten.

And no way in hell would she allow Cain Farrell to accomplish what fate hadn't managed to do.

She shifted forward instead of backing up, meeting him halfway and accepting the tablet. Her fingertips brushed his, but she kept her gaze glued to the screen, absorbing the tingling shock against her skin. She might not be able to do anything about her body's reaction to this man, but she didn't have to let him see the effect he had on her.

Focusing her attention on the device, she scanned the website he'd pulled up, recognizing it as one of the more popular columns that featured on-dits about Boston society. Huh. He didn't strike her as the kind of man who gave a damn about gossip. She frowned, but kept reading. Moments later, she sucked in an abrupt, hard breath.

What the... He *hadn't...*

But dammit, he had.

"I—" she stuttered, humiliation and anger burning through her like a blowtorch. "I didn't—"

"Didn't what?" Cain cut her off, the ice in his tone freezing her. "Didn't leak the news about our nonexistent engagement to the press? Didn't give an exclusive to this little gossip rag?"

"I didn't do it," she insisted, her fingers so tight around the tablet it was a wonder the screen didn't crack under the pressure. "I wouldn't without your agreement."

"So you'd have me believe you grew morals overnight?" He arched an eyebrow. "If you didn't leak this, then your father did. Not that it matters. The only thing that does matter is that I hadn't found the opportunity to tell my mother about our—" he paused, his lips twisting into a cruel sneer "—*arrangement* yet. Instead of hearing it from her son, she read it in that silly column. Do you know what it's like to look your mother in the eye and lie to her, Devon? Do you know how dirty that makes you feel?"

"No," she whispered. "I don't know what that's like. My mother died when I was ten."

Cain stiffened, and silence pounded in the room like a heartbeat. Throbbed with tension, with the ache of loss. At least on her part. What would her mother say about this situation? Would they even be here if she was alive? Would her father be the man he'd become?

So many what-ifs…

"You understood the pain I was feeling, you mentioned that in the garden," he murmured, his gaze roaming over her face, searching. She wanted to hide from that incisive scrutiny. He couldn't have her memories, couldn't have her pain. "I'm sorry about your mother, Devon. Mothers…" An emotion so stark, so dark, that the breath locked in her lungs flashed in his eyes. In the next instant, it disappeared, but she hadn't imagined it. Not when her chest echoed with it. "Mothers are special. And I'm sorry you lost yours."

"It's been sixteen years."

"You still miss her."

"I do," she rasped, the admission slipping from her without her permission.

She blinked against the sting of tears. *No, dammit.* No weakness. God, there wasn't much hope for her to survive this whole thing if she couldn't stop breaking her rules with this man.

Clearing her throat, she shoved the tablet at him. "Here." She barely waited for him to accept it, being careful that they didn't touch again. Smoothing her damp palms down her hips, she strode over to one of the windows and stared out at the view of downtown Boston and beyond.

A king. He was a king all the way up here at the top floor of this lofty building. Did that make them all peasants in his sight? Or did that make him distant and lonely, a prince in a gilded tower of his own making?

"I didn't place that gossip in the column. But I will apologize for my father's actions. Not that it will make much difference now."

"No, it won't," he agreed, the ice returning to his tone. "I hadn't decided what story to tell my mother about an impending marriage, much less why I haven't introduced her to a woman I've been seeing long enough to make my wife." His woodsy, fresh scent, heated by that big body, reached out to her, teasing her. Teasing her with what she craved, but her mind—her heart—knew it would be lethal for her to partake. "I would cut my own heart out before breaking my mother's. And telling her I'm entering the same loveless prison she endured with my father would accomplish that. So I had to lie and convince her I've fallen in love," he bit out. A caustic note hardened those words, telegraphing his opinion of falling in love with her. "And with the choice of hurting my mother or continuing this charade, I'm going to sell the hell out of it. Which means even though you see a walking dollar bill when you look at me, you better scrape together all your superb acting skills and pretend I'm the man you can't live without when you're in front of her. And for whoever else we need to convince so the truth never gets back to her."

The weight of her father's machinations landed hard in her chest. From one moment to the next, she couldn't breathe. As if all his schemes, lies and betrayals shrank the room, and she battled claustrophobia, scratching and clawing to escape. His needs, his goals, his greed demanded a price, but it was her and Cain who had to pay the cost.

And it was high.

"Mr. Farrell, Laurence Reese from Liberty Photography is here for your appointment." Charlene's voice dragged Devon from the dark hole she'd been sliding down, and she glanced at Cain's desk phone, almost grateful.

"Consider this your first casting call," Cain said, and

she blinked at the enigmatic statement, turning to watch him stride toward his desk.

"What?" she asked, confused.

He glanced over his shoulder at her, a cold, humorless smile curving his mouth. "Our engagement photos." Before she could reply—hell, *if* she could reply—he pressed a button on the phone. "Send him in, Charlene. Thank you." He started toward his office door but paused at her side. Lowering his head, he murmured, "I want every person who looks at these photos to swoon and fall in love with the idea of us. To crown us the next fucking Harry and Meghan. So better bring your A game, sweetheart."

His lips grazed the rim of her ear on each word, and she fought not to betray how even that slight caress sent desire spiraling through her.

Only when he continued across the room did she turn around, inhaling a gulp of air, her lungs on fire from the breath she'd been holding. Her heart thudded against her rib cage, a primal rhythm that echoed in her head, drowning out the conversation between Cain and the tall, thin man who entered the office. They shook hands, and when Laurence Reese glanced in her direction, she forced a smile to her lips. Though it felt brittle and phony, the gesture must've passed muster because the photographer returned her smile, his brown eyes warm.

Behind him, a crew poured into the office toting equipment. Devon hung back as the photographer and his assistants worked. In short order, they had cameras, tripods and reflective umbrellas set up. Cables snaked across the floor and Laurence even had his people set up a green screen on one side of the room. They performed in a well-organized unit, and it wasn't long before the photographer, camera hanging around his neck, directed them to stand in front of the window.

With Cain's permission, several people had moved his

massive desk out of the way, and Devon could imagine the picture would reflect a power couple with all of Boston stretched behind them like their kingdom.

And they said a picture was worth a thousand words. Right.

All of theirs would be lies.

"How about we start with you, Mr. Farrell, behind Ms. Cole. If you'll wrap your arms around her..." Laurence instructed, lifting his camera over his head.

Damn. *Damndamndamn.*

She couldn't move. Couldn't breathe. Cain. With his arms wrapped around her. She stiffened, tension starting at her toes and racing like a lightning bolt up her body until she stood so tight, one tap would probably send her tumbling forward. And shattering into pieces.

It occurred to her that the first time Cain embraced her would be just for the sake of the camera and public consumption. There was something seedy about it. And yet, a secret part of her that she'd buried so deep she barely acknowledged it hungered to be held by this man. Yearned to know how his body would cover her—shelter her. Protect her. And that part, which had been wounded by rejection, by deceit, by blows to its self-esteem, wasn't picky about how it happened.

A hard wall of expensive wool and muscle pressed to her back. She gasped, that initial contact smashing her paralysis. An electrical current zigzagged through her, making her body jerk. But strong, toned arms slid under hers and circled her waist, controlling the involuntary motion.

"Shh, easy," Cain rumbled in her ear, his head lowered over hers. To the photographer, it probably appeared as if he were affectionately nuzzling her. "You love my arms around you, remember? Want my hands on your body."

Oh God.

Her lashes fluttered, and she sank her teeth into her bottom lip, trapping the moan that crawled up her throat. His words elicited hot, erotic images of his arms holding her close in another setting. One with a wide bed, twisted sheets, air thick with the musky scent of sex. One where those big long-fingered hands swept over her bare skin, cupped her heavy breasts, pinched her beaded nipples... dipped between her trembling thighs...

"Yes, perfect," Laurence praised, his camera snapping away in rapid-fire succession. Startled, Devon lifted her hands, cupping them over Cain's. He immediately intertwined their fingers, and she couldn't help but look down. Their fingers looked like puzzle pieces finding homes; it struck her as beautiful. And for a stupid, nonsensical moment, tears stung her eyes. "Beautiful," the photographer murmured, edging closer to them, camera whirring and clicking. "Now look at me."

They followed his instructions for the next thirty minutes, and the half hour flew by in a haze of simmering desire and embarrassment. She tried to pretend it didn't faze her every time Cain cupped her elbow or pressed his chest to hers or curved an arm around her waist. Tried to act as if this was business as usual for a woman in love. And all the while she secretly prayed that the invasive and all-too-perceptive camera lens didn't capture the dueling emotions waging an epic battle inside her—uncertainty, lust, vulnerability, a ravenous hunger that surpassed the physical, a hunger for the closeness they were making a sham of.

A hunger for pretense to be reality.

Oh God, she needed this to be done. And not just the shoot, but this mess her father had dropped her into. She was a motherless child, a neglected daughter, a rejected woman. In other words, so starved for love that she'd easily—willingly—turn to this man for affection. For scraps of kindness, even knowing they were faked for the eyes of others...

A sob clawed at her throat, desperation squeezing her, trapping her like the restricting sleeves of a straitjacket—

Cain strode over to the photographer to view some of the pictures on the digital screen, and she took advantage of the reprieve. Whirling around, she bolted back to the window. She stared sightlessly out, gulping in huge breaths and shoving back the edges of panic.

No. No, dammit.

The admonishment rang in her head, bringing her back from the emotional edge.

She wasn't weak. She wasn't fragile or damaged. Donald hadn't broken her; she'd come out stronger for that. Smarter and not so naive. And Cain wouldn't finish what Donald had started.

She wouldn't allow him to.

"One more pose, if you don't mind," Laurence said, switching out cameras with one of his assistants. "How do you feel about a shot with a kiss?" He smiled. "Only if you're comfortable with it, though."

She turned from the window to find Cain's hooded, blue-gray gaze on her. Her breath snagged in her throat and inside her head, the "hell no" bounced around, deafening. But she remained silent, returning that stare, certain he would decline. He didn't want to kiss her. Hell, he'd pretty much told her their marriage, if they progressed that far, would be a cold one and she would have to find pleasure in someone else's bed—as he planned to do. So, surely he would shoot down this suggestion.

Any minute now.

"Where do you want us?" Cain asked Laurence, not removing his scrutiny from her.

That was *not* a refusal.

"In front of the green screen," he instructed them.

Cain slowly stretched his arm toward her, palm up. She stared at it, unmoving. But realizing everyone waited on her, she forced her feet forward…and slid her hand across his. Inexplicably, the nerves battering her calmed. Which made zero sense because he *was* the cause of those nerves.

Jesus, she was in so much trouble.

He quietly led her across the room to stand in front of the tall screen.

"Great," Laurence said. "Just be natural. Pretend we're not here."

Seriously? She could feel the eyes of every person in that room on her, on *them*. Her senses were so sharpened, she could hear their inhales, smell the clean notes of Laurence's Tom Ford aftershave. And if she glanced around, she'd glimpse the curiosity his team tried to hide behind their professionalism.

"Look at me," Cain murmured, low enough that it only carried to her ears. Unlike before when he'd issued orders, she couldn't help but obey. She lifted her gaze to his. "Your choice, Devon."

Her choice. He was giving her what had been stolen from him by her father and her, or so he believed. And yet, he was offering a choice to her when he could just take.

A longing so deep it verged on pain filled her. A longing for the impossible. For time to reverse itself and all the events that had occurred—her father's interference, this forced engagement—to have never happened. That the impromptu meeting in the garden had been the impetus for a true romance and this moment they shared right now was genuine instead of a phony prop for an equally phony relationship.

But even God couldn't undo what was. They couldn't go back. She couldn't have that fairy tale. Still… Maybe she could have an element of that fantasy. A kiss. A bit of romance. A little tenderness. It wasn't too much to ask—too much to take.

She nodded.

Heat flashed in his eyes like dry lightning, lending his wolf eyes an almost eerie glow. And in that instant, she identified with prey. But instead of running away, she edged closer, tipping her head back. And if she resembled a creature exposing its vulnerable neck? Well, she credited it to the surreality of this moment.

Cain lifted his hand, but instead of cupping her face as she expected, he gripped the knot of hair twisted behind her head and tugged. Before the gasp could leave her lips, he'd freed the heavy, long strands. Shocked, she stared up at him, unable to contain her shiver as his blunt-tipped fingers dragged over her scalp then tangled in the wavy mass.

"I'd wondered," he murmured, echoing the same sentiment she'd uttered to him back in the garden when she'd first seen his eyes.

"You wondered what?" she whispered.

His inspection shifted from his hands buried in her hair to her eyes. The unfiltered desire in his gaze punched her in the chest and, reeling, she grasped at anything to steady herself in the wake of it. Him. His waist, to be more exact. Her fingers dug into the firm flesh that seemed to sear her through his white dress shirt. Instead of snatching her hands away from the heat, she burrowed closer. Clung harder.

He didn't answer her, but his hold on her thick strands tightened, and he pulled, tugging her head back farther. She shouldn't like that tiny pricks danced across her scalp. Shouldn't have loosed that low, needy sound that telegraphed exactly how much she liked it. But she did both, and when Cain's eyes narrowed, lust flaring brighter, hotter, she couldn't regret either.

She anticipated a conquering, passionate onslaught when the kiss came. But he surprised her again. He brushed his lips over hers. A gentle caress. A tender pursuit. And *oh God*. How she wished he'd overwhelmed her with lust. It would've been less confusing. Less devastating. She could've chalked up a hungry siege to lust and anger. Could've responded with the same. But this? She sighed. Or maybe whimpered. Either way, she melted. Her lips parted, and she couldn't resist the lure of the mouth that could appear so hard and cruel, but in truth was so incredibly soft. And sensual. And beautiful.

Canting her head to the side, he molded that gorgeous mouth to hers, his tongue sweeping in, questioning even as he invited her to dance. And she did. No hesitation. With that decision, that surrender, the hunger she'd initially expected followed.

Now she understood why he'd gentled her first.

To prepare her for this.

He was a carnal marauder. A conqueror. And she, the willing captive. His for the seizing. And as he drove deep, licking, tangling and sucking, he razed a path of destruction through her senses. Through any past experience of what a kiss was or should be.

And she wanted more. *Needed* more.

"I think I have what I need." Laurence's voice, thick with amusement, penetrated the dense fog of lust that enshrouded her.

She stiffened, and Cain went rigid against her.

Mortification and despair roared to life within her, chasing away the passion that had blinded her to the fact that they had an audience. Mortification because she'd lost herself in his arms, had laid out her desire for him and in turn, offered him a tool to use against her. A damn novice's mistake. And in this game, she was far from a novice.

And despair because even now, anger crystallized his

light gaze. At her, at himself—she didn't know. Not that it mattered. His remorse and disgust were plain for her to glimpse, and for a foolish instant, she mourned the loss of the tender, sensual stranger who had drawn both hunger and wonder from her with his kiss.

"Are we finished here, then?" Cain asked, stepping away from her. The cold rushed in, wrapping her in its chilly embrace.

Pride constrained her arms at her sides, refusing to let her wrap them around herself in protection.

"Yes," Laurence nodded, apparently oblivious to the undercurrents of tension running between her and Cain. Or maybe he just interpreted it as sexual, considering the display they'd just put on. "I think you're going to be very pleased with the photos, Mr. Farrell."

Cain spoke with the photographer as he and his crew packed up, negating the need for her to engage in conversation. Thank God. Because she couldn't string two sentences together right now if she'd wanted to.

She glanced at Cain, scanning his tall, wide-shouldered frame, the powerful chest, flat stomach and long, muscular thighs. A sizzling coil of desire unfurled within her, and she raised her hand to her mouth, touching her trembling fingers to her tender lips.

As if he sensed the movement, Cain's regard shifted from Laurence to her. That gaze dropped to her mouth, and Devon dropped her arm as if caught mid-sin. Maybe thinking about wanting her fake fiancé to kiss the ever lovin' hell out of her wasn't on God's list of sins, but it was on hers.

Falling for the enemy might be a great romance trope, but this was real life. If she allowed Cain close, when he moved on, she wouldn't be left unscathed. And he would move on. If there was anything she'd learned since her mother's death it was that anyone could be ripped away at a whim.

Better she remember that the next time she wondered if his body looked as powerful without clothes as it did in them.

Starting now.

Seven

Cain remembered the first time he saw the *Mona Lisa*.

He'd been fifteen, and his father had taken him along on a business trip to Paris. It'd been boring as hell. For the five days they'd been in one of the most beautiful cities on earth, he'd spent ninety percent of it locked in conference rooms with his father and other businessmen. He hadn't cared about acquisitions or profits and losses. At fifteen, three things had consumed him: the Boston Red Sox, beating his best score on *Call of Duty* and getting to third base with Cassandra Ransom.

But then his father had allowed his assistant to take Cain on a tour of Paris. And he'd visited the Louvre and seen *her*. Mona Lisa. He'd spent at least an hour staring up at the painting of the mysterious Italian noblewoman with her dark beauty, wearing her enigmatic smile. The epitome of grace and yet, he always imagined that smile hinted at the woman's passion, joy, mischief. But especially her passion.

No flesh and blood woman had ever intrigued and captivated him as much as that piece of art.

Until now.

As Laurence and his staff exited his office, Cain ordered himself not to turn around and study the silent woman who hadn't moved from the wall where the green screen had stood. Not to turn and skim the interesting features only a blind man would call plain. Not to survey the breasts that had pressed against his chest, confirming every suspicion he'd had about their firmness and weight. Not to regard the almost dramatic flare of her full hips and the sensual thickness of her thighs. Not to stare at the mouth that had damn near brought him to his knees in front of an office full of people.

Jesus, the soft give of it, the heady, sultry taste of it—he'd lost control, forgotten about everything and everyone else except the woman sweetly surrendering to him, granting him her passion like a gift wrapped with a bow. That never happened with him, to him. *Ever.* And as he'd surfaced from the dark pool of lust, anger lit in him, but so did fear. Who had he become in those moments when he'd been drowning in her?

He'd suspected passion hot enough to reduce him to ash had existed behind that innocent demeanor. Had glimpsed it in the garden in those beautiful, deceptive eyes. And in the occasional flashes of temper and sarcasm. But to confirm it? To be on the receiving end of that lovely flame?

Goddamn. Since meeting her, his sleep had been disturbed with dreams of her. Now that he'd tasted her? He would be lucky if he ever slept again.

Clenching his jaw, he shut the door closed behind the last of the photography crew and crossed the room toward her. What else did she hide behind that Mona Lisa face? What else would he discover was a mask, a lie? If anything, today had shown him he could trust nothing about her.

The cherry on top of this shitty sundae would be for him to become a slave to his lust. To willfully turn a blind eye to her true nature just so he could be kissed by fire again. That's probably what her father intended.

Well, he was no one's puppet. Including his cock's.

"I should probably go—" Devon began.

"We need to—" he ground out simultaneously.

Whatever they would've said remained unfinished and hanging in the air as his door flew open and Achilles and Kenan strode in as if it was their office instead of his. Technically, they weren't wrong. Everything in this company belonged to them as much as it did him.

With that reminder, the bitterness he'd felt since the reading of Barron's will simmered to the surface. And spilled onto the men who'd barged into his life much as they'd done his office.

"Please, come in. My obviously closed door is always open," he drawled from between gritted teeth.

"Well, obviously," Kenan drawled back, a smile curving his mouth. His sharp gaze, identical to Cain's own, lit on Devon. "We heard a ridiculous rumor through the office gossip grapevine that you were in here with a photographer for an engagement photo shoot." He surveyed the room with an exaggerated turn of his head and body. "No photographer, but we do have a possible fiancée." Though his tone remained light and teasing, his gaze narrowed, and his smile hardened around the edges. "But that can't be true. Because surely Achilles and I wouldn't discover you were engaged to be married through the secretary pool? We would be devastated, right, Achilles?"

Achilles propped a shoulder against the wall, crossing his arms over his massive chest. "Devastated," he said, voice dry.

"Don't let the stoic face fool you. Inside, he's broken. As am I. So please clear it up for us, Cain. Is it true that you're getting married and we're the last to know? Like literally, behind the mail room clerk, last to know? And if so, why is it you didn't think it was any of our business? You know, being brothers and all."

"Brothers?" Devon gasped behind him.

He glanced over his shoulder, meeting her wide eyes. And sighed. "Devon, let me introduce you to my half brothers, Kenan Rhodes and Achilles Farrell." *Brothers* still seemed foreign on his tongue. Like a language he hadn't yet mastered. And wasn't sure he wanted to. "Kenan, Achilles, this is Devon Cole...my fiancée." It was a miracle he didn't choke on that title.

"A pleasure to meet you, Devon," Kenan greeted, his expression warming as he extended his hand toward her. Devon shook it, returning the warm gesture and smile.

And it was *not* jealousy that speared through Cain's rib cage at the pretty sight of it. He didn't *do* jealousy. And did *not* covet that warmth or wish it was directed at him.

"Devon." Achilles dipped his head, the mouth surrounded by his thick beard remaining flat. The man could never be called emotive.

"It's nice to meet you both," Devon said. "And I'm sorry about Cain not sharing the news about our engagement with you. I asked him not to tell anyone until we announced it in the paper. Call it being superstitious, but I didn't want to jinx anything." She wrinkled her nose, the gesture adorable. And damn believable even as she lied with a straight face. "He was just indulging me."

"I'm trying to picture an indulgent Cain." Kenan cocked his head and squinted. "I kind of like the look on you, brother."

Across the room, Achilles snorted.

"If you two are finished with the nosy busybodies act, can I have a private moment with Devon, please?" Cain growled, his patience with the two men ending.

Kenan tsked, shaking his head. "We would be eternally grateful if you could do something about his manners while you're at it, Devon. Welcome to the family."

Kenan twisted *family* as if it were some kind of private joke. And maybe it was. To call them his "brothers" was more than a stretch—it neared a tall tale. Still, the asshole pressed a kiss to Devon's cheek and had the audacity to flash a grin at Cain before exiting the office. With a chin lift, Achilles unfolded himself and followed their younger brother out.

"Would it be totally inappropriate for me to start singing 'Papa Was a Rolling Stone' right now?" Devon whispered.

Cain stared at her. Then snorted.

Instead of answering her question, though, he asked the one that had been plaguing him for the past few minutes. "Why did you lie to Kenan and Achilles?"

She shrugged. "I didn't want your brothers' feelings hurt because they believed you didn't tell them about the engagement. And I didn't want you to have to lie to another family member."

Astonishment whipped through him. Was this another trick, another tactic to make her appear less calculating than he knew her to be? It had to be. Otherwise, why did she care if Kenan or Achilles felt slighted by him? Why did it concern her at all?

He searched her face, her eyes for an ulterior motive. And as even as he did so, he couldn't get past how swollen her lips were—and how proud he felt that he was the cause.

"How are—" she faltered, glancing at the door. "You three are…"

"How are three men of different racial backgrounds, who are obviously strangers, brothers?" he finished for her.

She flushed but nodded.

"The miraculous story of the long-lost Farrell heirs was in the papers a couple of weeks ago. You didn't read about it?"

"It's better you find this out about me now instead of later. I honestly couldn't give a damn about business or society gossip. I go online to find out the latest reality TV news and spoilers about my favorite Netflix shows. Everything else is detrimental to my ass."

He arched an eyebrow. "Detrimental to your…ass?"

"Yes." She nodded. "Reading all the crap that's going on right now in the world makes me either sad or angry. And I'm an emotional eater. So, all the chips, ice cream and chocolate go straight to my ass. Therefore, no upsetting internet searching for me."

He stared at her. Blinked. Then fought down the bark of laughter that pressed at his throat. *This* was the woman from the garden. Funny. Candid. Fucking adorable.

Note to self: Stop handing her opportunities to be adorable.

"Achilles and Kenan are my father's illegitimate children," he said, guiding them back to her original question… and away from his memories of those stolen moments in the garden. "I didn't discover their existence until after he died." He told her about the meeting and the terms of his father's will. "So we're forced to stay together for one year to save my family's company."

"I take it back," she whispered. "Your father wasn't a rolling stone. He was an asshole."

Again, the urge to laugh shoved at his throat. "Yes," he agreed. "Yes, he was."

She shook her head, the strands of that thick, gorgeous hair falling over her shoulder. He stared at the brown-and-gold mass. Curiosity had needled him into tugging it free from the bun during the photo shoot. He hadn't expected its heaviness, its softness. Or that it would slide over his skin, between his hands like a caress. What would it feel like against his bare chest...his thighs? Would it stream like a caramel waterfall to her hips, stick to her damp skin while she rode him?

Lust shuddered through him.

He should never have touched her. Kissed her.

That had been a tactical error on his part. One he had to avoid committing again at all costs.

She was a danger that needed blinking neon caution signs.

"Why would he do that? Wait until so late in life to let you know you had brothers out there? Wouldn't you have wanted to know about Achilles and Kenan much earlier?" she asked.

Would he? When Cain was younger, he'd dreamed about having brothers or sisters. Someone who would be in the trenches with him. Maybe he wouldn't have felt so alone or isolated. But as he'd grown up, he'd stopped wishing for that. He wouldn't have wished his existence with Barron on an enemy much less a sibling.

"Knowing about them now or ten years ago wouldn't have changed anything," he said.

Maybe it'd been a blessing that he hadn't been aware of them. They would've been just two more people his father could've used against him. Like his mother.

"Barron had his own reasons for his actions. The least of them being manipulation and power," he added, then immediately cursed himself for revealing too much. No way in hell was he getting into a discussion about his hellish childhood with her.

With anyone.

"You can't mean that," she protested.

"About Barron? I damn well can."

"No." She shook her head. "About your brothers. I wish I had siblings. It would've meant someone who had your back. No matter what. No questions asked. It would've meant not being alone. What I wouldn't give to have that right now," she said softly.

So softly he had to wonder if she'd meant to voice the words aloud.

"Why are you alone, Devon? You might not have siblings, but what about family other than your father? You told me you came from a big family. What about them?"

She blinked. "You remember that?"

"I remember everything," he murmured.

About you. About that day.

He wished he didn't.

"Yes, I do have a large family. Between my father's and mother's sides, I have six aunts and four uncles. And a ton of cousins. I haven't seen them in years. Not since we moved from New Jersey."

Cain frowned. "New Jersey isn't across an ocean. It's not even five hours away. Why?"

Pain flickered in her eyes before her lashes lowered. But he caught the shadows it left.

"Initially, Dad's new firm demanded a lot of his time, so we didn't return to visit often. And then I guess everyone became busy because the phone calls slowed, then stopped, and we just lost touch." She shrugged a shoulder, but he didn't accept or believe the nonchalant gesture. Not for a minute. She missed that big Italian family she'd spoken of so affectionately in the garden. And he suspected there was more to the story than she was admitting.

And he also suspected that "more" started and ended with Gregory Cole.

"Oh God." Her low exclamation refocused his attention on her and not on his darkening thoughts. "That's why you were in the garden the day of the funeral," she breathed, eyes widening. "Your father is who you were damning." Her full lips twisted. "Not only did you lose your father, but you discovered he'd been lying to you for years. No wonder you were furious. I'm so sorry. You should've been saying goodbye, grieving. Not having the rug pulled out from under you."

"You were my saving grace that day," he murmured.

He hadn't intended to let that slip, either. Even if it was the truth.

"Until I wasn't," she said, voice as soft.

"Until you weren't," he agreed. "But I'm still thankful. You reminded me of one very important fact. If it seems too good to be true, then it is," he drawled.

Satisfaction should've filled him at her barely concealed flinch. It didn't. He hadn't stated the obvious to hurt her so much as to drive home that she couldn't be trusted. Those pretty green eyes and that disarming honesty had tricked him once. Now that he'd made the mistake of kissing her, he was even more susceptible to disregarding what he knew about her and her father for another taste.

At this point, when his body was in danger of launching a full-out rebellion, he *needed* her to be the woman capable of deception and blackmail, and not the soft, desirable woman who'd welcomed his mouth and domination.

"I have a meeting I need to prepare for," he said, sliding his hands in his front pockets—and away from temptation.

If his blatant dismissal affected her, she didn't reveal it. Nodding, she crossed the room for the purse she'd deposited on the visitors chair before the photographer arrived. She stood for several seconds, staring at him, lips parted as if words hovered there. But, after a moment, she gave her head a shake and exited the office without glancing backward. The soft snick of the lock reverberated in the room.

And he was glad she wasn't there to witness his flinch.

Eight

I'm in hell.

Cain surveyed the large formal dining room full of people. It reminded him too damn much of his father's funeral. The guest list included business moguls, society darlings, celebrities and even a few professional athletes. Food and alcohol that probably cost more than most people's yearly salary. A beautiful decor including antiques and artwork that had probably netted some interior designer a mint. The laughter and chatter from jeweled, tuxedoed and gowned guests.

Except this time, instead of celebrating a death, they were toasting his engagement.

Same thing, in his opinion.

The only good part about this trip to purgatory was that Gregory Cole had insisted the party be held in his Back Bay townhome instead of the mansion Cain had been forced to reside in for the next year. Any excuse he had to *not* spend time in that mausoleum, he grabbed.

Still, he had to hand it to Gregory. When the man threw a party, he didn't hold back. He'd gone all out to brag about his wealth and prowess to Boston society. Because regardless of what the invitations stated, this occasion wasn't about Cain and Devon. It was all about Gregory Cole. An opportunity to gather the very people he sought to impress in one place. This wasn't an engagement party but the beginning of his campaign to infiltrate their privileged, blue-blooded ranks. And like any good general, the man was a master strategist.

Disgust boiled inside Cain. He hated this. Hated the hypocrisy, the phoniness. And yet, here he stood, right in the midst of it, a hostage because of his loyalty to one person. The person he loved most in this world.

Emelia Farrell.

He scanned the room, and within seconds located his mother, as always, surrounded by a circle of admiring men and women. Though in her midfifties, in Cain's eyes, she hadn't aged a bit from the woman who'd read him bedtime stories when his father wasn't home to forbid her from coddling him. The woman who'd gifted him with his first camera on his twelfth birthday. The woman who'd yelled the loudest and longest when he'd graduated from both high school and college, when his father couldn't be bothered to attend either ceremony because of business trips. Time might've brushed her raven-black hair with touches of gray and grazed the corners of her eyes with lines, but it hadn't stooped the proud lines of her shoulders, hadn't dimmed the brightness of her blue eyes—or the love for him that shone there.

That love had brought her here tonight, to her ex-lover's home. Cain didn't know the details of her affair with Gregory, and he couldn't ask because she wasn't aware he possessed knowledge of it. Still, even if the relationship had ended amicably, Gregory now used it as a weapon against her and Cain. And damned if he would allow his mother to discover her affair with Gregory was the sword held to Cain's throat.

Unbidden, his focus shifted to the woman at his mother's side—his fiancée. Though his mother had met Devon for the first time tonight, she'd immediately taken to her. Even now, with their arms linked at the elbow, they appeared to be close friends instead of strangers who'd met only hours earlier. But how could his mother resist? Devon had assumed her friendly persona for the evening—the one that had snagged his attention. His mother had been enchanted and had told Cain so. Witnessing that delighted smile on her face—and the relief in her eyes—he hadn't possessed the heart to disappoint her by revealing Devon's true nature. How this engagement had more to do with mercenary greed rather than love.

As if sensing his perusal, Devon glanced away from the young man so animatedly talking to her and met Cain's gaze. Damn, those eyes. Capable of gleaming with amusement, then shadowed with sympathy and sadness, then glazing over with passion. Chameleon eyes. Gorgeous eyes. Secretive eyes.

Against his will, his attention dipped to her lush mouth, painted in a bold red that begged to be smeared. It called to him, just as her body did in a dark green, floor-length gown that should've been modest. But the material clinging to the high thrust of her breasts, the indent of her waist and the dramatic flare of her hips transformed the simple style into a billboard for a wet dream.

She was a princess holding court. Accepting all the attention and praise as her due. Regal and untouchable.

All lies.

Especially since he couldn't evict from his mind just how *touchable* she was.

"It's your engagement party, son." Gregory appeared

beside him, clapping Cain on the shoulder. "You should be enjoying yourself instead of standing over here in the corner. Go mingle. After all, these people are here to celebrate you and your bride-to-be."

Cain snorted. At both the man and the admonishment. "These are *your* guests, not mine. And considering I was informed of this little get-together a couple of days ago when the invitations had been mailed out a week earlier, count yourself grateful I'm here at all." He shrugged off the other man's hand on the pretense of lifting his tumbler of Scotch to his mouth. "And don't ever call me son."

Gregory's smile tightened and anger flashed in his eyes. "You're not thinking of causing a scene in my home, are you, Cain? I wouldn't advise it." Tucking his hands into his front pockets, Gregory turned and made a show of surveying the room. "I was delighted that your mother chose to attend. She looks as beautiful as I remember."

Rage barreled through Cain, licking at the restraints binding his control. His vision flickered to crimson, and for a moment, real fear that he would hurt this man flashed through him.

"Listen to me, Cole," Cain growled, waiting for Gregory to swing his smug smile back to him before continuing, "and listen well. Don't comment on my mother. Don't look in her direction. Don't even fucking think about her. You believe you have me by the short hairs with your blackmail scheme, but if you upset her—if I even suspect you hurt her feelings or breathed in her direction—I will raze your world to the ground, and I don't give a damn if I go down in flames with you."

"You're in no position to threaten me," Gregory snapped.

"Threaten you? Oh no, Cole. It's a promise."

The older man glared at him, a muscle ticking along his jaw. "I—"

"There you are, Cain." Kenan strode up to them, Achilles beside him.

The two of them cut a wide path between the thick throng of people, leaving glances in their wake that ranged from admiring to curious to smirks and whispers. This was the first public appearance of the Farrell Bastards with their legitimate brother, after all. Irritation rose within him, swift and bright.

"Smart to position yourself near the bar," Achilles rumbled, stepping past Cain and requesting a beer from the bartender.

"The man might not be much of a talker, but when he does speak, he makes perfect sense," Kenan praised with a grin. He stretched a hand toward Gregory. "Kenan Rhodes. It's nice to meet Cain's future father-in-law."

"Yes," Gregory said, accepting his hand. "I've heard so much about you and your brother. Thank you for coming tonight."

"Of course." Kenan nodded, still smiling. He must've inherited that charm from his birth mother because God knew neither Cain nor Achilles had received it from their father. "Would you mind if we steal Cain from you for a moment?"

"Sure thing." Gregory cupped Cain's shoulder once more and squeezed. "We'll continue our talk later, Cain."

He didn't bother replying and as soon as the man disappeared into the crowd, Kenan snorted. "I just met the man, but he has me wanting to take a dip in a bleach bath." He slid Cain a glance. "No offense."

"None taken." Cain sipped his Scotch. "Believe me."

"Good thing you're marrying his daughter and not him," Achilles added, pushing off the small bar. "Although, I have to wonder if you're really marrying anyone."

Shock whipped through Cain. "What are you talking about?"

"Devon. Your fiancée," Achilles said, his deep voice lowering. "She wasn't wearing a ring during your engagement photo shoot. When a man proposes it's normally with a ring."

Shit. He forced himself not to look in Devon's direction. Or glance down at her bare fingers. He hadn't thought of buying her a ring—it hadn't occurred to him. His gut twisted. Who else had noticed? Were they speculating even now about why Cain Farrell hadn't bought his new fiancée—the woman he was supposed to be hopelessly in love with—an engagement ring?

"I don't think anyone else has noticed. Or at least they aren't gossiping about it," Kenan said.

"At least not within our hearing," Achilles muttered, tipping his bottle up for a sip.

"Anything you'd like to share?" Kenan asked, cocking his head to the side and studying Cain with a narrowed gaze.

The truth shoved at his throat, catching him by surprise. But he remained silent. Old habits died hard. He'd been the keeper of his family's secrets for so many years that he was a professional at not sharing his burdens with others. If he didn't hand over information to people, they couldn't use it against him.

They couldn't pity him.

Kenan sighed. "Listen, Cain, I'm well aware you don't think of us as brothers. And you haven't known us long enough to trust us. But you don't have to trust Achilles and me for us to have your back. Whatever you need us to say or do, just tell us. We don't need to know what's going on or why. Until you're ready to share."

It would've meant someone who had your back. No matter what. No questions asked. It would've meant not being alone.

Devon's wistful words drifted to him.

Kenan was right; he didn't trust them. Given his childhood, he'd learned at too young an age not to have unconditional faith in anyone except his mother. But here stood the two men who shared his DNA and not much else, offering him their loyalty? What had Cain done to earn that?

They were fools to give it.

And yet the words to say so froze on his tongue.

"Thanks," he said. Clearing his throat, he scanned the room for Devon. He spotted his mother but his "fiancée" no longer stood by her side. "Have either of you seen Devon?" he asked, frowning.

"No," Achilles said. "Last I saw, her father pulled her away from your mother to speak with her. That was several minutes ago." He arched an eyebrow. "Why? Is everything okay?"

Cain coerced his lips into a smile. "Of course. If you'll excuse me."

He laid his drink on the bar and went in search of Devon and Gregory. What was so important that Gregory would leave his guests to talk to Devon?

Unease slid between Cain's ribs, lodging in his chest. It couldn't mean anything good.

For him.

"Dad, what's going on? Is everything okay?" Devon frowned as she followed her father into the library.

Not that she was complaining about getting a breather from the party. No, she was thankful for the reprieve. These social events were tedious and painful for her at the best of times. But to be the center of attention? The focus of speculative glances and pseudo whispers? Many of which wondered how *she*, a fat nobody, had managed to snag one of the most eligible bachelors in the city.

Yes. Torture.

Her father, on the other hand, was in his element. Already, the fruits of his scheming labors were coming to pass with the who's who of Boston society. He was a king sitting on his throne. All he'd had to do was blackmail a man and sacrifice his daughter's future to accomplish it.

She studied her father as he strode to the built-in bar on the other side of the library and prepared a drink. She tried not to allow bitterness to swallow her whole. The man who'd taught her how to ride a bike and then tenderly picked her up and wiped her tears after she fell—he couldn't have entirely disappeared. The man her mother had loved still had to exist. And because of those memories and occasional glimpses of that loving, supportive father... Because of her mother and the promise Devon had made to her...she couldn't give up on him. She had to believe the man he'd been wasn't completely *lost*.

"How're you and Cain getting along?" he asked, his back to her.

She frowned. "Fine, I suppose." How did he expect them to get along? Cain was being blackmailed. He viewed her as one of the conspirators. He loathed her.

Even if he kisses like he filed the patent on it.

She mentally shook her head. As if lust had anything to do with affection or love. Donald had taught her that.

"Fine? You'll have to do better than that." He faced her, his drink in hand. "Do you think people haven't noticed that you two seem distant toward one another? This is your engagement party and neither of you appear happy to be here. People talk. Then they'll start to speculate." He swirled the amber alcohol in his glass. "You need to try harder, Devon. After everything I've arranged on your behalf, you need to do better so all of my hard work doesn't go to waste. This relationship might not have been his idea, but if you put in a little more effort, he may forget about that. I need Cain happy. And that is your responsibility."

"Careful, Dad," Devon drawled. "With talk like that,

you're edging close to prostitution. And you're not pimping me out, are you?"

He uttered a sound somewhere between disgust and impatience. "Don't be ridiculous. This is all for you, for the children you'll one day have. So you will never have to endure what your mother and I did—poverty, powerlessness, invisibility. No one will look down on you, and I'm ensuring that. Is it pretty? No. But there's nothing fair about this world we live in. Even Cain understands that."

"I really think you believe that, Dad," she murmured, sadness hollowing out her chest. "But Mom would've been happy living in a Plainfield, New Jersey, duplex surrounded by family. And maybe we didn't live in a Back Bay townhome with money at our disposal, but we were happy. We had love, community and joy. We had each other. I don't care if other people accept me. Money can't buy that acceptance and it definitely can't provide what we had back in Plainfield."

"Spoken like a person who has never known what it is to work their fingers to the bone to provide for their family," he sneered. "But that is in the past. Your mother isn't here, and I'm going to provide for you in the way I see fit. Which brings me to another topic…" He lifted his glass and sipped from it, regarding her from over the rim. "It's come to my attention that Farrell International has a real estate project in the works near TD Garden and North Station. It includes a concert venue, shops, an office tower, hotels, condominiums in a five-hundred-unit, sixty-floor residential tower, as well as transit upgrades to North Station. Farrell is apparently accepting only a handful of investors for the development. I intend to be one of those investors."

She shook her head, shrugging. "I don't know what that has to do with me."

"Everything," he countered. Placing his unfinished drink on the bar behind him, he strode across the room and halted in front of her. "Right now, Cain isn't feeling very…charitable toward me."

Devon snorted. Now wasn't *that* the understatement of the millennium.

"That's where you come in. I need you to convince him to invite me to be an investor on the project."

The crack of laughter escaped her before she could contain it. "You're not serious?" Another incredulous chuckle climbed the back of her throat but then she narrowed her gaze on her father's darkening expression. "You *are* serious," she whispered, stunned. "Dad, that's cra—"

"Thanks to me, you are now engaged to one of the most powerful men in Boston—"

"I didn't ask you to do that for me. I want nothing to do with it," she interrupted.

"Thanks to me, you are the envy of every woman in this house, in this city," he continued, raising his voice and rolling over her protest. "The very least you can do is help me. A project this size would mean millions in profit for not just me but for all of my clients. To be in business with Farrell International would establish my company as one of the wealthiest and most successful boutique investment firms in the country. All you have to do is speak to Cain and use your influence to convince him to let me in on it."

"Influence?" She scoffed, slicing a hand between them. "What influence? He hates me just a little bit less than he hates you. And even if I did have that kind of sway with him, I wouldn't do it. I have no idea what you're holding over him, but isn't it enough that you're forcing him into a marriage he wants no part of? Now you want to trick him into a business deal? No." She shook her head, vehement. "You were just telling me how all of this is for me. This is about you, Dad. All you. And I won't be a part of taking more from Cain."

"Where's your loyalty?" he snarled, crowding closer

and jabbing a finger at her. "You are my daughter. Your first allegiance is to me, not to a man who wouldn't even know you existed if not for my hand pulling the strings. You owe me."

"I owe you?" she repeated on the tail end of a disbelieving chuckle. "And when do I stop paying, Dad? When is my bill wiped clean? When do I no longer need to whore myself out for your ambitions?"

Anger darkened his green eyes to nearly black pools and red mottled his skin. His mouth disappeared into a hard, angry line. He edged closer, looming over her. "Don't you ever talk to me like that—"

"Get the hell away from her."

Devon jolted. The seething fury in that voice had her jerking her head toward the library entrance. Her father stiffened, the corner of his mouth curling as he stepped back and turned to face Cain.

An avenging angel.

The words whispered through her head, and even though she acknowledged the sentiment as fanciful and silly, she couldn't erase it. With his powerful body, starkly beautiful face and an aura of righteous wrath, the only things missing were wings. She shivered. In apprehension? In fear? In…excitement? She didn't care to answer that question.

He stalked forward, and, oh God, part of her wanted to run to him, to burrow against that wide chest.

It was the need that kept her feet firmly rooted.

"This is family business, Cain," her father growled. "Which means it's none of yours."

"You made it my business when you forced your way into my life. When you threatened my mother's reputation. When you made your daughter collateral in a back-alley deal with my father. So no, Cole. Devon is my business."

Devon is my business.

The statement seemed to echo in the sudden stillness of

the room. It reverberated in her ears like a pulse. Pounded in her chest like an anvil. Throbbed low in her belly like an ache. To a person who'd spent the last sixteen years of her life never belonging to anything, anyone or anywhere, that announcement hit her like a drug. One she would be wise to resist.

"This is ridiculous," her father bit out. "I have guests."

Throwing one more glare at her, he stormed out of the library, the door closing with a heavy click. Silence vibrated in the room, so dense, she swore it pressed against her skin. Anger still clung to Cain, but it didn't alarm or frighten her. His outrage was on her behalf, not directed at her.

When was the last time someone had leaped to her defense? Had sought to protect instead of use her? For the second time in as many minutes, she shied away from answers she would regret.

"Has he ever put his hands on you?" Cain ground out, his predator eyes blazing bright.

"No," she whispered. Then clearing her throat, she shook her head for added emphasis. "No, he wouldn't do that. Whatever your opinion of him, he's never been physically abusive."

Being emotionally neglectful was another matter.

"You're not lying to me, are you, Devon?" he pressed, his gaze searching her face. She fought not to squirm under its inspection. "You're not just trying to protect him?"

Irritation surged within her, but something—call it intuition—suppressed the flash of impatience. Beneath the rigid lines of his face and the growl in his voice lurked... worry? No. It was deeper than that. More...visceral. It was darker. Her heart knocked against her sternum as a completely absurd thought crept into her head, twisted her belly.

Had Barron Farrell hurt Cain?

As soon as the thought flickered through her mind, she slapped it down. Impossible. God no. She had no proof of that whatsoever. In an insular ecosystem such as Boston society, surely she would've heard some kind of rumor.

You just don't want to imagine it's possible.

An image of a younger Cain shrinking away from a larger, malevolent figure shot inside her head before she could stop it. Cain in pain, scared, victimized... She clenched her fingers into fists, the sudden, fierce longing to strike out against that figure so strong, so intense, a tremble shivered through her.

But in the next instant, she silently ordered herself to calm down, to get it together. Cain had walked in on an argument between her and her father. Yes, his assumption had been wrong, but objectively she could understand why he'd come to that conclusion. None of that meant he was a victim of abuse himself.

Given her overactive imagination, maybe she needed to start writing fantasy novels.

"No, I'm not covering for him," she finally replied. "Cain, I promise you. I wouldn't lie to you about that."

He stared at her for several more moments before nodding, the movement stiff.

"What were you arguing about?" he demanded.

The truth pushed at her throat, but that loyalty her father accused her of not having shoved back. If she told Cain about her father's request, he would see it as another attempt to manipulate him, to extort him. Gregory held something over Cain, but the billionaire reminded her of a prowling beast, waiting for just the right opening to leap and devour. She refused to be the conduit for that opportunity. Gregory might not value prudence when it came to this man, but she did. And if she had to save her father from himself, then so be it.

But speaking of the something Gregory held over Cain...

She moved toward him even though every primal instinct shouted she should maintain a safe distance. Still, she didn't stop until only inches separated them, and she had to tilt her head back to peer up into his face. His earthy, woodsy scent filled her nose. His heat called out to her, enticed her to share it. Briefly, she closed her eyes, combatting the lure that was *him*.

"You said my father threatened your mother's reputation. What did you mean?" she asked, fairly certain he wouldn't grant her the truth. Since he believed her to be her father's accomplice, he probably assumed she knew and was engaging in a coy game.

He didn't reply, but stared down at her, ice chilling his eyes. She read the "fuck you" there before he uttered it.

But he didn't utter it.

"Your father and my mother had an affair several years ago. My parents' marriage was not a happy one. Since I was old enough to understand what their arguments meant, I knew Barron was unfaithful. When your father arrived at my office to tell me about the affair, I didn't judge her. She just made the mistake of having an affair with the wrong man."

He calls his father by his first name.

The words swirled in her head.

"Apparently, before Barron died, Gregory went to him with evidence of his affair with Mom. Videos, pictures, texts, emails. To keep it from going public, no doubt so he didn't look like a fool who couldn't satisfy his wife," Cain sneered, disgust dripping from his tone, "Barron signed a contract with your father. The terms were simple—Gregory remained quiet about the affair and agreed not to release any of his evidence to the press and my father would hand me over."

Oh God. She splayed her hand over her rapidly pounding heart. There was only one place for this to head. One. And part of her couldn't stand to hear it. The filthy by association part.

"The week after Barron's funeral, your father showed up with his contract, demanding I honor it, or he would ensure every trash tabloid and gossip site received those pictures, videos and texts. I either marry his daughter or sit by and watch my mother's reputation be ripped apart click by click, view by view. So, I agreed."

She gasped—disbelief, repulsion and pain struck her like tiny fists. White noise exploded in her head and bile scorched a path toward her throat. How could her father do that? How could he use Cain's *mother* as a bargaining chip? Would he have been so quick to do the same to her own mother? To his wife? Where did his boundaries lie? Or had greed and ambition obliterated all lines?

She was going to be sick. Her suddenly leaden feet stumbled back. She clutched a hand to her stomach, bending over at the waist.

Out of the corner of her eye, she caught Cain's movement toward her, but she shot out an arm, palm up in the age-old signal of stop. She couldn't bear a touch. Not when she was so fragile. One gentle wisp of air would shatter her.

But he didn't stop. He walked around her, and strong, muscular arms encircled her from behind, steadying her, holding her up when her legs threatened to give out. A rock-hard chest braced her while powerful thighs supported her. All that strength and brawn—for her, and she greedily, shamelessly, took advantage.

By sheer force of will, she swallowed and held off the overwhelming surge of nausea. But the effort left her trembling, shaking.

"I didn't know," she rasped, voice hoarse from the silent sobs that had torn at her throat. "I swear, I didn't know."

No wonder he hated her; in his eyes, she was complicit in the vile threat against his mother. To him, she was the selfish bitch who used any means necessary to marry a man for his connections. He couldn't know she was as much a hostage to her father's schemes as he was—and she couldn't tell him.

But would it even matter? She was the daughter of the man who was blackmailing him. She was stealing his future with a woman he could truly love.

"Easy, sweetheart. Just breathe. Follow me." He bent his head over hers, his mouth brushing her cheek. "In and out. In. And out." He inhaled and exhaled several slow, deep breaths. Without a conscious decision, she followed his lead. In. Out. In. Out. Eventually, her tempo matched his, and she calmed, relaxing back against him.

Only their breathing punctuated the air. Seconds passed into minutes. And at some point, as the back of her head rested against his collarbone, the cyclone of pain, anger and disillusionment segued into another kind of storm. One where she became aware of the carefully leashed power in the arm wrapped around her, just under her breasts.

One where she noticed how his long, hard legs surrounded hers. Where she noted how his chest rose and fell on a slightly faster rhythm, matching the hot blasts of air that grazed Devon's cheek.

Where the steely length of his cock nudged the rise of her behind and small of her back.

Where she fought not to arch and rub against that length. Fought and failed.

Tempting the beast was an act of lunacy. And yet, as his low rumble vibrated in her ear and against her back, she couldn't bring herself to give a damn.

The arm around her tightened and his free hand caressed her shoulder before trailing over her collarbone and then necklacing her throat. She gasped under the weight of that big palm and those long fingers, a thrill spiraling through her at the heaviness of his hold—at the possessiveness. He didn't squeeze, but he didn't have to. Soft pants broke on her lips as the flesh between her legs swelled, moistened, pulsed.

Like prey, she arched her neck, exposing her throat to him. Exposing her vulnerability to him.

Her lashes lifted and her eyes clashed with his sharp wolf's gaze. Unmistakable lust burned bright and the hunger there stoked the needy flames leaping and dancing inside her. And when he leaned his head down, she tipped her head back farther, rising on her tiptoes to meet the carnal beauty of his mouth.

Unlike the kiss during the engagement shoot, this one lacked gentleness. It was fury. Wild. Raw. So wet. A clashing of tongues, teeth and wills. Though she'd surrendered, she was not meek.

With a lick against the roof of his mouth, she dared him to duel with her. With a thrust and slide of her tongue she ordered him to give her more. With a hard suck she showed him she could take all that he dished out. That she *wanted* to take it.

His long fingers splayed higher on her throat, tilting her head to the side so he could dive deeper, claim all of her. She opened wider, offered him…everything.

She lifted an arm, grabbed the nape of his neck even as she arched like a tightly strung bow and rubbed over the thick column of flesh branding her. In answer, his grip tightened a fraction and his hips ground into her, enflaming the hot, grasping need inside her. She whimpered into his mouth, and he swallowed it, exchanging it for a groan.

The arm banding her torso loosened, but before she could object, his hand cupped her breast, molding it, plumping it. The material of her dress proved an inadequate barrier to his bold, questing fingers, and when he pinched her nipple, the electrical current jolted from her breasts to her sex. Her whimper morphed into a cry. But not one of pain.

God no. One of pleasure. So much pleasure. Almost too much. How was that possible? His thumb swept across the tip, circling, then tweaking. And as another bolt of ecstasy ripped through her, she didn't care about the logistics of how and why. Just that he. Didn't. Stop.

"Cain," she gasped against his lips. "Please."

He stiffened behind her, his hands on her, freezing. Silently, a wail of protest screamed in her head, momentarily deafening her. And she wanted to demand—hell, beg—that he continue what he'd started. To not leave her aching. Hurting.

But as if his name on her tongue had shattered their sensual haze, he snatched his arms away, leaving her adrift, confused by the sudden lack of contact. She shuddered, the cool air of the room reaching her now that the furnace of his body no longer surrounded her. In defense—in self-protection—she wrapped her arms around herself.

"That shouldn't have happened," he rumbled from behind her, and the words struck her like an icy blow. She should've expected his regret; she was the enemy, and unlike the engagement photo shoot, there were no witnesses here to convince. Of course, he wouldn't be thrilled about kissing her, touching her. And yet... A wounded throb pounded inside her chest, her stomach.

What was it about her that made it so hard for others to want her? Made it so easy for them to reject her? To leave?

A sob lodged itself in the base of her throat, but she refused it passage. With that kiss, she might have betrayed her attraction to him, but damn if she would hand over her pride, too. If he could be unaffected, so could she.

So *would* she.

Schooling her expression into an aloof mask, she turned to face him.

"A mistake on both our parts," she said, proud how her

voice didn't reflect the pain that still trembled inside her. "We'll both make sure there's not a repeat performance," she added, beating him to the "this can't happen again" speech.

Cain stared at her, and she couldn't keep her gaze from dipping to his swollen, damp mouth. Swollen and damp from her kiss. Despite the hurt pumping through her veins, lust stirred low in her belly. Dammit. She knew not to invest more into a relationship than the other person. That deficit had nearly destroyed her confidence, trampled her pride, battered her heart.

Texans remembered the Alamo. She remembered Donald.

Desire didn't equal affection. Didn't even equal *like*. And as hard as Cain's dick had been when pressed against her, he didn't care for her. Quite the contrary. If he had a choice—if her father granted him the choice—he would want nothing to do with her.

"Is that what that was? A performance?" he asked, and the rough texture of his tone rasped over her skin. "With no audience?"

"You're here, an audience of one. Besides, what else would it be? You're the one who told me to make my supposed love for you believable," she lied. "Consider that a dry run." She smiled, and it felt brittle and stiff. "We should return to the party. Any longer and people will wonder where we are."

But he didn't move. Just continued to study her in a way that threatened to carve away her emotional shield facade by facade, lie by lie.

"Right, we can't allow people to start gossiping about us," he drawled. "But do me one favor." He stepped forward and pressed his hard chest and thighs to hers, and his erection… She locked down the moan that rose within. His erection, still hard, still insistent, prodded her belly. Pride refused to let her shift backward. Refused to let him see how his aroused flesh had need clawing at her.

Before she could ask about the favor, he brushed his thumb across her bottom lip. Once, twice before pushing down on it.

"Don't replace your lipstick. One look at this swollen mouth and people will know I fucked it. That, too, is good for the validity of the performance."

His callous words had a dual effect—they angered her... and they had her sex tightening so hard, she squeezed her thighs against the erotic pull.

He dropped his hand and stepped back, placing distance between them. "After you," he mocked, sweeping an arm toward the library entrance. "We don't want to keep the masses waiting."

She ordered her legs to move, and thankfully, they followed her command. Not glancing at Cain, she strode toward the door, deliberately keeping her pace steady and casual.

Priority number one. Get through this farce of a party.

Priority number one-point-five. Patching up her defenses against Cain. That kiss had shaken them like boulders catapulted against stone barricades.

Because if she didn't, the consequences terrified her.

Not that he would get in.

But what she would let escape.

Her heart.

Nine

Cain pulled into a parking spot in front of the East Boston community center. Frowning, he nabbed his cell from the dashboard console and brought up Devon's text. He glanced at the address, then shifted his gaze to the GPS dash. Yes, it was the correct address.

Shutting off the engine of his Lexus RX 350, he exited the vehicle and surveyed the large red brick building set in the middle of the residential block. A couple of apartment buildings rose behind it and a city park sat across the street. A fenced-in playground, a couple of basketball courts and a paved lot painted blue with hopscotch blocks and a four-square game fanned out from the center. With it being well after dusk, no kids climbed the jungle gym. From the equipment that appeared old but well tended, the care and pride the administrators took in the center was apparent.

Still… Why did Devon ask him to meet her here? Was this a pet project and she intended to hit him up for a donation? At least the avarice would be for a good cause. He couldn't really fault her. When it came to obtaining funds for the charities she supported, his mother had been known to be rather cutthroat as well.

He held up his wrist and peered down at his watch. A little after six. If they were going to be on time for this dinner party her father was hosting—one Cain was attending only because several businessmen he knew were also going to be present—then they had to leave in the next twenty minutes. Which meant her pitch would have to wait for another time.

He approached the entrance to the building and, pulling the door open, stepped into the lobby. A semicircular desk manned by a security guard claimed one corner and a couple of tables cluttered with brochures took up another. A large corkboard took up one wall and artwork that ranged from childlike to more mature drawings covered it. The effect was professional yet welcoming. And warm. He could see only a corridor past the security desk, but the muffled sounds of voices and laughter echoed from that direction. There was happiness here, and safety.

"Can I help you, sir?" the older guard asked as Cain neared the desk.

"Yes, I'm here for Devon Cole. She's expecting me."

A smile brightened his face, as if just the mention of her name brought him pleasure. "Yes." He lifted a sign-in book and set it on the desktop. "You must be Mr. Farrell. Devon let me know you would be stopping by. Please log in your name and the time, and here's your visitor's badge." He slid a laminated card with a silver clip attached toward Cain.

After he finished entering his information and picked up the badge, the guard smiled once more. "She's in classroom number seven. Take this corridor to the end, go up the stairs and it's the last room on the right."

"Thank you." He nodded and started down the hall.

A sliver of anticipation slid through him, and he resented

the hell out of it. But he couldn't deny it. It'd been a couple of weeks since the sham engagement party—and that incendiary kiss in the library. A couple of weeks since his body had been his own. Every night he went to bed, she owned him. Because it was images of her in his mind as he stroked himself.

They'd made several public appearances since then, and each time he had to circle her waist, hold her to his side, pretend to be one half of an adoring couple. It was torture. That probably made him a masochist because every hit of her honey-and-citrus scent, every brush of her hip, every glance at that wicked mouth… Yeah, torture of the sweetest, dirtiest kind.

And yet, he held back. Didn't even try to cross the line they'd crossed that night. Finding her with her father—with Gregory looming over her like the bully Cain knew him to be—had triggered Cain. His memories. Those age-worn but still sensitive feelings of rage, helplessness, fear. Her assurances that Gregory had never physically abused her had mollified the anger, but comforting her, holding her, had transmuted the emotion to a ravenous need that incinerated his control. Burned through him with the speed and destruction of a forest fire.

God, she'd been sweet. And potent. And lethal to his resolve. To his vow never to be under the thumb of another person. To never be *weak*.

Devon might not have known what her father had used as a threat—he believed her about that; her reaction had been too real, too visceral—but lack of knowledge about the details didn't absolve her of responsibility. She was still a willing participant in her father's blackmail. Like he'd told her weeks ago, she could refuse to participate and the scheme would end. But she didn't. And so, giving in to the undeniable desire between them—her hungry mouth and taut nipples hadn't lied about that desire—would be akin to capitulating to manipulation. To once more submit to someone else's control, when he'd promised himself it would never happen again.

He would never be powerless again.

Barron Farrell had taught him early on that love was a convenient excuse to cuff another person's will, to strangle their individual and emotional freedom...to steal their choices.

Cain wanted no part of the promise of pleasure in Devon's eyes or the vulnerability she stirred in him.

The rise of voices behind a closed door dragged him from his thoughts, and he zeroed in on the number above it: 7. He grabbed the knob, and after a brief pause, twisted it and pulled the door open.

Desks that wouldn't have been out of place in a high school were arranged on either side of the classroom and Devon stood in the middle aisle. Neither she nor the kids—ranging from early teens to young adults—noticed him standing just inside the entrance. One half of the room celebrated with high fives and fist bumps while the other side groaned and yelled good-natured gibes.

"Okay, okay," Devon said, pushing her hands down in a "shush" motion. "Team Come At Me Bro, this is your chance to tie the score. Answer this question correctly or Team It's About to Go Down will be ahead by three hundred points." The kids quieted, and she faced the catcalling side. "Ready?" She held up a white card. "For three hundred points in the category of music. What is the name of the most famous left-handed guitarist?"

That's easy, Cain silently scoffed. *Jimi Hendrix.*

But the teens didn't immediately shout out the answer. They huddled together, furiously whispering. Then a young girl wearing a Hobbits Run Middle Earth T-shirt and beautiful dreads leaned in and murmured something to her team with an adamant wave of her hand. The other kids glanced at each other and shrugged.

Turning to Devon, the girl stood and stated loudly, "Jimi Hendrix."

Devon stared at her, letting a dramatic pause fall over the room. "You're correct."

Stunned, Cain found himself smiling and mentally cheering with the team as they broke out in loud victorious shouts and some kind of dancing that looked both jerky and coordinated.

His bark of laughter took both him and the others by surprise. The room fell silent as all eyes swung his way. For the first time in years, a bout of self-consciousness swelled inside him, but he met the thirty or so gazes fixed on him. One thing he remembered from high school—never show weakness. Thankfully, curiosity and surprise filled their stares instead of the calculation and pettiness he recalled from his younger years at the exclusive prep school Barron had insisted his son attend.

"Cain," Devon greeted, and then reached behind her to remove a cell phone from the pocket of her entirely-too-tight-for-his-sanity skinny jeans. Peeking down at the screen, she winced. "I'm sorry, I lost track of time. We were just finishing up here..."

"Uh-uh," a tall, blond boy from the opposing side objected. "We still have two more rounds to go. You can't just quit in the middle of Trivia Titans! This is war! And there's a pizza party at stake!"

Cain smothered a snort at the exaggerated protest and the outrage coloring the kid's declaration of battle.

Devon glanced at him, uncertainty flickering in her eyes. "Could you give me a few minutes to finish up here?"

"Yes." And then, before he could ask himself, "What the hell?" he shrugged out of his suit jacket and laid it across an empty desk. "Which team should I join?"

Shock widened her eyes and parted her pretty lips. With effort, he dragged his inspection from how soft and giving he knew that mouth to be and arrowed in on the team that included the *Lord of the Rings* fan. "Do you mind?" he prompted.

The teens stared at him in disbelief, some of them surveying his white shirt, blue-and-gray-striped tie, black dress pants and shoes. But in the next moment, almost to a person, they broke out in grins. "Hell no!" one boy yelled, waving him over.

"Justin," Devon reprimanded with a frown.

The boy shrugged, offering her a sheepish smile. "My bad, Ms. Cole. I mean, yes, sir. Please do join us." He threw the overdone invitation at Cain, who didn't bother to contain his chuckle.

Cain slid into a desk next to Justin, and a series of objections and boos rose from the other side.

"No fair," a younger teen girl yelled, eyes narrowed behind her bright blue eyeglass frames. "That means you have to play for us, Ms. Cole."

"I can't—"

"No problem, Ms. C," another student rose from Cain's team, her hand outstretched to Devon. "I'll take over the questions. Besides," she curled her lip in a mock sneer directed at the opposing side, "they need all the help they can get."

The noise level in the room rose to deafening as everyone started tossing out smack talk. In a couple of minutes, though, Devon had confiscated a desk across from Cain's adopted team and the trivia battle resumed.

"All right, Team It's About to Go Down. For two hundred points… In the category of sports. Who ran the world's first marathon?"

They answered correctly with Philippides, and the next forty-five minutes passed in a furious and often hilarious blur of questions, answers, cheers, taunts and laughter. As the *Lord of the Rings* fan, whose name he'd learned was DeAndrea, emitted a battle cry that would've made William Wallace envious, Cain realized with more than a little astonishment that he was having fun.

When was the last time he'd just enjoyed himself? When he laughed, relaxed and let go of the weight that had burdened his shoulders since—well, a long damn time.

It felt…good.

He glanced at Devon, who was clustered with her team, preparing for the next question. The kids gathered around her, throwing their arms around her shoulders with affection. They obviously loved her. Trusted her. What did they know that he didn't? This side of her—openly friendly and caring and funny—he hadn't glimpsed it since the garden. Not surprising given their recent history. But she gave that to these kids without reservation.

And Cain wanted it again. Craved it.

As if she sensed his regard, she lifted her head and met his gaze. Emerald eyes lit with humor. Pink flushing her cheekbones. Sensual lips curved in an easy smile. Thick hair that he dreamed of having tangled around him pulled back into a high ponytail.

She was beautiful.

Who was the real Devon Cole? This playful, warm woman? The manipulative, grasping social climber? The hurt daughter, horrified to the point of sickness at her father's actions? The passionate, greedy lover who'd burned in his arms?

"Hey, cut it out!" the girl with the blue glasses shouted, jabbing a finger in his direction. "No sending Ms. Cole the kissy eyes. You're the enemy!"

Devon's face flamed, and Cain grinned at her obvious embarrassment.

"That's her man, he can do whatever he wants," DeAndrea countered. "And all's fair in love and war."

It was official. The girl not only had fantastic taste in fiction, she was now his best friend and ally.

Laughter exploded from the back of the room. At some point, a crowd of kids and adults had crowded in to witness the competition.

Ten minutes later, Trivia Titans ended with Team Come At Me Bro, Cain's team, beating out Team It's About to Go Down by one hundred points. He waited until the cheers and yells had died down before lifting his hands.

"In thanks for letting me join in and for Ms. Cole for inviting me down here, I'm treating everyone to a pizza party. The entire community center."

The kids who hadn't participated in the competition jumped to their feet, adding their shouts to the others. Several more minutes passed before Devon calmed them down and instructed them to meet their parents downstairs or get ready for the center's van to carry them home.

As the kids filed out, they clapped their hands to his in high fives or bumped fists with him. A few hugged him, and his chest tightened at all the signs of acceptance.

When the door closed behind the last child, Devon turned to him, her hands clasped in front of her. The smile she'd worn for the last hour remained, but no longer reached her shuttered gaze. He instantly regretted the loss of that friendly, unguarded grin.

"Thank you for the pizza party, Cain. You didn't have to do that." She shook her head as she set about straightening the desks. "And I don't think you realize what you signed up for. Those kids can *eat*." She chuckled.

"I remember the hollow leg I had at that age. Especially for pizza. But no need to thank me. It's the least I can do for the fun they gave me this evening. It's…been a while," he murmured, crossing the room and helping her rearrange the desks.

"What's 'a while'?" she asked.

He paused, glancing over at her, but she continued with her task, not meeting his eyes. Used to keeping his own council for so long, the words lodged in his throat. But, straightening, he waited until she paused as well and turned, locking gazes with him.

"Longer than I can remember," he murmured.

She studied him, her scrutiny almost uncomfortable.

"I'm sorry for that, Cain," she said, and he restrained his instinctive flinch at the compassion in her voice. "But I'm glad you could find it here. That the kids could give those moments to you."

Not just the kids.

He locked down the words, but he couldn't deny the truth of them.

Turning away from her—and himself—he resumed straightening the desks. But he couldn't suppress his curiosity about her. About this side of her.

"When I walked in here, I expected you to pitch for a donation, not be the host to a trivia throwdown. Most women I know focus their energy on raising funds for an organization or sitting on its board, not getting their hands dirty. What are you doing here, Devon?"

"I work here."

He paused, surprise shooting through him. "Volunteer, you mean?"

A ghost of a smile teased the corner of her mouth before she shook her head. "No, I mean I work here. Draw a paycheck. I'm the youth coordinator for the community center."

Giving her his complete attention, he crossed his arms over his chest and frowned. "Why?"

"Why do I work here? Because this place is important to the community. It provides not only after-school care, but much needed services for children and senior citizens. The center is a safe place—"

"No." He waved his hand through the air. "Why do you need to work here? You can't convince me Gregory doesn't provide for his own daughter."

"I don't need to—well, I take that back. Yes, I do. This is where I belong, where I'm useful and have a purpose. These kids don't just need me, I need them, too. But a paycheck isn't just about money. It's insurance, security and stability. It's independence. I earned this job on my own merit, and no one can take it away from me." A shadow passed over her face, momentarily darkening her eyes. "At least not without a fight."

"What are you saying?" he asked, unease and suspicion crowding into his mind. "Has your father threatened not to support you? To kick you out? To get you fired?"

Gregory Cole had gone to extreme and illegal lengths to obtain an advantageous match for his daughter. He knew the man had no moral compass.

She shrugged a shoulder and gave a short shake of her head before striding over to the large desk in the front of the room. "Everyone's capable of anything under the right circumstance," she tossed out, her voice nonchalant. But the tension transforming her normally graceful movements into stiff ones belied that tone.

What did that mean? Was she referring to her father…or him? Guilt swarmed inside him, buzzing, stinging.

But dammit, they weren't friends. Weren't allies.

The battle lines had been drawn between them when she and her father had extorted him. For the last few weeks, he'd been fighting for autonomy over his professional and personal life. No one had ever accused him of fighting dirty, but when it came to never again being that powerless boy, he would get down in the mud and roll around in it.

Yet, the urge to pull her into his arms, to comfort her, to apologize, lingered like a grimy aftertaste.

"Who are you, Devon?" he murmured, the question out before he realized it had even formed in his head.

But he didn't rescind it.

She stared at him, her expressive eyes unreadable. Then that same small smile, this one containing a touch of wistfulness, teased her mouth before dropping away. "You don't really want to know the answer to that, Cain," she replied softly.

Before he could demand clarification, she pulled open the desk drawer and removed her purse. "My dress is in my office. Just give me twenty minutes to change, and I'll be ready to go."

He nodded, quiet as he followed her from the classroom.

This woman was an enigma. A beautiful, seductive enigma. And while he'd always loved to solve puzzles, she was one he would be better off leaving a mystery.

Ten

Devon glanced at the ornate clock mounted on the foyer wall.

6:28.

Cain should be arriving any moment for another night out—another performance as the loving, happily engaged couple. Cupping her left hand, she brushed her fingertips over the gorgeous four-carat, princess cut diamond ring encircling her finger. Any woman would be delighted to receive it—including her. Not ostentatious, but elegant, with small, flower-shaped emeralds decorating the band and adding a touch of whimsy. Oh yes, it was a dream ring, and she would be a liar if she claimed the sight of it hadn't squeezed her heart.

But in the next moment, a deep sadness had filled her.

Because the ring was a lie.

Another lie in a chain of them that slowly strangled her more and more each day. And each time she slipped it on her finger, the weight of it became heavier and heavier. A constant reminder that she was so enmeshed in this sordid mess that her father had created, she couldn't inhale a breath that didn't contain the acrid, bitter tang of deception.

And ever since Cain had visited the community center two weeks ago and revealed the man who existed beneath the cold, embittered executive, the act had become even harder to perpetrate. The truth had become more difficult to confine.

When he'd asked her who she really was... Her throat had ached with restraining a plea for him to see her. Take a hard look past his preconceptions and really *see* her. The need to inform him that he wasn't the only victim of her father's blackmail clawed at her. But she'd glanced around the empty classroom, envisioned how it'd appeared only minutes earlier, packed with excited kids safe from the dangerous lures of the streets, learning and having a ball.

And she'd remained silent.

Because confessing to Cain would've been for her sake alone. Being quiet was for the teens she loved, the staff who devoted their time and hearts, the community who depended on the center's existence.

So she continued to play her role. Continued to participate in this charade of a romance that at times careened too dangerously close to feeling real.

She wouldn't emerge from this unscathed. And that terrified her almost as much as losing the community center.

Her left hand curled into a fist, the lights from the foyer's chandelier bouncing off the diamond.

Oh yes. Beautiful lies.

The doorbell chimed, snatching her from her morose thoughts. Swiping her damp palms down her thighs, she moved forward and unlocked the door. She didn't need to glance through the video monitor; she expected only one person this evening.

Pulling open the door, she revealed Cain standing on

the other side. His bright gaze met hers before dipping to the black high-waisted cocktail dress with the daring square neckline and roaming down to the stilettos with a delicate ankle strap. When his regard returned to her face, she sucked in a low breath at the heat flickering in those beautiful depths. The same warmth tingled her skin, swirled low in her belly...instigated a sweet, acute ache between her legs.

Her body had no shame when it came to this man.

And he hadn't even touched her.

Yet.

Her body already braced itself for the solicitous presses of his hand to the small of her back, the sensual cupping of the nape of her neck, the possessive curl of his arm around her waist. By the time he returned her home after these little outings, she resembled a noodle—wet and damn near limp with desire.

If she didn't know for a fact that the man despised her, she would accuse him of diabolically torturing her with the sex he exuded like a pheromone.

"You look beautiful," Cain said, the deep inflection a rough caress over her skin.

It wasn't the first time he'd complimented her, but it never failed to leave her flustered and a bit disbelieving. Cain might not possess the reputation of a playboy, but previous to their "engagement," he had been caught by photographers with women on his arm. Women who looked nothing like her. Tall, slender, sophisticated, worldly.

Not short, full-figured, a little naive. Especially when it came to this world he navigated with the precision and skill of a shark piloting through dark, predator-infested waters. She harbored zero doubts that if her father hadn't manipulated and schemed, that meeting in Cain's garden would've been their first and last. He wouldn't have sought her out.

Wouldn't have kissed her as if she had become his air, food and shelter—everything he needed to survive.

More lies.

"Thank you," she murmured, turning and picking up the coat she'd tossed over the chair. Before she could slide into it, Cain stepped forward and gently but firmly took the garment from her. He held it up, and she slipped her arms through the sleeves. "Thanks," she repeated, tying the belt. "I'm ready."

Nodding, he grasped her elbow and steered her out of the house. Minutes later, they pulled away from the curb and joined Back Bay's Saturday night traffic. She stared out the window, lost in her thoughts, but soon realized they were headed in the opposite direction of downtown and the reception for the gallery opening. Her father had issued the invitation as one of his clients owned the art gallery. In other words, he wanted to flaunt his association with Cain like a national flag.

"Cain, unless this is an unusual shortcut, this isn't the way to the reception."

He glanced over at her, his gaze hooded. "We're skipping it."

She blinked. Stared at him. Or his sharp profile since he'd returned his attention to the road. "But…" she stuttered.

Oh, Dad isn't going to like this.

As if he read her mind, Cain stated, "I told your father once before that just because he barks doesn't mean I heel. I've attended several of the other events because they were beneficial to me. Tonight, he intends to prance me around the room like a show pony, and I'm not anyone's stud. Besides," he added, shooting another undecipherable look in her direction. "I made other plans."

She didn't ask what those plans were.

Jesus, his refusal to kowtow to her father shouldn't be

so damn *hot*. No man of her acquaintance had ever dared to defy Gregory Cole. Quite the opposite—they catered to him. Donald had pursued her just to get to her father. But Cain's attitude? She would never have to worry if Gregory's appeal was stronger than hers. Never have to fear his ulterior motives.

Ludicrous given their circumstances, but there was something...freeing in that knowledge. Freeing and just damn *hot*.

By the time she got herself together, Cain arrived at a home—if one could call a stately, historic mansion a home—she recognized.

"Your house?" She tore her gaze from the monolith of old Beacon Hill wealth to throw a confused glance at Cain. But he didn't answer her. He shoved open his car door and rounded the hood to open hers. "Cain?" she pressed, sliding her palm across the one he extended toward her.

"Dinner, Devon," he replied, drawing her from the vehicle and shutting the door behind her. "Trust me."

Oh God no.

She realized the comment had been offhand, but it resounded in her head.

She wasn't that far gone. To trust him would be to make herself vulnerable to him, and that would never happen.

As he guided her past the iron gate and up the walk and front steps, the cold, intimidating grandness of the place struck her again as it had the day of Barron Farrell's funeral. White stone with large bay windows, lit sconces and turrets that reminded her of a castle, the postcolonial mansion overlooked the Public Garden like a silent sentinel.

"I can't believe you grew up here," she breathed. Yes, she sounded like an awed tourist, but so what. It wasn't every day a person encountered something straight out of *Game of Thrones*. "This house is...wow. I heard someone mention—" okay, so it'd been her father "—that it's been in your family for generations."

"Yes, four generations of Farrells have dwelled in these hallowed halls," he said, his voice so flat, so…careful around the obviously mocking words, that she jerked her head from the inspection of the iron flower boxes to study him. Nothing.

That's what greeted her—nothing.

Not a sardonic lift of an eyebrow. Not one of his patented jaded smiles. Not a flicker of emotion as he stood under the mounted glass lamp next to the front door. Just a blank, impenetrable mask. Her stomach twisted with unease. She was missing something here. Something important…

"Over the years, each generation has added to or renovated it. Now it has six bedrooms and bathrooms, four powder rooms, ten fireplaces, an elevator, a rooftop heated pool and garden. There's also a covered patio, three decks, library, media room complete with a home theater, a gym and wine cellar." He rattled off the details and amenities matter-of-factly, impersonally.

"What did you add to it?" she whispered.

He dipped his head, meeting her gaze for the first time since they'd approached the house. "Nothing," he stated, the blunt declaration inviting no questions.

Her heart thudded against her chest, and the same dark sense of dread that had swamped her in the library the night of their engagement party welled up, wrapping its fingers around her throat. Because before Cain turned from her to unlock the front door, she'd caught a bleakness in his eyes. The sight of it stole her breath, sent alarm pounding in her veins.

Something is not right here…

Cain clasped her hand in his and led her into his home and the foyer that could've graced any palace. Marble floor, crystal chandelier, artwork, beautiful but impractical furniture. It was a showplace that testified to the wealth of its owner. And Cain didn't appear fazed by any of it. His lack of reaction—pride, pleasure, admiration—could be attributed to him growing up here and being immune to it.

But she doubted that was the reason.

An older man in a black suit and white shirt appeared seemingly out of thin air. Even though he didn't stand much taller than her five foot four inches, his military posture lent him the height of a giant.

"I'm sorry I wasn't here to open the door, Mr. Farrell," he apologized, holding his arms out for their coats. "I didn't hear the bell."

"Because I didn't ring it, Ben," Cain replied, his tone and gaze warming. "I have a key, and I'm sure you have more important things to do than running to answer a door I'm fully capable of opening myself." He settled a hand between Devon's shoulder blades, and as if her body recognized the claim her mind rebelled against, she shifted closer to him. "Ben, let me introduce you to my fiancée, Devon Cole. Devon, I'd like you to meet Benjamin Dennis. He's been with my family longer than I have. And he's calling me 'Mr. Farrell' just for your benefit. Usually it's something else less flattering with more colorful language," Cain teased with a snort.

"If you say so, sir," Benjamin drawled, and Devon grinned. "It's a pleasure to meet you, Ms. Cole." He inclined his head, draping their coats over an arm. He swept the other toward the long corridor to the right of the grand staircase. "Your guests are in the great room."

Guests? She frowned. Hadn't Cain said they were having dinner? She'd assumed it would be the two of them.

"Thanks, Ben." Gently applying pressure to her shoulder blades, Cain guided her forward. "This way, Devon."

Still confused, she nonetheless slipped into her polite, social mask—the one she donned when placed in the position of having to talk to people she didn't know. The one she wore while silently counting down the seconds before she could escape.

But the moment she stepped into the entrance of the huge room that could double as a small ballroom, that facade crumbled like dry leaves under a boot.

"Zio Marco. Zia Angela," she breathed, her gaze roaming over the beloved faces of her uncle and aunt. She blinked. But no, they still stood there. More lines around their mouths and eyes, a little more gray hair. But here. Still not believing she was seeing their faces after more than six years, she shifted to the others in the room. "Carla. Beth. Manny." Her cousins. And all of her parents' brothers and sisters and their children. Happiness, shock and a fear that if she glanced away from them, they would disappear swirled inside her. It grew and grew, spinning faster and faster until her chest ached, her throat seized and her eyes stung. "I can't believe... What are you doing here?"

"Devon," her aunt Angela said, dark eyes shining with tears as she moved forward, arms outstretched.

Devon almost ran forward, meeting her halfway. Angela drew Devon close, hugging her. The scent of powder and spices embraced her as well, transporting her back to her childhood. She closed her eyes, pressing her cheek to Angela's shoulder, her arms tightening around the woman who looked so much like her mother both joy and grief pulsed inside her veins.

"We've missed you so much. So much." Leaning back, her mother's sister clasped Devon's face between her soft palms and smiled wide. "When your man called and told us you were engaged, then invited us to see you and meet him, how could we not come?"

Cain... Cradling her aunt's hands, she drew them down and whipped around to face Cain, who remained in the entrance. "You arranged all of this? For me?" she whispered.

"Arranged it?" Zio Marco boomed, appearing beside his wife and throwing an arm around her. "He flew all of us in, put us up in a hotel and provided a limo to bring us here. This one must really love you to shell out money like that just to see you smile, eh?"

God, she'd missed her uncle's lack of filter. She grinned, tears tracking down her cheeks even as a sliver of pain slid between her ribs.

This one must really love you to shell out money like that just to see you smile...

She couldn't begin to grasp why Cain had done this for her but love surely hadn't been the motivation. Right now, though, with her aunts, uncles and cousins noisily gathering around her, she didn't care.

"Have you met Cain yet?" she asked. Twisting at the waist, she stretched her arm toward him, palm up. His gaze settled on hers, and she caught the flicker of emotion that appeared then disappeared before she could decipher it. Still, he strode forward, enclosing her hand in his and stepping to her side. "Everyone, this is Cain Farrell, my fiancé and the person who made all this possible." She squeezed his fingers. "Cain, this is...everyone." She laughed, so much joy inside her, it seemed impossible that her body contained it.

Cain greeted her relatives, and never having met a stranger, they pulled him into the fold without reservation or hesitation—which included hugging him, slapping him on the back, grilling him about his sports allegiances and asking if he had any bachelor friends. This from Zia Stella, who had three daughters. Devon chuckled, enjoying Cain's faintly overwhelmed expression.

No, she didn't understand why he'd gone through all the trouble for tonight.

But he'd given her the best gift.

Family.

Eleven

"I can't thank you enough," Devon said to Cain...again. For probably the fifteenth time.

And she would say it fifteen more.

Even though her relatives had left five minutes ago, after a boisterous and prolonged goodbye with promises to get together tomorrow morning before they left for New Jersey, Cain's house still seemed to ring with their voices. "I'll never forget this night. I—" She shook her head, and once more, murmured, "Thank you."

Cain nodded. "You're welcome, Devon." He studied her for a moment, his blue-gray eyes shuttered yet intense. "Would you like a drink? Or I can take you home now."

That invitation shouldn't sound like an offer to sin. Issued from Cain, it most likely wasn't. But that knowledge didn't prevent a hot pulse of desire from playing slip 'n' slide through her veins. It was late; if she possessed an iota of intelligence and self-preservation, she would decline the nightcap and head home. But enough wine had flowed this evening and she still rode high on the delight of being with her family. Both were enough to justify any unwise decisions she made tonight. Besides, it was a drink. She could handle one drink without committing any acts she would regret in the morning.

"Do you have any more of the wine from dinner? The Moscato?" she asked.

"Of course," he said, striding out of the foyer.

She followed him to a smaller, more intimate room than the one they'd been gathered in for most of the evening. A couple of couches, a cozy sitting area with chairs and a low table, a huge fireplace with a stone mantel, and a built-in bar occupied the space. Choosing one of the large armchairs in front of the low-burning flames, she sank down into it as Cain approached her with a wineglass. He lowered to the matching chair across from her, and for the next several moments, they sipped in silence, the muted crackle of wood the only sound.

"You weren't exaggerating when you said you came from a big, loud family," Cain said, peering at her over the rim of his tumbler.

She laughed. "And honestly, I think they went easy on you because they didn't want to scare you off before we get married."

As soon as the words exited her mouth, she mentally winced. *Before we get married* seemed to echo in the room over and over, ratcheting up in volume. God, she hadn't meant to say that. Especially since she still hadn't given up on finding a way out for both of them. How she would accomplish that feat? No clue. She stared down into the depths of her glass as if it held the solution.

"No one mentioned your father. They didn't appear to find it strange that he wasn't there," he added, his scrutiny fixed on her.

Another land mine of a subject. *I don't want to talk about him. Not here and now*, she silently yelled. But Cain had brought up her father, and after all he'd done for her, she couldn't *not* reply.

"I'm not surprised," she admitted softly, shifting her gaze to the fireplace so he couldn't glimpse her shame. "At one time, we were all very close. Even given our family's size, we still managed to be tight. Holidays, birthdays, communions, graduations, hell just because—we spent our days together. The locations might change, but not the people. We were especially close to Uncle Marco and Aunt Angela, my mother's older sister, since they and their family lived on the other side of us in our duplex. But that changed after Mom died. Everything changed," she whispered.

Taking a fortifying drink, she inhaled a deep breath and continued, "I lost Mom, and I lost Dad, too. He used to be such a jokester as well as protective and loving. I couldn't have asked for a better father, a more caring father. But after she died, he became angry, stern and work obsessed. It's like he transferred all the love and grief into building his business. Now I think he worked so hard so he could divorce himself from the life he'd shared with Mom. If he couldn't have her then he would erect an existence that was dramatically different from the one he'd shared with her. He accomplished what he set out to do."

Underneath her joy tonight had lurked a bittersweet sadness. For the memories. For all she'd lost. For the distance she'd allowed to spring between her and her relatives out of a misplaced loyalty to her father. He'd essentially forced her to choose; she'd chosen her remaining living parent.

"The more successful Dad's business became, the more he distanced himself from our family. First, it was moving out of the duplex. Then out of Plainfield. Then out of New Jersey. He cut them out of his life as efficiently and effectively as slicing off a limb. They no longer fit who Gregory Cole had shaped himself into, didn't fit into the world he'd created."

"What about you? He decided to purge his life of them, why did you have to?" Cain demanded, leaning forward and propping his elbows on his thighs, cupping the squat glass in his strong hands. She focused on those hands so she wouldn't catch the condemnation in his eyes.

"I didn't have to," she said, guilt and embarrassment thickening her voice. "Dad only had me. Mom died and he no longer had his brothers, sisters or in-laws, even though, yes, that was by his own decision. It was just us. And..." She swallowed hard, battling the conditioned response to defend her father even when he was indefensible. Inhaling a shuddering breath, she shoved the truth past her suddenly constricted throat. "And I promised my mother on her deathbed that I would look after my dad. And that included not abandoning him even though he'd abandoned his family."

Abandoned me.

"I didn't know your mother, but from how your aunts and uncles spoke about her at dinner, I feel like I'm more familiar with her than I was before tonight. A woman who loved to cook huge meals, so she feeds everyone... A woman whose heart and joy were her child and husband and providing a haven for them... A woman who has been gone for over fifteen years, but who her family still remembers with love and reverence... That woman wouldn't have wanted her daughter to not know the safety and happiness of family. And she didn't intend for you to carry the burden of your father's decisions or make them your own. No child— whether two or eighty-two—should be placed in that ugly and unfair position."

She stared at him, trembling. An automatic objection to his assurance swelled in her but desperation silenced it.

Desperation to grab on to those words and absorb them as truth. Desperation to be freed by them.

Closing her eyes, she willed the stinging to recede. Her fingers tightened around the wineglass, and afraid of shattering it in her grip, she set it on the low table between their chairs.

"Devon, look at me." The low, tender command contained a thread of steel, and she obeyed it. "When I called your aunt, do you know what she said after I told her who I was?" She shook her head, unable to voice anything. In the firelight, his bright gaze softened. "She said she'd been waiting for this phone call. She hadn't known who it would come from or when it would happen, but that she never doubted she would one day have you back. Not once did she give up on you, and there was no bitterness, no resentment. Just pure happiness that she would see you again. Sweetheart," he murmured, "they don't blame you. So stop beating yourself up."

"Why did you do this?" she blurted out. One, because the question had been nagging her all evening. And two, she needed a distraction before she asked him to hold her.

He was the last person she should be asking for comfort.

But in this moment, he was the only one she wanted.

How pathetic did that make her?

"At the community center, you gave me a few moments of happiness. Maybe I wanted to do the same for you. Or…" He glanced at the fireplace, and in its light, she noted the jump of a muscle along the clenched line of his jaw. "This house has never been a…happy one. Maybe I was just being selfish and wanted to steal some of what you have with your family. Even if for a little while."

Images of his cold expression, of the desolation in his eyes as they approached his home earlier flashed in her mind. What had happened here?

Longer than I can remember. That had been his response when she'd asked him how long it'd been since he'd truly enjoyed himself. For someone who possessed wealth, power and a blue blood pedigree, he seemed so isolated...so lonely.

It was wrong. This man who had sent dozens of pizzas to a center full of kids, granting them great memories, should be offered the same selflessness in return. This man who would surrender his own happiness and future to protect his mother from humiliation should be given the same protection. This man who'd reunited her with her family just to bring her joy was deserving of that same joy.

Even if for a little while, as he'd said.

Her pulse pounded under her skin, the blood in her veins suddenly screaming, hot and *alive*. She could do that for him.

Staring at him, at the slight frown that indented his brows, at the thick fringe of lashes that hid the emotion in his beautiful eyes...at the bold, carnal slant of his firm mouth...

She *needed* to do that for him.

Her breath whistled through her lungs, but she still slid to the edge of her chair. Then lower, to her knees.

As if Cain caught her movement out of his peripheral vision, his head jerked around, his wolf's gaze narrowing on her. Surprise glinted in the bright depths. Surprise and hunger. Oh God, so much hunger. Its heat warmed her skin more than the flames from the fireplace, and for a moment, she hesitated.

Would that intensity consume her? Leave her as ash?

Yes.

The answer was immediate and unequivocal.

And it would be her fault. She knew the consequences of playing with fire. She could turn back now before she crawled too far onto this path. She could end this, return to her seat and blame this impulsive decision on the wine...

She shifted forward on her knees—in supplication.

He didn't move except for the flare of his nostrils. Did he scent the desire that threatened to incinerate her? Silly question, but here, with lust an invisible string between them, yanking her closer, she could afford a bit of whimsy. It kept her from focusing on the reality of what she courted—a sexual animal who could easily devour her.

The short, negligible distance between her chair and his seemed to stretch for miles, but she finally reached him. Settling her hands on his knees, she applied pressure, widening his thighs. He allowed it, his muscles bunching then relaxing as he slowly opened for her, straightening when she claimed more space for herself. Only when his legs bracketed either side of her torso did she stop.

And she slid her arms around his waist, pressing her cheek to the wide, solid expanse of his chest.

Cain stiffened, but she didn't loosen her embrace, didn't pull back. Desire continued to throb inside her but even more than she craved his mouth on her, she craved holding him. She needed to offer him the comfort he'd so selflessly given her. And whether he admitted it or not, he needed to be held.

In slow increments, his arms rose. Wrapped around her. Tightened. Gripped.

His big body curled over hers, sheltering her even as he clung to her. With her height—or lack of it—his frame nearly doubled over to hold her close. The position couldn't have been comfortable, but he didn't let go. No, he buried his face in the crook of her neck, his heavy puffs of air bathing her skin. Each beat of her pulse transmitted an insatiable greed through her, but she closed her eyes, focusing on the power of the body surrounding her. On the fresh, earth-and-wood scent filling her nose. She inhaled, already taking him inside her.

An inarticulate groan rumbled up and out of him, and

she felt the vibration before the sound reached her ears. He jerked out of her embrace with an almost painful wrench and glared down at her, face taut over his sharp cheekbones, his mouth a hard, cruel line.

"What do you want from me?" he snapped, chest rising and falling as if he'd just barreled across a great distance.

"What are you willing to give?" she asked, not intimidated by the abrupt switch in his emotions. Not hindered by the soft voice in her head that warned she was turning into one of those people willing to settle for scraps. She shushed that voice. Afraid if she didn't, she would realize it was right.

"Nothing," he growled, his fingers tunneling under the loose knot at the back of her head, tugging on the strands and freeing them. "Everything," he hissed, tone rougher... angrier.

With her or himself? She couldn't tell. And in that second, with his blunt fingertips dragging down her scalp and pleasure sucking her into its depths, she didn't care. Just as long as he didn't let her surface.

"And what are you willing to give me, Devon?" he challenged, trailing a caress from the dip in her collarbone, up the front of her throat, over her chin and to her lips. Leaving fire in its wake. His other hand, twisted in her hair, drew her head back farther, arching her neck tighter as he traced the outline of her mouth. As his finger breached her, sliding over her tongue and then withdrawing to paint her trembling flesh with her own moisture.

"What I can afford to," she whispered, the answer containing a raw honesty she hadn't meant to reveal.

But from the heat blazing in his eyes like a strike of lightning, he coveted it.

"I'll take it," he said then crushed his mouth to hers.

On a ragged moan, she opened for him, welcomed the demanding thrust of his tongue. Eagerly, she returned the hard, rough sucking. He came at her like a starving man and she was his only sustenance. Not gentle, no manners. Just ravenous and desperate. Wild.

She tore away, gulping in a breath, but he didn't allow it. He followed her, his lips covering hers again, almost bruising in their greed. The hand not gripping her hair lowered to her neck, circling the front and mimicking the caress from the library. And just like then, lust flared hotter, brighter. Her nipples beaded under her dress, and she cupped her breasts, squeezed, attempting to alleviate the ache.

"Dammit, that's pretty," Cain praised, lifting his head and staring down at her kneading hands. He palmed her arms and guided her to her feet. Instinctively, Devon grasped for his shoulders, but he cuffed her wrists and returned her hands to her chest. "Don't stop," he ordered, waiting until she resumed her self-ministrations before freeing his grip.

His searing gaze only ratcheted up the clawing need raging through her, not easing it. Whimpering, she rubbed her thumbs over the distended tips, barely aware of him removing her shoes and tugging down her zipper. Air kissed the skin of her back, and she gasped. He drew the sleeves down her arms, her bra swiftly following, and seconds later, she stood half-naked in front of him.

It occurred to her that she should feel some embarrassment being so bared and vulnerable. Especially when her figure resembled nothing close to those of the women she'd seen him with. But, as he stared down at her breasts, the pure lust in those blue-gray eyes banished any doubts or insecurities that would've crept in.

He wanted her.

No matter what had brought them together. No matter how much he might resent this and her later... He wanted her.

And for now, it was enough. Had to be.

For both of them.

"So beautiful," he murmured, stroking up her waist and pausing just under her breasts. Leaning forward, he brushed his lips over her jaw, sweeping another caress just under her ear. "Tell me to touch you, sweetheart. Tell me to give us both what we need."

"Touch me," she whispered. No hesitation. No reservation. "Give us both what we need. And don't hold back."

If tonight was going to be all they had before returning to opposing sides, then she wanted no regrets.

She wanted the everything he'd promised her.

A growl rolled out of him, and his hands rose, claiming her breasts. "I was right." He squeezed her flesh, plumping it, molding it to his palms. Biting her bottom lip to hold back the tiny scream scaling her throat, she settled for sinking her nails into his forearms. And holding on. His gaze lifted from her nipples to her mouth, and then higher to meet her eyes. "You more than fill my hands. I can't number how many times I've woken up, my fist around my dick, picturing it. Wondering if my imagination neared reality. It didn't. Reality is so much better."

Before the shock that he dreamed about her could ebb, his mouth was on her. Tugging, sucking deep, swirling, giving her the barest graze of his teeth. She clutched him—clawed at him—her head thrown back as every swipe of his tongue, every pull on the beaded, overly sensitive tip, echoed in her sex.

This had always been pleasurable in the past, but *God...* He shoved her toward the precarious edge of orgasm, and until this moment, she hadn't known it was possible to come from a man's mouth on her breasts.

No, not a man.

Cain.

His ravenous mouth shifted, and cool air teased her wet flesh as he engulfed the other aching peak. Whimper after whimper escaped her, and she arched higher, harder into him, granting him access to all of her. Wordlessly begging him to take more, give her more.

And he did.

Just as she demanded, he didn't hold back, and the first tight contraction in her sex took her by surprise. She gasped, then cried out, her thighs tightening, hips jerking as pleasure swelled and cracked.

Harsh puffs of air wheezed out of her lungs, and she shook not just with the orgasm that gripped her, but with shock. That had never happened to her. And before she could tamp it down, a thread of despair wormed its way into her head. Sex wouldn't be the same after this. Already he'd redefined the experience, exposing her to things about herself, her body that she hadn't understood. Now Cain would be the yardstick by which she measured every person after him.

And she suspected—feared—no one would measure up.

His rough chuckle tickled her skin as he lifted his head, lips slightly reddened and damp. Lust blazed in his bright eyes. Lust and a glowing satisfaction. "You need another one, don't you, sweetheart?" he damn near purred, his thumbs still whisking back and forth over her nipples, making her shift and twist underneath his tormenting hands. "That just took the edge off."

Helplessly, she nodded. Because, dammit, she still *hurt*.

He pressed a hard, but thoroughly erotic kiss to her mouth, his tongue diving deep and rubbing against hers, obliterating all thought except for the hunger he ignited within her. Each parry and thrust was an explicit promise of what he still had in store for her. She opened wider for him and slid her hands through his hair. Gripping them, she guided his head, tilting it, so she could do her fair share of conquering. His dark groan telegraphed his approval.

One moment, she stood there, devouring his mouth, and in the next, the world upended as Cain wrapped his arms around her, hauled her off her feet and bore her to the thickly carpeted floor. By the time she regained her breath, he'd tugged the dress gathered at her waist down her legs. Black lace panties quickly followed. Only the flames and his searing hot gaze licked over her skin, heating her.

She shivered, and a belated bout of modesty materialized. One hand fluttered restlessly over her chest—which made zero sense considering he'd just had his lips and tongue there—and the other settled on her rounded belly, inching toward the soaked, swollen flesh between her thighs. She was so exposed. So naked. So vulnerable. Emphasized even more by the suit he still wore. He'd shed her of her armor, put every imperfection and insecurity of hers on display. But he remained as guarded, as *safe* as ever.

She didn't like it.

"Take it off," she croaked.

She hadn't planned on issuing that order, and from the stillness of his big frame, he hadn't expected it either. Maybe he didn't appreciate it, if the narrowing of his eyes provided any indication. But she didn't rescind the demand. They needed to be on equal footing tonight. It was all she would accept.

"The suit," she clarified. "Take it off."

He didn't move, and for an instant, panic bubbled within her chest. Had she gone too far? Would he walk away? A man so used to power and being in charge probably didn't take kindly to another person attempting to wrestle control from him. Well, it would hurt, but if he chose to leave, then he did. Tonight was about what they both needed, not just what he needed.

But her worries dissipated as he wrenched his tie from side to side, loosening the knot. The material fluttered to the floor. And his jacket, shirt, socks and shoes followed. At the sight of his wide, powerful chest and shoulders, and his ruthlessly toned arms, she swallowed past a constricted throat. Constricted with the rawest, most primitive need that had ever gripped her.

He was...perfect.

From the jut of his collarbone, to the dusting of dark hair over his pectorals, to the intriguing, dusky dip of his navel, on to the silky line bisecting his corrugated abs that disappeared under the band of his pants.

Sculpted art. Battle-ready warrior.

And for tonight, *mine*.

Oh, she should be terrified at how that one word resonated inside her. Instead, her fingertips itched to trace every beautiful inch of him.

But his hooded stare pinned her in place as his hands fell to the top of his pants. Without removing his gaze from her, he unbuttoned and unzipped his pants, then shoved them down his muscular thighs. She had just enough time to soak in his beauty clothed only in tight black boxer briefs when he pushed those down, too.

And *oh my God...*

Had she thought him stunning before? She'd been mistaken.

Stripped of the layers of civility, the true primal, beautiful animal was revealed. If anything, the cloak of his suits muted the power so evident in his big, naked body. She stared. Couldn't help it. Even that part of him—almost brutish with its wide, flared cap and thick, veined column—was gorgeous. And her mouth watered for a taste. To see if the virility that emanated from him possessed a particular flavor...

She didn't realize she'd shifted to her elbows, prepared to discover the truth for herself, until he knelt between her legs and pressed a palm to her shoulder, gently lowering her back down. A graze of lips over her neck, a kiss to each nipple, a nip of her stomach, a lick of her hip bone... Alarm scaled in her chest as understanding struck her. Belatedly, she scrabbled for his shoulders, but he moved out of her reach.

In her experience, oral sex seemed a chore for men. And in return, it'd never been that much of a pleasurable act because their impatience hindered her from truly enjoying it. The thought of disappointing Cain with her lack of reaction sent a trill of panic through her. Why couldn't they just get to the main event? Him inside her—

Oh...

Cain dragged a long, luxurious lick up the center of her, circling the pulsing nub cresting the top of her sex. Pleasure bolted through her and her hips punched upward, meeting his tongue and lips. A groan ripped free from her, and a full-body shudder worked its way over her.

"God, you taste good," Cain muttered, delivering another hot suck. Another flick. "The only thing I wanted more than this was to be buried so fucking deep inside you. And breathing. Maybe. If I could have this every day—" another soft and brutal lick "—breathing might be optional."

His words whirled in her head, echoed in her chest even as Cain's mouth yanked her under his erotic spell. She tunneled her fingers in his hair, gripping the strands as he feasted on her. His hum vibrated against her flesh, and it hit her that he was *enjoying it*. Enjoying *her.*

He claimed every inch of her with his greedy strokes, licks and swirls. She lost herself in the dark pool of ecstasy, willingly going under with each nibble and lap.

"Cain," she rasped. Hell, pleaded.

In reply, he drew her into his mouth, sucked hard and thrust a finger inside her.

She flew.

She seized, the rapture tearing at her, splintering her. The piercing sound of her cry reverberated in the room, and she couldn't be embarrassed about it. Not when pleasure unlike any she'd known arced through her in jagged waves. She could barely breathe past it, her frame trembling as it ebbed.

Lethargy soaked into her muscles, but then the sight of Cain snatching his jacket close, retrieving his billfold from the inside pocket and removing a small foil packet ignited the simmering heat in her veins, in her flesh.

He stared down at her, bright eyes an almost unholy glow, skin pulled taut over his cheekbones, his glistening mouth hard. With deft movements, he sheathed himself and she lifted her arms, reaching for him. Inviting him. Welcoming him.

His hands flattened on either side of her hips, and he crawled over her, not stopping until his mouth hovered above hers. And when he crashed his lips to hers, his tongue sliding over hers, dueling, making her taste herself on him, she didn't resist. No, she took, took, took.

"Ask me to come in," he growled against her.

She circled her arms around his neck and rolled her desperate, throbbing sex over him. "Please," she whimpered, nipping his chin, his bottom lip and kissing the sting from both of them. "Come inside me. Make the emptiness go away."

No sooner did the plea escape her, than he plunged. Stretching her. Filling her.

Branding her.

Nothing could've prepared her for him. For the strength of him. The power of him. Of this sense of completion.

"Breathe, sweetheart," he grated in her ear. And on a gust, she released the breath she hadn't known she'd been holding, her pulse thumping in her ears. "You okay?" He brushed a kiss over her brow, the bridge of her nose and finally, her mouth. "I won't move until you tell me to."

She shifted beneath him, and *oh God*. "Move," she gasped. Winding her legs around his waist, she undulated beneath him, and another cry broke free. "Move now."

He didn't ask her if she was sure, just took her at her word. Like the reins tethering his control had snapped, he withdrew from her until only the tip stretched her opening. Then buried himself inside her, propelling a scream from her lungs.

"So good," she breathed. "Too good."

"Never," he grunted, his hips grinding against hers, directly over the bundle of nerves where pleasure coiled and pulsed. "It's never too good."

Curling a hand behind her neck, he crushed his mouth to hers, taking her lips even as his steel-hard flesh took her body. He drove into her, riding her, molding her to him so that she fit only him. Craved only him. As she arched beneath him, writhing and bucking, she knew, *knew*, that he'd ruined her for anyone else. No one had ever made her feel as if she were dying and being reborn at the same time.

She dug her fingernails into his taut shoulders, moaning into his mouth. He swallowed the sound and gave her back his own in return. There wasn't any way she could survive this. Not intact. But as he powered into her, hooking a hand under her knee and pushing her leg toward her chest so he could bury himself deeper, she couldn't care.

"Cain." She jerked her head back, pressed it against the floor. "Please."

"Look at me," he growled, pinching her chin and tugging her back down to meet his lust-brightened eyes. "Look at me and let go."

With his dark command and a grind of the base of his cock over her sex, she did. She let go and shattered. Just fragmented into so many pieces it should've scared her. But she felt only the purity of pleasure…and freedom.

She fell into the abyss, and as Cain stiffened and thrust in broken, desperate strokes, she knew neither one of them would be alone.

At least not for tonight.

Twelve

Cain studied the road before him, the white dotted lines blurring under his focus. At one o'clock in the morning, Boston might not have been asleep but little traffic cluttered the streets from Beacon Hill to Back Bay. The drive should take only ten minutes. But with the woman sitting silently beside him in the car and the tension thick, the trip stretched for much longer.

He couldn't decide if he longed for this drive to be over, or to prolong it until he could empty himself of the confusion, remorse, guilt—and *need*—stretching him so thin one move might snap him in two.

Goddammit, he should've never touched her.

Never put his mouth on her.

Never slid dee~~p in~~

both embrac

Been drai

Deve

left h

And yet, as he'd eased out of her, regretting the loss of her snug, quivering sex, he'd been…alive. For the first time in, God, so many years. Blood had sung through his veins as if he'd just returned from battle. He'd been euphoric and yes, at peace.

He'd had sex before. And it'd been pleasurable, fun, even dirty at times. But never had it humbled him. Invigorated him. Twisted him in so many knots he resembled a snarled ball of yarn.

Never had it begun with a hug that nearly broke him so every secret, every fear and longing poured out of the cracks.

But then, he'd never had sex with Devon Cole before.

It couldn't happen again.

Touching the curves that had been driving him crazy from their first meeting and mapping their sweetness with his hands and mouth had been a beautiful mistake. But it'd been a mistake nonetheless.

He'd lowered his guard, made himself vulnerable in a way that was just short of unforgivable. With any other woman, sex would've been a natural, biological release. But Devon was far from "any other woman." She was the daughter of the man who blackmailed him and threatened his mother. She was the daughter complicit in her father's machinations, and even though she hadn't issued the ultimatum, she benefited from Gregory's deceit and schemes.

Cain couldn't forgive or forget that. Only a fool would turn a blind eye to the wolf snarling and snapping at his ___ d though he'd been played for one by Devon in his _____ that error again. Bar- ____ sed his son, _____ hildren—

_____ me,"

Devon said, her low, husky voice like a cannon blast in the silence of the car.

He yanked his attention from the road and glanced at her. But Devon stared out the passenger-side window, giving him a view of the long, thick hair tumbling over her shoulders and back.

"I just have one question for you," she said.

"What is it?" he asked, not denying her assertion that he regretted being with her.

Material rustled, and when he shifted another look in her direction, she'd turned to face him. Shadows danced over her face, casting her in both darkness and the light from the streetlamps. But her careful, composed expression betrayed none of her thoughts.

Resentment ignited inside his chest before he deliberately snuffed it out. A part of him wanted her to appear as agitated and unsettled as he felt.

"You once listed the things I wouldn't receive from you in this…arrangement. Fidelity was one of them. You would have sex with other women, but not with me." She inhaled, and Cain fought the urge to wrap a hand around the nape of her neck, draw her close. He tightened his grip on the steering wheel, the other hand on his thigh curling into a fist. "Tonight," she continued, "was that about you using me to further stick it to my father? Do I need to prepare myself to have this thrown in his face—and mine—at some point? Because if so, I—"

"Let's get one thing straight, sweetheart," he growled, cutting her off. "Your father uses wo—
tle games—I don't. Y—
Devon. You ca—
night was —
had *not*—

A —

so dense with desire it pressed against his skin. His cock twitched against his thigh.

Damn, this was his fault.

He shouldn't have mentioned her coming for him, because now he swore he could feel the phantom spasms of her slick flesh around him. The craving to have it again, to have her surrounding him, burned him.

Hungering for his enemy's daughter only spelled trouble. So no matter how hard his dick throbbed and complained, tonight had been the first and last time.

"I believe you," she murmured.

He shot her a glare. "Then you're a fool," he snapped. Ignoring her sharp intake of breath, he pressed her. "You and I aren't friends. We aren't lovers. Tonight might not have been about your father but that doesn't mean I won't destroy him and fuck the casualties. Even if one of those casualties is you. Don't believe me. Don't trust me. Because I damn sure don't trust you or Gregory."

He thrust his free hand through his hair, grinding his teeth together. *Lie.* The word whistled through his head. His father had been that ruthless. That coldhearted, to allow an innocent to be harmed in the course of business.

All his life, Cain's one goal hadn't been to run Farrell International as its CEO. It had been to be nothing like Barron Farrell.

But she isn't innocent.

Images of her in the garden, at the community center, of her crawling across that floor to hug him flickered across _____ flashes. That Devon contradicted the _____ ing room, who'd stood _____ Gregory's plans. _____ few hours _____ ired the

Once, that knowledge had enraged him, hauling out the emotional baggage of his childhood.

Now, though? Now he was just…*tired*.

"I'm not naive, Cain," she said, turning back to the window. He hated the even tone that betrayed none of the hurt he'd heard in that little gasp. "I trusted you with my body tonight, but nothing else. I'm not a fool now, but I was once upon a time. And thank you for the reminder of what could happen if I forget that."

What the hell are you talking about? Who were you a fool for? What happened to put that hollow note in your voice?

The barrage of questions slammed a path toward his throat, clamoring to emerge and desperate for her answers. But he locked them down. He didn't have the right to ask. But that didn't prevent a dark, ugly emotion with claws from tearing at him.

Jealousy.

He didn't even bother with the pretense of denying its existence. The snarling, green-eyed beast in him wanted, *demanded* she confess this other man's name, the details of what he'd done…if she'd loved him.

Dammit.

He scrubbed a hand down his face, his five-o'clock shadow abrading his palm. He had no claims on her, regardless of the contract his father and Gregory had signed.

He needed distance, space to get himself back in check. Under control. Yes, control was key. Not losing his temper with his father or betraying any of his hurt had become an art form for Cain. After years of practice, not losing it over a woman he'd known for a handful of weeks was child's play.

"Good," he said, guiding his car down her quiet, dark street. "We're in agreement, then. Tonight was a mistake. One we can't repeat."

His life contained enough complications with brothers

he barely knew, a company to run and an inheritance to lock down.

And a mausoleum of a house to return to with only screaming childhood ghosts for company.

No, he didn't need anything else on his plate. Like an inappropriate and inconvenient fascination for a woman with eyes like emeralds, a Mona Lisa face and the curves of a goddess.

"Of course," Devon said. "Business as usual. We both know how good I am at following orders."

The comment referred to how she so easily conformed to her father's dictates, but that's not how his body interpreted it.

Don't stop.

Breathe, sweetheart.

Look at me and let go.

She'd followed those orders so sweetly, too.

Lust rippled through him when he remembered how he'd obeyed hers as well.

Take it off.

Her husky, sensual words echoed in his ears, and he steeled himself against the wave of need that crashed over him. Silently uttering a curse, he jerked the gearshift into Park and damn near bolted out of the car.

Distance and space. Distance and space.

The two words became his mantra as he rounded the car to open her door. But she'd already pushed it open and stepped out, heading for the front steps of the townhome.

"You don't need to walk me to the door," she objected in that cool voice that set his teeth on edge. Even though it was what he needed to keep her in the neat box where he'd placed her.

"I'm walking you to the door, Devon," he ground out, his hand hovering over the small of her back. But after a moment, he lowered it. Better off not tempting fate by touching her at all. Not with their mingled scents still clinging to his skin. "You're not some booty call that's dropped off at the curb."

"I'm not a friend. I'm not a lover. And now I'm not a booty call," she said, fishing her key out of her purse and sliding it into the slot. "I'm beginning to wonder who or what I am." She grabbed the knob and twisted. Even as his mind ordered him to avoid putting his hands on her, he cupped her elbow, halting her.

She didn't turn around, and he didn't force her to. Instead, he edged closer until his chest pressed to her back and his reawakened cock nudged the rise of her ass. He clenched his jaw against the pleasure and pain of the contact. Against the insatiable animal inside him that roared for more.

He lowered his head. "You're a beautiful, unwanted, sexy-as-fuck complication," he growled.

Then he stepped back. Away from temptation. Away from whatever pull she had on his will and his body.

Away from her.

Without looking back, he strode down the steps and the front walk to his car. Once he was inside the safe confines of the vehicle, he glanced at Devon, standing in the doorway. Due to the distance and the shadows, he couldn't decipher every feature of her face, couldn't see her eyes. There was no possible way she could note his regard through the heavily tinted windows, but only when he stared at her, did she walk through the entrance and close the door behind her.

Shutting herself in.

Shutting him out.

Thirteen

Being up at eight o'clock on a Sunday morning should have been considered a punishable offense, but having breakfast with her family before they returned to New Jersey pardoned her crime.

She smiled, excitement and happiness spilling over as she pulled on her jacket and descended the stairs to the foyer. Already, she'd talked to her aunt Angela, and the other woman's steady flow of chatter and laughter had been infectious. Devon had needed to finally tell her aunt that she had to hang up and get dressed or she would be late meeting them at their hotel.

Devon shook her head, her smile faltering. When Zia Angela had informed her of the exact hotel where they were staying, she'd swallowed a surprised gasp. The five-star hotel catered to the wealthiest and most famous, and Cain had arranged for her huge family to stay there like they were royalty. Regardless of how their evening had ended last night after having sex, she was so grateful to him for his treatment of her family.

And no, she preferred not to dwell on that awkward, cold ride home. As soon as the sweat dried on their skin, he'd seemed eager to be rid of her. And his insistence that what had been special to her was nothing but a momentary lapse in judgment—that she was a *beautiful, unwanted, sexy-as-fuck complication*—had scored her deeper than it should have. Deeper than she wanted to admit.

It'd required every bit of acting ability she possessed not to loose her anger, or worse, her tears.

She'd *known*.

God, she'd known that he could inflict damage on her. But she'd convinced herself that she wouldn't lower her guard.

All the good that'd done her.

Pausing on the bottom step, she briefly closed her eyes. She wanted to rail against Cain, to accuse him of using her. But…she couldn't. This—the hollow, gut-punched feeling weighing her down—could, and should, be laid entirely at her feet.

Donald had taught her to believe her eyes, her logic, not her heart. For hours last night, she'd stared up at her ceiling, unable to sleep, silently reprimanding herself for forgetting.

She wouldn't forget again.

"Devon, good. You're awake." Her father drew to a stop at the base of the staircase, his gaze skimming over her short leather jacket, white T-shirt, jeans and ankle boots. "Where are you going so early?"

The "looking like that" remained unsaid but was heard loud and clear.

She considered lying. Confrontation did not top her list of favorite things, especially with her father. But she'd given in to her father once where her family was concerned and lost them for years. Not again.

"I'm headed downtown to meet up with Zia Angela, Zio Marco and the rest of the family for breakfast."

Shock blanked his handsome features. But then anger poured in, mottling his cheeks and thinning his mouth. "Excuse me?"

"I said that I'm—"

"I heard you," he snapped, slicing a hand through the air. "But I don't want to believe it's true. What are *they* doing here in Boston?"

She detested the derision in his voice when referring to his brothers and sisters—his wife's family—as if they were beneath him. All because they were poor, and he now had money and a home in a certain zip code.

"They're here because Cain invited them here, and because I wanted to see them. We all had dinner together last night, and it would've been wonderful if you'd been there, too. They miss you."

"Is that why you two didn't show up at the opening last night? Because you were entertaining them?" His lips twisted into an ugly sneer. "Cain had no business interfering in our family affairs. Your aunts and uncles don't belong here, not in our world. And I thought you understood that, Devon."

"*Our family*, Dad?" Devon shook her head, loosing a short, incredulous laugh. "I understand that I distanced myself from them to please you, even if it hurt me. Even if I missed them with every breath. Besides you, they are my last connection to Mom. They're yours, too, but maybe that's why you cut them out of our lives. Because you don't want to be reminded of Mom. And because you resent them for reminding you of where we came from. Of why all these blue-blooded assholes won't accept us into their inner circle." She stepped down, meeting her father's glare even though that same fear of disappointing him pumped through her veins. "Well, you can continue to deny their existence, but I'm not going to throw away this chance of getting to know them again. And if that upsets you, well…"

She shrugged and started past her father, but he grasped her elbow. "We're not finished with this conversation. But I have more important matters to discuss with you. Come to my study."

He released her and, pivoting sharply on his heel, stalked down the hall.

I don't have time for this.

Pulling her cell phone from her back pocket, she peered down at the screen. If she left in ten minutes, she would just make it to the hotel on time. She glanced at the front door, then huffing out a breath, turned and followed her father. Nine minutes. That's all she would give him.

"Close the door behind you," he ordered as she stepped into the study.

She did as he requested and crossed the room to his desk. "Could we make this quick, Dad? I don't want to be late."

"It will take as long as it takes," he snapped, his fingers drumming impatiently on the desktop. "This takes precedence over your breakfast." He paused, studying her. "Where are you with convincing Cain to invite me to be an investor on his real estate project?"

She stared at him, disbelief and frustration seething inside her. "Really? Are you serious?" she demanded. "I told you I wouldn't bring that up to him, and I didn't. Cain wants nothing to do with you, and there's nothing I could say to convince him otherwise even if I wanted to. Which I don't."

"We discussed this," he persisted, waving off her response as if it were an annoying pest. "You have more influence than you believe. Where's your confidence? And Cain bringing his future father-in-law into his business deals would only bolster the appearance of solidarity and a happy union. *Think*, Devon. Stop being so passive."

Five…four…three… She inhaled a deep breath and forcibly shoved her temper down. Losing it never worked when dealing with her father.

"Cain doesn't care about appearances. He doesn't want—"

"I don't give a damn what he wants," he barked, jabbing a finger into the desk. "I need this, Devon. It's not like he doesn't have other projects. This is any other deal for him, while it means everything to me. To us. To my business."

"Dad," she whispered, dread and foreboding squirming in her stomach. "What are you talking about? What's going on?"

He looked away from her, jaw clenched tight. Several seconds later, he returned his narrowed regard to her, and the anger and—*Oh God*—flicker of fear in his green eyes deepened her unease. "I've made several…unwise investments over the last couple of years, and they've had devastating effects on the firm. Our financial situation is dire. I need a new, reliable project guaranteed to bring in profit for my clients and the company. If I don't…"

Ruin. Bankruptcy. Scandal.

Panic and worry for her father churned inside her. "Oh Dad. I'm so sorry. I had no idea…"

"Now you do," he said, voice clipped. Then he sighed, and for a moment, he looked so tired, so beaten down, that she took a step toward him, needing to hug him, offer some comfort. But his face hardened, and he hiked up his chin, his stare pinning her in place. "You understand now why I need you to persuade him to let me in on this deal. And if you can't convince him, then find some way to obtain the bidding information so I can submit a proposal with a winning bid."

Disgust and horror expelled any sympathy for her father. "You can't mean that, Dad," she rasped. "You can't possibly mean that."

"Devon, you will do this. I'm your father and your first

priority. Your loyalty doesn't belong to a man you've known for weeks, and who would toss you aside in a hot second if not for me forcing him to stay with you. Everything you have right now is because of me. Including that man. Like I told you before, you owe me. Your allegiance. Your duty. Your *life*. All of it, you owe to me."

"And what if the cost is too high?" she demanded, his words splinters that burrowed deep. She didn't need to be reminded of Cain's disdain, his desire to be free of her. Last night had demonstrated that quite clearly. "This isn't about loyalty. This is about your need for more, more, more. More wealth. More status. More connections. More recognition. You've already sunk so low as to use a man's mother to blackmail him into bending to your will. Now you want me to deceive him, spy on him, *steal* from him. What about my integrity? My soul? Because they would be the price I paid if I went through with your plan. And let's be clear. I'm. Not."

"Stop being so dramatic," he sneered and yanked open a drawer, withdrawing a sheet of paper and sliding it across the desk toward her. "Pick it up, read it."

Hesitant, she complied. A list of about twenty names partially covered the sheet. She recognized a few of them as prominent businessmen, but that was it.

"What is this?" she asked, lifting her attention from the paper and meeting her father's gaze.

A smugness curved his lips. That expression could mean nothing good for her.

"That is only a partial list of the donors for your community center, but they are the ones who have donated the most money. It will only take one call from me and a word about how their funds are being mismanaged. All it will require is one person to start withdrawing their money before the others fall like dominoes. And Devon, that person will be me. The center won't continue without the financial support of its benefactors." He nodded toward the paper she now clutched in her hands like a lifeline.

The names on that list comprised the life support for the place she loved. The place that was the heartbeat of its neighborhood.

"It's your choice," her father continued, arrogance and a sickening self-satisfaction reeking from him like a pungent cologne. "Either do this small favor for me and save your family's company and future. Or stand by and watch me dismantle the center dollar by dollar."

She'd asked herself before who her father had become? Now she had the answer.

He was no longer her mother's husband.

He was a cruel stranger who had passed down his DNA.

Without another word to him, she pivoted and exited the study. Escaped him.

But there was no avoiding the sordid choice he'd left her with.

Either she destroyed lives by eliminating employment, classes, services and a haven for children and seniors.

Or she betrayed a man who despised her family and didn't trust her in the first place.

A breath shuddered out of her, and a vise constricted her chest, her ribs and lungs.

By the time this was over, Cain would hate her even more.

Fourteen

"We have the updated plans and numbers on the North Station project. I've emailed them to you. For those dinosaurs who insist on paper copies, I have those, too."

Laughter filled the room as Karina Douglas, Farrell International's chief financial officer, stood at the head of the conference room table and waved toward the pile of manila folders. "I've also forwarded the latest proposals and bids and a projection for the next three years required to finish the construction and leasing."

Cain tapped his inbox on his tablet and located the email. He opened the attachment and in seconds, numbers filled the screen. This project would mean a very healthy profit for not just Farrell but its investors and stockholders. But the information might as well have been written in hieroglyphics. Nothing made sense or snagged his attention for very long.

Not exactly the truth.

There was one person who monopolized his thoughts

and attention. Had thoroughly hijacked his focus so not even work offered an escape. Which was unprecedented. No person or thing had ever interfered with work before. He hadn't allowed it. But since Saturday night—since he'd dropped Devon off at her house with both of them still smelling of sex—he didn't have a choice.

Devon Cole had become his own personal ghost. And she haunted him when he was awake and during the few hours of sleep he managed to snatch.

His fingers tightened around the stylus, and it pressed into his skin. Nearly forty-eight hours had passed since he'd last seen her, and he could still hear her moans in his ears. Still feel the impatient, demanding twist of her body under his. Still smell the perfume of her need. Still taste that perfume on his tongue.

But even more, her sharp gasp as he coldly called her a fool for trusting him rattled in his ears like phantom chains. Her contained expression and shuttered emerald eyes floated across his mind.

Goddamn, he needed an exorcist if he were going to focus or sleep again.

"Cain."

He jerked up his head from his blind study of the report to find the men and women around the table staring at him, including Karina, Achilles and Kenan. He avoided the two men's scrutiny, not just uncomfortable with what he might see in their identical gazes, but with what he might inadvertently reveal to them.

"I'm sorry." He cleared his throat. "I was studying the numbers."

Karina nodded. "I suggested each of us review the proposals and bids then reconvene next week with the top five. And we can narrow it down to three from there."

"Sounds good." Cain tapped the screen and closed the email out. "Is there anything else?" A murmur of noes filled the room, and moments later, the meeting ended, and everyone filed out.

Sighing, Cain followed minutes later. As he headed toward his office, his thoughts again reverted to Devon. What was he going to do? Saturday night, he'd had big intentions of maintaining a safe distance, never crossing that line again. But the past two days had rendered those objectives laughable—and impossible.

He wanted her.

All of the reasons why he should uphold the boundaries he'd placed on this "relationship" remained valid. Now more than ever, since they'd thrown sex into the mix. But that logic took a suicidal leap out the window when up against his memories of that night, the smile of pure joy that had lit her face when she'd seen her family. Or when the brand of her sweet, selfless embrace taunted him with a bone-deep longing he refused to name—was too terrified to name.

No, he couldn't go on much longer like this, he decided, sweeping a glance over his executive assistant's empty chair and desk. He had to make a choice. Either he stick to the facade of a loving fiancé in public and preserve a careful and polite distance in private… Or he surrender to his dark, carnal urges and fuck Devon out of his system.

Pulling open his closed office door, he strode inside, jaw clenched. Only one of those options didn't spell disaster. Only one made sense—

Devon rose from the couch in his sitting area, her emerald eyes slamming into his.

"Cain," she said, her sultry tone soothing the agitation crackling under his skin—and hardening his body to the point of pain. "I'm sorry to show up uninvited, but there was something I needed to speak with you about. Your assistant said I could come in and wait for you…"

She continued speaking, but a dull roar had exploded in

his head. And it pounded in his chest, his gut...his cock. Seeing her in the flesh as if she'd been conjured straight out of his dirty fantasies, wearing a black turtleneck dress that clung to every lush curve, all that gorgeous brown-and-gold hair tumbling around her shoulders and playing hide-and-seek with her beautiful breasts...

His will caved, and he buckled under the weight of his lust.

Dropping his files and tablet to the floor, he stalked across the office. With each step, every warning shed from him like dirt knocked off a boot. By the time he stood in front of her, her green eyes were wide with surprise and simmering with heat.

He was not the CEO of Farrell International. Or a member of one of the oldest, wealthiest families in Boston. He wasn't a son, a brother, not even a bought fiancé.

He was just a man condensed to the basest, most primal parts of himself.

Hunger. Need.

Survival.

Because if he didn't get inside Devon, he would damn sure cease to exist.

Lifting his hands, he cupped her face, tilted it back. His thumbs swept over her high, rounded cheekbones, skimming the tender skin under her amazing eyes.

"Cain," she whispered, her fingers circling his wrists. But she didn't tug him away. Just held on.

His answer was to take. Her mouth. Her gasp. Her breath.

Her.

He molded his lips to hers, dragging his teeth along the soft, damp skin. Smoothing any sting he might've caused with his tongue, then plunging inside her. God, it had been only two days since he'd last savored her, but it might as well have been two weeks, two centuries.

She tasted like sunlight and darkness. Purity and sin.
His salvation, his damnation.

With a growl, he licked and sucked. Thrusted and re-treated. Teased and taunted. Worshipped and consumed.
He couldn't get enough of her. Of the wet tangle and slide
of their tongues. Of her breathy moans and whimpers. Of
the restless tightening and loosening of her hands on him.

"What are you willing to give me, Devon?" he asked
against her mouth, repeating the same question he'd posed
Saturday night.

Her lashes lifted, revealing her passion-glazed eyes. Her
damp lips, already swollen from his kiss, trembled. And the
sign of her vulnerability squeezed both his heart and his
dick. He pressed a soft kiss to her mouth, nipping lightly,
and her ragged inhale rippled over his skin.

"What do you want?" she finally said.

"Everything," he murmured. "I'm a greedy bastard. I
want everything."

Her eyes closed, and once more, the sweetness of her
breath bathed his mouth, and he tasted her kiss. With a sigh
that was part surrender, part need, she loosened her grip
on him and slowly sank to her knees.

Shock and a desperate, tearing hunger ripped through
him, leaving him in aching, conflicted shreds. Aching, be-cause her hands fumbled with the band on his suit pants, re-leasing the tab and lowering the zipper. His flesh throbbed,
damn near begging to be freed and touched, stroked…
swallowed.

Conflicted, because he didn't expect this intimacy from
her. Didn't want her to feel pressured to give it to him.

Even though, goddamn, he craved it. Had dreamed about
just this.

"Devon, sweetheart." He laid one hand over her hand
at his zipper and cradled her cheek with the other. "You
don't have to do this." He swept his thumb over her bottom

lip, already seeing his cock weighing it down in his mind. Shaking his head, he briefly squeezed his eyes closed, his grip on her hands inadvertently tightening. "Let me—"

"I don't have to do anything," she said, sliding her hand out from under his…and gripping him through his boxer briefs. Stroking. A shiver worked its way through his body, his hips bucking into her grasp. He might come from that alone, that delicate little hand on him. "I *want* to. Are you going to let me, Cain?"

Sometimes, Devon appeared so damn innocent. And then there were other times, like now, when she transformed into a siren capable of luring him to crash against her. To come apart for her.

"Yes, I'm going to let you put your pretty mouth on me," he said, slipping both hands into her hair, tunneling through the thick strands of heavy silk. "Undo me, Devon."

She dipped her hand inside his underwear and cradled his hot, thick flesh. He hissed, his body locking up, going rigid. Pleasure pierced him like a scorching knife, cutting through him, laying him open to her eager touch and the excited glitter in those green eyes. With a low hum that he didn't even think she was aware of releasing, she jerked his boxer briefs lower on his hips, fully exposing him to her hands, gaze and *damn*, her mouth.

That beautiful, sinful tease of a mouth parted, slid over him, taking him inside. So wet. So warm. So *good*. She fisted the lower half of him, pumping while she tormented the top half with her lips and tongue.

"Sweetheart," he rasped, his voice the consistency of freshly churned gravel. "Open wider for me. Please." Yes, he was begging and couldn't care.

She did as he asked, and using his grasp on her head, he held her still and drove into her mouth, his hips rocking forward almost of their own accord. Reaching for the back of her throat on the smooth runway of her tongue. A familiar, but totally new sizzle zipped up his spine, then ran back down as his tip nudged that narrow channel. He groaned, gritting his teeth as she became a lightning rod for the pleasure rippling through him like an electrical current.

"No," he growled to himself, jerking free of her. "Inside." Cupping her under her arms, he yanked her to her feet, trying to be gentle, but undoubtedly failing. "I want to come inside you."

In seconds, he had them on the couch, her panties in his back pocket, her straddled over his thighs and a condom rolled down his erection. Air powered out of his lungs in deep, serrated rasps, and he silently ordered himself to slow down, to not hold her so forcefully. To not bruise her with his barely tempered strength and lust.

Maybe it made him a caveman throwback, but he would take pride in marking her soft, golden skin with their passion. So when she looked at her body the next morning, she would know that for these few stolen moments, she belonged to him. Yeah, he wouldn't mind that. But he didn't want to hurt her. He'd rather cut off his hands first.

She shivered above him, her fingernails biting into him through his suit jacket. This might be the hottest encounter he'd experienced since he'd been introduced to screwing at sixteen. Both of them were still fully clothed, only her glistening sex, thick, gorgeous thighs and his dick were exposed. The redolent musk of their passion perfumed the air, their breath punctuating the silence.

"Are you going to take me in?" he murmured, the strain rippling through his muscles.

Please take me in, Devon.

The plea scraped at the back of his throat, but pride locked it away. Pride and fear of saying too much. Revealing too much.

With their gazes locked, she slowly lowered onto him, her flesh parting, quivering, adjusting…accepting.

Only when she was fully seated on him, squeezing him like a gloved fist, did she lean forward, press her lips to his and whisper, "Yes, Cain. I'll take you in."

A swell of murky emotion—light and dark, joy and pain, need and fear—coalesced in his chest, spinning out until it nearly swallowed him along with the teeth-clenching pleasure. Deliberately, he shoved everything down—everything but the pleasure. He let it bend him, consume him, as she slid up his dick, those tiny feminine muscles fluttering around him. He didn't move, handing over full control, but his fingers dented her hips with the effort of not slamming her back down. And goddamn, did she reward him for holding off. She gifted him with an equally slow and torturous glide back down, dragging a long groan—hell, a stone's throw from a whimper—out of him.

"Again, sweetheart," he grunted. "I need more." God, did she give him more.

She rode him.

Fucked him.

Broke him.

Her breathless cries and dirty moans stroked his flesh. But with each roll of her hips, each pulse around him and over him, she shoved him closer and closer to release. He held on like a man hanging on to a crumbling cliff by his fingernails.

"Touch me," Devon croaked against his neck. "Please touch me."

He understood her pained request even as her channel spasmed around him. Reaching between them, he rubbed his thumb once, twice, three times over the stiff button of nerves at the top of her sex. Her body clamped down on him, seizing him in a strangling embrace.

As she came undone, quivering and sucking him impossibly deeper, he gripped her tight, held her aloft and pounded inside her, chasing the perfection that loomed so close. Pleasure arced through him in fire-hot, blazing strikes. They struck his spine, his lower back, the soles of his feet, his dick.

Devon took his thrusts, her arms wrapped around his shoulders, her teeth sinking into the base of his throat. And it was that bite, the erotic sting of it, her marking of him, that sent him cracking wide down the middle. Thank God for the soundproofing of his office, because his hoarse shout rebounded off the walls, echoing in his head.

And even as he let go of his passion, his control, he held on to her.

Fifteen

Devon hovered on the bottom step of the grand staircase that spiraled far above her. The light purple and gray of the day's dying light streamed into the equally grand foyer of the Beacon Hill mansion. Part of her wanted nothing more than to jog back up the steps, head back down the hall to the room she'd just exited and climb back into the big bed with the tangled covers and sheets.

Cain's bed. Cain's sheets.

But they were both responsible for tangling them.

A shaky breath escaped her, and she pressed her palm to her fluttering stomach. Silly, considering all that she'd been doing with him since they left Farrell International hours ago. Heat crawled up her throat and poured into her face when she recalled how she'd fallen to her knees for him, let him fill her mouth and then her body *in his office*.

Again, silly she should be embarrassed given what she'd been allowing him to do to her since—and what she'd done to him in return. But when it came to Cain Farrell, nothing made sense. Not her decisions. Not her logic. Not her lack of control. Not this magnetic, almost *desperate* pull toward him.

She'd gone to Farrell to broach the subject of his real estate deal. Shame slithered through her. Yes, she'd had every intention of lobbying on her father's behalf. And when Cain's assistant had allowed her to wait in his empty office, she'd stared at his desk, so close to skirting around it and searching the massive piece of furniture and his computer for anything regarding the project. Ultimately though, she couldn't sink quite *that* low.

But when Cain stalked into the cavernous room, all thoughts about real estate and her father bolted from her head. Not two nights earlier, she'd vowed not to be vulnerable with Cain again. But it'd been the glimmer of confusion and need in his blue-gray gaze—the same emotions so rife inside her—that had spurred her surrender to him, his kiss, his touch. Even knowing it would lead to only more problems, more mistakes.

And here she stood, in Cain's house, tumbling deeper and deeper into the quagmire that was their "relationship."

"What are you doing down here?" Cain appeared before her, his powerful chest bare, wearing only a black pair of lounging pants that clung to his narrow hips like a jealous lover. "I was going to bring food up to you." His gaze surveyed her from the unruly, freshly sexed hair, over his white dress shirt that she'd slipped on and down to her painted toes. She fidgeted, aware that she'd become *that* woman—the one who wore her man's clothes just to be closer to him, to be surrounded by his scent.

Only Cain wasn't her man. Not truly.

"Are you hungry?"

The simmer of heat brightening his eyes kindled the same embers of desire in her. Beneath the fine cotton, her nipples beaded and the flesh between her legs softened, swelled. She opened her mouth, about to tell him "not for food," when her stomach growled. Loudly.

For the first time, a real, full-fledged smile curved his mouth, the amusement reflected in his gaze. Her breath snagged in her lungs at the beauty of it. She marveled that it was directed at her.

"Come on." He clasped her hand in his and guided her off the last step. "It's not much given my culinary skills, but it should be enough to suppress the rebellion." His chin dipped toward her stomach.

In spite of the flush transforming her face into a fire hazard, she laughed and followed him to the kitchen.

Contrary to his assertion of "not much," the spread of cold cuts, cheeses, bread, vegetables and fruit impressed her. They fixed thick sandwiches and settled at the table in the surprisingly cozy nook to dine.

Surreal. It seemed so surreal that she sat with Cain like any ordinary couple eating homemade deli sandwiches. He asked about her family, and she told him about spending time with them before they left, which led to childhood stories. They laughed together, and *God*, the sound of that low, deep timbre shouldn't cause her belly to bottom out or her heart to seize and beat in triple time.

Oh no.

This didn't bode well for her. At all. But she didn't get up and leave. Instead, she stayed and savored every moment. Hoarding it away.

Later, Cain gathered their dishes and carried them to the sink. On bare feet, she rose from her chair and padded to the huge bay windows that covered the back wall. Though night had fully chased away dusk, soft light from gas lampposts provided a shadowed view of the garden where they'd met weeks ago. Funny how such a serendipitous meeting would lead them here.

Well, that meeting, her father and his damn contract.

Not going to think about him. Not now. Not here.

"It's so beautiful," she murmured, lifting a hand, fingers splayed and hovering over the pristine glass. As if she could reach right through it and touch the carefully tended hedges and flowers.

"It was my mother's," Cain said quietly. She started, not having heard him come up behind her. But his reflection towered over her in the glass mirroring their images. "It was the only change my father allowed her to make to the house that's been in his family for generations. Even now, I don't know why he did. Maybe because it added to the property value," he mused, his voice and the accompanying chuckle bearing a bitter note.

The question that had been nagging her since they'd arrived at his house Saturday night danced on her tongue. And not for the first time. She'd quelled the urge to ask on those previous occasions, but tonight... With the walls they'd both erected to protect themselves a little more nebulous, she risked it.

"Why do you hate this house so much?" she whispered to his reflection.

Silence met her, and inwardly, she winced, regretting the impulse to intrude on his past. Damn her and her curiosity.

"I'm sorry. I shouldn't have—"

"My father abused me when I was younger. This house was my prison and personal hell."

Horror and a wailing grief welled inside her, and she whimpered at the pain. She tried to whirl around, to wrap her arms around him, but two big hands on her shoulders prevented the movement. Cain didn't let her turn around, but kept her facing forward, his chest pressed to her back. She ached to hold him, but this wasn't about her.

However he needed to get through his story, she would respect it.

"Barron was never an affectionate man. He ran our family the same way he did the company—in total control, calculating, manipulative and ruthless. If not for my mother, there wouldn't have been any love or warmth in this house. But he started beating me when I turned seven, and even her love couldn't protect me. He called it 'making a man out of me.' All I understood was there must've been something so defective, so horrible about me that he would backhand me as soon as talk to me. But as bad as the physical abuse was, the emotional and mental violence was worse. Never knowing what awaited me when I came home from school or when he arrived from work. Trying to be perfect, when no matter how hard I tried, I could never achieve it. Suffering from stomachaches and headaches from the stress. Throwing up whenever he summoned me to the library. Because I knew what awaited me there. And nobody could stop him. Nobody could save me," he murmured.

Devon closed her eyes, biting her lip to hold back the tears stinging her eyes. She hated Barron Farrell in this moment. Detested him for hurting his son. For putting that distant note in the voice of the man the boy had become. As if retelling this story pained him so much he had to speak as if it had happened to someone else.

Oh yes. She hated Barron.

"Did he abuse your mother, too?" she whispered.

"Not physically, no. But he cheated and flaunted his infidelities in her face. Belittled her, called her names… I often wondered why he bothered to marry and have children, and the only reason I can come up with is he wanted victims to torture. My mother could've left, could've divorced him. But that would've meant leaving me behind because there was no way Barron would've let her have custody. So she stayed until I was old enough to defend myself. Not long after I graduated college and moved out of this house, she divorced my father, and I never returned here. Until the funeral."

No wonder he'd been in that garden. Having to return to this hellish place… She frowned at their reflections. "Why stay here then? It's obvious to me that you can't stand stepping foot in here."

"Because it's another stipulation of my father's will," he explained. "I have to live here for a year or risk losing Farrell International."

"That bastard," she hissed, fury a living thing inside her. "It wasn't enough that he tortured you as a child, but he's still trying to manipulate you from the grave." She shook her head. "After the year is up, you should turn this place into a home for women and children who are victims of domestic violence. Give them a place to transition between a shelter and being on their own. That would show him from wherever he is now… And just for the record, I don't think he's looking *down* on us," she muttered.

His low laughter rumbled against her back and he rubbed his chin over the top of her head. The casual display of affection had longing for what could never be lodging in her throat. The reminder sent splinters of pain digging beneath her skin. Especially in light of what he'd just revealed.

"I'm sorry for all you suffered, Cain," she said softly, covering the hand on her shoulder, threading their fingers together. "That man has stolen so much from you. Your childhood. Your innocence. Your brothers. And you didn't deserve any of that. I can't imagine…" She shook her head, her grasp on him tightening. "The man you've become now is a testimony to the character and strength your father had no hope of ever possessing. Then, after spending years choiceless and powerless, my father comes along and tries to strip both from you again. I'm so sorry," she rasped, now fully comprehending why Cain hated her father—and her—so much. He'd survived his horror of a childhood, claimed his power and control, and then they came along to remind him of the hell he'd endured.

Spinning around, she faced him, forced herself to meet the scalpel-like gaze that seemed to peer to the very soul of her.

"I have something to tell you."

Her father had warned her not to reveal the truth to Cain, but given what he'd just confessed, there was no way she could continue deceiving him. She owed him the truth.

"You asked me why I didn't walk away from this deal between our fathers." His eyes narrowed slightly, but she inhaled a deep breath and continued before losing her nerve. "He threatened the community center. If I didn't go through with the engagement and marriage, he wouldn't just have me fired, but would revoke his financial support and convince other much needed donors to do the same. I didn't care so much about my job, but too many other people depend on the center. I couldn't tell you before now because Dad…" She trailed off, shrugged. "Anyway, I thought you should know—"

He cupped her face, cutting off the flow of words. His mouth slanted over hers, voracious and demanding. With a moan, she tilted her head back, opening wider for the erotic onslaught, circling her arms around him and clutching his back for purchase.

His hands fell away from her cheeks, and bending his knees, he grasped the backs of her thighs and hiked her high in the air. Instinctively, she wrapped her legs around his waist, shifting her arms to his neck. And when he laid her out on the kitchen table like a meal he couldn't wait to devour, she surrendered to his passion. To the need that his kiss had ignited in her.

But even as he removed his shirt from her and drew her

nipple into his mouth, she couldn't silence the voice that whispered Cain would never be able to see past her father's sins to love her.

Which presented one hell of a problem.

Because she'd fallen in love with him.

Sixteen

"Cain," Ben called from the doorway of the study.

Cain glanced up from gathering files to bring to the office. The office he was late going in to. The minutes ticked closer and closer to ten, and he had an eleven-thirty meeting. Usually, he arrived at Farrell before anyone else except the security guards, but not this morning. And he couldn't complain. Not when the reason for him being late had just slipped from his bed a few hours earlier.

A smile tugged at his mouth as heat slid through him. There'd been a time when he would've never allowed a woman to interfere with his business life. But with Devon? The woman had thrown him curveballs from the moment they met. And he couldn't regret running a little late if it meant waking up curled around her curvy little body, her scent in his nose and his sheets.

Especially considering her confession the night before.

It shouldn't have surprised him that Gregory Cole would blackmail his own daughter, but it had. The man had no lows to which he wouldn't sink. And though hearing her admission sickened Cain, it'd also hauled a huge weight off his chest. Until it lifted, he hadn't realized just how much her supposed complicity with her father had eaten at him. The relief and emotional intensity from unloading his own past on her had triggered a lust that he'd worked out on the kitchen table. Another unprecedented event for him.

A contradiction of emotions had warred within him as he'd dropped her off at her home that morning. An almost overwhelming need to call her back, to stay another day in bed, locked away from the demands of the world. And a sense of…fear.

Because at some point, Devon had infiltrated his carefully constructed guard and become important.

And yeah, that was terrifying.

He still couldn't fully trust her.

Maybe it was because of all he'd suffered as a child or who her father was, but he had a difficult time letting anyone close. Her. Kenan and Achilles. Even his mother, to a degree. Yet, none of them threatened his cocoon of self-preservation, his equilibrium, his control.

Not like Devon.

"Cain," Ben said again.

He shook his head, shooting his butler an apologetic smile. "I'm sorry, Ben. Yes?"

"There's a Gregory Cole here. He said you would see him even though he showed up uninvited."

That fast, anger kindled. Damn, the balls on this man. "Send him in."

Ben nodded and ducked out. Moments later, Gregory strode in, and it required every bit of Cain's control to remain behind the desk. His father and Gregory were two of a kind, and just being in the same room had Cain itching to take another shower. After he slammed him against the wall.

"What are you doing here, Cole?" Cain asked, voice cold and impatient. "Showing up where you're not wanted or invited is becoming a bad habit for you."

The man's smile remained in place although his green eyes glinted with irritation. "Considering we're soon to be family, we shouldn't stand on formality," Gregory said. He gestured to one of the chairs in front of Cain's desk. "May I sit?"

"No," Cain clipped out. "I'm headed into the office. So whatever you came here to say, you need to make it quick."

"Fine." Gregory tugged at his cuff, the movement stiff. "I heard about the North Station project Farrell International is heading. I want in as an investor."

Cain blinked. Stared at the other man. Then barked out a disbelieving laugh. "You're joking." When Gregory's mouth hardened, his shoulders going rigid underneath his flawlessly tailored jacket, Cain laughed again. "You're not joking." He shook his head. "I can't trust you, but you think I would do business with you? Ask my partners to trust you?"

"My firm is above reproach—"

"No," Cain interrupted, voice flat. "And if you still don't understand that. Hell no. Now—" he stuffed folders into his leather case "—if that's all you came over here for…"

"I didn't want to go here, but if Devon had convinced you as I asked her to, then this wouldn't be necessary." Gregory tsked, mock regret coloring his voice.

Unease crept into Cain's chest, clenching his gut.

If Devon had convinced him as he'd asked?

"What are you talking about?"

"If Devon had used her influence, then I wouldn't have to once more use the…information I have to convince you to let me in on this project. But here we are." Gregory spread his hands wide, palms up. "Now, I can come to your office later to talk details."

Rage, fueled by betrayal, rushed swift and hot through

him. Rage at Gregory extorting him again. Proving that Cain would never be out from under this man's thumb. Cain would forever be at his mercy as long as he possessed that inflammatory material on his mother. And Devon… She'd known all along about her father's intentions to infiltrate this project. And she'd said *nothing*. All the time they'd spent together, she could've but hadn't. The sting of that betrayal burrowed deep, past skin and bone to the part of him he'd vowed no one would ever hurt again.

Giving in again wasn't an option. He'd already done it once, and it landed him here—a fish caught on a never-ending hook. But, dammit. How could he get out of this? What was his next move?

His mind raced with a possible solution. Anything that would free him from this man and his deceitful daughter. One thing he treasured above all was loyalty. And feeling safe with a person. She'd betrayed both. Maybe he didn't have a way of escape now, but by God, he would find one.

"So what's your decision, Cain?" Gregory pressed. The smug smile on his face telegraphed his confidence that he'd won Cain's cooperation.

Well, he could go screw himself.

"The answer is not a chance in hell," he ground out, glaring at Gregory. Anger, pain and disillusionment poisoned his blood. "It isn't enough to force your daughter on me. Now you want to force your way into my family business as well."

"I certainly have no intention of being forced on anyone."

Pain blazed a white-hot path through her, and for a moment, she could barely breathe past it. But she forced her feet forward, entering Cain's study and approaching her father and the man she'd just admitted to loving the night before.

The man who had just made it infinitely clear that he wanted nothing to do with her.

Oh God, that hurt.

Forcing a calm to her expression that was a complete lie, she stopped in front of Cain's desk and dropped the thick manila folder in her hand on top.

"Devon," her father snapped. "What are you doing here?"

"Setting everything right," she replied. "I hate to break it to you, Dad, but the engagement—if you could ever really call it that—is done. I'm calling it off."

"What?" he demanded, stalking to her side. "What are you talking about, girl?"

She didn't reply to her father, nor did she remove her gaze from Cain's. His eyes simmered with anger, and her heart constricted, pain flaring in her chest. She'd overheard his conversation with her father. Knew what he thought. Even after last night. He still believed her capable of betraying him. She would never be trustworthy in his eyes. Would always be the burden he'd just called her.

Well, she was no one's burden, no one's liability.

Not anymore.

"Take it," she whispered, nudging it closer with a fingertip. "You're free. And so am I."

"Devon." Her father gripped her arm and turned her to face him. Crimson slashed across his cheekbones, fury and worry warring for dominance in his eyes. "What did you do?"

"What I should've done when you first started all of this, Dad. After you left for work this morning, I opened your safe," she murmured, regret a heavy weight on her shoulders. "It didn't take me long to figure out the combination." She huffed out a humorless laugh. "Mom's birthday. Seems almost sacrilegious to use anything about her in relation to what you've done. But I found everything you had on

Cain's mother. It's in that file." She waved a hand toward Cain's desk. "I have to be honest. I didn't expect either of you to be here. I intended to just leave this here for you, Cain, and talk to you later, Dad. But since you both are, we can get this over with now. Two birds with one stone, and all that. It's done. This is all finished."

"How could you?" Gregory yelled, dropping his hand and stepping away from her as if she disgusted him. "I'm your father, and you betray me like this? For a man who doesn't even want anything to do with you?"

She took that truthful jab, absorbed it and pushed on. "You betrayed me first," she shot back, straightening her shoulders and hiking her chin. "I've been nothing but a puppet to you. A pawn to move around on your chessboard. I'm through, Dad. I'm your daughter. And it's all I've wanted to be for a very, very long time. But if you can't be my father—the father who loved and accepted me, who thought I was perfect even when I clearly wasn't, who thought the sun rose and fell on me simply because he loved me—then we can't have a relationship anymore. I'll love you from a distance rather than be involved in a toxicity that drains me of my self-worth and confidence."

"You're no daughter of mine," her father stated, the ice in his voice piercing her clean through, and then he pivoted on his heel and stormed out.

She absorbed that verbal blow, too.

"Devon," Cain said, and she returned her attention to him, holding up a hand, palm out.

"No. Both you and my father have said more than enough," she said, referring to the conversation she overheard. "For too long, I've passively allowed myself to go along with the men in my life. To be toyed with and maneuvered like a plaything. I'm done. There was a time I loved a man who didn't love me in return, who used me. You might not want an 'in' like Donald did, but I won't be your surrogate for venting your anger. I've never betrayed you. Never hurt you. I've only…"

Loved you.

But she held back those words. No, he couldn't have that from her. Her heart might be shattering because of how much he filled it to breaking, but when she walked out of here, it would be with her pride. He couldn't have that either.

"I'm through paying for someone else's sins. I've been paying the price with my father for my mother dying and leaving him. I've paid the price for being too blind to see when a man wanted my father's favor more than he wanted me. And with you, I'm paying for being his daughter. You've never seen me as more than that, Cain. And initially, I couldn't blame you. But after getting to know me… After spending time with me… After being in me…" Her voice cracked on the reminder of how tender and loving he'd been with her, and how it'd all been a lie. "You once asked me who I really was. I hoped you would come to see that, know me for myself. But you never will. I will always be a reminder of the man who blackmailed you and threatened your mother. I'm so much more than that. And I'm tired of trying to prove it to you."

"Devon," Cain murmured, and for the first time his gaze softened, losing the edge that had been there since she'd intruded into the study. "I know who you are."

"Too late," she whispered, loving him and resenting him for saying that to her now. "I don't believe you. I saw your face, your eyes when I walked in here. You thought I had sided with my father. The truth is he did ask me to approach you about that deal. He even instructed me to steal the info on it. But I couldn't do that to you. And had I known he would attempt to blackmail you again, I would've told you about his desire to be in on the project. That's my mistake— a mistake. The truth is, Cain, you can never trust me."

He didn't contradict her, which proved her wrong. She *could* hurt worse.

"I've been down this road before, Cain. I'll put it in terms you might understand better. I've invested all of myself into a man I loved who couldn't give me the same in return. I'd rather be alone, giving one hundred percent to myself, than receiving fifty from someone else. I'm worth one hundred. I deserve it."

She stared at him for a moment longer, soaked in every feature of his beautiful, hard face because it might be the last time. Then she turned and left.

Without looking back.

Seventeen

A hard rap reverberated on the study door, but before he could growl for Ben to go away, the door swung open. Kenan and Achilles strode in.

Dammit.

Cain ground his teeth together and he leaned back in his office chair, not uttering a word as the two men approached the desk. It'd been three days since he'd been to the office—three days since his confrontation with Gregory Cole and Devon.

Devon.

Jesus, just the echo of her name in his head had him wanting to reach for the bottle of Scotch. Drinking himself into oblivion had temporarily helped him forget the dagger-sharp agony Devon's words had sliced into him. But he could only down so much liquor. And after he'd crawled into the shower and dressed the next morning, he'd locked himself in the study, replacing Scotch with work. He could've gone in to the office—it would've made sense to escape the scene of the crime, so to speak. Call it punishment, but he remained in here, where the echoes of her remained to torment him, castigate him for the wrongs he'd committed.

I've been down this road before, Cain... I've invested all of myself into a man I loved who couldn't give me the same in return.

He briefly squeezed his eyes shut, but the action couldn't purge the impassioned statement from his head. He'd been analyzing it over and over like there was a puzzle buried in those words. She'd obviously been hurt before but could she possibly love...?

He shook his head. No, she didn't. And there was no point in even considering it.

"So this is where you've been hiding yourself," Kenan said, dropping into one of the visitors chairs in front of his desk. Achilles took up his post across from them, propping a shoulder against the wall. "We were trying to be patient and give you time to get over your Heathcliff impersonation, but apparently, you need a kick in the ass."

Cain snorted. "Heathcliff?"

"What?" Kenan shrugged. "I read."

"You look like shit," Achilles rumbled, and the blunt assessment had Cain's spine snapping straight.

"I didn't ask either of you for your opinion or to come over here. What do you want? Shouldn't you be at work?" he growled.

Kenan arched an eyebrow. "Shouldn't you? I thought you'd be too worried to leave the bastard Farrells at the office without your careful supervision." He tsked. "Falling down on the job, Cain."

"Are you trying to piss me off? Because it's working," Cain said, not bothering to keep the menace out of his voice.

"Good," Achilles grunted. "Then maybe you can get that stick out of your ass about every-fucking-thing and stop treating us like the enemy. We want to be here as much as you want us here."

"I doubt that," Cain snapped. "You two think you're doing me a favor by staying here, because you have to give up a year of your life? Try thirty-two. Thirty-two years of hell living, working with and suffering at the hands of a cold, manipulative, vicious bastard. Yes, I want you here. Would've begged you to stay here because everything I endured with that man had to mean something."

The words exploded from him in an ugly, bitter torrent that he couldn't stop. Kenan stared at him, and Achilles slowly pushed away from the wall, straightening.

"What does that mean, Cain?" Achilles growled.

Unlike the previous times, the truth burned a trail up his throat, and he didn't hold it back. Couldn't. Didn't want to. Not anymore.

He told them everything—about his childhood with their father, the abuse, even about Gregory Cole's blackmail and his relationship with Devon. Through it all, Kenan and Achilles remained silent, not asking questions, just allowing Cain to purge his soul in a way he hadn't even done with Devon. When he finished, his breath grated against his throat, and the labored sound echoed in the quiet room.

Achilles moved toward him in his oddly graceful gait, and in moments, he'd pulled Cain into his arms, holding him tight. It should've been weird, being embraced by this giant, but no. It was…family. Tears burned his eyes as the burden of anger and bitterness that he'd borne since the reading of that damn will crumbled and fell. And for the first time since they all met in this house, he could call this man brother.

"I'm sorry, Cain," Achilles muttered in his ear. "I'm sorry you had to suffer that shit. None of us should."

The curious choice of words struck Cain, and he suspected that maybe his younger brother could more than sympathize with him about being on the end of an abusive person.

Achilles neither confirmed nor denied anything, but released Cain with a squeeze of his shoulder.

"Now I want to dig the bastard up, kill him and then bury him all over again," Kenan spat, standing in front of the desk. He shook his head, his blue-gray eyes shadowed. "I'm sorry, Cain. About everything." A muscle ticked along his jaw, and his mouth hardened. "I knew something was off about Gregory Cole. And I'm not going to lie, I had my suspicions about the relationship with Devon. But you only need to be around her for five minutes to realize she's not like her father. She proved that by going against him to give you the material on your mother." His voice lowered but didn't lose the adamant edge. "I know we haven't been in each other's lives for very long, but you are my brother. And so I'm going to tell you this—you fucked up by letting her walk away."

"I didn't *let* her walk away," Cain insisted. "And she was right about one thing. I don't know if I could trust her. I don't know…" How to explain that his greatest fear wasn't losing the company. It wasn't even leaving his mother exposed to Gregory's extortion.

It was letting someone in, loving them, and being hurt by them.

It was opening his heart and being deemed unworthy… unlovable. That fear had kept him from committing to anyone or anything except his job. Because the work, the company, he could control. Other people? Their hearts? Hell, his own heart? No.

"If you can't trust her, then who?" Achilles insisted. "I get it, Cain." In his eyes, identical to Cain's, he again saw the shadows that deepened his suspicion about his brother's past. "But you deserve happiness if any of us do. And she's it for you. I don't care how this started, we saw how she looked at you…and how you looked at her. Don't continue letting your father control and manipulate you from the grave."

That man has stolen so much from you. Your childhood. Your innocence. Your brothers.

Achilles, Kenan, Devon… They were right. Barron had stolen so much more than his childhood. He'd robbed Cain of his ability to believe in the innate goodness in people. If the man who was supposed to love and protect him had hurt him so deeply, had destroyed his trust, how could he have faith in, depend on, others?

He couldn't. He could only trust himself.

But not with Devon.

From that first meeting in his mother's garden, she'd shown him compassion, kindness, humor, given him comfort. Him, a stranger to her at the time.

He'd asked who she really was. The shy, funny woman from the garden? The loyal daughter? The gentle, loving youth coordinator? The passionate lover?

His answer: all of them.

And he loved each one.

God, did he love her.

Maybe he had from the moment she admitted to wondering about the color of his eyes. Or when she'd called out everyone in that god-awful party for being ghoulish when he'd needed comfort.

The exact second didn't matter. What did was that he'd allowed her to leave him without any intention of brightening his life again.

"I fucked up," he whispered.

"Yeah, you did," Achilles agreed, nodding.

"But luckily you have something on your side now that you didn't before," Kenan announced.

Cain frowned. "What?"

Kenan spread his arms wide. "Me," he scoffed.

Achilles snorted, and Cain laughed. An honest-to-God, full-belly laugh from a place that had been locked up tight for so long.

He felt good. He felt…free.

He had his brothers.

Now he had to go find the woman he loved and convince her to give him another chance.

He had nothing to lose, and the world to gain.

Because Devon was his world.

Eighteen

Devon sighed as she entered the lobby of the community center. A fatigued but good sigh. It'd been a long day, but she loved those. Especially now. They tired her out, didn't leave her time to think. And by the time she arrived home—home now being her apartment in Charlestown—she ate whatever takeout she picked up and dropped into bed.

For the first time, she was on her own—no, that wasn't true. The past weekend, she'd driven the five hours to New Jersey to spend the weekend with her family. It'd been like stepping back into the past when everything had been innocent and happy. Being with her aunts, uncles and cousins had been a balm to her battered soul. The only hairy moment had been when her aunt had asked about Cain and her father. But in the end, she'd been so tempted to unload everything. But in the end, she'd just said they were both fine and left it at that.

been, she didn't want to tarnish his image in his brothers' and sisters' eyes.

She might have walked out of all of this with a broken heart and a permanent rift with her father, but at least she had her family back. She called that a win.

Even if she stared at the ceiling for hours with burning eyes before falling to sleep from sheer exhaustion. Only to dream about a beautiful man with wolf eyes.

It'd been a week since she'd last seen Cain. Time. That's all she needed to get over him. And she would. One day.

"Finally leaving for the evening, Devon?" Harry, the security guard on duty, called out to her.

She smiled at the older man. "Finally," she said. "And there's a Netflix binge with my name on it."

He laughed. "My wife just watched that show starring the Superman guy. Except he has white hair like that elf from *The Lord of the Rings*. She loved it. A little too much, if you ask me."

Devon grinned. "Tell her she has great taste." Waving goodbye, she exited the building, headed down the sidewalk toward the small parking lot. Tomorrow started the basketball tournament so she would need to arrive early to—

"Devon."

She swallowed down a yelp and raised her fist, keys poking out between her fingers. But then she saw the man pushing off the brick building and taking steps in her direction.

Shock ricocheted through her, and she couldn't move. Couldn't do anything but stare at Cain as he approached her. Against her will, she scanned the starkly beautiful lines of his face. Met the gaze that never failed to send her pulse pounding. Her fingers itched to stroke the full, sensual mouth and the rock-hard line of his jaw. She curled those traitorous fingers into her palm.

"Cain," she rasped. Paused, and cleared her thro
"What are you doing here?"

He slid his hands in his front pockets, the action stretching his shirt over his wide chest. God, she tried not to notice. "I'm here for you."

Not "to see you." But "for you."

What did that mean?

Didn't matter. She didn't care—*couldn't* care.

"You need to go," she said, injecting steel into her voice that she fought to feel. But with him standing there in front of her, the resolve not to touch him, not to get within five feet of him wavered. *He hurt you, dammit*, she hissed at her wayward, glutton-for-punishment heart. And as much as she longed to curl up against his chest, she refused to settle for scraps of his affection or love. "Really, just leave."

"Devon," he said, and after a brief hesitation, shifted forward. Under the light of the streetlamp, she caught the faint shadows under his eyes. They reminded her of how she looked in the morning after a sleepless night, before she applied concealer. "I don't have the right to ask this but please, hear me out. And if you still want me to walk away and never bother you again, I will."

It was the "please" that gave her pause. A man like Cain didn't say it often. With a jerk of her chin, she nodded. But instead of talking, he lowered his head, studying the sidewalk. Finally, he released a soft, self-deprecating chuckle.

"I had what I wanted to say all planned out. It was going to be simple and straight to the point. Kenan has connections at Boston University and wanted me to come here with the marching band." He lifted his head, and surprise rippled through her again at the sight of the true smile curving his mouth. As did the casual mention of his half brother. "But I turned him down. Even if they were going to play 'I Will Always Love You.'" She rocked back at that admission, her lips parting on a wheeze of breath, but Cain continued. "I don't need gimmicks to tell you I'm sorry. damn ashamed of how I treated you. It was unfair, assigning someone else's sins to you. I, more than anyone, understand we're not our parents. And you…" He huffed out a breath, his voice taking on a reverent tone that belonged to works of art, to prayers, not her. Especially not from him.

But it was there. For her.

"You're the best of all of us. Beautiful. Kind. Selfless. So damn brave it terrifies and shames me. Loyal. And *mine*."

She stumbled back a step, rocked by that impassioned claim. Self-preservation made a last-ditch effort to save her from herself, and she raised her arm, palm out. "Stop. I don't want to hear any more. I can't…"

But Cain didn't listen to her. He strode forward until her hand pressed to his chest. And dammit, her fingers rebelled again by curling into the dense muscle. He covered her hand with his bigger one, holding her to him.

"You were right, Devon. You deserve one hundred percent of a person. Their fidelity, their security, their protection, their passion, their heart. Their soul. And, sweetheart, you have all of that from me. You've owned me for so long, but I was too afraid to let you in, to risk you seeing the real me and deciding I wasn't worthy enough. I was afraid to trust that my heart was held by the gentlest of hands—that it had found its home. *You own me, Devon*," he repeated on a jagged whisper. "And maybe because of how I've hurt you, I'm not worthy of you, but I promise I won't stop trying to be. You are worth the fight. Because I love you."

Her body jerked as those three words jolted through her like an electrical current.

Her mind rebelled even as her heart nearly leaped out of her chest to throw itself at him. He couldn't love her. He couldn't because she wanted him to—so damn much. She wasn't aware of shaking her head until he nodded.

"Yes, I do. I love you, Devon." He lifted the hand holding hers captive and stroked his fingers d cheek. Then he reached into his pants pocket and withdrew a small gold key. He extended it toward her.

"What is this?" She accepted it but didn't remove her gaze from his.

"It's the key to a safety-deposit box containing all the information on my mother that you took from your father's safe. I'm handing it back to you. There's no one else I trust more to keep it safe. To protect not just me, but my family. You're not your father, Devon, and I'll never look at you and see him. I only see the woman I trust and love beyond reason or explanation."

Her fingers curled around the key, pressing it to her heart. The heart that wholly belonged to him.

"I love you," she whispered. "I love you so much."

She removed her hand from his chest to throw both her arms around him and hold on. And she would never let go. She was his, and he was all hers.

"Sweetheart." He cupped her chin and tilted her head back, brushing his lips over her temple, her cheek, her nose and finally, her mouth. "Say it again."

"I love you. I love you. I love you," she chanted, then laughing, threw her head back and shouted to the sky, "I love you."

Chuckling, he buried his face against her throat, his words muffled, but she didn't need to hear him to know he whispered a vow of love. Of forever.

"One thing," she said. Cain lifted his head, cradling her face in both of his palms.

"Anything."

"Next time you come groveling—because given who we are, I'm pretty sure there will be a next time—I want the marching band."

His bark of laughter echoed in the air, and hers joined _ _ reveled in that sound of joy, savored it, knowing it the first of many for them.

"Come home with me," he murmured. "Come make new memories with me and exorcise the old ones."

"Yes," she replied without hesitation, placing a soft, tender kiss to his lips. She stared into his wolf eyes and basked under the love gleaming there for her. "New memories. And tomorrow—" she held up the key "—we have a fire to build."

"I think that will be our first real date," he teased, sweeping his thumb over her bottom lip. "I can't wait."

And as he lowered his head and took her mouth again, she couldn't wait either.

For tonight.

For the date.

For their forever.

* * * * *

COMING SOON!

We really hope you enjoyed reading this book.
If you're looking for more romance, be sure to
head to the shops when new books are
available on

Thursday 12th
November

To see which titles are coming soon, please visit

millsandboon.co.uk/nextmonth